THE
ELEMENTS

LOST IN TIME

N R SPEAKMAN

Printed in the United Kingdom.

For more information, or to book an event, contact:
(nrspeakman_writer@outlook.com & nrspeakman.com)
http://www.nrspeakman.com

Book design by Niamh Speakman
Cover design by Niamh Speakman

ISBN - Paperback : 979-8307155431
Independently published

Book 2

First Edition : January 2025

THE ELEMENTS

LOST IN TIME

To the people we've lost.

LOST IN TIME

PART 1

The only real mistake
is learning nothing

1

Return to Bleakwood

They say the hardest part about loving someone is letting them go. But those who say that have never truly lost someone. Because it's not so much the absence of that person which causes the most pain.

No!

In fact, the hardest part about losing someone is the constant regret which follows. The constant question – what if?

What if you could change the past?

What if you could go back in time?

What if a mistake could be fixed?

And what if a tragedy could be undone?

This was exactly the case for Eleanor Walker.

But even though this life was all Eleanor had ever known, she couldn't help but wonder what her life might have been like if the Elements had never been found.

It was impossible to ignore, for that night marked the beginning of her family's descent into misfortune. All the lies, the heartbreak, and the tragedies that followed all led back to that one night on the 1st of November 1996.

Part of Eleanor felt silly feeling so sad about this. She couldn't understand how she could miss a father she never knew. Yet somehow, even her own reflection would cut away at her. It only reminded Eleanor of John Walker. And even if a part of it made her smile, seeing her father's eyes stare out of the mirror and knowing that she was John Walker's daughter – proud of everything he stood for and everything he sacrificed to protect the world from Nyx - she couldn't help but feel so much anger. Anger for never having met him.

Eleanor had never grasped the gravity of a single moment until that fateful night. She sometimes wondered in the tiniest moments when she was alone and staring awake at her bedroom ceiling about how random chance was, just like the roll of a dice, you could never be sure how it would turn out. But surely if that were the case, then the whole world must have been built on billions of random events. Or maybe nothing ever really happened by accident. What if all of history had been planned out before she'd even been born?

It made her ponder deeply about whether she had any choice of her own – whether anyone did. Was free will just a fairy tale people told themselves? And if that were the case, then who made the decisions?

Or maybe, just maybe, there was one amongst the millions upon millions of possibilities that John Walker could have lived. That thought just made her stomach curl even more, thinking that somewhere out there amongst many possibilities Eleanor Walker could have grown up with a mother and a father. But she couldn't begin to imagine what that life would be like. To have a life so ordinary that it seemed as much a stranger to her as a random person in the street. Her entire life could have been so different, and yet, fate had other plans.

LOST IN TIME

*

She couldn't deny, the past few months living with Dr. Asterio, the twins' crazy and eccentric uncle, had made that summer one of the best Eleanor had ever had. Of course, living way out in the countryside meant catching any action was a little harder to come by. But after the madness of her last year at Bleakwood school, a little bit of peace and quiet had been just what Eleanor had needed.

After months of silence, there had been no word of Nyx all summer. It was as if he'd disappeared into the darkness, just as he had done after killing her father fourteen years ago, and there was no reason why he wouldn't do the same this time. The Dr had promised to tell Eleanor the second he heard any news, but there was still a hopeful part of Eleanor that believed Nyx wouldn't come back at all. Was Nyx truly gone, buried beneath the wreckage of Bleakwood School? Or was he lurking in the shadows, biding his time, waiting for the perfect moment to strike? Logic told her that he was still alive—he had escaped death before, emerging stronger each time. But what scared her most was the whisper of doubt slithering into her mind: If he returned, would she have the strength to face him again?

Eleanor clutched the Light Element so tightly her fingers ached, the cool surface pressed against her palm as if it were the only thing tethering her to reality. She had carried it with her every day, studied it relentlessly, lost herself in its shifting mysteries—from sunrise to sunset, from page to page of the old, black leather book that held secrets older than time itself.

Dr. Asterio had told her the script that appeared in the book was ancient, far beyond the comprehension of any historian, written in a dialect so obscure it predated even the earliest hieroglyphics. No human alive had seen it—except him. But Eleanor doubted even he could fully grasp the depth of its knowledge. Because when she stared at the pages long enough, the symbols no longer seemed alien. They whispered to her—not in words, but in flashes of understanding that bled directly into her mind. She didn't read the book so much as feel it, each passage unravelling its mysteries inside her like creeping threads of light.

Was it a gift? Or a curse? The question had gnawed at her all summer, winding through her thoughts like ivy, tightening around her every time she closed the book and felt reality crash back in. Because without the Light Element, she was just Eleanor Walker. Just a girl. Just ordinary.

But the ordinary was unbearable. Without the Element, the weight of everything—of loss, of doubt, of the gnawing, twisting anger—crashed over her like a tidal wave. It wasn't gradual. It was instant, like waking too soon from anaesthesia, the moment before consciousness sharpens where the world feels too loud, too heavy, too real.

And then there was Nyx.

His face had become a spectre on every television screen, his name an echo in every news report. They called him public enemy number one, the most wanted man in the country. The authorities had pinned his image across every broadcast, hoping that if they saturated the country with him, someone—some desperate soul in the fringes of society—would give him up. Someone had to have seen him. Someone had to know where he was hiding.

But no one did. And deep down, Eleanor wondered if she should be relieved. Because if Nyx was found, it wouldn't be by someone capable of stopping him. No ordinary human could stand against him. Not without a force to match his own. And Eleanor knew—knew with the kind of certainty that twisted her stomach—that the only power strong enough to counter the Dark Element was the one burning inside her own hands.

That was why she had spent the summer clinging to it, drowning herself in its energy, trying desperately to understand how to wield it. But even as she read its ancient scripts, even as she peeled back layer after layer of its mysteries, there was a nagging fear clawing at the edges of her resolve.

Nyx had wielded the Dark Element for fourteen years. He had mastered it, twisted it, bled his will into it until it became an extension of himself. Eleanor had barely begun to grasp the Light Element's power—she was nothing compared to him.

And if he returned... if he found her...

Would she be strong enough? Would she be enough?

Eleanor pressed her forehead against the cold glass, letting the rhythmic clatter of the train lull her into something resembling peace. The countryside blurred past in streaks of green and gold, its serenity a stark contrast to the restlessness twisting inside her. She focused on it—the rolling hills, the quiet streams—anything but the thoughts clawing at the edges of her mind.

Distraction was necessary.

She wasn't sure when it had become her way of coping. It was easier to focus on the landscape, easier to pretend the tension in her chest wasn't there. Because the moment she stopped, the moment she allowed herself to dwell, something flickered beneath the surface. Memories. Uncertainties. The lingering, unspoken fear of what she might one day become.

She was not thinking about that.

Bleakwood rose in the distance, its cobblestone streets and towering spires standing timeless against the horizon. To anyone else, it looked unchanged. But Eleanor saw what others didn't—the fractures, the remnants of what had been left behind. The battle had carved itself into the town, etched into the walls, hidden in the wary glances of those who had lived through it. And though time had passed, though the world had moved forward, she knew it hadn't truly healed. Not really.

Neither had she.

She ignored that thought as quickly as it came.

The train pulled into the station, metal screeching against steel, and Eleanor stood, gathering her things with careful precision. She latched onto the familiar motions—step off the train, nod at familiar faces, keep moving forward. Routine. Focus. Distraction.

She could do normal.

But even with one eye staring at the trunk of her suitcase she couldn't pretend as through she hadn't noticed the swarm of reporters scattered all around the town, their cameras swallowing its cobblestone streets, their voices turning its people into nothing more than entertainment, like animals on a nature documentary.

By the time Eleanor stepped into the dense undergrowth opposite the great lake, the presence of police officers had swelled—tenfold, maybe more. Their watchful eyes, their rigid stances, the low murmur of radios—it was meant to be reassuring. But instead, it felt suffocating.

Something was wrong.

The returning students might not have pinpointed it at first. It was subtle, creeping—just a feeling. But eventually, they would all notice. The west side of Bleakwood School was askew, the once-stately structure now slumped ever so slightly, like an aging man bent over a walking cane. Its grandeur had not faded, but the scars remained.

A section of stone was gone, swallowed by the wreckage of that night—the night when the first-floor chemistry lab had been destroyed. Some would recall it only faintly, a distant catastrophe, a headline long forgotten.

But for Eleanor, it was fresh. A memory carved so deeply into her mind that it might as well have been yesterday. The sharp scent of burning, the fractured screams, the heat licking at her skin—the chaos of her battle against Nyx lived in her bones, thrumming beneath the surface.

She forced herself to breathe, to keep moving.

Ahead, waiting beneath the shadow of the school's towering spires, stood Dr. Asterio. His expression softened the moment his eyes met hers, the weight of something unspoken settling in the space between them.

Relief.

But Eleanor wasn't sure if it was his—or her own

"Eleanor!"

She let him embrace her, let herself lean into it—for just a moment. Then she pulled back, forcing a smile, forcing herself to be fine.

"Come in, come in. We have much to discuss."

That was good. Discussion was good.

The office was warm, lined with shelves stacked with ancient books, their spines cracked with age. The fire flickered against the stone walls, filling the room with the scent of burnt wood and old parchment—things solid, unchanging, real.

"How are you holding up?" Dr. Asterio asked, settling into his chair.

Eleanor traced the edges of the cushion beneath her fingertips, grounding herself. Distraction. Routine. Answer the question.

"I'm managing," she said. Not a lie. Not really.

Dr. Asterio studied her carefully, the sharpness in his gaze cutting through the mask she wore. He always knew when she wasn't saying something.

"You have your father's strength," he said gently, and something tightened in Eleanor's throat.

She forced herself to breathe.

Did she?

Or was she just pretending she did?

She met his gaze. "I hope so."

Dr. Asterio knelt beside his desk, rummaging through the drawer with familiar absentmindedness. Papers rustled, the metallic clink of keys against wood echoing in the quiet. Eleanor watched, feeling an unexpected swell of anticipation rising in her chest—an unfamiliar but welcome feeling.

At last, he plucked a single key from the mess, holding it up triumphantly.

"Here it is," he said, handing it to her. "I pulled a few strings, but I managed to get you in the same dormitory as last year. Number 23, right?"

Eleanor's fingers curled around the cool metal, a grin twitching at the corners of her mouth. The first real smile she had felt in weeks.

"I've been told that your friends, Chris and Maddison, have already moved into their rooms."

Eleanor's chest tightened with something unexpectedly warm. She hadn't seen them all summer—their messages had been brief, fragmented by the weight of everything that had happened. But she had felt their absence keenly, like a missing limb.

Dr. Asterio's voice held amusement now.

"And I hope it's not too much trouble, but given your experience with the twins, I believe they've taken up the spare bedroom." He gave her a knowing look. "I'd wish you good luck, but knowing the twins, I think you're going to need a lot more than luck."

Eleanor laughed, a quiet but genuine sound—the first time she had truly let herself feel anything close to excitement.

"I appreciate it," she said.

As she turned the key over in her palm, the weight of returning to Bleakwood settled more firmly around her—but this time, it wasn't suffocating.

This time, it felt a little like coming home.

2

Reunited

E leanor's steps slowed as she made her way through the dimly lit corridors of Bleakwood School. The familiar stone walls pressed in around her, where every corner held remnants of last year—moments of laughter, moments of fear. She wasn't sure which weighed heavier.

The excitement of seeing Chris and Maddison again should have been enough to ease the tightening in her chest. It almost was. But beneath that excitement lay a quiet unease—an unspoken question that lingered at the edges of her mind. What would this year bring?

She tightened her grip on the key, running her fingers over its worn edges, grounding herself.

The door to dormitory 23 stood before her now. For a moment, she hesitated, her breath steadying as she slipped the key into the lock. The familiar click sounded, and with a creak, the door swung open.

Inside, it was the same—but different.

Chris and Maddison were mid-conversation, sorting through their belongings, their presence filling the space with the effortless energy Eleanor had missed.

"Eleanor!" Maddison's voice was bright, her arms wrapping around her before Eleanor had the chance to react. The warmth of the hug was grounding, pulling Eleanor fully into the present.

"It's so good to see you!"

Chris smirked from across the room, offering a casual salute. "Welcome back. Ready for another year of absolute chaos?"

Eleanor chuckled, the familiar banter settling something inside her. This. This was normal.

"I think so," she admitted. "It's good to be back."

She barely had time to set down her things before the door burst open again.

Tom and Jenny. The twins.

A whirlwind of energy and mischief, filling the space before Eleanor even had time to greet them properly.

"Eleanor! Long time, no see!" Tom exclaimed, slapping her hand in a quick high-five.

Jenny grinned, eyes sparkling with barely contained excitement. "Hope you're ready for some wild adventures," she teased, throwing a playful wink in her direction.

Eleanor smiled, truly smiled—something that had felt foreign in recent weeks. Despite the looming responsibilities of fourth year, despite everything still lingering beneath the surface, she knew this—these people—were her anchor.

As the evening stretched on, they gathered in the common room, warmth radiating from the fireplace, laughter threading through the air. The shadows of past months receded, if only for a while.

"So," Eleanor asked, settling deeper into her chair, "what have you two been up to all summer?"

Chris leaned back, that familiar impish grin playing at his lips. "Oh, the usual. My parents dragged me to Asia for work."

Eleanor raised an eyebrow, intrigued. "That sounds interesting."

Chris scoffed. "Not really. I was stuck in a hotel most of the time. Apparently, most of the places they visited were 'too dangerous for a fourteen-year-old kid.' Honestly, after last year, you'd think they'd trust me to handle danger."

Maddison rolled her eyes, suppressing a smile. They all knew the truth—knew that Chris had faced things far worse than any foreign city could offer.

"And what about everything that happened last year?" Eleanor asked carefully. "Did they believe any of it?"

Chris's grin faltered, his fingers tapping idly against the armrest. "Barely," he admitted. "Even after Maddison printed out all the articles on Nyx and the Elements, they just called it 'kids with overactive imaginations.' Like none of it mattered."

Eleanor's gaze sharpened. "And what about the news? Nyx is literally public enemy number one."

Chris shrugged. "British news isn't exactly easy to come by in Japan," he muttered, then quickly changed the subject, pulling out a strange treat wrapped in a crystalline shell. "But I did find this in one of the markets. Best thing you'll ever taste—guaranteed."

Eleanor hesitated before accepting the offering. The texture was unexpected—crumbly on the outside, yet the centre melted into something chewy, salty-sweet. A burst of flavour she hadn't anticipated.

"It's… actually really good," she admitted, earning a smug grin from Chris.

"That's what I've been telling people!"

Maddison shook her head with mock exasperation. "He exaggerates everything."

The laughter was easy, the kind that settled into her bones. But then—

Tom, who had been unusually quiet, finally spoke.

"Speaking of danger... have you heard anything about Nyx? Is he still out there?"

The air shifted.

The warmth receded.

Eleanor's fingers curled slightly against the armrest, steadying herself.

"No one's seen him all summer," she said slowly. "It's like he vanished. But I know he's still out there. Somewhere."

A quiet settled between them, a knowing quiet.

They weren't naive.

They understood what that meant.

Chris was the first to break the silence, his voice steady, certain. "Whatever happens, Eleanor, we've got your back. We've faced him before, and we'll do it again. Together."

Eleanor met his gaze, feeling the truth of his words settle deep within her. She exhaled, then turned to the twins, nudging the conversation forward. "And you two? What chaos have you been causing all summer?"

Jenny's grin returned, bright and mischievous.

"Oh, where do we even start?"

Tom leaned forward, eager now.

"We've been working on new inventions. You'll love this."

Eleanor arched a brow. "Let me guess. It explodes?"

Jenny burst into laughter. "Not quite... but we've been testing some new gelignite in the woods. More controlled this time. Only burns within a meter radius."

Eleanor's thoughts flickered back to the destruction left by their last invention, a memory carved into the school's foundation.

She barely had time to react before Tom added, more seriously now, more cautiously.

"You won't believe what we found, though."

Eleanor's stomach tightened.

"What?"

Jenny leaned in, lowering her voice to a hushed whisper. "We found something buried beneath the trees. A stone slab, covered in strange carvings."

Eleanor sat forward, pulse quickening. "Carvings? What kind of markings?"

Tom shrugged, his fingers drumming idly against his knee. "No idea. But whatever it is, it's old. Really old."

Maddison, arms crossed, shot them both a disapproving look. "Leave it to you two to find something ancient and immediately want to destroy it." Her cheeks flushed with frustration, a reaction Chris found oddly adorable—not that she appreciated that fact.

Tom, undeterred, leaned forward. "Then why was it buried?" His tone was sharp, challenging. "Someone went to a lot of trouble to hide it. And if it was forgotten for this long, maybe it holds something important." He paused, a mischievous glint sparking in his eyes. "Besides, we won't know what it is unless we break it open."

Maddison groaned, shaking her head. "That's just you two all over. First instinct? Blow it up. You're as bad as the Romans—if something ancient and mysterious exists, your immediate reaction is to destroy it."

Tom merely shrugged, clearly unbothered by the comparison. Destruction was, after all, a force of discovery in its own way. It was why most professors at Bleakwood had resigned themselves to the chaos that came with the twins. The only people who had ever managed to keep them in check were Professor Dougan—and begrudgingly—Singleton.

Then, as if fuelled by renewed enthusiasm, Tom leaned closer, eyes gleaming. "Speaking of discoveries, Eleanor—why don't you show us some of the tricks you've learned with the Light Element?"

Eleanor hesitated, her fingers brushing over the weathered pages of the leather-bound book she had studied all summer. She had hardly written to them during those months, which was only natural when living in the middle of nowhere, far from civilization. But now, she could feel all eyes on her—expectant, eager—waiting for her to reveal something extraordinary.

"I don't know, Tom," she murmured, voice quiet but firm. "I'm still learning. I haven't mastered it yet."

Tom's grin widened. "Come on. Just a little demonstration. We're all friends here."

Eleanor sighed, feeling the weight of their expectant gazes. But deep down, a small flicker of excitement stirred within her.

"Alright," she relented, "but don't expect anything grand. I've only been able to create holographic-like images. Nothing solid yet."

The group leaned in as Eleanor closed her eyes, drawing the warmth of the Light Element into her palms. It pulsed through her veins, like threads of golden energy weaving into her fingertips.

Slowly, a glow formed between her hands—soft at first, like a candle's flame, then growing brighter, more defined. Shapes began to form—a delicate shimmer taking shape, shifting into something small, fluttering—a butterfly. Its wings, translucent and edged in gold, beat softly as it drifted into the air, tracing faint trails of light as it moved.

Maddison gasped softly. "That's incredible, Eleanor."

Eleanor smiled, watching the glowing insect hover through the space. "It's just a hologram," she admitted. "No physical form. But it's still pretty cool, right?"

Tom, eyes wide with intrigue, nodded enthusiastically. "Do you think different Elements let you do different things?"

Eleanor thought for a moment, tilting her head. "It's possible. The Light Element seems to be more about creation and illumination. Maybe other Elements focus on manipulation. The Dark Element, for example, might allow control over shadows—or even the ability to form illusions, just as Nyx had done."

The butterfly hovered between them, pulsing softly.

Then—suddenly—the glow shifted.

The golden hue flickered, morphing into a pale blue.

Eleanor stiffened. Something wasn't right.

The butterfly's wings began to distort, edges sharpening, twisting—until slowly, letters began to form within them. One by one, symbols aligned, reconstructing into a message that hung in the air.

Eleanor, come to the headmaster's office immediately.

Silence swallowed the room.

Eleanor's breath caught in her throat.

"What does that mean?" she whispered, unease curling at the edges of her voice.

Maddison stared at the glowing letters, eyes dark with uncertainty. "It sounds like a message from Singleton. But *how* and *why* would he use the Light Element to communicate with you?"

They each turned to Eleanor, expecting her to know the answer. But after having spent all summer practicing to use its power, nothing like this had ever happened before. Supposedly there were many things she still had to learn.

Chris leaned in, his usual smirk absent, replaced by quiet concern. "Maybe it's something urgent."

Maddison nodded. "It makes sense—if he only wanted you to receive it."

Jenny, for once, looked serious. "You should go, Eleanor. We'll be here if you need us."

Eleanor swallowed, forcing herself to stay composed. She couldn't shake the feeling that something was wrong.

"You're right," she said slowly, standing, before turning to Chris alone. "But I need you to look after the Light Element for me."

Chris frowned. "You never go anywhere without it."

It was true. After everything that had happened with Nyx last year, she preferred to keep its warm glow close to her chest. Just having it by her side was a small comfort—a rare certainty in a world filled with unknowns.

Eleanor exhaled, gripping the artifact tightly one last time before handing it over.

"True," she admitted. "But I've learned not to trust anything. For all I know, the message is a trap. If Nyx wanted to lure me out alone, this is exactly how he'd do it." She couldn't afford to take that risk.

As she made her way through the school, the spiral staircase loomed ahead. Descending, a sharp gust of wind curled around her ankles, carrying the scent of damp stone and unsettled dust. The first floor had been under construction for months, yet little progress had been made—scorched flooring and crumbled brick told a story of stalled reconstruction attempts.

Near the headmaster's office, construction workers milled about, their conversations a low hum beneath the flickering torches overhead. Their presence made her uneasy—not because they were a threat, but because they were oblivious to what had transpired here last year. They didn't understand the battle that had raged through these halls. To them, Bleakwood was just another job, another paycheck.

Eleanor squared her shoulders, willing herself forward as the heavy door to Singleton's office loomed ahead. Though she hesitated for only a fraction of a second, the pause was enough to remind her of the gravity of what lay beyond. Taking a steadying breath, she pressed her palm against the handle and pushed it open.

"Come in," a voice called from within.

She stepped inside, and immediately, the change in atmosphere struck her. The space felt colder than she remembered, stripped of the debris that had once cluttered the floor, leaving behind an unsettling emptiness. The room was too clean, too precise, as if someone had deliberately erased all evidence of the chaos that had unfolded there. And yet, despite the illusion of order, Eleanor could feel it—the echoes of that night, lingering beneath the surface, waiting for someone to acknowledge them.

Her gaze swept across the room, landing on the three figures gathered by the desk. A sharp pang of unease tightened in her chest as she swallowed, her grip on the doorframe firmer than necessary.

This was no ordinary meeting. Whatever was about to happen—she knew it would change everything.

"Miss Walker, I see you got my message." Singleton's voice came from the back of the room, calm but laced with something unreadable.

Eleanor barely had time to process his words before her attention snapped to the two unfamiliar men standing beside him. Their rigid posture, the heavy badges glinting from their belts—police.

Her stomach twisted into knots.

Why were the police here?

She was still grasping for answers when the chair across from her spun around, revealing a familiar face.

"Dr. Asterio?" Eleanor frowned, her voice taut with confusion as her eyes flicked between him and the equally stiff figure standing at his side—Professor Dougan. Neither of them spoke, their expressions carefully guarded, but the tension in the room was palpable.

Something was very wrong.

"I see you've come alone," Singleton observed, his tone neutral yet weighted with meaning.

Eleanor shifted, an unsettling awareness creeping over her as she registered the absence of the Light Element from her side. It had always been with her, a quiet reassurance, but now, without it, she felt exposed—like stepping into battle without armour.

Singleton leaned forward slightly, his fingers steepled as he studied her. "Do you want to explain how you managed to send a message using the Elements?"

So, he had noticed.

But of course, Singleton was not one to reveal his thoughts so easily. He only smirked, offering no further explanation, his silence deliberate. Secrets were his currency, and he wasn't about to give them away for free.

A charged stillness settled over the room, thick with unspoken implications, before Singleton's expression grew more serious.

"Miss Walker," he said carefully—too carefully. "After discussions with the chief of police, we have come to the decision that, for your own safety, you should not remain at Bleakwood this year."

The words landed like a slap.

Eleanor went rigid, the shock rolling through her in waves.

No. No. No.

"You can't be serious," she hissed, the initial disbelief quickly giving way to anger. "NO. Hell NO!" Eleanor hardly ever cursed—but this warranted it.

Dr. Asterio exhaled, already bracing for her reaction. "I've been asked to home tutor you—until we deem it safe for you to return."

Eleanor whipped toward him, frustration burning in her chest. "Dr., please. You can't possibly think this is necessary."

Dr. Asterio opened his mouth, hesitation flickering in his eyes, but before he could say anything, Dougan spoke first.

"Eleanor..." she began cautiously.

Eleanor cut her off before she could soften the blow. "You want to sweep me under the rug. Erase me. Just lock me away and hope the problem disappears?" Her voice climbed, her heartbeat pounding against her ribs as she forced herself to breathe through the frustration. "I was the one who helped stop Nyx last time. If he comes for Chris, for Maddison, for anyone—what do you think will happen to them?"

Silence.

Too long. Too heavy.

Singleton's stare remained unreadable as he finally responded, his voice calm but firm. "They will be protected. But the threat to you is greater."

Eleanor inhaled sharply, the words twisting inside her. "You think?" she echoed, Maddison's unmistakable assertiveness slipping into her tone. "And if you're wrong? I'm not going to sit back and let fear dictate my life."

Singleton didn't flinch. "Miss Walker, you don't understand—"

Dr. Asterio reached out, gripping his arm as he spoke quietly. "Mike, it's her choice. We can't force her to do anything."

Singleton's jaw tightened, irritation cracking through his carefully composed mask. "If I had any sense, I would have expelled you for insubordination. Then the choice wouldn't be yours at all."

The words hung between them, heavy and sharp.

Eleanor refused to blink first.

Then, as if dismissing the conversation entirely, Singleton pivoted.

"Professor Dougan, see Miss Walker out."

Eleanor barely held back a scoff. Just like that?

Singleton continued, his voice clipped. "Dr. Asterio and I have paperwork to finalise. If you insist on staying at Bleakwood, Miss Walker, and playing the *hero*, as foolish as that is, then at least the Dr. can keep a closer eye on you..."

A pause.

"...As your new Antique studies professor."

Eleanor nearly laughed at the sheer absurdity of it. "Antique studies isn't one of my classes."

"Let's call it a compromise." Singleton's smirk curled, calculated. "If you attend both your usual studies and my additional lessons, I will allow you to remain in Bleakwood."

Everything inside her screamed to argue. To fight back.

But logic and restraint eventually won.

Eleanor clenched her teeth. "Fine."

The moment she stepped into the corridor, frustration burned beneath her skin, curling in her fists. Heat licked at her palms, deepening the red in her fingers.

Eleanor turned the corner, her head down, murmuring to herself—until she walked straight into someone coming from the opposite direction.

Oliver Morningstar, Maddison's older brother, had been carrying a precariously stacked pile of newspapers and hadn't seen her approaching. The collision sent the papers scattering around them.

Eleanor stumbled backward, blinking in shock. Of all the people she could have run into, he was the last person she'd have expected.

3

I've got news for you

Eleanor barely registered Oliver's words at first—her mind still reeling from Singleton's ultimatum. Her pulse pounded in her ears, the anger from that meeting still boiling over. They wanted her gone. Pushed aside. Hidden away like a liability.

She refused to accept it.

Oliver studied her carefully, his gaze flickering to the faint redness on her face. "Eleanor, what's wrong?"

"They want to send me away," she muttered, voice tight with frustration. "They think Bleakwood is too dangerous for me. Singleton and Dr. Asterio want to home tutor me."

Oliver's frown deepened, his expression hardening. "That's ridiculous. You've done more to protect this place than anyone else." He hesitated, jaw tightening. "If it weren't for you, I'd still be-"

He stopped, shaking his head as if dismissing the thought.

Eleanor sighed, forcing herself to breathe through the frustration curling in her chest. "I know. But they think it's for the best."

Oliver shook his head, determination flashing in his eyes. "You can't let them do that. You belong here. Besides, I've got news that might cheer you up."

Eleanor glanced at him, curiosity flickering despite herself. "News?"

He handed her a freshly printed copy of *V.E.N.U.S*, Maddison's greatest achievement—her relentless passion project in the aftermath of last year's chaos.

Oliver's lips curled into a grin, excitement gleaming in his eyes. "I got offered a place at the Royal Institute of International Affairs."

Eleanor blinked. "In the British Government?"

He nodded briskly.

"And Maddison's been offered an internship with the British Telegraph because of the success with *V.E.N.U.S.* She doesn't know anyone else is aware... until now." He pointed to the front page, Maddison's face plastered across it for the world to see.

Eleanor's eyes widened, then a slow smirk tugged at her lips. "Oh, she's going to love that," she teased, the sarcasm laced with amusement.

Though Maddison had earned her reputation as 'The Firecracker', she had never been comfortable with attention on herself—especially this much.

The two walked toward the centre of the school, Oliver scanning the corridor until his eyes landed on their target.

"There she is," he muttered, nodding toward Maddison—lost-looking, scanning the crowd in confusion.

"I asked her to meet me here," Oliver explained, mischief threading into his voice. "She has no idea I added her picture to the issue."

Eleanor chuckled. This was going to be interesting.

"Maddy!" Oliver called, waving her over.

Maddison met his gaze and immediately broke into a wide grin, quickening her pace. Perched on her shoulder was Oliver's pet parrot, Peter—his feathers gleaming crimson against the light.

"Ollie!" she called back, leaning in for a tight hug.

Eleanor couldn't help but notice how much closer the siblings had grown since last year—since the attack. Oliver had become more protective, more present, spending every moment he could with Maddison before his final year at Bleakwood ended.

Maddison pulled back, eyeing her brother curiously. "Why did you want me to bring Peter?"

Peter gave a soft squawk, fluttering his wings before hopping from her shoulder onto Oliver's. His hooked beak nestled against Oliver's cheek, amber eyes scanning the surroundings.

Oliver smirked. "I thought you and Peter might want to take a look at this."

He unfurled a rolled-up newspaper from the pile behind him, handing it to Maddison.

The moment her eyes landed on the front page, they widened into two round orbs of pure horror.

"What is this?" she gasped.

"I figured, given all the work you've put into the paper, you deserve a chance in the spotlight for once."

A stunned silence.

Then, the faintest trace of a smile—small, reluctant, but real.

And then—

"Many Maddy's! Many Maddy's! Many Maddy's!" squawked Peter, his voice piercing through the corridor.

Oliver winced as the parrot flapped his wings wildly, fixated on all the copies of Maddison's face scattered across the hallway.

Students rushed up the staircase in clusters, grabbing newspapers as they passed, their excited chatter filling the air with an almost electric energy. Laughter spilled from a group of girls perched on the stairwell, their eyes glued to Maddison's feature as they eagerly dissected every word.

Maddison exhaled sharply, rubbing her temples as frustration flickered across her face. "I am going to kill you."

Oliver merely grinned, entirely unapologetic.

Eleanor laughed, shaking her head. "At least I added a column about Professor Horridge's latest disaster to distract them from your feature."

She didn't need to read it to know—everyone knew. Ever since Nyx's betrayal had left the school scrambling to fill the Chemistry professor's position, poor Professor Horridge, who was strictly a biology expert, had been drowning under the pressure of handling the extra classes. And, as expected, chaos had followed.

Just last week, she had accidentally mixed the wrong chemicals together, triggering an explosion of fluorescent neon powder that had coated the classroom walls—and any unfortunate students caught in the crossfire—in a blinding shade of yellow.

Classic Horridge.

Classic Bleakwood.

Eleanor let out a small chuckle, the familiarity of it all grounding her for a brief moment—until her gaze flickered across the corridor and landed on something unexpected.

By the stone statues near the entrance hall, a group of first years huddled together, their hushed laughter curling through the air like whispers carried by the wind. They stood out against the crowds, their nervous energy giving them away almost immediately. So small. So wide-eyed. So completely unaware of everything that was to come.

Eleanor watched them for a moment, a wistful tug settling in her chest as she wondered—had she ever been that young? That innocent? Had there ever been a time when she wasn't looking over her shoulder, waiting for the next disaster to strike?

A nostalgic smile played at the corners of her lips.

Then—

Movement.

Across the hallway, just beyond the sea of students weaving their way through the entrance, a figure slipped through the main doors, clad in a long white cloak, their back turned to the crowd.

Eleanor blinked, her pulse hitching for just a second.

The crowd shifted, bodies pressing forward, her view blocked for no more than a heartbeat—and yet, when the paths cleared, the figure was gone.

A strange unease crept along her spine, cold and unwelcome.

She turned to Oliver, her brow furrowed. "Have the prefects changed their uniform?"

Oliver frowned, visibly confused. "Not that I know of."

"That's weird," Eleanor muttered, scanning the space where the figure had been only moments ago. "I swear I saw someone wearing a white prefect robe."

Oliver and Maddison followed her gaze, searching for whatever had caught her attention—but the corridor was as it had been before, busy and bustling, nothing out of place.

Oliver shrugged, his easy-going nature dismissing the tension. "Probably a first year getting their costume ready for Halloween. You wouldn't believe the outfits I've seen students wearing lately," he continued, shaking his head. "But I guess that comes with the role of head prefect."

Bleakwood had seen changes. The biggest being that—for the first time in three years—James Callaghan was no longer head prefect.

His father had forbidden him from returning to Bleakwood unless he was stripped of all prefect duties and placed under the highest quality protection money could buy.

A Callaghan move, for sure.

But for once, Eleanor almost felt sorry for him. Almost.

Callaghan was as much a prisoner to his father's authority as she was to the attention constantly surrounding her.

Before she could dwell on it any further, a voice cut through her thoughts like an arrow hitting its mark.

"You're Eleanor Walker, right?"

She barely had time to react before a swarm of first years engulfed her, their eager faces wide with admiration, excitement radiating from them like heat off a flame.

Too much. Too fast.

Her pulse spiked, her instincts kicking in as her eyes flickered toward Oliver in a silent plea.

He stepped in without hesitation.

"All right, give her some space," Oliver said, his tone firm but patient as he gently ushered the younger students back. "Eleanor needs room to breathe."

The first years hesitated, their enthusiasm faltering just slightly—but after a moment, they finally dispersed, their chatter fading into the hum of the corridor.

Eleanor let out a quiet breath, grateful for the reprieve.

"Thanks, Oliver," she murmured, running a hand through her hair, the weight of attention settling heavily on her shoulders. "Guess being famous has its downsides."

Oliver chuckled, patting her shoulder with an easy grin. "You'll get used to it. Besides, not every day someone gets to be a hero."

Eleanor rolled her eyes. Hero.

"I'm just trying to survive, like everyone else."

Before Oliver could respond, a familiar voice broke through the crowd.

"Eleanor! There you are!"

Chris burst through the sea of students, slightly breathless, excitement flickering in his eyes like the first spark of a flame.

Maddison raised an eyebrow, unimpressed. "Chris, were you running?"

Chris nodded, still panting heavily. A bead of sweat dripped down his temple, evidence of his haste.

Eleanor wasted no time. She pulled Maddison and Chris closer, her fingers tightening around their sleeves as urgency crackled in her voice.

"If you're both here," she whispered, her breath a thread of unease, "who's watching the Light Element? Please don't say the twins."

Chris quickly shook his head, sensing the tension in her question. "Not the twins. Don't worry, we found a safe place for it."

A wave of relief washed over Eleanor, her shoulders loosening just slightly. Thank goodness.

"But," Chris continued, his voice shifting as the weight of his next words changed the energy between them, "you'll never guess what we found."

Maddison's eyes flickered with curiosity, her posture sharpening. "What?"

Chris grinned, excitement barely contained. "Remember that strange tunnel we followed Singleton down last year? When we thought he was behind the attacks?"

Maddison frowned, rifling through memories, searching for the moment. "Yeah?"

Chris leaned in, his voice dropping just slightly, as if the mere mention carried an unseen weight. "Well, after our earlier discussion, the twins ran off to blow off steam in the forest. And you won't believe what they found."

A flicker of recognition sparked in Maddison's gaze, her intuition kicking in like second nature. She exhaled sharply, lips curling into a knowing smirk.

"Another tunnel," she said.

32

Chris groaned, throwing his hands up in exasperation. "How did you know I was going to say that?"

Maddison's smirk deepened, effortless confidence threading through her expression. "Chris. You should know by now that I know you all too well."

The others chuckled, the tension momentarily giving way to easy camaraderie.

Chris rocked slightly on his heels, still thrumming with anticipation, his excitement infectious. "Whatever. If you want to see it—I'll show you."

He took a deliberate step back, dragging out the moment with playful suspense, his grin widening, mischief glinting in his eyes.

"But..." he teased, drawing out the word, "you'll have to follow me."

Then—the bell rang.

Oliver groaned and checked the time. "I've got class. You two go on without me," he said, disappointment flickering across his face. Of all things, exploring historic passageways was exactly the kind of adventure he would have loved.

Maddison, however, wasn't dwelling on her brother's misfortune. Instead, she latched onto Chris's arm with the energy of an impatient child.

"You heard my brother," she declared. "What are you waiting for? *Let's GO!*"

Chris barely had time to react before Maddison dragged him toward the exit, her grip firm, her pace relentless. "I can't wait to write about this in my next article," she muttered to herself, excitement practically vibrating off her.

Eleanor followed, catching up just as they navigated Bleakwood's winding corridors, slipping past oblivious students— students completely unaware of the secrets buried beneath their feet.

"I can't believe you found another tunnel," Eleanor admitted, keeping pace with Chris's jogging.

Chris nodded eagerly. "Yeah, and this one's different. Feels... older. Like no one's stepped inside it for centuries."

The trio pushed into the forest, dense foliage brushing against their arms, twigs snapping beneath their hurried footsteps. The scent of pine thickened the air, grounding them in the moment.

Then—they saw it.

The stone slab.

Eleanor's breath hitched. It shimmered under the shifting sunlight, intricate symbols etched deep into its surface, their patterns unfamiliar yet commanding.

"Here it is," Chris said, barely containing his excitement. "We almost missed it."

Chris pushed aside the overgrown vines, their thick, tangled stems resisting for a moment before finally giving way, revealing the entrance—an unyielding void of darkness, a hollow, black tunnel sinking deep into the earth. The opening gaped before them, as if daring them to step inside.

Maddison leaned forward, pulse quickening—not just with fear, but with a deep, unshakable curiosity that made her fingers twitch against the flashlight in her grip. She had always been drawn to the unknown, compelled by the thrill of discovery, and this was no different.

"What do you think is down there?" she whispered, her voice barely audible, as if speaking too loudly might wake something buried within the depths.

Eleanor, ever cautious, placed a firm hand on Maddison's shoulder, grounding her before she let her excitement pull her too far ahead. "We need to be careful," she warned, her voice steady, a quiet but unshakable reminder of the dangers they couldn't yet see. "We don't know what we're dealing with."

Chris's eyes gleamed under the dim moonlight filtering through the leaves above them, the anticipation crackling in his expression. "Ready?"

Maddison didn't hesitate. With a sharp click, she flicked on her flashlight, its beam cutting through the darkness, slicing through the air like a blade.

"Let's do it."

The trio stepped inside.

Darkness swallowed them whole, thick and consuming. The air shifted around them, heavy with dust and the scent of forgotten time, the weight of history pressing down on their shoulders. The tunnel walls, lined with rough-hewn stone, felt impossibly ancient, as if they had been waiting—watching—undisturbed for centuries.

Then—the tunnel widened.

A vast chamber stretched before them, eerie in its silence, its emptiness humming with something unspoken. Strange symbols clawed across the walls, jagged carvings twisting into indecipherable shapes that seemed almost alive beneath the flickering light of Maddison's flashlight. Eleanor squinted, straining to make sense of the markings, her mind racing to piece together their meaning.

And then—

"BOO!"

Two figures lunged out of the shadows, their laughter ripping through the air.

Chris shrieked—a high-pitched, utterly humiliating sound that echoed off the chamber walls before his feet slipped in the thick mud beneath him.

And then—

Flat on his back.

Soggy trench-like mud everywhere.

Maddison and Eleanor didn't flinch.

The twins, however, collapsed into laughter, their voices bouncing wildly off the cavern walls, their amusement utterly uncontained.

"GOTCHA!" they howled, their identical grins wide with triumph.

Chris groaned, lifting his arms just enough to glance down at the massive brown stain streaking across his new jeans. He was going to have to burn them.

"You—are the worst," he muttered, his voice dripping with betrayal.

Tom shrugged, entirely unbothered, his smirk unwavering. "We didn't think you'd actually be scared. You knew we were down here."

Chris blushed, his pride suffering more than his clothes.

Jenny smirked, arms crossed over her chest as she studied him. "So?" she prodded. "Did you find anything while you were gone?"

Tom shook his head, his grin fading slightly, replaced with something more serious. "Not really. These tunnels are caved in. Gonna take a while to shift the rubble."

A slow grin stretched across both twins' faces—identical, mischievous, brimming with unspoken plans.

"Good thing we brought shovels."

Eleanor stared at them, her brain short-circuiting for just a moment before she found her voice.

"...Why were you carrying shovels around?" Then, she thought better of it, shaking her head before they could answer. "Never mind. I don't want to know."

The twins? Always up to something. They had only been back a matter of days, and already, they had returned to their usual chaos.

As Tom and Jenny launched into their self-imposed excavation with a level of enthusiasm only they could muster, Eleanor turned to Maddison, her voice quieter now, more serious, laced with an unspoken weight.

"We need to keep this discovery to ourselves."

Maddison held her gaze, searching for the reason behind Eleanor's caution, and for a brief moment, she hesitated. But then—slowly, deliberately—she nodded.

"You're right."

But then, as if the thought had snuck up on her, her eyes flickered with realization.

"...What am I supposed to write about in the meantime?"

Chris, always ready to stir the pot, grinned, the mischief returning to his expression.

"You could always do another feature on Eleanor?"

Eleanor's stomach dropped, the suggestion hitting her like a stone. Absolutely not.

"How about the Halloween party?" she suggested, hoping—praying—that it might drag the conversation in any direction that didn't involve her. "That's bound to get everyone talking."

Maddison folded her arms, considering the alternative, her mind rifling through options. After a long pause, she sighed, a reluctant acceptance settling in her features.

"Fine. I suppose that'll have to do."

4

Professor Asterio

O ver the next month, Bleakwood was alive with energy as preparations for the Halloween party took over. Banners appeared overnight, pumpkins lined the corridors, and the scent of spiced lattes drifted through the air from the school cafés. Students lounged in the courtyard or sprawled by the lake, soaking in the crisp autumn breeze, their chatter filled with costume plans and wild guesses about who would have the best scare of the night.

Maddison, ever the relentless journalist, had thrown herself into her latest article, dissecting every detail of the upcoming event with her usual wit and flair. She had an uncanny ability to make even the most mundane preparations sound like breaking news, and somehow, it had worked—the school was buzzing.

Meanwhile, Eleanor's schedule had become impossibly full, something Chris and Maddison had long since stopped questioning.

MONDAY
9 o'clock, Spanish
10 o'clock, Advanced Chemistry
11 o'clock, Biology

Lunch

1 o'clock, Ancient artifacts ... courtesy of Singleton's twisted sense of compromise, and though it wasn't the worst class, Eleanor couldn't shake the feeling that she was being monitored.

And then—there was the other thing.

The feeling she couldn't quite place.

It wasn't obvious. Not enough for anyone else to notice. Just small things, too small to be worth mentioning, too fleeting to hold weight. A subtle shift in her surroundings, barely significant, yet undeniably present.

Her pen wasn't where she had left it. Her textbooks kept rearranging themselves, as if nudged by an unseen hand. The silver pendant tucked away in her drawer—one she rarely touched, one that should have been exactly as she left it—had been moved. Just slightly.

At first, she barely noticed.

She brushed it off, convincing herself it was nothing, just exhaustion making her forgetful, her mind playing tricks on her, warping details in the haze of long nights and restless sleep.

But then—the pattern continued.

Again and again.

Unsettling in its persistence.

Still, it wasn't enough to bring up to anyone. Not yet.

She pushed the thought aside as she stepped into Ancient Artifacts, arriving just in time for Dr. Asterio to glance up and smile at her in greeting.

"Eleanor, glad you could make it."

She frowned slightly, her brows knitting together in mild confusion. She wasn't late.

Was she?

She didn't dwell on the thought, brushing the unease away as Dr. Asterio lifted a shimmering golden statue for the class to admire, the artifact gleaming under the torchlight, its surface catching the glow like liquid sunlight.

"This piece originates from Tibet," he explained, slowly turning it in the light so the intricate details could be fully appreciated. "Take note of the precision in the moulding, the careful inscriptions etched into the surface—this sculpture wasn't crafted using traditional techniques. The Tibetans developed a highly advanced process known as sublimation, blending carbon crystal with liquefied metal to achieve this distinct polished effect."

Murmurs of appreciation rippled through the students, the quiet hum of fascination filling the room.

Maddison, always ready with an educated guess, shot up her hand, her eyes tracing the fine details with practiced ease. "900?" she guessed, her voice laced with confidence.

Dr. Asterio nodded, an approving glint in his gaze. "Close. 996, to be precise."

Maddison huffed, scrutinizing the carvings with renewed focus before passing the artifact to Eleanor.

Eleanor took it carefully, her fingers pressing against the cool surface of the gold, the metal smooth beneath her touch. The emerald eyes embedded in the statue shimmered under the flickering light—too sharp, too watchful, as if they could see more than they should.

A strange unease flickered through her, an almost imperceptible shiver ghosting along her spine.

She blinked, shaking off the feeling, and passed the artifact along before she could dwell on it.

The lesson continued, with each artifact unveiling another layer of history, offering glimpses into the lives and craftsmanship of civilizations long past.

Then—

Dr. Asterio's voice rose slightly above the quiet murmur of discussion.

"Everyone, I'd like you to meet our new student."

Eleanor glanced up.

A boy stood near the front of the room, relaxed, his stance effortlessly confident, his expression marked by quiet assurance.

"Theo Decker," he introduced himself, turning toward the class with an easy grin, his eyes scanning the faces before him.

Eleanor reached out and shook his hand, feeling the firm steadiness of his grip. There was something measured in his manner, something curious behind his gaze, as if he were already assessing the energy of the room, cataloguing details with practiced ease.

Dr. Asterio, not pausing for introductions to linger, pressed forward with the lesson. "For today's activity, I'll be handing out artifacts for analysis. Your task is to determine which civilization each piece might have originated from and—more importantly— interpret the emotions the artist was attempting to convey through its design."

Theo, still smiling, shifted his attention to Eleanor and Maddison, the easy charm in his expression never wavering.

"You don't mind if I group with you, do you?"

"Not at all," Eleanor replied without hesitation, moving over to make space for him at their table.

Dr. Asterio motioned her forward, carefully stacking statues along his desk, preparing them for distribution.

Theo leaned slightly closer, his posture casual, his eyes studying her with quiet interest.

"So, you're Eleanor Walker?" he asked before settling in the seat beside her.

She nodded, already knowing where this was going.

"You're a bit of a legend around here, I'm guessing."

Eleanor rolled her eyes, though a grin tugged at her lips. "You could say that."

Theo smirked. "Bet you're tired of people asking by now."

Eleanor chuckled, shrugging. "You can say that again."

A loud throat-clearing interrupted them. Maddison thrust out her hand, posture firm—too firm.

"And I'm Maddison Morningstar," she announced, voice sharp with authority.

Theo blinked, momentarily startled, but took her hand politely.

"Just so we're clear," Maddison added, "I'm in charge of the facts around here."

Eleanor groaned, burying her face in her hands.

Theo laughed. "Oh, right. Didn't realize there were official roles."

Eleanor shook her head. "Ignore her. You don't have to stay quiet if you know the answer."

Maddison scoffed, arms crossed. "Please. I bet you don't even know what famous Aztec statue was used in over a hundred human sacrifices."

Theo didn't even pause.

"The Elda Grad de Familial, known as the winged bat. People thought it was a messenger of the gods."

Maddison narrowed her eyes. "Lucky guess."

Eleanor sighed, steering the conversation forward. "So, you're into historical relics?"

At that, Theo brightened, enthusiasm sparking in his eyes.

"My family's collected relics for thirteen generations. Coins, medieval weapons—you name it. My great-great-grandfather was an archaeologist who started the collection himself."

Eleanor's curiosity sharpened. "That's incredible! Do you have a favourite piece?"

Theo paused, considering.

"Probably a ceremonial dagger from the Roman Empire. The craftsmanship is unreal. Plus, there's a legend attached to it."

"Legend?" Maddison, despite herself, leaned in.

Theo nodded. "It supposedly belonged to a Roman general who was betrayed by his own men. The dagger is rumoured to be cursed—anyone who holds it will meet the same fate."

Eleanor shivered—though, strangely, excitement danced in her stomach.

Before the conversation could continue, Dr. Asterio clapped his hands.

"All right, class! Let's reconvene."

Eleanor, Maddison, and Theo stepped forward, presenting their analysis.

Dr. Asterio nodded in approval.

Fantastic insights. Brilliant observations.

Eleanor caught Theo's eye.

He felt different.

Not in the way most students did—not like someone trying to figure her out, trying to make sense of the rumours people whispered about. Instead, his curiosity felt... genuine.

But as she turned back toward her desk, passing Maddison a smug look, something shifted in the corner of her vision.

A shadow.

Just outside the window.

Her pulse hesitated for half a second.

Then, just as quickly, she brushed it off, a sudden crash echoed through the hallway, followed by the unmistakable sound of raised voices.

Eleanor barely had time to process the noise before Maddison was already on her feet, Theo right behind her.

Chris skidded to the doorway, eyes wide. "What the hell was that?"

Another shout—louder this time—cut through the air.

Without hesitation, they bolted out of Dr. Asterio's classroom and into the stairwell.

Chaos.

Fifth year students Gregory and Ezra were at each other's throats—shoving, yelling, fists clenched. A group of students had already gathered on the steps, some shouting for them to stop, others watching in stunned fascination.

Gregory's face was pale with anger—not the reckless, arrogant fury Eleanor had expected.

Ezra lunged at him with unfiltered force, sending Gregory stumbling backward. His heel caught nothing but air, and for a split second, Eleanor was certain he was going to fall. Instinct took over before thought—she surged forward, her fingers closing around the fabric of his sleeve, stopping his descent just in time.

The moment her hand made contact, something odd prickled through the space between them—a fleeting charge, a raw static lingering in the air like a storm that hadn't broken yet. Eleanor's chest tightened, though she couldn't place why, and when she glanced toward Ezra, he had stepped back, blinking fast, his breath uneven, as if some invisible thread had been yanked between them.

Then—Dr. Asterio spoke.

"Enough."

It was a single word, but it cut through the tension like a blade.

Gregory froze in place, his stance solidifying beneath him, while Ezra straightened, his expression smoothing over as if nothing had happened. Around them, the students stilled, their murmurs fading, their gazes darting between the trio with a mix of curiosity and caution.

Dr. Asterio stepped forward, his gaze sharp, flickering between Ezra and Gregory like he was piecing together something neither of them had said out loud.

"What is going on?"

Silence.

Eleanor could feel the weight of his scrutiny, like he had seen something he wasn't meant to, something lingering just beneath the surface. She glanced toward Ezra, expecting irritation, embarrassment—anything—but his posture remained tense, his hands curling into fists at his sides, though whether from frustration or something else, she couldn't tell.

His eyes flickered, unfocused for half a second, like there was something running through his mind—something just out of reach.

Then, as if shaken from a trance, he looked at Eleanor.

And something shifted.

It wasn't fear. Not really.

It was something deeper.

Something unsettled.

Ezra stared past her shoulder, like there was something there that nobody else could see before muttering something under his breath, but not in English, but in a language she didn't quite understand.

Without warning, Professor Dougan appeared.

Eleanor hadn't seen her approach, hadn't heard her footsteps, yet there she was, standing tall, authoritative, her presence effortlessly commanding the space.

She didn't ask questions. She didn't linger.

She simply turned to the boys, expression unreadable, and gestured for them to follow.

"You two. With me. Now."

Ezra hesitated, his jaw tightening for just a fraction of a second before he stepped forward, still watching the left of Eleanor's shoulder.

Maddison shook her head as she watched them leave, her voice barely above a whisper.

"That was... really weird."

Eleanor let out a slow breath, trying to anchor herself in the normalcy of the moment, though something about it still clung to her skin like static.

"Yeah," she murmured, gaze lingering on the spot where Ezra had stood. "Too weird."

The hallway lights flickered.

Not a sudden blink, but a slow, deliberate dimming—like something was siphoning the warmth from the room.

The temperature dipped, subtle but noticeable, and Eleanor caught the way Maddison rubbed her arms, her fingers trailing across her skin as if she had just stepped into the heart of winter.

Eleanor turned back to find the rest of Asterio's class staring at her. They weren't gossiping between each other as most students did after a fight, but they just stood there, perfectly still...

... watching.

A chill crept up Eleanor's spine. Was she imagining things? Was she just being paranoid? Or was there something really wrong, not just with Ezra or the fight, but Bleakwood itself?

5

Night of Broken Glass

The library was dimly lit, the flickering flames from the fireplace casting dancing shadows on the walls. Eleanor, Maddison, and Chris sat around a large wooden table, their books and notes spread out before them. The warmth of the fire provided a comforting contrast to the cold, dark night outside.

"I see Professor Dougan is still as generous as always with the homework," Maddison remarked, her tone laced with sarcasm.

Chris thumped his head on the table. "You can say that again," he groaned, flicking his pen on and off. "I don't understand any of this."

Maddison snatched the textbook from under Chris, her eyes scanning the page. "Let me see," she said.

Chris watched her, a look of helplessness on his face. "I've been staring at this for hours, and it still doesn't make any sense."

Maddison sighed and tapped her finger on the page. "Alright, let's break this down. The question is asking about the causes of the French Revolution. You need to focus on the economic, social, and political factors."

Chris nodded slowly, trying to follow along. "Okay, but what does that mean exactly?"

Maddison rolled her eyes playfully. "It means you need to talk about how the financial crisis, the inequality between the estates, and the influence of Enlightenment ideas all contributed to the revolution. For example, the financial crisis was caused by France's involvement in expensive wars and the lavish spending of the monarchy."

Chris groaned, "Can't you just do it for me?"

Maddison's eyes widened, "Not at all. That would be cheating, Chris!"

"But nobody would know, it would be our little secret."

"You would know. When they ask you this question in the exam, do you think I'll be there to help you?"

Chris half mulled over the idea.

"No, Chris. The answer is no," she said with a lecturing stare. "Those who cheat, only cheat themselves."

"I'm okay with that," he muttered, curling over the textbook like a naughty puppy.

Eleanor looked up from her history book, her eyes reflecting the firelight. "Have you ever heard of Kristallnacht?" she asked, her voice soft but filled with a sombre tone.

Maddison glanced up; curiosity piqued. "Isn't that German?" she asked.

Eleanor nodded, reading more into the book, "They call it the Night of the Broken Glass. The Nazis instigated a wave of anti-Jewish violence all over Germany and Austria. Over 200 synagogues were destroyed, people were attacked and killed, Jews were dragged out of their homes. Leaving the streets littered with broken glass."

Chris gazed across, his brow furrowed, "Hence the name Broken Glass?"

Eleanor nodded, her gaze drifting to the fire. "It just got me thinking, about the terrifying things that ordinary people can do when driven by fear and hatred. The Nazis managed to manipulate and incite fear in the population, turning neighbours against each other. People who once lived side by side in peace became enemies overnight."

Chris shivered, pulling his sweater tighter around him. "It's hard to imagine how people could be so cruel. But I guess fear can make people do terrible things. When the person in charge is drunk with power and lies for their own personal gains, even the best of people will believe anything. In the wrong hands, ordinary people can be the most dangerous weapon of all."

Maddison nodded thoughtfully, thinking more about how their world today differed from life during the Nazi's control. "Did you know there are still some rich and powerful families alive across the world today," she began to explain.

"From the Nazis?" Chris exclaimed, his jaw dropping and nearly intaking all the soot blowing through the air.

Maddison strongly shook her head, "NO! Don't be daft!" she scolded, "They were destroyed and for good reason. But when one power goes, there are always people who look to fill the void they left." She corrected.

As they continued their discussion, the librarian, Mrs. Thompson, who had been quietly shelving books nearby, approached their table. She was an elderly woman with kind eyes and a gentle demeanour. She had overheard their conversation and felt compelled to share her own story.

"I couldn't help but overhear your discussion," Mrs. Thompson said softly, her voice carrying a hint of nostalgia. "I was only a child when the war took place, but I remember the aftermath vividly."

The trio looked up, their attention fully captured by the librarian's words. Eleanor gestured for her to join them, and Mrs. Thompson pulled up a chair, settling in by the fire.

"My family lived in a small village in England," she began, her eyes distant as she recalled the past. "The war brought so much destruction and fear. I remember the nights spent in the bomb shelters, the sound of sirens wailing, and the uncertainty of whether we would see the light of day again."

She paused, her voice trembling slightly. "But what struck me the most was how ordinary people, driven by fear and propaganda, could turn against each other. Neighbours who once shared meals and laughter became suspicious and hostile. The fear of spies and traitors was so pervasive that it tore communities apart."

Mrs. Thompson's eyes glistened with unshed tears. "After the war, the destruction was everywhere. Buildings reduced to rubble, families torn apart, and a sense of loss that hung heavy in the air. It took years to rebuild, not just the physical structures, but the trust."

Eleanor, Maddison, and Chris listened intently, their hearts heavy with the weight of her words.

"We must never forget the lessons of the past," Mrs. Thompson continued, her voice firm. "But after all we are only human. And when we get angry and scared, we have a history of doing stupid things."

6

Omen

E leanor's vision blurred, disjointed shapes flickering in and out of focus—ruins stretching endlessly, shadows twisting against firelit skies, the jagged outlines of crumbling towers splitting apart as the world collapsed around her, folding into itself. The air was thick, heavy with the scent of smoke and destruction, the distant crackling of flames barely audible over the relentless pounding in her ears.

Her breath came in ragged bursts, her heartbeat hammering violently against her ribs, a frantic rhythm drowning out the chaos around her.

Where was she?

Something wet clung to her fingers—warm, sticky.

She lifted her hands, the motion slow, deliberate, almost unwilling, and her pulse stalled for half a second.

Blood.

Her chest tightened, her mind scrambling to process the sight, but panic surged faster than logic, flooding through her veins as adrenaline pushed her muscles to react—except her legs felt impossibly heavy, weighted as if the very air around her had thickened, pressing in, suffocating, making movement feel like an impossible feat.

The world twisted, shifting too fast, reality bending under an unseen force, and then suddenly—bodies.

Motionless.

Their faces were familiar. Too familiar.

Maddison. Chris. Oliver. Jenny. Tom.

Mangled. Bloody. Dead.

A strangled breath escaped her throat, breaking into something between a gasp and a plea, but she refused to believe it, refused to accept what her eyes were telling her.

This wasn't real.

It couldn't be.

Then—

Nyx stepped forward, the wicked gleam in his eyes cutting through the chaos like a blade, sharp and deliberate, holding the kind of certainty that made Eleanor's stomach churn.

As she stumbled backward, the ground beneath her feet suddenly became unstable, shifting unpredictably, threatening to give way beneath her. It felt as though she were standing at the edge of something vast and unknowable, something she could neither control nor escape, the sheer weight of it pressing against her lungs.

The Light Element pulsed faintly in Nyx's grip. But—how?

How did he have it?

Her fingers clenched instinctively, a desperate reflex to reclaim what had already been lost, but even before she looked, before her mind fully caught up with the moment, she knew.

It was gone.

Nyx tilted his head slightly, his expression steady, measured, his smile curling at the edges—slow, deliberate, almost amused.

"You did well, Eleanor," he murmured, his voice quiet, too quiet, the gentleness twisting into something far worse.

Eleanor shook her head, sharp, frantic, her breath catching in her throat. "No."

This wasn't her doing. It couldn't be.

She would never kill her friends. She would never hand him the Light Element.

Nyx's grin widened, his presence unwavering, his gaze holding the kind of certainty that sent a fresh wave of panic rushing through her.

"But you did," he countered, his voice effortlessly assured, dripping with conviction. "You handed it over willingly."

Eleanor's gaze snapped to the Light Element in his grasp, watching in horror as the longer he held it, the darker it became, the glow fading, the light draining from its core, as if he were pulling every ounce of energy from it, consuming it from the inside out.

Had she really given it away—to him?

A flicker of movement stirred at the edges of the broken ruins, barely visible in the dim, firelit haze.

She stiffened, breath catching again, pulse stuttering unevenly.

Something was there.

A figure emerged from the shadows.

Her own reflection.

But not her.

Not really.

She tried to move, to pull away, to force herself into action, but her reflection stepped closer, its hands reaching outward, pressing into her chest, pushing through her skin, slipping inside—

And suddenly, she was watching.

Watching herself laugh.

Watching herself stand beside Nyx and smile—but not her smile. Not her at all.

She wasn't herself anymore.

*

A sharp gasp shattered the silence as Eleanor jolted upright, breath coming in uneven, ragged bursts. Her chest heaved, struggling to steady itself beneath the crushing weight of the dream—so vivid, so real, she could have sworn it had been.

Sweat clung to her skin, damp and uncomfortable. Her pulse pounded a frantic rhythm against her ribs, adrenaline still coursing through her veins despite the familiar stillness surrounding her.

Slowly, shapes emerged—the outlines of her bedroom sharpened, the soft glow of candlelight flickered from her bedside table, curtains swayed in the night breeze, and the distant murmurs of Bleakwood settled into its usual quiet. She scanned her eyes over the floor several times but saw nothing out of the ordinary.

No blood stained the fabric.

No ruins crumbled around her.

No lifeless bodies lay strewn across the ground.

It took her a moment to convince herself—it was only a dream.

Everything was exactly as she had left it.

Except—

"Eleanor?"

She twisted around, pulse still hammering.

Chris stood in the doorway, concern deep in his expression, his silhouette framed by the dim glow of the hallway.

"You alright?"

Eleanor swallowed, forcing herself to breathe, to gather the scattered pieces of herself.

"Chris—" she hesitated, gripping the blanket edges as if they could tether her to reality. "What are you doing up?"

"I heard a noise come from your room." The he pointed to the ground where a shattered glass shards were scattered. She must have knocked over the lamp in her sleep. Eleanor rubbed over her knuckles, expecting to feel the sting of impact, but—nothing. No pain. No evidence that she'd touched anything.

"I was just having a nightmare."

"A nightmare?" All the colour seemed to drain out of Chris's rosy flushed cheeks. "Like last year?"

Because the last time Eleanor had suffered from night terrors, it had been right around the same time Nyx started poisoning students with Devilsroot, warping their minds, twisting their bodies into something barely recognizable. It had been a warning then, a sign of something stirring beneath the surface—and now, it was happening again.

Eleanor exhaled slowly, rubbing her temple as the remnants of sleep still clung to her like a veil she couldn't quite shake. "You ever have that moment—when you wake up, but you're not completely sure if you're actually awake? Like you're caught somewhere between two dreams, hovering in that strange space where everything feels too real to be imagined but too surreal to be reality?"

Chris's expression shifted, a flicker of understanding crossing his face as he considered her words. "You mean like a dream inside a dream?"

Eleanor nodded, swallowing against the unease still tightening in her throat.

Chris took a slow, measured step forward, his posture changing as something in the atmosphere grew heavier, more uncertain. "Yeah," he murmured carefully, his voice quieter now, as if speaking too loudly might break whatever fragile illusion held them in place. "Like you never really wake up. Like you're just trapped in it."

Eleanor's pulse quickened as she turned her gaze toward the Light Element again, watching it with growing intensity. She could have sworn—just for a second—that the glow beneath it flickered, an almost imperceptible shift that sent a shiver down her spine.

Chris settled beside her, lowering himself onto the edge of her bed with deliberate slowness. His voice was softer now, gentle but weighted. "Eleanor—what did you dream about?"

She hesitated, her fingers twitching against the fabric of her sheets, gripping them tighter as if holding onto something tangible might anchor her in reality. The truth was, she wasn't sure she wanted to answer. Because in that moment, no matter how much she tried to convince herself, she still didn't know if she was truly awake.

Not for a single moment.

7

Lacrosse

T he thought of Nyx still clung to her mind, lingering in the quiet moments when she found herself alone. There had been no news—no updates, no confirmation of his whereabouts. Nothing to prove he was still out there, but nothing to suggest he wasn't.

And that was the worst part.

The not knowing.

While the rest of Bleakwood carried on—students filling classrooms, exams looming, Halloween decorations brightening the streets—Eleanor couldn't shake the feeling that she was missing something, like she was meant to be looking elsewhere.

Like something was watching her.

Every time she tried to catch sight of it, a flicker of white movement vanished just out of reach, nothing more than a ghost in her peripheral vision. A trick of the light, maybe. A reflection, perhaps.

Or something worse.

She didn't trust it.

And until she knew where Nyx was, her senses were on high alert.

At breakfast, the Great Hall was alive with chatter, the sounds of shifting plates and laughter filling the space. Eleanor sat across from Maddison and Chris at their usual table, but her mind wasn't really there.

She scanned the room, taking in every strange detail, everything that might seem out of place.

"Earth to Eleanor," Maddison said, waving a hand in front of her face. "You okay?"

Eleanor blinked, snapping back to reality. "Yeah, sorry. Just thinking about something."

Chris leaned in, mischief glinting in his eyes. "And has that SOMETHING got anything to do with the twins' tunnel discovery? Or the nightmare from last night?"

Eleanor hesitated.

Chris sighed dramatically, shoving the last bite of his egg muffin into his mouth.

Eleanor shouldn't have been surprised that Chris had told her. He had a terrible poker face and Maddison was the best at coaxing out the truth. Once she got a whiff of a mystery, she couldn't let it rest until she'd unburied the truth.

"Speaking of nightmares, you know who gives me the creeps-that old librarian." Chris blurted out to break the tension.

Maddison didn't hesitate to whack his shoulder.

"Chris! She'd an old lady, have some respect."

"Then why is she always creeping up on me when I'm trying to work."

"She's probably just lonely! That's what happens when you get to that age."

Eleanor barely registered their back-and-forth, her mind elsewhere, fingers absently toying with the edge of her spoon.

"I was thinking," she murmured, half to herself, before straightening. "I think we should talk to Theo."

Chris blinked at her, his expression blank, while Maddison, mid-sip, choked spectacularly on her water.

"Theo?" she coughed, struggling to regain composure. "That's a terrible idea."

There wasn't even a trace of hesitation in her tone—just immediate, unimpressed dismissal.

Eleanor sighed. It wasn't as ridiculous as Maddison was making it out to be.

With Nyx's knowledge of historical artifacts and Singleton and Asterio's relentless attempts to keep her in the dark about certain peculiarities, maybe Theo could help. He seemed to know things— things they weren't being told.

But Maddison was already shaking her head.

"We hardly know him, Eleanor," she pointed out. "You want to just loop him into our biggest secret?"

Eleanor frowned. "I just think it might help us understand more about the Elements."

Chris finally found his voice, though he still looked vaguely concerned.

"And what if he knows something we don't want him knowing?"

Maddison pointed at Chris, as if he had just made her point for her.

"Exactly."

Eleanor huffed, crossing her arms.

"It's not like I'm suggesting we give him a step-by-step guide on how to use the Elements," she muttered. "I just think he might know something useful."

Maddison didn't budge.

Chris still looked sceptical.

And Eleanor couldn't shake the feeling that, one way or another, Theo was going to end up involved in all this anyway.

Whether they wanted him to be or not. The more time he spent around them, it was only a matter of time before he caught sight of something weird or overheard a part of their conversation about the Element.

Eleanor wasn't sure whether to argue or let it go. But Maddison's attention had already shifted.

A slow grin spread across her face.

"Speaking of big secrets—Chris, why don't you tell Eleanor what you've signed up for?"

Chris froze, mid-bite.

Maddison pounced.

"Oh, he hesitated—so I'll tell her." She grabbed Chris around the shoulders, squeezing him like an overbearing older sister.

Eleanor watched, intrigued.

"Chris is trying out for the lacrosse team," Maddison announced, almost gleefully.

Eleanor nearly choked on her cereal, coughing violently as the milk burned its way down her throat. She wiped at her watery eyes, still catching her breath after her near-death experience that she hadn't expected first thing in the morning. Finally managing to speak, she glanced at him, her voice laced with scepticism. "Do you even know how to play?"

"Of course I do." Chris replied, rather quickly but there was a small stutter laced in his words, "As a matter of fact, I'm going to make frontline."

Maddison snorted, shaking her head in amusement. "You just learned what frontline means, Chris."

Chris, undeterred, ignored her entirely, puffing out his chest as if sheer confidence alone could make up for his lack of experience.

It was clear that Chris was searching for something— something beyond just the game.

He wanted to prove something.

Not to them.

To himself.

Eleanor leaned back, crossing her arms as she hid the small, knowing smile curling at the corners of her lips.

"Well," she murmured, voice tinged with amusement, "this is going to be fun to watch."

Chris grinned, unbothered, his energy unshaken. "I was born for this."

Eleanor had no doubt that it would be entertaining. Whether it would end well, however, was an entirely different question.

*

Later that afternoon, the trio made their way to the lacrosse field. Chris had spent far too long in the boys changing room. The odd squeals and groans echoed through the walls as tried to squeeze himself into his sports gear, to the point that Eleanor and Maddison had nearly sent someone in after him, convinced he'd suffocated beneath the padding.

By the time he finally emerged, the players had gathered on the field, stretching and preparing for try-outs. Eleanor and Maddison found seats along the sidelines, watching as the hopefuls lined up.

Of course, they were here to support Chris—but Maddison had her own reasons.

Her crush, Daniel, was also trying out. And compared to Chris, he was built like a titan.

Chris barely came up to Daniel's shoulder, and when Daniel stretched his arms fully outward, they practically matched Chris's entire torso in width.

Still, Chris looked determined.

The whistle blew. The ball soared through the air.

And Chris fumbled spectacularly.

Still repositioning his head guard, he wasn't watching the play—and instead of catching the ball, it hit him square in the chest, sending him sprawling onto the grass.

Maddison groaned. Eleanor winced.

"Knight! Keep your eye on the ball!" Professor Black bellowed, frustration thick in his voice.

Chris scrambled upright, brushing himself off, his face cherry-red with embarrassment.

What followed was a disaster—a wild swinging of his lacrosse stick that managed to injure nearly half the lineup before he even got possession of the ball.

Players shouted complaints.

Another whack to the shin.

The ball came flying toward him again—and this time, it bounced off his helmet with a thunderous crack.

Eleanor stood abruptly. "He's getting massacred out there."

Then—out of nowhere—Player Number Eleven swept in, effortlessly manoeuvring past the defence, twisting into a perfect somersault before landing the shot of the century.

"Nice shot, Decker!" Professor Black called out, clearly impressed.

Theo grinned, high fiving his teammates.

Meanwhile, Chris could barely stand without unintentionally weaponizing his lacrosse stick.

The rest of the team eyed him wearily, rubbing the fresh bruises where Chris had accidentally smacked them mid-play.

Professor Black sighed. "Knight, how about you try in goal? I think the team has had enough bruising for one session."

Chris nodded, eager to redeem himself.

But—it only got worse.

The opposing team moved like a well-oiled machine, weaving through the field with sharp precision, passing the ball effortlessly between them. Every attempt Chris made to block a shot ended in failure, his reflexes just a second too slow, his footing just a fraction off-balance.

Ball after ball soared past him.

Swing after swing ended in nothing but empty air.

The frustration in his teammates grew unmistakable, their movements growing sharper, their patience wearing thin. He could feel it—the tension tightening like a coil, the unspoken disappointment lingering in the air around him.

And then—the moment of truth.

Theo gained possession of the ball, manoeuvring across the field with practiced ease. He barely seemed to struggle as he sidestepped defenders, cutting through their ranks like they were little more than paper obstacles. The path ahead of him opened up in an instant, the goal clear, unobstructed.

Chris's body locked up, his eyes fixed on Theo, heart hammering against his ribs.

This was it.

His last chance to make a difference.

A reckless, desperate thought surged through him, louder than logic, drowning out every warning sign in his mind.

Before he could stop himself, he charged.

Straight at Theo.

Straight at Daniel—who was still guarding the goal.

"Chris, NO!" Eleanor shouted, but it was too late.

Chris barrelled into Theo and Daniel with the force of an avalanche, sending all three of them flying into the goal, tearing the net clean off its frame before momentum carried them further—

Straight into Bleakwood's lake.

The icy water swallowed them whole, and the entire sideline collectively gasped.

When they surfaced—soaked, mud-smeared, and thoroughly miserable—Professor Black looked ready to detonate.

"Knight!" he thundered. "The goalie is supposed to stay in goal—not go charging down the field!"

Chris avoided Eleanor's gaze, still dripping wet.

Daniel grinned despite himself. "You'd make a brilliant wingman. That charge was epic—you swept me clean off my feet."

Theo finally spoke, unshaken. "No hard feelings, Chris."

Chris managed a weak smile. "Agreed."

Then—chaos struck again.

A stray ball went flying through the air—straight for Daniel's face—but before impact, a lacrosse stick swooped out of nowhere, catching the ball with perfect precision.

Eleanor blinked.

Maddison stood, stick raised, expression unbothered.

"You!" Professor Black called out to her, clearly impressed. "Have you ever thought about trying out for the team?"

Maddison twirled the stick effortlessly, tossing the ball back straight into the net—with impossible accuracy.

"No thanks," she said smoothly. "I prefer sports with actual skill—like fencing and archery. Not really into the whole sweaty jersey thing."

Daniel gawked at her.

"You're, like, really good."

"Five years of karate. Twelve years of fencing," she explained. "My parents made me do it. But I'm too busy now—internship and all."

Professor Black nodded, impressed. "Well, if you ever change your mind, the team could use someone with your skills."

Then, turning back to the players—

"Alright, Parish and Decker, you're on defence. And as for you, Charles—"

"...Actually, it's Chris."

Professor Black chuckled, clapping Chris's shoulder. "Let's see what you're like in defence—you seem good at taking a hit."

Chris blinked at his soaked clothes, the water dripping onto the grass.

"What, like this?"

Professor Black laughed heartily. "It's fine! Just run around— you'll dry off in no time."

Chris waddled toward the court, completely miserable, as the whistle blew.

Eleanor bit back a laugh, watching him struggle against soggy underpants.

Then—just as the game resumed—

A shout echoed across the field.

Eleanor turned, spotting Sammy Shrew—one of the smaller fourth years—cornered by Henry Kensington, Bleakwood's resident bully.

Of course, Henry's two lackeys loomed close behind, snickering, waiting for the inevitable.

Henry sneered, folding his arms. "Move, Shrew. You're in my way."

Eleanor braced herself, expecting Sammy to crumble, to retreat the way he always did—but he didn't.

Instead, for the first time, he held his ground, though his hands shook slightly.

Eleanor straightened, sensing something different.

Henry leaned forward, smirking. "Have you finally grown a backbone? You think you're tough enough to go up against me? Once a coward, always a coward."

Sammy inhaled sharply.

Eleanor could see it—the hesitation, the battle in his mind, the part of him that wanted to run—but then, through trembling breaths, he forced out—

"N-n-no! Y-you're not going to keep pushing me around anymore!"

Henry's grin widened.

"Oh? And who's going to stop me, y-y-you?" he mocked, mimicking Sammy's stammer with cruel precision.

And then an idea struck.

Eleanor's fingers brushed against the Light Element in her pocket, a new thought sparking to life. She didn't need force. She didn't need to intervene outright. All she needed was a little illusion, she thought to herself, as she focused on channelling its energy and weaving the trick just enough for Henry to see it—

A holographic mouse flickered to life beside Sammy.

Henry's face drained of colour.

His entire body stiffened.

Three rapid steps backward, his heel catching on the uneven floor, nearly sending him stumbling.

The second Eleanor smirked, Maddison caught on instantly and began biting back laughter.

And Sammy—realising what had just happened—stepped forward, confidence filling his face, with a wide grin splitting across his features.

Henry couldn't backpedal fast enough. Then, without another word, he turned and fled, much to the amusement of every witness nearby.

Eleanor let the illusion fade, her heart racing, an unexpected thrill sparking through her veins. For the first time, Bleakwood wasn't just changing for the worse. Maybe—just maybe—it meant there was still hope left if the likes of Sammy Shrew could stand up to Henry Kensington.

8

Friendships

Four weeks into the new school year, and Eleanor was already drowning in work. Taking on an extra class had turned into more of a nightmare than she anticipated, all while juggling time with her friends and practicing with the Light Element.

She was improving.

She could now conjure multiple images at once—though each session left her drained, collapsing onto the dormitory couch with a pint of orange juice. It was the only thing that seemed to bring her blood sugars back up.

But it was worth it.

Her control was strengthening. She had managed to maintain an illusion for up to ten minutes—which, of course, immediately landed her in the middle of one of the twins' ridiculous schemes.

Professor Dougan's distraction? Courtesy of Eleanor.

Their prank supplies sneaked into the forest unnoticed? Also, courtesy of Eleanor.

Her circle of friends, as chaotic as it was, kept her grounded.

Though lately, she had noticed small changes among them.

Chris seemed a lot quieter, often lost in thought. He wasn't as eager to jump into every conversation as usual—something about him felt like he was figuring things out in his own head.

Maddison, on the other hand, was more driven than ever, her ambition bordering on obsession, as if she was chasing something just out of reach. Her journalistic mind was bubbling more furiously than Eleanor had ever seen it before.

And as for Eleanor...

...Nyx hadn't resurfaced, and that fact alone made Eleanor uneasy. No news. No sightings. No hints. It wasn't so much of a comfort to her, as it was a warning. And she knew better than to let her guard down.

Still, the energy at Bleakwood was alive with excitement—Halloween party preparations, wild costume ideas, an eerie undercurrent that lurked beneath the surface of all the fun.

One evening, the trio sat by the lake, the golden sunset painting the rippling water and the crisp autumn air wrapping around them.

Maddison casually brought up the topic that had been buzzing around campus all week.

"So, what are we all dressing up as?"

Chris grinned. "I'm going as a highwayman. Got a killer costume ready."

Maddison smirked. "I'm going as a vampire queen. Full velvet cape, fangs—the works."

Eleanor chuckled. "I haven't decided yet. Any suggestions?"

Then—a voice from behind them.

A presence they hadn't noticed before.

Theo leaned in with a mischievous glint in his eye. "How about an ancient warrior? With your knowledge of history, you'd be perfect."

Eleanor laughed. "I like that idea. Maybe I'll go as a Celtic warrior."

Chris straightened slightly, silent now, his stance shifting ever so slightly as he eyed Theo.

"Theo," Eleanor started, sensing the tension, "this is my friend, Chris. Chris, this is Theo. I know you two have already met."

Chris hesitated, then took Theo's outstretched hand.

"Nice to properly meet you, Chris. No hard feelings about try-outs," Theo said smoothly.

Chris held the handshake for a beat longer than necessary, then nodded. "No hard feelings."

Theo turned to Eleanor. "Eleanor has told me a lot about you."

Chris raised a sceptical brow. "Really? Funny. She hasn't mentioned much about you."

Theo chuckled, unfazed. "Probably because we only see each other two hours a week for Dr. Asterio's artifact studies class. Not much time to chat."

"So, what are you going as, Theo?" Maddison asked, sipping her coffee.

Theo leaned back against the tree, considering it carefully.

"I've been toying with a few ideas," he admitted. "Maybe a medieval king, with armour and a sword. Would be fitting, given my family's collection of historical artifacts."

Chris, still reserved, stepped forward slightly. "Solid choice. So, you're into history too, huh?"

Theo smiled. "Yeah, you could say that." He turned to Eleanor, eyes glinting. "I don't suppose you'd want to revise together—we can geek out over ancient artifacts."

Maddison barely looked up from her phone before she abruptly stood.

"Jenny just texted—meet her ASAP," she announced.

Theo furrowed his brows. "Oh? What's happened?"

Eleanor offered a reassuring smile. "Probably just needs help with something."

Theo, ever earnest, spoke up immediately.

"Maybe I could come along and lend a hand."

Before Eleanor could respond, Chris stepped in, firm, controlled.

"Sorry, Theo. Maybe another time."

And that was that.

The trio raced off toward the cliff top, descending the stone steps with urgency, the sound of their footsteps echoing.

Jenny was waiting beneath the cloisters, eyes wide, bouncing slightly on the balls of her feet.

"You'll like this," she grinned, excitement radiating off her.

"What's going on?" Eleanor asked, curiosity piqued.

Jenny leaned in.

"Tom and I finally got through the rubble in the tunnel—and you won't believe what we found."

Eleanor's stomach tightened, anticipation humming beneath her ribs.

Chris had already gone inside with Tom.

But first—

Jenny smirked, eyes bright with mischief.

"But first, you might want to put this on." Jenny thrust two construction worker-style hard hats toward Eleanor and Maddison.

Eleanor eyed them warily, holding hers up. "Where exactly did you get these?"

Jenny waved off the question as if it was completely irrelevant. "Oh, you know, they were just lying around on the first floor." She shrugged, adjusting her own helmet. "I figured the workers wouldn't miss a few."

Maddison let out a sharp scoff, crossing her arms. "Jenny, that's literally stealing."

Jenny grinned unapologetically. "Borrowing. We'll give them back... eventually."

Maddison rolled her eyes, but Eleanor had already slipped hers on, the cold press of the plastic against her scalp grounding her.

Her heart raced with anticipation.

Whatever Jenny and Tom had uncovered—it had to be big.

Finally, Eleanor exhaled, voice steady despite the flutter of nerves building in her chest.

"Alright," she said. "Let's see what you've found."

Jenny didn't wait—she turned on her heel, leading them through a narrow passageway, the walls lined with crumbling stone and thick, damp moss.

The temperature dropped as they ventured deeper, the flickering light casting eerie shadows that slithered along the rough stone.

Ahead, the faint, echoing voices of Chris and Tom rang through the tunnel, which sounded giddy and excited, that could only be compared to the reaction of two giddy schoolboys.

9

The Twins' Discovery

"Look at this."

Chris's flashlight cut through the darkness, illuminating a section of the tunnel wall. The beam landed on ancient markings, their edges worn and fractured by time.

"These symbols are old, but this writing…" He narrowed his eyes, tracing the fresh inscriptions carved directly over the ancient ones. "This is new. Someone's been down here recently."

Eleanor's stomach tightened.

Tom, already buzzing with excitement, pulled Chris closer, his grin stretched wide.

"You're way behind, mate," he chuckled. "Jenny and I have been mapping these tunnels for weeks. And get this—one of them runs straight under the Black Lake."

Chris's eyes widened. "No way."

Tom nodded furiously. "Yeah! And who knows where else they might lead?"

Chris exchanged a glance with Eleanor before grinning. "Then let's find out."

The twins rubbed their hands together in anticipation, practically bouncing on their heels.

Then—a sudden beam of light sliced through the tunnel, followed by a familiar voice.

"Hey, you two idiots—what the hell are you doing?"

Jenny emerged from the passage, flashlight held high.

"You're one to talk," Tom quipped, smirking.

Maddison and Eleanor caught up to them, Maddison tilting her head, inspecting the surroundings with curious caution.

"What have you found so far?" she asked, her flashlight beam sweeping across the rough stone walls.

"More than we bargained for," Chris replied, still grinning. "Tom says they've been mapping these tunnels for weeks. And one of them runs straight under the lake."

Eleanor's eyebrows shot up. That was both fascinating and a little alarming.

Tom waved off her concern with a careless shrug. "Alarming? It's an adventure! Who knows what secrets these tunnels hold?"

Jenny nodded enthusiastically, her voice laced with excitement.

Maddison's expression hardened, the practical side of her taking over.

"Some of these tunnels look unstable," she pointed out. "If we're really going to explore them, we need to be prepared."

Chris nodded, for once taking her seriously. "Agreed. We should gather supplies—flashlights, ropes, food, water—in case we get stuck down here for a while."

Then—his signature grin returned.

"Or, you know—we turn this place into our own hideout."

Eleanor scoffed. "A hideout? What are we now, vigilantes?"

Chris shrugged playfully, but Jenny leaned in conspiratorially.

"I don't know about you, but we could use a place to hide from Professor Dougan every once in a while."

Tom slapped his hands together, eyes gleaming. "Agreed."

The twins performed their iconic handshake, sealing the deal before anyone could object.

Maddison, ever the planner, pulled out a notepad, scribbling a quick list. "Fine. But let's split up—Eleanor and I will gather supplies while you lot keep mapping the tunnels. Meet back here in an hour."

Eleanor glanced at the others.

"And no wandering off alone, okay? We stick together."

The twins nodded, but the mischief in their eyes suggested Eleanor's warning had already been ignored.

Still, she couldn't help but smile. As she and Maddison headed back to the surface, Chris, Tom, and Jenny pushed deeper into the tunnels. The further they ventured, the colder the air became, thick with damp earth and the faint scent of rusting metal.

Jenny meticulously marked their progress, while Chris and Tom scanned the walls—flashlights bouncing off layers of stonework that shifted in design. Some parts were rough, ancient, carved by hand.

But then—it changed.

Chris reached out, brushing his fingers over the brick and steel reinforcements.

"This isn't old," he muttered. "This is modern construction."

Jenny shone her flashlight along the ceiling, revealing support beams that didn't belong in tunnels this ancient.

"This isn't just a forgotten passage," she realized. "Someone built something down here. And then—buried it."

The realization hung between them, heavy and unanswered.

Then—Tom stopped.

"Look at this."

His light landed on a massive metal door, its edges sealed like a vault.

Chris stepped forward, inspecting the intricate lock mechanism.

"Of course, it's locked," he muttered. "But I bet we can get in."

Jenny reached into her bag, pulled out a set of lockpicks, and handed them over.

Chris took them with mock confidence. "Watch and learn."

He worked at the lock, his breath shallow, tension thick in the air.

Jenny and Tom kept watch, their flashlights revealing faint scorch marks on the walls, as if something had been burned away long ago.

Then—

Click.

The panel to their left hissed open and just beyond it was a slab of metal, covered in layers of dust. The twins brushed it off, revealing a black panel—sleek, polished—far too high-tech to be more than fifty years old. Chris then peered through a small latch on the door, his voice echoing.

"This place is unreal," he whispered. "Who built this?"

Jenny ran her hand across the smooth metal, frowning. "It's like it was deliberately hidden."

Eleanor and Maddison arrived, arms full of supplies, just in time to see the massive vault before them.

"Looks like you found something big," Eleanor said, stepping forward.

Chris nodded, his grin returning. "We just need to get in."

Tom and Jenny tried tugging on the door.

Maddison scoffed. "That's not going to work—it's deadlock sealed."

Eleanor leaned against the panel beside the door, shaking her head.

"Maddison's right, it's not just going to suddenly—"

Then—

A beep. A green light.

The panel lit up, displaying two words: ACCESS GRANTED.

Eleanor froze.

How come it had let her in? As Eleanor pulled her hand away, a little startled, she honestly didn't know. Perhaps the mechanism simply worn down after years—decades—of being buried beneath rubble? That was the only logical explanation.

The bolts slid sideways, dust hissing from beneath them.

Tom, who had been lying flat to inspect the gap under the door, jumped upright as the ground shook.

The handle rose.

The door squealed open.

Tom couldn't stop grinning. But as the five of them crept inside they were oddly disappointed by the dead end of rocks and rubble that they found. Small bolder folded on top of each other to form a small pyramid at the far end.

I was expecting something more impressive," sighed the twins in unison, their voices carrying through the dimly lit cavern.

Still, Tom's expression shifted as he glanced around, taking in the towering stone walls and the faint scent of earth that lingered in the air. "This place is perfect for a secret hideout," he added, his voice echoing slightly against the cavern's rough edges.

"And an even better place to test our inventions," Jenny chimed in, nodding eagerly as she exchanged a gleeful look with her brother. Their excitement was unmistakable, a spark of mischief gleaming in their eyes.

Maddison folded her arms, unimpressed, and scoffed. "Sure—if you want the entire foundation of Bleakwood School to come crashing down on top of us."

Tom laughed, shaking his head, a grin tugging at his lips. "Come on, Maddison. Have a little faith in us. We're not that reckless."

The statement hung in the air just long enough for Eleanor, Maddison, and Chris to share a glance—each of them hardly reassured.

But Eleanor's mind was elsewhere, turning over the same unanswered question.

Who built this place?

And why was it hidden?

Before she could voice her thoughts, a sudden scuffling noise echoed from deeper within the tunnel—not them.

Eleanor froze.

Chris turned, his flashlight sweeping across the passageway, casting long shadows against the walls.

Then—a figure stepped forward, emerging from the darkness like he'd been waiting for this moment.

Henry Kensington.

Eleanor's stomach dropped instantly.

His expression twisted into a grin, all sharp edges and triumph, his posture radiating smug satisfaction.

"Well, well, well." He crossed his arms, surveying the group like a predator that had cornered its prey. "I knew something was off about you lot."

Maddison groaned, already exasperated. "For goodness' sake, why are you even here?"

Henry shrugged, entirely unbothered by their frustration.

"I followed you," he admitted, no shame in his tone whatsoever. "You think I didn't notice you sneaking around?"

Chris let out an exaggerated sigh, rubbing his temples like he was already over this conversation before it had even properly started.

"And what exactly do you want, Henry?"

Henry smirked, his eyes flickering toward the open door—the metal vault that led into something they hadn't fully explored yet.

"This is restricted," he said slowly, letting the weight of the word settle, dragging out the moment just to watch their reactions.

Jenny scoffed, unimpressed. "Yeah? And who exactly restricted it?"

Henry's grin widened.

"Singleton."

Of course. Singleton. The man who always had his hands in whatever secrets Bleakwood tried to bury.

Before anyone could react, Henry took one last satisfied look at their horrified expressions—then turned on his heel and sprinted back up the passageway, the sound of his footsteps fading fast.

Maddison cursed under her breath, already moving to chase after him—but Eleanor grabbed her arm, holding her back, because it was pointless. He was already gone.

And they all knew exactly where he was headed.

"That little rat is going straight to Singleton," Eleanor muttered, her pulse hammering.

And now, thanks to Henry, Singleton would know exactly what they'd found.

10

Truth

The group stood stiffly before his desk, the eerie glow of his desk lamp casting elongated shadows against the walls. Eleanor could feel Singleton's piercing gaze settle on each of them, assessing, calculating. Henry Kensington sat smugly to one side, arms folded, his satisfaction radiating off him. But it lasted only a moment. Singleton slowly leaned back in his chair, exhaling through his nose.

"I don't know where you students get these ridiculous notions," he said smoothly, his voice deceptively calm.

"The tunnels beneath Bleakwood," he continued, "were nothing more than failed storage passages from an older section of the school's foundation. They were deemed unstable decades ago, sealed for safety purposes, and have no relevance to anything you'd find of historical significance."

Eleanor bit the inside of her cheek to stop herself from protesting.

Singleton wasn't just hiding something—he looked nervous.

"Your unauthorised entry into a restricted part of the school is a serious infraction," Singleton went on, narrowing his eyes. "But given the lack of damage and your clear ignorance, I will extend leniency—this time."

Henry, who had been waiting for them to be dragged through the mud, snapped upright in protest.

"That's it? That's all you're going to do?" he sputtered. "They were sneaking around places they had no right to be in, and you're letting them off with a warning?"

Singleton's gaze shifted, now trained on Henry with an unsettling steadiness.

Eleanor wasn't sure, but she could have sworn that for just a second, Singleton looked mildly displeased that Henry had spoken up.

The room tensed, the atmosphere curling inward.

Singleton slowly straightened in his chair, placing his hands flat on his desk. "Mr. Kensington," he said coolly, "I don't recall asking for your input."

Henry hesitated, confidence flickering.

Singleton's fingers tapped once against the wood, thoughtful, precise. Then—his voice dropped ever so slightly.

"You followed them into the tunnels, did you not?"

Henry blinked. "Well, yeah, but—"

Singleton tilted his head slightly, and Henry's smug demeanour crumbled immediately.

"In that case," Singleton said, smoothly turning over a blank disciplinary form, "I will extend your punishment twice over for knowingly entering a restricted area. Since you felt so strongly about rules being enforced, I would hate for you to be left out of the consequences."

Henry gawked, his protest dying in his throat.

Chris coughed to hide his laughter.

Tom smirked.

Jenny folded her arms, satisfaction gleaming in her expression.

"Detention for the next two weeks, Mr. Kensington," Singleton concluded, filling out the form in neat, calculated strokes. "Perhaps that will remind you where your priorities should lie."

Henry, red-faced and fuming, glowered at his newly assigned detention slip while Eleanor, Chris, Maddison, Jenny, and the twins stood in calculated silence, unwilling to provoke Singleton further.

Just when Eleanor thought the conversation was over, a sharp knock rattled the door.

Singleton exhaled slowly, as though the patience he had left was dwindling at an alarming rate.

"Enter," he said curtly, barely lifting his gaze.

The door swung open, revealing a stocky construction worker, his uniform stained with dust and grease. He looked hesitant, as if stepping into Singleton's office alone was its own punishment.

"Sir—sorry to interrupt—but we need clearance to proceed with the next phase of the demolition."

Singleton's eye twitched ever so slightly.

"You mean the next phase of the restoration work?" he corrected, his voice cooler than before.

The worker shifted uncomfortably, realizing his mistake too late

"Yes, sir. The restoration work," he amended quickly.

Singleton stood, moving toward the window, his fingers pressed firmly behind his back.

"You are behind schedule," he muttered, almost to himself. "This school should be rid of those tunnels before the next term even begins."

Eleanor stiffened, exchanging a glance with Maddison. Chris caught on too, brow furrowing

"Rid of them?"

Not just sealed—removed entirely?

What exactly were the construction workers doing? Or more specifically what had Singleton asked them to do? It was certainly not restoration of the chemistry lab. They would have at least seen some progress by now.

Singleton's head tilted ever so slightly, a flicker of annoyance passing through his otherwise unreadable expression.

"I wasn't aware I needed to explain myself to a student, Knight," he remarked.

Chris held up his hands. "Just curious."

Singleton turned his attention back to the worker. "Whatever remains of them down there—remove it. I don't care how it's done, just do it quickly."

Eleanor's stomach twisted.

The worker gave a hurried nod, mumbling his agreement before quickly retreating from the office.

Singleton exhaled sharply. "Now, if there are no further interruptions," he said smoothly, his gaze locking onto the group.

The unspoken message was clear—they had been dismissed.

One by one, they filed out, but just as Eleanor stepped past the threshold, she risked one last glance back at Singleton.

He was still standing by the window, staring out toward the school grounds, his expression unreadable.

But his fingers...

They were curled tightly behind his back, as if he was crossing his fingers. Something about this entire situation unsettled him as much as it did her. And that worried her more than anything else. Because Singleton was a man of control. And right now—Eleanor wasn't sure he had any at all.

As the group made their way down the hallway, Chris finally broke the silence.

"He's lying," he muttered.

Jenny nodded. "Of course he is. He's always lying."

Maddison exhaled, pulling her jacket tighter around herself. She doubted that Singleton's sole concern was the risk to health and safety that those tunnels posed.

They already knew he was aware that the tunnels existed, especially after using them as a cut through to Shadow Wing alley last year, but what they still couldn't grasp was why he wanted them gone? And why all of a sudden?

Was it all the high-tech equipment he wanted buried?

Maddison squared her shoulders, determination flickering in her expression. "We need to figure it out—before it disappears for good."

Eleanor, walking slightly behind, found her gaze drifting back toward the spiralled staircase which led down to Singleton's office.

For the first time in weeks, she felt completely at a loss for words. How had Singleton just let them walk away? No punishment, no threats, no carefully worded warning meant to instil fear.

It didn't make sense.

If Singleton had even the slightest suspicion that they had stepped out of line last year—he would have made sure they felt it. He would have devised the most calculated, ruthless punishment possible, ensuring they never dared to cross him again.

And yet, now? Nothing.

Maybe Singleton was losing his touch.

Then again, strange behaviour from him wasn't exactly unusual—not where Eleanor was concerned.

At last, she turned to Maddison as they rounded the corner, lowering her voice. "We need someone close to Singleton."

Maddison frowned, crossing her arms. "And by 'we'—you mean me, don't you?"

Eleanor sighed. "You can use your internship as a cover."

Chris raised a brow, catching on. "You want Maddison to pretend she's covering some new article."

Maddison rolled her eyes. "Why am I always the one getting roped into things?"

Eleanor ignored the complaint. "Say you need material—something to keep students entertained, something that'll stop them from looking too closely into things that Singleton doesn't want uncovered."

Eleanor knew that when it came down to it, the one thing that was more precious to Singleton than anything else was his reputation.

Maddison's brow furrowed. "And while I'm busy feeding people fake news, you want me to watch Singleton?"

Jenny smirked. "Better you than us. He already hates Chris."

Chris scoffed. "Yeah, well, I hate him back, so it works out."

Maddison sighed, considering. This went against everything Maddison stood for as a journalist "Alright. Fine. But he's not an idiot, Eleanor. He'll know I'm listening."

Eleanor nodded. "That's the point."

Maddison's eyes narrowed. "He won't let anything slip if I'm around."

Eleanor allowed herself a small grin. "Not deliberately."

Maddison pressed her lips together, rolling the thought over in her head.

This wasn't just casual snooping—Singleton was dangerous in a way that wasn't obvious, and getting too close to him meant stepping into territory they didn't fully understand yet.

"Alright," she finally said, straightening. "I'll play nice. Make it look like I'm just digging for a story—keep it harmless."

Eleanor nodded. "Just don't push too hard. If he catches on..."

Maddison smirked, but there was a flicker of unease behind it. "What, you think he'll have me erased?"

Chris scoffed. "Singleton doesn't work like that. He doesn't need to erase people." He shrugged. "He makes sure they never find what they're looking for."

Jenny crossed her arms, thoughtful. "You mean he's good at diverting attention?"

Chris nodded. "Exactly."

Eleanor studied them all carefully. If Singleton had secrets worth burying, then Maddison was walking into something without knowing how deep it actually went.

"You need to watch his movements, where he goes, who he speaks to," Eleanor said, shifting slightly. "Try to catch what he isn't outright saying."

Maddison sighed dramatically, tossing her hair back. "So I'm just supposed to shadow him and hope he slips up?"

Eleanor tilted her head. "Not hope. Expect."

Maddison narrowed her eyes but didn't argue.

Then—Chris hesitated, glancing toward Eleanor.

"You ever wonder," he muttered, voice quieter, "what actually is down there? The tunnels? I mean, Singleton isn't just trying to seal them—he's trying to erase them entirely."

The statement lingered, heavier than before.

Eleanor swallowed. "Yeah. I do wonder."

And the worst part?

She wasn't sure she wanted to know the answer. Not yet. Not until they were ready for it.

11

Kristallnacht

T he past week had been a blur of late-night research sessions, whispered discussions, and careful manoeuvring around Singleton's ever-watchful presence.

Maddison had taken Eleanor's advice, getting close to Singleton under the guise of her journalism internship—but instead of keeping things surface-level, she had accidentally walked into a real story.

At first, the journalist society had treated her like just another student intern, expecting her to write up meaningless school announcements like better soap in the girls' bathrooms or thieving first years ransacking the kitchen of all cakes and sweet treats. But then, during one of her meetings with the editorial team, something shifted.

After overhearing reports of a series of strange thefts across the country, Maddison decided to investigate the case herself. When she caught the scent of a mystery, she couldn't rest until she had unravelled it.

She had already interviewed every journalist working on the top-secret story—under false pretences, of course. At first, it had worked like a charm. She managed to sneak copies of their articles, combing through them for any hints or overlooked clues.

That is, until the chief editor noticed.

Before she knew it, she was being summoned to Singleton's office. At first, she braced herself for a lecture to stay out of it. Or maybe even a punishment. But when she arrived, the chief wasn't waiting with disapproval.

Instead, he sat there with a large briefcase resting beside him—and an amused, almost bedazzled smirk curling at the edge of his lips. While Singleton remained perfectly still and unfeeling.

"You're persistent, Maddison."

The words came from Mr. Graham, the lead editor—an aging but sharp-eyed man who had spent far too long working in journalism to be easily impressed.

Maddison sat stiffly in her chair, fully aware of Singleton's presence beside Graham. She blinked, straightening in her chair. "Uh... thanks?"

Graham smirked. "That wasn't necessarily a compliment." He leaned back, glancing at Singleton, before continuing, "But I'll admit—you're not wasting your time here, are you?"

Maddison kept her face neutral, though she could feel Singleton watching for a reaction.

"Not really," she replied.

Graham pulled out a slim folder, sliding it across the desk. But before Maddison could reach for it, Singleton's hand pressed against the cover—holding it there for just a second longer than necessary.

It wasn't just hesitation.

It was reluctance.

Maddison suppressed the urge to clench her jaw, while Singleton slowly lifted his hand. His fingers tensing slightly before pulling away.

Maddison took the file, placing it under her arm.

"Thank you," she said, standing smoothly.

Graham nodded, but Singleton remained stone-faced, his fingers curling ever so slightly against the edge of his desk.

Maddison didn't look back as she walked toward the door.

As soon as she stepped into the corridor, Eleanor was already there, waiting.

"Well?" Eleanor asked, pushing off the wall. "What did he want?"

Maddison exhaled, until a readily brewing smile appeared on her face, before glancing down at the folder. "He gave me this."

Eleanor eyed the file like it had secrets buried in its spine. "What's in it?"

Maddison hesitated before handing it over.

"Official records," she muttered, the words barely escaping her lips.

That meant he trusted her with all the redacted information too sensitive to be revealed to the public. The thought settled heavily in her mind. They must have been truly desperate if they had turned to a student for help.

Eleanor flipped through the pages, scanning details quickly. Her brow furrowed.

Blueprints of factories. Planning permits for several companies across the country. Expedited construction orders. But...

Nothing that could explain why Singleton seemed reluctant for them to know about this.

Nothing that justified his sudden desperation to destroy the network of tunnels beneath Bleakwood.

Nothing about what used to be there before they were sealed.

Nothing on what Singleton was actually afraid of.

Eleanor snapped the file shut, gripping it tightly, frustration tightening in her chest. "This isn't enough."

Maddison sighed, crossing her arms, her expression troubled. "I know. But there hasn't been much progress on the construction work since the break-in at the main factory two miles from here."

Eleanor's head snapped up, eyes narrowing. "What?"

Without hesitation, Maddison unfolded the front page of the file, her finger skimming over a buried paragraph, eyes darting across the text. "Apparently, thieves made off with a handful of equipment—not enough to halt the project entirely, but enough to stir up concern among the stockholders."

Eleanor raised an eyebrow, suspicion creeping into her voice. "Stockholders?"

Maddison nodded, her tone growing sharper. "Some wealthy contractor who funds the business from their own pocket, hoping to turn a profit."

Then—her voice faltered.

Her eyes widened.

Her finger skimmed faster, scanning the page with increasing urgency.

Eleanor's heart picked up pace. "What?" She leaned in, tension prickling at the back of her neck. "Have you found something?"

Maddison let out a sharp breath, flipping the file toward Eleanor, shoving it into her hands. "Do you recognize this name?" Her voice was demanding, her finger jabbing at a single bolded line of text.

The moment Eleanor's eyes landed on it, her stomach dropped.

"No way."

Her hands tightened around the page, as if gripping it could steady her thoughts, could ground her in a reality that suddenly felt far too unstable.

She read the name aloud, because a part of her refused to believe it was real, refused to acknowledge that it had been hiding in plain sight the entire time.

"Decker Incorporated."

Slowly, she looked up at Maddison, who was grinning like a Cheshire cat, thrilled by the discovery, yet fully aware of the weight it carried.

Eleanor exhaled sharply, heart pounding, realization settling over her like a storm.

"I think we need to have a word with Theo."

*

It wasn't long before they'd made their way through the school, storming with intent. As the bell rang, signalling the end of the lesson, Theo stepped out of his classroom, completely oblivious—until Maddison collared him, shoving him against the nearest wall with a force fuelled by frustration.

"What's up?" Theo blinked, caught off guard.

Maddison didn't waste time. She thrust the report into his hands, jabbing a finger at his family's name printed in bold ink.

"When were you going to tell us that your family—the high-end collectors—are Decker Incorporated?"

Theo stared at the paper, confusion flickering across his face.

"I thought you knew," he said, as if it was common knowledge. "Most people recognise my name straight away."

Maddison huffed, clearly unimpressed.

"Maddison, calm down," Eleanor interrupted, placing a steadying hand on her arm. Then, taking a deep breath, she turned to Theo. "Do you know anything about the thefts happening within these companies?"

Theo shrugged, adjusting his bag strap.

"Sort of," he admitted. "I heard them mention the loss in profits, but my family doesn't tell me much. I don't think they want me to worry. Besides, it's not a big deal—thefts happen all the time."

Maddison's grip tightened.

"But disappearances?"

Theo tensed.

"What?"

Maddison stepped in closer, her voice low, sharp.

"Several workers, connected to your family's company, have turned up to work one day—and vanished the next. Explain that."

Theo's eyes widened, his throat tightening as panic surged through him.

"I—I don't know!" His voice shook, frustration tangled with confusion. "My family doesn't tell me that sort of stuff. Honestly? I don't even think they noticed when I transferred to Bleakwood. They hardly acknowledge me when I'm in the house—let alone halfway across the country."

For the first time, Eleanor felt a flicker of sympathy for him that went deep into her skin. She knew what it was like—to be forgotten.

"I swear I have never heard of any disappearances." He said.

But Maddison wasn't letting go. Her grip tightened around the files in her hands, her voice sharp and accusatory.

"Five! There have been at least five disappearances of ordinary works. How do you explain that?"

Theo shook his head slowly, his breath coming in uneven, shallow bursts as frustration and uncertainty tightened in his chest.

"Like I said—I don't know anything about that."

Maddison shoved the files toward him, flipping through the pages with a fury that matched the urgency in her voice.

"First—a bank in London. Then—an antiques company in Edinburgh importing foreign goods. A construction company in Wales, a satellite station in Northumberland, and now a factory on the other side of Bleakwood town."

She looked up, eyes blazing with frustration.

"What do you think the connection is?"

Theo stammered, his mind scrambling for answers, but Maddison pressed harder, her words cutting through the thick air between them.

"You! Your family! They fund each of these companies." Her voice rose, charged with exasperation. "Five locations. Five thefts. Five disappearances. That's not a coincidence, Theo—that's a pattern."

Theo's expression darkened, something shifting behind his eyes as the realization settled.

"But…" His voice dropped, his gaze flicking between the papers as he scanned the information again. Slowly, something clicked. "…That's not all that's happening."

Eleanor and Maddison exchanged tense glances, their focus locking onto him.

"What do you mean?" Eleanor pressed, stepping closer.

Theo exhaled, his fingers tightening around the report.

"They're getting closer."

Eleanor's breath hitched. Grabbing a pen, she marked the locations one by one in the order of their disappearance dates, the ink forming a pattern that crept closer—closer—toward Bleakwood.

And then—

A loud, shattering crash ripped through the uneasy quiet of the corridor.

Glass exploded from the windows, debris scattering as shards rained onto the stone floor. Students screamed, their voices splitting the air as they scrambled out of classrooms, fear carved into their faces.

Professor Flickwitt quivered as he emerged from his room, his complexion pale, his hands trembling at his sides. Professor Black stormed forward, his voice booming over the chaos.

"What the hell is going on?"

Eleanor, Maddison, and Theo shook glass shards from their backs, their minds racing through a blur of adrenaline and shock.

"Is everyone okay?" Eleanor called out, her gaze darting across the wreckage, scanning faces for injury.

There were nods. Unsteady breaths. The lingering shock reflected in wide-eyed expressions.

Maddison's hands trembled as she spoke. "That wasn't the wind."

Chris, who had appeared amidst the commotion, turned toward the wreckage alongside Eleanor. Their pulses pounded in their fists as they stepped toward the shattered window, the cool air pressing against their skin.

There wasn't even a breeze.

The trees stood eerily still, their branches frozen in place, their leaves unmoving.

Then—

Movement.

A figure in a black cloak moved swiftly across the school grounds, its silhouette barely visible against the dim light as it raced toward the cliff top.

"There's someone out there!" Eleanor's voice rang out, sharp with alarm.

Without a second thought, she launched herself forward into a sprint, her friends reacting instantly and charging after her, their footsteps echoing through the hallways as they rushed past classrooms and lockers. They didn't slow as they burst through the open gates, the cool night air hitting them like a wall, but Eleanor's focus never wavered.

The figure was fast, vanishing into the dense cover of trees ahead, their movements precise and practiced—but Eleanor refused to let them slip away.

Then, out of nowhere, Chris lunged.

With full force, he collided with the fleeing figure, sending them tumbling onto the grass in a tangled struggle of limbs and desperate movement. They twisted and fought, their body writhing in an attempt to escape his grasp, but Chris held firm, his grip unyielding.

Moments later, Eleanor and Maddison skidded to a stop beside them, their breaths coming in ragged gasps as they took in the scene before them. Chris, unwavering, reached for the hood and pulled it back, revealing the face beneath—a boy no older than they were, his expression defiant, his dark eyes flashing with something unreadable.

Recognition struck Eleanor instantly. Ezra. The boy who had been in that fight earlier in the term.

Steadying herself, she stepped forward, her voice measured but edged with tension.

"Who are you working for, Ezra?"

None of them believed for a second that a fourth-year student had acted alone.

Ezra's lips curled into a smirk. His gaze, unwavering, burned with quiet certainty.

"We are the future," he said smoothly, his voice carrying a weight beyond his years. "We are The Order of Shadows."

12

The Order of Shadows

The air was thick with tension, the kind that pressed down on Eleanor's chest and tightened every breath. Ezra, barely older than them, sat panting, his fingers raw from grappling with Chris who stood above him, jaw tense. Maddison crossed her arms, expression dark, while Eleanor knelt, her gaze drilling into his hollow eyes.

"Tell us about The Order of Shadows," Chris demanded, voice sharp. "What are you doing in Bleakwood?"

The boy sniggered, wiping sweat from his forehead with the back of his hand.

"Look at you," he muttered, shaking his head, "scrambling around, chasing your own tails in search of answers."

Maddison stepped forward abruptly, shoving Chris aside. "Give him here."

The boy grinned, unfazed. "And let me guess, if he's good cop, that makes you bad cop?"

Maddison's expression was cold, dangerous. "I'm a Morningstar."

The boy arched a brow, still smirking. "Am I supposed to be impressed?"

"No," Maddison said smoothly. "Just terrified—if you know what's good for you."

Before the boy could react, Maddison grabbed his wrist and kicked his legs over the cliff's edge.

A startled yell tore from his throat as his body swung violently over the twenty-foot drop, arms flailing until his fingers latched onto a thick protruding tree root.

The waves crashed violently against the jagged rocks below.

Maddison crouched, leaning over the edge. "Grab hold of that if you don't want to plummet to your death. It'd make for a very unattractive corpse."

The boy's face was pale, his breath coming in frantic gasps as he clung to the root.

"Now—tell us everything we need to know."

"Maddison!" Eleanor gasped, stepping forward.

Chris looked equally horrified but didn't stop her.

The boy's voice shook, his grip tightening. "Okay, okay! I'll tell you everything! Just pull me up first!"

With effort, Eleanor, Maddison, and Chris hauled him back up, their muscles straining. When they finally collapsed onto the grass, panting, the silence was suffocating.

The boy coughed, rubbing his sore wrists, gaze flickering between them. "The Order is a group for people sick of watching the world burn while the powerful sit back and do nothing. They destroy us—take everything we own, use up all the Earth's resources until there's nothing left. They don't have the right to lead."

Eleanor's stomach twisted. "And who does? You?"

The boy's grin returned. "Not us. Our righteous leader—Nyx."

Eleanor's pulse spiked sharply, sending a rush of adrenaline through her veins.

Just as she'd feared.

Nyx.

She had known, deep down, that it wasn't over—that his influence lingered, that his plans stretched far beyond what they had uncovered.

Maddison scoffed, crossing her arms and fixing the boy with a sharp, unwavering stare. "So what exactly *is* your plan? Throw bricks through windows? Attack innocent people until—what, you start a war?"

The boy laughed, shaking his head as though the very idea amused him. "Don't be ridiculous. Leader Nyx doesn't *want* war."

"No?" Eleanor leaned in slightly, her voice dangerously soft, each word measured with careful precision. "He just wants to mould the world in his own image."

The boy's confident smirk faltered for the first time. His lips parted as if to deny it—but he didn't.

"I'd rather die than let Nyx take the Light Element," Eleanor stated firmly, her voice unwavering.

At that, the boy's laughter shifted—losing its amusement, turning hysterical, sharp, unhinged. It rang out across the cliffs, bouncing off the jagged rock as Eleanor, Maddison, and Chris exchanged uneasy glances, tension crackling in the air between them.

"Nyx doesn't *want* the Light Element anymore," he muttered under his breath. "Why would he—when he could have the Key to Time?" And then, just as suddenly as it had begun, his laughter cut off. His mouth snapped shut, his body stiffening, as though he had realized he had said too much.

Eleanor stiffened, her body tensing instinctively.

Maddison lunged forward without hesitation, her voice sharp. "What did you just say?"

The boy's eyes widened in panic. He hadn't meant to say it. He knew it. They knew it.

Chris stepped closer, his expression darkening, his voice sharp with urgency. "What is his plan?"

A surge of anger coursed through Eleanor, rising fast, pushing past her hesitation. Without thinking, she clenched her fist around the boy's shirt, pulling him slightly forward.

His face turned red as he gasped for air, struggling against the sudden pressure.

"Somewhere underground," he choked out between ragged breaths. "Leader Nyx said that's where we'll find the Key to Time."

Eleanor loosened her grip just enough for him to breathe properly, but not enough to release him entirely.

"What is this key?" she demanded, her voice steady despite the storm of emotions tightening in her chest. "A weapon? A tool?"

The boy swallowed hard, his throat bobbing as he tried to steady himself. "Long ago, three powerful objects were given to humanity," he explained, his words strained. "The Element of Darkness. The Element of Light..." He exhaled sharply, his next words carrying undeniable weight. "And now, our leader seeks the Element of Time."

Eleanor's vision blurred for a brief moment as confusion crashed over her like an unforgiving wave.

"The Time Element was *lost*!" she shot back, disbelief laced in every syllable.

The boy's smirk was weak, but certain. "No."

Eleanor shook her head, trying to process his words, trying to make sense of something that shouldn't be possible. "What?"

Maddison's eyes burned with fury, her hands twitching at her sides. "He's *lying*! Let's hang him off the cliff again until he tells the truth!"

For once, Eleanor didn't disagree.

The boy panicked. "No, please! I *swear* it's the truth!"

Maddison sneered, unimpressed. "Right. Like we'd believe a radical like you."

But Eleanor studied him carefully—his wide pupils, his trembling fingers, his shallow, uneven breaths.

She wasn't so sure.

"I don't think he's lying," she murmured, her voice quiet but firm.

Maddison scoffed. "Maybe he's just *faking* it."

Eleanor ignored her, kneeling beside the boy, lowering her voice to a whisper. She leaned in closer, so close that her words barely had to carry. "Listen carefully," she said, keeping her tone calm, controlled. "Right now, I'm the only thing stopping Maddison from letting you hang until your palms start bleeding. If you want to avoid *that*—then you'll tell me the truth."

The boy nodded quickly, swallowing hard, his breath still uneven.

Eleanor held his gaze, unrelenting.

"Where is Nyx?"

"I—I don't know," the boy stammered, his voice breaking slightly. "But I *do* know where he will be."

Maddison arched a brow, unimpressed. "Go on."

The boy hesitated, looking around as if piecing something together in real time, as if realizing something himself for the first time.

"That's why the Order came here," he muttered, the words barely above a breath.

Eleanor felt her blood turn cold.

"He's in Bleakwood."

The boy nodded frantically, every movement laced with anxious desperation.

Eleanor turned to Maddison and Chris, horror settling deep in her expression.

"Which means... the Time Element is *here*."

Chris's head spun as the weight of the revelation hit him. "How could it be?"

Eleanor's fingers tightened around the file in her grasp. According to legend, the Time Element had vanished centuries ago, lost without a trace.

But if Nyx believed it was here—

Then he was coming for it.

Eleanor exhaled slowly, locking eyes with Maddison, their silent understanding shared in a single glance.

"We need to talk to Dr. Asterio."

Because whatever was buried beneath Bleakwood had just become the most dangerous thing in the world.

13

Confession

"**I** didn't lie to you Eleanor—not technically.**"** Dr Asterio began to say, "We never found the Time Element in the same tomb as the Dark and Light Elements..."

Asterio's voice was heavy, thick with something unfinished.

"...But one month after, there was a second expedition— funded by the Royal British Society to Athens—where the third Element was uncovered inside an old Greek burial chamber."

Eleanor's throat tightened.

She barely heard Maddison inhale sharply beside her.

"Why didn't you tell me this?" Eleanor asked, her voice shaking, edged with betrayal.

Asterio exhaled, rubbing the bridge of his nose. "Because by that point, I had already left the others."

She watched him closely—every hesitation, every flicker of something he didn't want her to see.

"At first, when it was just the four of us—me, Singleton, John, and Nyx—everything was normal."

Eleanor's stomach twisted at the sound of his name.

Nyx.

Asterio's voice hardened.

"But after we returned from Egypt, something changed in him. He became obsessed with finding the Time Element. He wouldn't say why. And it started to frighten me."

Eleanor swallowed, the weight of those words settling heavily in her chest.

Obsessed.

She knew what that looked like.

She had seen it—felt it—in the way his gaze lingered too long, in the sharp intensity behind his words, in the way he had carefully threaded himself into her trust, weaving a narrative so seamless, so convincing, that for a time, she had believed that he had truly cared.

Asterio wasn't finished.

"I believe he's been growing support. I have an old friend who works for the Telegraph who's been investigating the recent disappearances across the country. I recommended Maddison to help with the research."

Eleanor's head snapped toward Maddison, her chest tightening.

"All this time," she whispered, "your internship with the journalist agency was really you secretly working for the Dr?"

For the first time ever, Maddison stumbled over her words.

"I'm sorry, Eleanor. I wanted to tell you, but Asterio made me promise to keep it between us."

Eleanor's jaw clenched.

The lies.

The secrets.

From day one, Asterio had tried to keep her away from Bleakwood. From Nyx. And now—even Maddison had been hiding things.

Asterio pressed forward. "We believe these disappearances were just the start."

What did he mean the start? The start of what?

In the next breath they all watched as Asterio's expression darkened.

"We suspect Nyx has been growing support in young people across the country—forming a rebellious group who call themselves *The Order of Shadows*."

Eleanor stiffened. Hearing the name said aloud by the Dr made it sit even heavier in her chest.

This Order of Shadows had been leading raids all over the country for the past six months, something else the Dr had failed to mention. Eleanor wondered why she hadn't heard about it in the news, but she guessed if the police believed they were random, they had no reason to piece them all together. But the truth was, every raid was targeted. Each of them on storage vaults housing digging tools, weapons and mining equipment.

Maddison sucked in a breath, her eyes widening as the words settled. "Mining equipment?"

Asterio gave a slow, measured nod, his expression unreadable. "We believe Nyx is searching for the Time Element. And with the rate at which he's been gathering recruits, I expect him to make his move sometime within the next six months."

Eleanor's pulse pounded in her ears, a relentless beat against the rising uncertainty twisting through her. She swallowed hard, trying to steady herself, but the weight of his words made it nearly impossible to think straight. "You've been keeping tabs on him?"

Asterio hesitated, a flicker of something indecipherable crossing his face before he gave a small, almost reluctant nod.

Her stomach twisted sharply, the sudden wave of unease almost suffocating. "How long have you known Nyx was behind the disappearances?"

Asterio's gaze flickered, a brief moment of hesitation before he met her stare head-on, his voice carefully measured when he finally spoke. "There's only so much I can tell you, Eleanor."

She hated that answer.

That wasn't enough. Not even close.

This wasn't some insignificant piece of school gossip, something they could dismiss or ignore. This was Nyx—his actions, his plans, his looming presence growing stronger with every passing day, and yet Asterio had chosen to keep her in the dark.

Eleanor felt her anger rising, hot and steady, burning just beneath her skin. Why? Why hadn't he told her? He had promised—promised to keep her safe, to stand beside her, to ensure she wasn't left vulnerable. How did withholding this information possibly help? How did leaving her unaware of Nyx's movements make anything safer?

Asterio's expression softened, and for the first time, Eleanor glimpsed something raw beneath his composed exterior—regret, quiet and undeniable.

She swallowed, then squared her shoulders. "Were you afraid I'd be a liability? That if Nyx got a hold of me, he'd force me to spill all your secrets?"

Asterio's eyes darkened, "No," he murmured, his voice barely louder than a whisper. "Never you, Eleanor."

But that didn't ease the knot tightening in her chest. She knew the depths of Nyx's manipulation, the way he could twist himself into people's minds, warping reality until even the strongest began to doubt themselves. And Eleanor understood—on some level— that Asterio was trying to be kind about it, to soften the edges of a truth he didn't want her to bear alone.

Still, her breath hitched, fury curling beneath her ribs, simmering with an intensity she couldn't shake. Even though she knew what he meant, even though she understood why he had kept this from her, the sting of it remained. She had trusted him. She had let herself believe that he saw her as an ally, not as a weakness to be protected from Nyx's reach. Yet no matter what she said, no matter how she tried to rationalize it, Asterio's fear wasn't just of Nyx's power—it was of the destruction he could unleash.

Eleanor's voice hardened, her anger pressing against the edges of her control. "You said Nyx's obsession with the Elements was one of the reasons you left."

She narrowed her eyes. "What was the other?"

Asterio swallowed, his gaze momentarily flickering before settling back into something unreadable.

"Because he did to me exactly what he did to you... in a way."

Maddison stiffened beside her. "He manipulated you?"

Asterio exhaled slowly, the weight of his past pressing into his words, making them quieter, thinner—fragile in a way Eleanor had never seen before. "In a way... he broke our hearts."

Silence crashed over the room, thick and deafening, swallowing whatever disbelief might have lingered. And suddenly, everything made sense. Eleanor could see it as clearly as if the pieces had fallen into place before her eyes. Asterio hadn't been keeping secrets out of selfishness—he had been protecting her.

She inhaled sharply, then narrowed her gaze. "And by 'our,' you mean Singleton, don't you?"

Asterio flinched, his reaction giving her the answer before he even spoke.

Then, after what felt like an eternity, he nodded.

Chris shifted, tapping his pen against the table, shifting the mood, pulling the weight of the conversation onto something else. "If the Time Element was brought to Bleakwood, why would it be underground?"

Asterio's jaw tightened, his expression growing darker. "Two days after it arrived, John Walker confronted Nyx. That same night—the base collapsed."

Eleanor's breath stilled.

John.

Her father.

His work—the very thing that had consumed him for years, the thing he had dedicated his life to—had buried him beneath Bleakwood.

Asterio inhaled deeply before speaking again, his voice firm, unyielding. "Eleanor, if Nyx gets the Time Element—it will be the end of the world as we know it."

Her heartbeat slammed against her ribs, the panic rising faster than she could contain it. "What do you mean?"

Asterio's expression hardened, his eyes filled with something Eleanor could only describe as certainty—and dread.

"The Time Element alters reality," he said, his voice measured, careful, as if speaking the words too quickly would make them more real. "If Nyx gets his hands on it, he could rewrite history. Undo his mistakes. But at a price."

Chris stiffened, tension coiling in his posture. "What kind of price?"

Asterio's voice was barely a whisper, carrying an eerie finality that settled in Eleanor's bones.

"Every change erases the present. The bigger the shift—the greater the loss. He could erase entire timelines. Including ours."

Eleanor felt the world tilt beneath her feet, the weight of his words crashing down all at once.

Her stomach twisted violently, her breath uneven.

Nyx wasn't just searching for the Time Element. He was looking to change everything. And if they didn't stop him—if they couldn't stop him—there was a real chance they might never exist at all.

Then—the door swung open.

Singleton stepped inside, his sharp gaze sweeping across the room, his posture rigid, his expression unreadable. Whatever news he carried, it was bad. Serious enough that he had decided Eleanor needed to hear it, despite everything. Or maybe, just maybe, after all that had been revealed, the game of keeping her in the dark had ended the moment she learned the truth about the Order of Shadows.

His gaze locked onto hers, firm and unwavering.

"It appears, Miss Morningstar," he said, his voice clipped, precise, measured, "Mr. Graham, the journalist from The Telegraph, hasn't been seen since leaving Bleakwood."

The weight of his words settled heavily over them.

A cold wave rippled through the space.

Graham had been expected in London—but had never arrived.

No one needed to say it aloud.

Nyx was already covering his tracks.

Singleton's stare sharpened, his tone unwavering. "You need to be careful. It's clear Nyx is taking steps to eliminate loose ends."

Eleanor met his gaze and held it, refusing to let fear break her resolve. She understood exactly what he was telling her, but that didn't mean she wanted to hear it.

"So what?" she challenged, voice firm, defiant. "You want me to run and hide?"

Singleton smirked faintly, his response smooth, unbothered. "Run. Leap. Fly away if you have to," he mused, his tone as effortless as ever. "My offer to take you out of Bleakwood still stands."

But Eleanor remained unmoving, unwavering.

LOST IN TIME

She wasn't running. Not this time. Not ever.

14

Silenced

I 'll meet you back at the dormitory Eleanor. Maddison said as she raced off up the corridor. There are just a few articles I need to grab I won't be too long."

Singelton and Asterio were goodness knows where. Having raced off moments ago, with a plan they weren't ready to tell Eleanor, Chris or Maddison. But Eleanor needed to get back to the dormitory as soon as possible. She felt uneasy having left the Light Element unprotected. It was a mistake to think she could ever go without carrying it.

Maddison's fingers trembled slightly as she unlocked the door to the media society with a spare key she had borrowed from the professor's office. They wouldn't notice if one spare key went missing.

Pushing aside stray papers on the desk, her eyes darting between reports, trying to fit the documents into her bag. The blueprints, the reports. If Singleton was right and Mr Graham had been taken by Nyx, then these documents might be the only copy.

It didn't take more than thirty minutes to gather everything she needed. But by then, the air outside had turned icy and dreary.

A thick mist was rolling in from the east as Maddison stepped out of the school's office, clutching her bag tightly. Her mind buzzed with the revelations she had uncovered.

Just as she was about to reach the bottom of the path, a figure stepped out in a black robe with a metallic badge sparkling in the streetlight. At first her stomach dropped until she looked upon its face which had an infuriating look of authority.

Oliver.

"Maddison, we need to talk," he said, voice firm, cutting through the quiet.

Maddison huffed, adjusting her grip on her bag. "I can't right now, Oliver. I'm in the middle of something important."

She stepped sideways to pass him—but he caught her arm, his grip firm, not rough.

"You've been acting strange lately," Oliver pressed, his brows knitted in concern. "I know you're up to something dangerous, and I'm worried about you."

Maddison sighed, her patience wearing thin. "I appreciate your concern, but I have to do this. I'm close to uncovering the truth about the disappearances. This story could be the start of my career, just like your research on the Elements last year was the start of yours."

Oliver's expression darkened, his jaw tightening. "And what if you get hurt? Or worse?"

"I—" Maddison opened her mouth, but he cut her off.

"I won't be here next year to look out for you."

His words hit harder than she expected, lodged deep beneath the sharp urgency of the moment.

But before she could respond—

A black van screeched to a halt, tires skidding loudly against the pavement.

Her chest tightened as two burly men in dark clothing sprang from the shadows, their movements practiced and precise, leaving no doubt that they weren't here by chance. One of them seized her, fingers digging into her arm as he snarled, "Get in."

Oliver shouted her name, lunging forward in a desperate attempt to reach her, but Maddison's body reacted before her mind could process the danger. Adrenaline surged through her, fuelling her actions like instinct. She dropped her weight, twisting sharply, and with a burst of force, her knee slammed into the man's shin just as her elbow collided with his ribs.

The second man lunged for her—his grip just missing its target.

But Maddison spun, her boot connecting sharply with his groin, the force of the impact sending him stumbling backward with a strangled gasp of pain.

"Get her!" the first man shouted, already recovering fast.

Maddison didn't hesitate. She turned and ran, breath coming in short, uneven bursts, each desperate footfall echoing loudly against the stone path. Her heartbeat thundered in her ears as she darted behind the van, pulse hammering, feet pounding against the pavement with relentless force.

Then—

A blinding light erupted ahead, brilliant and sudden.

"Maddison!" Eleanor's voice cut through the chaos like a blade—sharp, commanding, impossible to ignore.

Maddison skidded to a halt, her pulse leaping violently in her chest.

Standing at the centre of the road, Eleanor held the Light Element in her hand, its glow pulsing steadily, power radiating outward in waves of crackling energy.

She lifted her arm, channelling the magic—

And before them—

A radiant eagle burst into life, its wings unfurling wide, spanning the entire length of the parking lot, its brilliant form illuminating the darkness with an otherworldly intensity.

The men froze, their faces contorting with horror, eyes wide and uncomprehending as the creature let out a deafening, ear-splitting screech, the eerie glow of its gaze locking onto them.

A step backward—then another. Panic flooded their expressions as they stumbled away, scrambling to put distance between themselves and the impossible sight before them.

"What the hell is that?" one of them stammered, voice shaking, fear curling through every syllable.

Eleanor stepped forward, her posture unwavering, her voice cold, devoid of hesitation. "Leave now," she warned, words deliberate, measured, unyielding, "and you might live to see another day."

They didn't pause to consider their odds.

With frantic movements, they scrambled into the van, doors slamming shut, tires screeching against the pavement as they sped away into the fog, disappearing like ghosts into the night.

Maddison's knees buckled, giving out beneath her as she collapsed onto the pavement, breath still coming in ragged, uneven gasps, adrenaline crashing through her system in relentless waves.

Eleanor rushed to her side, Oliver right behind her, his face pale, ashen with the weight of what had just happened.

"Are you okay?" Eleanor asked, voice lined with concern, eyes scanning Maddison for any sign of injury.

Maddison nodded despite the tremor still lingering in her limbs, her body unable to shake the lingering tension of the fight, the fear that had momentarily threatened to consume her.

Oliver's expression hardened, his gaze sharp, calculating. "Who were they, Maddison? What did they want?"

She swallowed, the answer sitting heavy on her tongue before she finally spoke. "Me, I think."

Oliver's eyes locked onto hers, searching, assessing.

"The Order knows I'm onto them."

Eleanor's breath caught in her throat. It was the only explanation—one that sent an unsettling wave of realization rolling through her. Which meant that Nyx wasn't far behind. If he hadn't already figured it out, if he hadn't already set this in motion—

Then maybe, just maybe, he was the one who had sent them in the first place.

Silence hung between them, thick, unspoken fears swirling in the space between words.

Eleanor's expression hardened. They needed to regroup. Only back in the dormitory were they truly safe from watchful eyes. As Oliver took Maddison by the shoulder and helped her up, she hobbled back on a pulled muscle. Even with all of her martial art skills, she hadn't been prepared to react so quickly.

Back inside, the tension refused to lift.

Oliver rushed to close the curtains, constant aware of everything happening around him while Maddison finally placed her documents on the table centre for all to see.

For Eleanor, it was strange to see something other than the usual files filled with evidence about her father's death occupying that space.

Chris was supposedly on his way back, but there was no telling how long he would take—meanwhile Eleanor's attention drifted elsewhere.

A soft whisper curled through the hallway.

She glanced from Maddison to Oliver, waiting for the perfect moment to slip out unnoticed.

At the end of the corridor—the mirror waited.

Eleanor checked once more that her friends weren't watching before she exhaled slowly, turning sharply toward the reflection.

And there it was.

The grinning shadow of herself, waiting, watching with a knowing and eerie smile. So now you want my help? it spoke in a voice that was both hers and yet distinctly different.

"No, I want you to leave me alone, but since that is never going to happen..." Eleanor trailed off, her frustration palpable.

Okay, okay... It paused, as if savouring the moment. You want to find Nyx, right?

Eleanor folded her arms. The reflection's gaze was intense, almost hypnotic, like a force pulling at her thoughts.

If it wasn't for me, you'd never have gotten a handle on the Light Element's powers, right? Its voice curled around her, low and knowing. *Well, what if I told you there are other ways of tracking an Element holder?*

Eleanor tensed, but curiosity outweighed caution. "I'm listening," she said, even as unease prickled at the back of her mind.

The reflection tilted its head, its grin sharp. *Each Element grants different abilities, but they are all linked. Used correctly, they emit an energy signature—completely undetectable by normal technology. But if you hold one Element, you can use it to find another.*

Eleanor's breath hitched as realization struck. "And since Nyx holds the Dark Element, I can trace everywhere he's been."

The reflection's grin widened. *Precisely.* Then, its expression darkened. *But be careful, Eleanor. The Light Element is powerful—but so is the Dark. You must be ready for whatever you uncover.*

She took a slow, steadying breath, pushing aside the doubt threatening to take hold.

The reflection's eyes gleamed—pride and something far more sinister flickering within them. *Good luck, Eleanor.* The words were smooth, but hollow, as if luck was the last thing it expected her to have.

As the reflection faded, leaving only her own familiar image staring back, Eleanor turned sharply on her heel. Her pulse was pounding. She had a weapon now—a way forward.

Rejoining Maddison and Oliver, she quickly explained. "We can use the Light Element to trace Nyx. It gives off an energy signature—we just need to focus and follow the trail."

Maddison's eyes sparked with hope. "That's brilliant! This could be the breakthrough we need."

Oliver, ever the cautious one, frowned. "But it sounds dangerous. Are you sure you're ready for this?"

Eleanor squared her shoulders. "I have to be. We all do. This is our best chance to find Nyx—and find out what he's planning before he has a chance to strike again."

Before the words had fully settled, the door burst open. Chris stumbled inside, breathless but determined. "I got your message. What's the plan?"

Eleanor met his gaze, feeling a buzz of energy—sharp and electric. "We're going to track Nyx using the Light Element. It's risky, but it's our best shot."

15

The Light Element

Eleanor held the Light Element tightly, its warmth pulsing against her skin, threading its energy through her veins. The air in the room was heavy with hesitation. This was happening fast—maybe too fast.

Oliver had argued for a careful approach, a solid plan. He wanted time to think things through. But playing it safe wouldn't get them anywhere. If they weren't willing to take risks, Nyx would stay ahead, always finding new ways to hunt them down. They couldn't live in fear forever, constantly looking over their shoulders.

They stood in a perfect circle, Eleanor at its heart. All eyes were on her.

Chris gripped a fire extinguisher—one he'd bought after the twins had moved into their dorm, as if expecting disaster at every turn. Maddison was tense, muscles coiled, prepared to take down whatever threatened them. Oliver stood nearest to the wall, his fingers brushing against the stone, as though he needed something solid to anchor himself.

This is it.

There was no turning back now.

Over their shallow breaths, Eleanor closed her eyes, steadying herself. She had learned how to channel the Element's energy—but this was unlike anything she had ever tried before. She didn't know what would happen. She only hoped her reflection had been telling the truth.

She prayed the Element wouldn't explode in her hands.

In an instant, she felt the connection—like flipping a switch. A sudden pulse ran through her, linking her thoughts to the flow of energy. Its power hummed inside her, weaving through every fibre of her being.

For now, it seemed to be working.

But she didn't want to jinx it just yet.

The next step—seeking out Nyx—meant searching for the Dark Element itself. She had learned that each Element carried its own unique signature—light, warmth, happiness. It made sense that the Dark Element would be the complete opposite.

She pulled at the deepest parts of her mind, searching for anything painful or unsettling—memories of Nyx.

A strange tingling ran up her fingers, sharp like needles. Something in the flow of energy twisted, shifting. A ripple.

As she concentrated, bursts of colour flickered behind her closed eyelids—quick flashes, like fragments of film moving too fast to grasp.

The images came faster now, flashes of colour and movement just beyond her grasp.

Her heart pounded, wild and uneven. If she could just focus—just steady her thoughts—maybe they would sharpen, revealing something real.

She wasn't even sure if it was working.

Nyx. Nyx. Nyx. She repeated his name like a mantra. *Show me where you are. Show me what you're planning.*

A blur of green and brown filled her mind—fractured, disjointed, slipping through her fingers before she could make sense of it.

Not enough.

She had to dig deeper.

Gritting her teeth, she braced herself against the storm crashing through her mind. Wave after wave, each one slamming into her lungs and leaving her gasping for air.

She had to hold on—just a little longer. The images in her mind were sharpening, growing clearer, pulling her in.

Then came the scent. Damp earth, crushed leaves, thick with decay. It clung to her senses, almost suffocating. But that wasn't enough. It wasn't a breakthrough. Most of the world was covered in soil and plants—this wasn't the answer she was looking for.

She had hoped she wouldn't have to do this. But she had no choice now—no time to hesitate.

Summoning every ounce of strength she had left, she reached deep into the darkest corners of her mind and clawed out the most painful memory she could find.

She wasn't even sure if it was real or just some twisted nightmare. But in the depths of her subconscious, she saw them— her friends' bodies, lifeless, sprawled across the ground. All because of *her*.

Just as the images began to sharpen, a searing pain tore through her head, shattering her concentration like glass splintering into pieces.

She gasped, clutching her temples as the Light Element in her hand grew hotter, the burn creeping up her fingers. It felt like a thousand needles stabbing into her mind, each one pushing deeper, threatening to tear her apart.

Through the chaos, she heard a voice shouting. *Let it go!*

But she was so close—so close to finding the answer.

"No! I can do this!" she screamed, her voice raw, desperate.

Maddison shook her head and reached out to close the book. It was clear Eleanor couldn't think straight. Someone needed to step in and put a stop to this, but Chris held her back. "What are you doing?" Maddison questioned over the swirling sound of energy, it was barely heard, "It could kill her!"

But Chris replied with a stare that needed no words, one that said, she can do this, you have trust her.

Eleanor was now caught in a whirlwind of chaotic visions. But it didn't matter how hard she tried, it still felt like an invisible force was preventing her from seeing the whole picture. Like the visions couldn't quite come into focus.

A sudden, blinding light exploded in her vision and the book dropped out of her hands, causing her to collapse onto her hands and knees. For a moment all Eleanor could see was stars swirling in her eyes. For a moment she thoughts she'd gone blind until she saw Maddison standing over her with that all too familiar worried look.

Oliver quickly slammed the book cover shut, concealing the light inside as if to protect it from whatever unseen force had attacked Eleanor.

Eleanor groaned, her body aching from the impact. "I... I couldn't hold it. The pain... it was too much."

Maddison gently helped her sit up, her touch reassuring. Her covered with concern, "What did you see?" she asked softly.

Eleanor took a shaky breath, her mind still reeling from the experience. "I saw Nyx in a desolate wasteland, an underground lair filled with ancient artifacts, and a hidden passage in a misty forest. But I couldn't hold on. The Light Element... it was too powerful."

Oliver looked at the Light Element, now lying dim on the floor, his eyes narrowing in thought. "Maybe you're not supposed to do this alone. Maybe the Element's power is too much for one person to handle."

Eleanor nodded, wincing as she moved. "You're right.

"But none of us can use it, it doesn't work with us." Chris said solemnly.

At that moment, Eleanor caught a glimpse of her reflection in the nearby window. It didn't just mirror her—it *mocked* her, winking with a wicked smile, its lips curling into a knowing smirk. A flicker of anger stirred within her. The reflection's presence was a constant reminder of her failures.

Beside her, Oliver picked up the Light Element, turning it carefully in his hands, studying its surface with quiet focus.

Eleanor had poured everything she had into it, pushing herself to harness its power, yet still—it hadn't been enough.

The Elements weren't like ordinary forces of nature. They didn't follow the rules of science as they knew them. They existed beyond all of that, bound to something greater—an energy beyond their world, beyond human comprehension, beyond anything they had ever encountered before.

If it had worked like how a television tuned into a specific channel or how a radio frequency could be amplified to pick up a signal, then the solution would have been far simpler. But there was just a switch they could flip to make the Elements more powerful

They responded to something deeper.

Something *driven by emotion.*

Something *alive.*

Oliver's eyes narrowed slightly as he turned the Element in his hands, considering its weight, its presence, the hum of power barely perceptible beneath its surface.

Then, after a moment, his expression shifted.

"I might have an idea," he announced.

The others frowned.

"Ever since Nyx pretended to be our Chemistry professor last year, I wondered how he'd managed to use the power of the Dark Element to disguise his appearance every day without completely tiring him out. Here's what I found. In the story of the 'Four Princes' when the Elements were first bestowed upon humanity, each Element was chosen by the prince who connected most to its powers."

Eleanor recalled Dr. Asterio explaining the same thing to her at the end of last year. Nyx had been able to wield the Dark Element because it fed on strong emotions—power, ambition, and the relentless desire to dominate. His hunger for control was exactly the kind of force that fuelled it.

"I think the Elements respond to emotion."

"Emotion?" Maddison questioned.

"What, so it's like some high-powered mood ring?" Chris scoffed, chuckling under his breath.

Oliver rolled his eyes, perfectly mimicking his sister's signature unimpressed expression. "When you tried using the Light Element before, did it get more painful the harder you pushed?"

Eleanor thought about it for a moment. "I guess," she admitted.

"The Light Element is all about hope and goodness, right?" Oliver continued.

"Right."

"So, try again. But this time, focus on the happiest memories you have."

Eleanor picked up the Light Element once more, feeling its gentle warmth against her palm. She took a deep breath, closing her eyes, steadying herself, willing her emotions to settle. The idea that feelings could amplify the power of the Elements fascinated her—but it also made her wary.

She focused on Oliver's words, letting them guide her.

Eleanor cast her mind back to the moments that had filled her with joy and hope—the thrill of adventures in Bleakwood, the unbreakable bond she had forged with her friends. She recalled laughing with Maddison and Oliver, their camaraderie a steady light in even the darkest times. She thought of Christmases spent with the Harrisons, the warmth of their home, the embrace of their family, and the love that had always made her feel safe.

As the memories washed over her, she felt the Light Element respond. Its glow brightened, pulsing gently in her palm, and a deep sense of calm and strength settled within her. She focused, channelling that energy, pushing past her doubts, searching for the signature of the Dark Element.

Visions swirled in her mind once more, but this time they were vivid, sharp, and undeniable. She saw Nyx, shrouded in shadows, his form consumed by darkness. Yet even through the haze, she could sense his emotions—anger, desperation, an unrelenting hunger for control.

Then, the image shifted. She saw towering stone walls stretching into the dim glow, their surfaces adorned with intricate carvings that flickered beneath the amber light. Crates of weapons and explosives lined the space, a chilling display of destruction—enough firepower to wipe out an entire town.

And Eleanor felt the chill settle into her bones as she realized exactly what it was.

Power.

She felt herself being drawn toward the energy signature of the Dark Element, its pull growing stronger, its presence pressing against her senses. The pain returned, sharper and more insistent, but she held on, refusing to let go and kept her mind focused on her friends and the light buzz filling her chest. She saw flashes of Nyx's face, his eyes black and soleless.

The vision shifted to the misty forest, the air thick with humidity. Nyx stood before a grove of trees; a massive stone doorway hidden among them. The runes on the doorway glowed faintly, and Eleanor felt a sense of foreboding. She could smell the damp earth and hear the rustle of leaves as a breeze passed through the trees. It was as though Eleanor was looking through his eyes, seeing the world from his vantage point. She looked around to find something that would give away where Nyx was hiding out. A landmark or signpost. But wherever he was, it wasn't somewhere you'd find on a map.

Then, as if somehow Nyx could sense her presence, his perspective shifted. He turned slowly toward a nearby tree, his expression darkening. "Nice try, Eleanor," he muttered, his voice dripping with menace.

Eleanor's voice dropped. Crap! How could he know she was watching. Someone he could sense that she was rummaging around in his mind.

In one swift motion, he swung his fist at the tree with such force that it felt like a seismic wave reverberated through the air. Eleanor was suddenly yanked backward, her whole body feeling as though it had been violently pulled from her own. The sensation was disorienting and painful, like being torn from the fabric of reality itself.

Eleanor's vision blurred as she was thrown back into their dormitory surrounded by Oliver, Chris and Maddison, her body crashing against the wall with a bone-jarring thud. The shock of the impact knocked the breath from her lungs, and she lay there for a moment, dazed and struggling to process what had just happened.

"Eleanor... Eleanor..."

Maddison's voice pierced through the haze, and she was gently shaking her awake. Eleanor's eyelids fluttered open, her vision slowly coming into focus. The first thing she saw was Maddison's relieved face before she was enveloped in a massive hug.

"I told you she'd be okay," Chris said, though his voice was strained with worry. He was met with a hard, dagger-like stare from Maddison.

Eleanor was still panting, her breath coming in ragged gasps. She felt a grin curl up the corners of her lips as the adrenaline slowly subsided. "I saw him," she managed to whisper, her voice filled with both awe and dread. "All those disappearing people... they're not disappearing at all. I think they're working with Nyx. Helping him to build an army."

Maddison's eyes widened in horror. "An army? But for what purpose?"

Chris knelt down beside Eleanor, his face serious. "If Nyx is building an army, it means he's planning something big. Something that could threaten all of us."

Eleanor nodded, her mind racing with the implications of her vision. "He's amassing power. The weapons, the explosives, the people... he's preparing for something catastrophic."

Eleanor stood in front of the mirror in her dormitory, the Light Element resting on the table beside her. The room was dimly lit, the only light coming from the faint glow of the Element. She stared at her reflection, feeling a riling through her blood as her back rolled o er a thousand needles from the impact. The reflection stared back, its eyes glinting with a knowing, almost mocking expression. Almost as if it knew what was going to happen and was enjoying every single second of it.

16

The Weight of Secrets

Eleanor sat by the window in Dr. Asterio's study, the soft patter of rain outside mingling with the quiet rustle of turning pages. The room was steeped in memories—old books, faint herbal scents, and remnants of experiments long past. Yet tonight, beneath the gentle drumming of rain, an undercurrent of tension whispered through the halls, hinting at secrets too deep to ignore.

A few steps away, the voices of Dr. Asterio and Professor Singleton had dropped into a hushed, urgent tone. They leaned close near the doorway, their words charged with unspoken regret and the bitter residue of old love. Eleanor listened, feeling that their conversation was carefully cloaked in meaning—a dialogue not meant for her ears. More than once, she caught the unsettling sensation of unseen eyes watching from dark corners. Unbeknownst to her, Dr. Asterio kept a discreet vigil from behind heavy drapes, his protective gaze ensuring that she remained shielded from truths that might only bring pain.

Singleton's tone was edged with bitterness and lost affection as he broke the silence. "How long are you planning to keep this up, Asterio? You can't shelter her from the truth forever."

"I'm not, Mike," Asterio replied, his voice steady but tinged with sadness. "I'm trying to protect her from you."

Every word cut through her, stirring something deep in Eleanor's heart. The way they kept saying "her" echoed in her mind—she knew immediately they meant her. Yet, rather than feeling reduced to an object without her own thoughts, it made her feel startlingly real and seen.

Dr. Asterio's reply was calm and measured, but beneath his steady tone lay a quiet tenderness. "I'm not hiding from the truth—I'm keeping her safe," he said, his voice heavy with guilt and the promise of protection. After a long, choking silence, he added, "From you."

For years, the weight of not being there when John needed him had haunted him relentlessly.

"You think I don't care about her?" Singleton's voice was filled with bitterness, a raw edge to his words. "You think I don't regret what happened to John?" Asterio's silence spoke volumes. Eleanor could almost feel the weight of his unspoken words, the burden of guilt and sorrow that he carried.

"John was my friend too," Singleton continued, his voice breaking with emotion. "I would have done anything to save him."

A beat of silence passed between them, heavy with memories and things unsaid. "And yet, here we are."

As Asterio said this she saw Singleton's eyes flash with frustration.

"How dare you even say that, when you weren't even there" Singleton shot back, his eyes blazing with anger and hurt.

"Is that why you hate me so much?" Asterio asked softly, his voice carrying a rare trace of vulnerability that made Eleanor's heart tighten. There was a long, heavy pause. For the first time, Eleanor saw Singleton struggle with his words, as if each one was weighed down by regret. "It doesn't matter what you think of me. Just once, you have to set your own feelings aside."

Singleton scoffed, his tone icy. "I don't think anything of you."

But Eleanor sensed the truth behind his harsh words. The mask Singleton wore so meticulously concealed a fragile core—a small, stubborn spark of vulnerability that no matter how high he built his walls, refused to be completely extinguished.

"Is that why you're so cruel?" Asterio pressed gently, his eyes searching Singleton's face. "You seem to delight in the pain you cause, making everyone believe you have no compassion—no feelings at all."

"Don't be ridiculous," Singleton snapped, pushing the idea aside with a dismissive wave of his hand.

"Then why?" Asterio shot back, his voice firm and direct. "Why act as if you care for no one, as if your heart is locked away forever?"

In an explosive rush of raw emotion, Singleton yelled, "Because the last time I let my guard down, my closest friend died. I had to watch him die alone, and then you came back—as if nothing had changed. You left me, left us to endure all that loss on our own!" His voice quivered, and in that moment Eleanor saw deep, unfiltered pain flash across his eyes—a pain that had not been hidden, however briefly, behind his habitual hardness.

Singleton's voice cracked, and Eleanor could see the raw pain in his eyes. Almost as if a veil was lifting, a part of Singleton's personality, one that clearly hadn't surfaced for a long, long time, came forth with great intensity. Asterio looked at Singleton, his eyes filled with a mixture of sorrow and longing. "I loved you once, Mike," he confessed, his voice barely above a whisper. Eleanor's heart skipped a beat. She knew she shouldn't listen in. Singleton and Asterio wouldn't want her to. But after hearing their confession, leaving was the last thing Eleanor wanted to do.

"Really." Singleton scoffed, his voice dripping with sarcasm. "Well, you had a terrible way of showing it, ghosting me for thirteen years."

"I can't say I don't have regrets, of course I do. Every month for thirteen years I wrote you a letter. I can't tell you I didn't think about sending them, but I knew if I did, then if Nyx somehow traced it back to me, he would find the Light Element and John Walker would have died for nothing," Asterio explained, his voice filled with anguish.

Singleton's eyes softened for a moment, but then he shook his head, his expression hardening once more. "You should have trusted me. We could have faced Nyx together. Instead, you left me to deal with the fallout alone."

Asterio took a step closer, his eyes pleading. "I was scared, Mike. Scared of what Nyx had become. I thought I was protecting you by staying away." Singleton returned an icy cold stare. "You know your affection for Eleanor won't make up for your past mistakes. You need to realise, she isn't John."

Dr. Asterio turned, grabbed Singleton's hands, a ghostly white shade passing over his face, more than its usual sickeningly pale colour.

All the while, Eleanor was thinking of her parents. She couldn't remember seeing them together, but the look in their eyes was unmistakable. In her mind, it was a look that was burnt into everyone's DNA. It was a language as old as time. A way of speaking that needed no words at all.

Then, without warning, Singleton bolted away like a wounded animal, leaving Dr. Asterio standing alone, his heart aching in the silence.

17

Into the Forest

E arly the next morning, long before the first rays of sunlight touched the rooftops of Bleakwood, Eleanor slipped out of the dormitory, drawn by an unshakable pull she couldn't ignore. The air was crisp with the lingering chill of the night, and the damp earth beneath her boots sent a quiet shiver up her spine as she made her way toward the open clearing by the lake. It was the only time of day that none of the professors were out patrolling the grounds.

She had spent the hours before dawn trying—again and again—to harness the Light Element, hoping to unearth something more of Nyx's current location, wherever that might be. Anything that might make her feel useful.

But no matter how many times she tried, no matter how fiercely she focused, her mind kept circling back to the same vision—the same overwhelming images of dense greenery, sprawling plant life, towering forests teeming with something just beyond her reach, just as Nyx always seemed to be.

Of course, it was a long shot to think that the images she saw had any real meaning, but she was damned if she *wasn't* going to check it out.

There were half a billion trees across the country, the images could have been from anyone of them, or none at all. They could have been the effect of chemicals in her brain firing off her neurons as the Light Element's power had overwhelmed her. But something about the plants she'd seen, maybe it was the species of trees, Eleanor couldn't seem to shake the feeling – what if the reason the police had never found Nyx was that he'd never really left Bleakwood. What if all this time they'd been searching across the country, he'd in fact been hiding here this whole time, right under their noses.

"Eleanor!" a familiar voice rang softly from behind. She turned to find Oliver standing there, his ever-present pet parrot perched on his shoulder. His quiet steps had been so gentle that she hadn't noticed him until he was right beside her.

"I thought it was you," he said, his tone a mix of surprise and genuine concern. "I'm surprised to see you out here alone. Where are the others?"

For the past few days, Chris and the others hadn't known about her morning adventures. They would simply have something to say, trying to convince her that it wasn't safe.

"They're asleep," Eleanor replied coolly. Free from the watchful eyes of guardians—despite what Singleton or Dr. Asterio might think—she had proven she could stand on her own, day after day, without needing constant supervision.

"And you?" she asked, turning the spotlight back on him.

He exhaled deeply. "Prefect meeting," he said with a shake of his head. "Whoever thought a meeting before sunrise was a brilliant idea deserves to be ridiculed."

Eleanor smirked. "I'd volunteer," she teased.

A grin spread across his face. "Now that I've escaped that misery, I have nothing planned for the next couple of hours. Care for some company?"

After a moment's hesitation, barely noticeable, he got his answer: "Sure."

The relief on Oliver's face was immediate—bright and eager. Though he'd never admit it out loud, he secretly loved being around Eleanor. It made him feel like he was part of the adventures. Part of the team. Part of their inner circle.

"And what are we doing?" he asked.

Eleanor turned and pointed toward a cluster of trees ahead. "Do you see that forest?"

Oliver nodded slowly.

"We're going to search it. Every little bit of it."

Oliver blinked in surprise. "Every bit?" he repeated, his eyes widening as he surveyed the tangled expanse ahead. "That's at least two miles to cover."

Eleanor had already set off toward the tree line, leaving behind the slight tremor of doubt in Oliver's voice. Only then did Oliver notice her determined pace, and he quickened his step to catch up.

As they stepped under the canopy, the air grew cool and damp, filled with the rich scent of pine and soft, overturned earth. Each snap of a twig and every rustle of a leaf sent a ripple of tension through Eleanor's nerves, but she pressed on, determined not to let her fear interfere.

When they reached the edge of the woods, Eleanor stopped and turned. "Let's split up," she said with quiet authority. "We'll cover more ground that way. Meet back here in an hour."

Oliver's eyes searched hers, uncertainty flickering briefly on his face. "And what exactly are we looking for?" he asked in a low voice.

"Nyx," she replied simply.

For a moment, his expression went blank as he absorbed the gravity of her words. Then, with a firm nod, he set off in the opposite direction. In that instant, they were swallowed by the forest, each step carrying them deeper into the unknown.

Eleanor moved cautiously, her eyes scanning the ground for any signs of disturbance. She had to keep her voice low. If she was to truly keep her hears open for any noise or signs of life, she had to use all of her senses.

Her eyes kept close to the ground. She took note of every overturned rock, every broken branch, and every patch of disturbed earth, hoping to find something that would confirm the presence of someone else. Someone that might have been living out here, out of sight of the locals, the professor and especially the police. It was the perfect place to stay hidden. The forest was vast, and there were countless places where Nyx could have hidden. She couldn't shake the feeling that she was missing something, that the answers were just out of reach.

As the minutes ticked by, Eleanor's frustration grew. She couldn't help but feel a sense of urgency, knowing that Nyx could be plotting something dangerous while she was biding her time away. Following the biggest leap, she could make just because it made her feel useful, like her actions actually meant something.

She glanced towards the school. Though she had almost reached the outskirts of the village, the towering stone spire still loomed in the distance. Out here, uneven stone bricks jutted from the ground, making her stumble. The forest pressed in on her, its tangled branches closing like grasping fingers. The familiar path was fading, swallowed by wild undergrowth, and the air around her had turned sharp and cold.

After what felt like an eternity, Eleanor heard a rustling in the bushes ahead. She tensed, her heart pounding in her chest, but it was only Oliver, emerging from the underbrush with a look of disappointment on his face.

"Anything?" he asked.

Eleanor shook her head. "Nothing. You?"

"Same here," Oliver replied. "I checked the entire eastern perimeter, but I didn't find any signs of Nyx."

Peter squawked loudly, flapping his wings in agitation. Eleanor and Oliver exchanged a glance, their frustration mirrored in each other's eyes.

"Maybe we're looking in the wrong place, or maybe he's just too good at covering his tracks."

Oliver placed a reassuring hand on her shoulder. "We'll find him, Eleanor," he said. "We just have to keep looking."

Eleanor nodded, grateful for his support. "You're right," she said. "Let's head back and regroup. We'll come up with a new plan."

Just as they were about to turn back, Peter squawked again, this time more insistently. He flapped his wings and took off, flying deeper into the forest. Eleanor and Oliver exchanged a surprised glance before hurrying after him.

Peter led them to a secluded area of the forest, where the trees grew thicker, and the underbrush was denser. The parrot landed on a low branch, squawking and flapping his wings excitedly.

Eleanor and Oliver pushed through the dense foliage, their hearts pounding with anticipation. As they emerged into a small clearing, they saw it—a closed-off passage covered by branches and twigs. The ground around it was disturbed, with footprints in the mud leading to the entrance.

"This is it," Eleanor said, yanking aside a thick branch. "Nyx has been here. I can't believe it. I was right."

Oliver's eyes flicked over the disturbed ground. Eleanor crouched, tossing aside tangled roots and dirt, exposing a narrow tunnel mouth. A gust of stale air rushed up to meet her, thick with damp earth and rot. She swallowed hard.

"Let's go," she murmured, lowering her body down and leaving Oliver a few feet above. The air inside overcame her nostrils with a musty, cool, and damp scent. The walls, far below the surface, were adorned with mounted roots and moss, clinging to the ancient stone. Her footsteps clattered to the ground, echoing softly in the confined space.

Oliver slipped down after her. Something small and dark blurred past his vision, followed by a bluster of air. He reared his head up to catch the faintest glimmer of Peter's lustrous feathers passing overhead.

"You have a plan if we find Nyx, right?" Oliver asked.

Eleanor hesitated. The memory of her last encounter with Nyx rushed back—the way he had whispered, *We'll meet again.*

She wasn't naïve. She had always known their paths would cross again. But she had assumed she'd be ready, that she'd have the advantage this time. She had imagined herself prepared— finally living up to the expectations everyone had of her.

But now? She had no plan. No strategy. No idea what she would do if Nyx actually stood before her—or if they ran into the men who had tried to take Maddison.

It hit her all at once. She hadn't thought about *any* of it.

This was just like last year. First, she ran off chasing some wild idea and nearly got her friend hurt—so close to disaster.

Her fingers moved to her side on instinct, reaching for the Light Element—only to remember she'd left it back in her dormitory. She swallowed a curse.

At the time, it had seemed like the smartest choice. If she didn't have it on her, Nyx couldn't steal it. But now? Now, she had no way to defend herself. They were completely exposed.

The thought made her want to squeeze her eyes shut, but she forced herself to keep them open. The further they went, the deeper the darkness grew. Their only guide was the rough, clammy surface of the cobblestone wall beneath their fingertips and the weak flicker of torchlight that barely stretched across the uneven ground. It helped them avoid immediate obstacles, but there was no telling what lay ahead.

Eleanor focused on the tree roots bursting through the ceiling above. They curled like skeletal fingers, clutching at the stale underground air. The scent of petrichor mixed with damp soil, rot, and something sharper—something metallic. It lingered on her tongue, humming at the edges like electricity. A charge in the air, almost like batteries. But they were far below ground. There shouldn't have been any electricity down here. And yet, the sensation crawled beneath her skin, an unsettling whisper of something unnatural waiting in the depths.

Eleanor swallowed against the unease rising in her throat. They were too deep now. Too deep to turn back. The weight of the tunnel pressed in, as though the stone itself were aware of their presence.

Then—movement.

A scrape. A whisper of something shifting ahead.

She froze. Her breath hitched in her throat. "Did you hear that?"

Oliver stiffened beside her, fingers twitching toward his belt. "Yeah."

Silence thickened. The tunnel itself seemed to hold its breath.

They advanced, slow, calculated, following the source of the sound. The passage sloped upward, the incline steep, treacherous beneath their feet. The wet stone groaned under their weight. Water dripped somewhere, the sound strangely rhythmic—like footsteps echoing just behind them.

Light flickered ahead.

The dark thinned, revealing fractured brick, rusted pipes, remnants of something human. Eleanor pushed forward, her pulse hammering.

Then, she stopped dead.

Bleakwood School.

They had emerged into the ruins of the first-floor chemistry lab.

The sight slammed into her like a blow. The lab was exactly as she had left it—burned, broken, abandoned. The explosion's scars remained, untouched. Glass shards glittered like jagged teeth. The air reeked of scorched chemicals, though the fire had long since died.

The weight of memory pressed against her chest. This was where she had battled Nyx. Where the explosion had torn through the walls -still far beyond repair.

"This is how Nyx escaped," Eleanor murmured, voice hollow.

Oliver scanned the wreckage, jaw set. "No one would've thought to check for a tunnel."

Eleanor's pulse quickened. A new thought wormed into her mind—cold, sharp. "Except Singleton," she muttered.

Oliver's head snapped toward her.

"He knew," Eleanor continued, anger rising like bile. "This whole time. He knew how Nyx got out, and he never said a word."

Oliver cursed under his breath. "That sneaky—"

Peter squawked.

Sharp. Urgent.

The parrot flapped violently, talons scraping against the charred table, his wings slicing through the stale air. Eleanor and Oliver snapped toward him. He wasn't just agitated—he was warning them. His gaze locked onto the mess of crumpled papers, his beady eyes fixed, unwavering.

Eleanor didn't hesitate. She tore through the scattered blueprints, dust billowing into the dim light. Her fingers brushed against the brittle edge of something buried beneath the mess—a map.

Not just any map.

Her stomach tightened.

It was identical to the one Maddison had received from Mr. Graham. The same careful lines. The same paths and corridors woven through Bleakwood's foundations. But this version—this one was altered.

Red circles bled across the paper. Indicators. Entrances. Exits.

Oliver leaned over her shoulder, his breath shallow. "These weren't on Maddison's map."

Eleanor swallowed hard. Someone had been keeping track. Marking routes. Mapping out escape points—hidden pathways no one should have known existed.

Peter let out another cry, sharper this time, his feathers bristling. Eleanor's pulse spiked.

They weren't alone.

Something was coming.

Suddenly, a small, black shape darted out from the shadows, causing Peter to squawk even louder. Eleanor and Oliver both let out a sigh of relief as their eyes fell upon Cole, Professor Dougan's fury companion.

Oliver chuckled, shaking his head. "You gave us quite a scare, Cole," he said, reaching out to pet the cat.

Just then, they heard a voice behind them. "What the hell are you two doing here?" Professor Dougan's voice echoed through the room, filled with a mix of surprise and irritation.

Eleanor and Oliver turned to see Professor Dougan standing in the doorway, her hands on her hips and a stern expression on her face. Cole trotted over to her, rubbing against her legs.

Eleanor's throat tightened. "We—we were just—"

Oliver stepped in, lifting the map as if it would justify their presence. "We were following a lead." His tone was steady and authoritative, leaning on his prefect status in the hope it might soften their punishment.

Dougan's eyes narrowed, lingering on the marked-up map. The silence stretched unbearably long. Then, her expression shifted, a subtle crease forming between her brows.

"I see," she murmured, her voice measured now. But then, her gaze locked on Eleanor, stern. "You shouldn't be here. Not alone. Not you."

Eleanor bristled. "I—"

"We know," Oliver cut in smoothly, his tone earnest, trying to keep the conversation on safe ground.

Dougan exhaled, rubbing her temples. For a moment, it seemed she was debating whether to press the issue further. Then, she sighed. "Very well. Back to your dormitories—now." A beat. "And I won't speak of this again."

Relief edged in, but frustration still gnawed at Eleanor. Oliver nudged her gently, urging her toward the door, but just as she stepped past the threshold, Dougan's hand caught her arm, firm but not unkind.

"Just so you know, Eleanor," she said, voice lower now, measured. "I don't always agree with Singleton's way of doing things. But when he told me I might find you here, I almost didn't believe him."

Eleanor blinked, startled.

Dougan's lips pressed into a thin line. "It seems he knows you better than you think."

Eleanor's stomach twisted—not just at Dougan's words, but at the implication beneath them. Singleton wasn't merely watching her. He was anticipating her, predicting her choices before she even made them.

Her throat felt tight. Whatever game Singleton was playing, she just hoped he wasn't doing it at the expense of everyone she cared about.

18

Distractions

What did Singleton want from her? Did he expect her to interfere—or was he testing her restraint? Whatever his plan was, he had a cruel way of showing it. No warnings. No instructions. Just this unsettling game of cat and mouse, where she wasn't sure if she was the hunter or the prey.

For the first time in what felt like forever, she had a string of free periods stretching across the rest of the week.

It wasn't a coincidence. It couldn't be.

She suspected that Singleton had carved out this time for her—deliberately.

The only question was: why?

Was it an act of kindness? No that was absurd, Singleton was anything but kind. There must be more to his actions, but whatever that was, Eleanor couldn't figure it out.

It was vexing seeing how little attention he paid her this year, not unlike the last. How could he suddenly go from making her his pet project to letting her run around the school without any restraints or warnings.

But she was done thinking about what Singleton wanted her to do. It was exhausting. To live at the whim of someone else reminded Eleanor of her time in Merridone. Growing up, there was always a right and a wrong way of doing things. Of course, most of the time Eleanor often did more of the don'ts rather than the dos.

Besides, she had enough on her plate. The twins were off goodness-knows-where, sneaking through tunnels and nearly bringing down buildings in the process. And with Chris joining the lacrosse team, it meant constantly running back and forth from the hospital wing with an ice pack in hand.

The moment her final class of term ended, she grabbed her coat and headed for the sports fields, hoping to catch the last few minutes of Chris's training session.

The biggest Lacross match was due to take place just before the end of term. But everyone knew only the top players would play on the official team. And if Chris wanted a spot, he'd have to prove himself, which meant doing a lot more to impress the coach, Professor Black, than he already had.

The field was a battlefield of mud. Every breath Chris took came out in thick clouds in the morning chill. His teammates jogged in place to keep warm, their cut-off sleeves and shorts leaving their skin exposed to the biting wind. The coach's whistle split the air, and the players sprang into motion.

Chris bolted across the field, muscles burning. He had to be sharper, faster—better than Theo.

But the soaked ground had other plans. His shoes skidded in the mud, sending him stumbling—again. The professor's booming laughter rang out from the sidelines.

"Knight! Watch your footing!" Black called, amusement curling at the edges of his words. "I get a special kind of joy watching you hit the mud."

Maybe it was the way he flailed his arms like a cartoon character or the resounding thud that shook the ground when he hit the grass—limbs sprawled out like a fish out of water. Either way, Chris was done with it.

He gritted his teeth, frustration simmering beneath the surface. His problem wasn't skill, or at least that's what he kept on telling people. It was his gear, he would say. But a decent pair of cleats didn't come cheap, and Chris didn't have spare cash lying around. He was barely scraping by on the last few pounds from last year's birthday money, stretching it out as long as he could.

For months, he'd played in worn-down shoes, slipping whenever the field was wet. The fabric at the toes had split open, the spikes worn down so much they practically dug into the sole. He'd tried asking his parents for help, but they were always busy— jetting across the world for work, unreachable when he actually needed them.

Each fall on the field, each scuffed knee, was a reminder that he was on his own. Always just short of measuring up.

By the time practice ended, Chris trudged off the field, caked in mud from head to toe, looking like he'd just crawled out of a military drill. Eleanor and Maddison were waiting by the bleachers, their faces etched with concern.

Maddison spoke first. "Hey, Chris. How was practice?" Although she already knew the answer.

Chris forced a tight smile. "Same as always."

Eleanor frowned. "You look like you lost a fight with the field."

Chris exhaled sharply. "It's impossible to keep up." He shrugged while yanking off his pathetic excuse of a shoe. "I might as well just give up to Theo. He's far better. He has the best gear and everyone likes him far better than me."

Eleanor and Maddison exchanged a glance. Chris never said it outright, but they could see it—the weight pressing on him, the exhaustion from constantly trying and still falling short.

Eleanor nudged his arm, offering a small smile. "Let's take a trip into town. Get your mind off it."

Chris hesitated, fingers tightening around his ruined shoe. Then, after a beat, he sighed. "Yeah. That sounds good."

They wandered into town, the crisp autumn air biting at their cheeks. Leaves spun in golden bursts around their feet, caught in the breeze like scattered coins. The streets buzzed with life— Halloween decorations draped across storefronts, paper ghosts dangling from lampposts, the scent of cinnamon and pumpkin spice curling through the air like a warm embrace.

Their first stop was a bookstore. Eleanor ran her fingers along the spines of mystery novels, lost in the titles, while Chris flipped through the latest sci-fi releases, his shoulders slowly relaxing.

Next—the bakery. A deep warmth settled over them as they sank into chairs, their hands wrapped around steaming pumpkin spice lattes, the sugar from cinnamon rolls melting on their tongues. The simple comfort worked, if only for a little while.

But then—Eleanor paused outside a sports shop. "Look," she said, nodding toward the window display. "Lacrosse gear. On sale."

Chris followed her gaze, his pulse quickening at the sight of fresh cleats lined neatly beneath a sign boasting discounted prices.

"Maybe I can save up," he muttered, more to himself than anyone else.

Maddison scoffed lightly, rolling her eyes as she reached into her pocket. "Don't worry. I've got it."

Chris blinked as she pulled out a roll of crisp bills and handed them over to the cashier without hesitation. He stared, stunned. He had never seen that much money in one place before.

Chris's throat tightened. "No, I can't let you do that."

Eleanor understood his hesitation. Though she came from a family much like Maddison's—one with more wealth than they cared to admit—she knew Chris had never wanted Maddison to feel like he was only friends with her because of her money.

But Maddison didn't wait for him to argue further. She darted toward the shop door, clutching the folded notes in her fist.

Chris reacted instantly, reaching out to grab her shoulder, trying to pull her back. "Maddison, seriously—"

She turned to face him, unfazed, her expression firm. "Chris, let me do this for you." Her tone carried no pity, only certainty, as if it was ridiculous to think her view of him would change because he accepted help.

"I can't," he muttered.

She rolled her eyes. "Well, it's not up to you. For the sake of the team, I'm doing us all a favour."

With a bright, self-assured smile, Maddison flicked her long brown hair over one shoulder, her perfect curls bouncing slightly beneath her fur-lined bobble hat. She tucked a loose strand behind her ear, then strode inside, selecting the best pair of cleats the store had to offer without even bothering to haggle over the price.

When she handed the box to Chris, a genuine smile broke across his face, reaching his eyes. "Thanks, Mads." He hesitated, voice faltering before he forced out, "I'll pay you back."

Maddison waved him off. "Don't bother. Call it an early Christmas present."

Chris blinked, warmth swelling in his chest. Then, before he could overthink it, he pulled her into a tight hug. "You're the best."

Maddison laughed, returning the embrace with ease. "There is one thing you could do for me, though."

Chris pulled back slightly, eyeing her warily. "What's that?"

Her eyes sparkled with mischief. "Go out there and kick the other teams butt." She paused, smirking. "And when you win the finals, you owe me an exclusive interview."

Chris grinned, shaking her hand firmly. "Deal."

19

All Hallows Eve

"All Hallows' Eve," Singleton announced, his voice dripping with disdain. "Mischief Night, Tricker Night—or, as I prefer to call it, the worst night of the year."

Giggles rippled through the classroom, but the laughter quickly died as Singleton turned his icy gaze on them.

"It's bad enough that every year my assistant's office gets egged." Flickwitt peered nervously from behind Singleton, his small frame dwarfed by the towering headmaster. "A man's home is supposed to be his castle," Singleton continued, his voice slithering through the room like a cold wind, "not a flipping omelette."

Eleanor couldn't get the image of Singleton sat on a throne inside a tall stone castle, surrounded by a draw bridge and moat filled with blood thirsty alligators, ready to eat anyone who dared cross it's path.

While for the rest of students, Halloween fever had gripped Bleakwood school. Candy bowls littered the halls, students carved pumpkins with reckless enthusiasm, and the arts team frantically added last-minute flourishes to the evening's decorations. The corridors buzzed with costume debates, whispered plans, and the unmistakable scent of spiced treats. But Singleton's mere presence was enough to drain all lingering traces of mischief from the air.

"If I catch so much as a whisper of a prank—if I so much as suspect any of you thinking about pulling one—I will personally see to it that your nights for the rest of the term are spent in detention. Five hours. Every night."

He slammed his palms onto the twins' desk, making the entire room flinch. "I mean it!"

The laughter had long vanished. A few students exchanged nervous glances, but no one dared challenge him.

"Good," Singleton said, his tone shifting to something eerily calm. "Now, onto more pressing matters. The Halloween Ball is tonight, and I expect every one of you to behave. This is a school event, and I will not have it ruined."

Flickwitt cleared his throat, nodding along furiously. "Yes, yes, absolutely—no mischief."

First-years were oblivious to Flickwitt's long-standing role as Bleakwood's most consistent Halloween victim. But those who had been around long enough knew the truth—he was a magnet for pranks. His skittish nature made him an easy target, and year after year, students took full advantage.

One year, his office had been filled floor-to-ceiling with balloons. It had taken him hours to pop his way to his desk.

Another year, it was transformed into a haunted house—creepy music, mechanical ghosts, and dozens of fake spiders strategically placed to trigger his deepest fears.

Flickwitt lived in a perpetual state of terror during October.

Singleton's gaze swept over them one final time before he stepped back. "Dismissed."

LOST IN TIME

As students poured out of the classroom, Eleanor found herself stuck between excitement and apprehension. Bleakwood's Halloween events were legendary—but this year, it felt different.

Chris sidled up beside her. "Are you thinking what I'm thinking?"

"Are you thinking what I'm thinking?"

Eleanor raised an eyebrow. "That we should all avoid any pranks and stay out of trouble?"

Jenny grinned mischievously, her eyes sparkling with excitement. "That would be the sensible thing to do. But as it happens, sensible is overrated."

Eleanor sighed, a small smile tugging at her lips. "You never learn, do you?"

Tom's grin matched his sisters'. "Where's the fun in playing it safe?"

Eleanor groaned, but she couldn't help smiling.

Before they could say anything more, chaos erupted in the corridor.

Professor Dougan burst from her office, steam rising from her hair, frothy extinguisher foam clinging to her robes. Students froze, mouths hanging open, stunned into silence.

Then—the twins broke.

Dougan's appearance sent them into breathless fits of laughter, clutching their stomachs as they doubled over.

"Speaking of pranks," Jenny wheezed, barely able to speak.

Chris and Eleanor exchanged glances, both struggling to contain their own amusement.

"Please don't tell me that was you two." Eleanor groaned, already knowing the answer.

"At least no one saw them do it," Chris muttered, voice low.

Jenny opened her mouth to respond—

BANG!

A firecracker erupted from Dougan's office, sending sparks skittering across the marble floor. The words *Happy Halloween, from T & J!* unfurled in shimmering, glittering streamers before dissolving into smoke.

The hallway froze. Students pressed back against the walls, eyes darting between the chaos and the inevitable explosion of fury that was coming.

Dougan didn't disappoint.

Her eyes blazed, her cheeks turning a shade of red that—if possible—looked hotter than the firecracker that had just gone off.

"YOU TWO!"

The corridor split as students instinctively backed away, clearing a path for Tom and Jenny—who exchanged one look, breathless from laughter.

"We'll catch you later," Tom said, inching toward the exit. "We've got some running to do."

Jenny grinned. "Good thing we found that hidden passage by the stairwell."

Steam all but rose from Dougan's robes as she lunged forward, but the twins were already gone, their laughter echoing down the hall like mischievous ghosts.

Eleanor and Chris stood frozen for a beat, watching the scene unravel further as a group of uniformed officers patrolling the grounds cautiously poked their heads around the corner.

Chris groaned. "Please tell me they're not going to be here all night."

Eleanor smirked. "Well, considering the twins just sent Dougan running down the corridor covered in extinguisher foam, I'd say Singleton isn't taking any chances."

Chris sighed. "It's Halloween, not a hostage situation. What's next? Searchlights? Guard dogs?"

Eleanor chuckled. "Wouldn't rule it out."

They both glanced toward the retreating figures of Tom and Jenny, disappearing into the depths of the building like shadows at dusk.

Chris shook his head. "Let's just hope they don't do anything to make things worse."

Eleanor let out a soft laugh. "Yeah. Let's hope."

Without another word, they turned and headed for their dorms, keeping a low profile and praying that the rest of the night would—by some miracle—remain uneventful.

20

The Masquerade Ball

As evening descended, Eleanor adjusted her hat in the mirror, tilting it just enough to give her that perfect highwaywoman look. The black Stetson cast a dramatic shadow over her sharp gaze, the sleek mask framing her features with an air of mystery. Her holstered prop pistol sat snug against her hip, completing the illusion of a rogue outlaw, a fugitive slipping through the cracks of history. A thrill of anticipation ran through her veins.

"Ready for the ball?" Chris's voice echoed from the hallway.

"Almost!" she called back, tugging her hat down one last time before grabbing her mask and stepping into the corridor.

Chris, dressed in a similarly costume, leaned against the doorframe with a knowing grin. His coat swished as he shifted, the faint glint of silver buttons catching the dim hallway light.

It had become tradition for them to dress in matching costumes every year. It was part of what made Halloween exciting. Not so much the candy and tricks, that was just for little kiddies, but the thrill of being able to stay up until midnight dressed as someone or something completely different from yourself. It was a way of slipping into another life for a night. And for Eleanor, it was one of the only times she could pretend to be another face in the crowd without the risk of being gawked at by first-years or tormented by Henry Kensington.

"You look like trouble," he said, eyes glinting. "I hardly would have recognised you."

Eleanor smirked. "That was the goal."

While she and Chris stuck to their tradition, Maddison had decided to go off-theme this year. No one knew exactly what she was planning, but one thing was certain—it would be extravagant and impossible to miss. They were sure to know the moment they saw her.

Eleanor turned around. "Mind giving me a hand with my mask?"

Chris fastened the strap, making sure it fit snugly. Eleanor checked her reflection in the mirror and smiled. No one would recognize her now.

Chris held out his hand. "Shall we?"

She slipped her hand into his. "We shall."

The halls were alive with energy, a symphony of excitement rippling through the crowd. Costumes of all kinds drifted past— glittering masks, cloaks sweeping the floor, horns curling from the heads of mischievous devils. Lace and velvet twirled in hushed conversation, the air thrumming with anticipation.

Upon approach, Jack-o'-lanterns flickered from every shrub and archway, their carved expressions twisting in the shifting candlelight—some mischievous, others downright sinister. It set the cliff top alight with and orange glow that drowned out the darkness.

In each window and balcony overlooking the entrance stone gargoyle carvings lurked with gleaming eyes, watching the crowd like hunters waiting for the perfect moment to strike. Skeleton hung down from the walls and just by the doors, for a fleeting second, Eleanor swore she saw something truly *unnatural* slip through the crowd. But with so many strange this wandering the ground this evening, it wasn't surprising.

They were excited to join the fun, but as they neared the entrance, they took notice at a long line, a within that towards the back a familiar voice cut through the spellbinding chaos.

"Eleanor, you made it!"

She turned to see Oliver, his silver-and-blue sequin mask glittering in the moon light.

"Oliver!" Eleanor beamed, taking in his outfit—a carefully pieced-together explorer's attire, complete with a weathered satchel and aged leather gloves.

"You've outdone yourself," she said, impressed.

Oliver grinned and gave an overly dramatic bow. "Why, thank you, thank you."

Chris squinted at him. "What... exactly are you supposed to be?"

"Howard Carter," Oliver declared proudly, his cheeks flushed with excitement. "The legendary archaeologist."

Chris blinked. "Right."

"And let me guess, are you a pirate?"

Oliver studied him closely. Considering the boots, the long coat, and that dramatic stance, it was reasonable guess to make.

But Chris just sighed. "It was supposed to be Dick Turpin."

Silence.

Oliver cleared his throat, eyes flicking toward the entrance. "I see Maddison's here," he said quickly, desperate to shift the conversation.

Eleanor turned just in time to see Maddison gliding at least thirty people ahead of them, arm in arm with Daniel Parish.

Maddison had fully embraced the vampire aesthetic, and she looked *every bit* the royalty of the night. Her long purple gown shimmered as she moved, catching the light like liquid amethyst. Her dark braids were woven with strands of deep crimson, tiny gems glinting between them like droplets of blood. Dramatic eyeliner framed her piercing gaze, and her blood-red lips completed the look of effortless elegance and power.

Daniel, towering beside her, carried himself with the quiet confidence of a true night stalker. His tailored tuxedo hugged his frame perfectly, the crimson-lined cape giving him an unmistakable appearance of count Dracula, making the two of them the perfect vampire duo.

Beneath his crisp white shirt, Eleanor could see the defined contours of his frame—lean, strong, effortlessly confident. Judging by the way a cluster of students practically melted at his presence, he knew the effect he had. Maddison, ever the realist, caught his wandering gaze and answered with a sharp slap to his shoulder.

Classic Maddison.

Each of them watched as Daniel, usually composed, turned an unmistakable shade of pink—visible even under the thick layer of white, greasy face paint.

Before Eleanor could soak in more, the line surged forward. Chris, who had been wondering for a while, finally voiced the question lingering in the air.

"What exactly are we waiting for?"

Oliver raised a brow, surprised they hadn't put it together.

"The haunted trail. It's new this year. No way into the main building without going through it first."

Whatever had grabbed Oliver's attention yanked him away in the next breath. He spun, scanning the grounds—probably some first-years stirring up trouble down by the lake.

"Duty calls," he muttered before striding off in that direction, just ahead of the wandering officers patrolling the area.

The line shuffled forward again, and soon, Eleanor and Chris stood at the front. A thick mist curled around the entrance like ghostly fingers reaching for them. Eerie lights flickered between twisted tree branches, casting shifting shadows that seemed to breathe. Above them, the sign loomed—aged, cracked, barely holding itself together.

Welcome to the Haunted Trail. **ENTER IF YOU DARE.**

Chris chuckled. "Well, that's subtle."

The moment they stepped onto the path, the air shifted. The scent of damp earth filled their noses, and whispers—low, echoing, barely there—drifted through the trees.

A skeletal figure moved in the shadows.

Then, out of the mist, a ghostly bride emerged.

Her tattered white gown trailed behind her, shifting unnaturally with no wind to guide it. Her face was pale, her eyes hollow. When she spoke, her voice was nothing more than a breath—a whisper carried on the air.

Chris shuddered. "Okay. That's creepy."

Eleanor's spine tingled as the bride drifted closer, her gaze locked on them.

Then, without warning—she lunged.

Chris yelped, grabbing Eleanor's arm as they stumbled backward. The bride stopped just short, her lips curling into an unsettling smile before vanishing into the mist.

Eleanor let out a nervous laugh. "Well. That was—"

Before she could finish, a blood-curdling scream rang out from deeper in the trail.

Chris stiffened. "Uh. Maybe we should reconsider this."

Eleanor grinned. "Where's the fun in that?"

The mist curled around their ankles as they pressed forward, every step swallowed by the eerie silence between distant, echoing whispers. Just ahead, a pair of glowing eyes flashed in the dark. A werewolf—a towering silhouette with wild fur and piercing golden eyes—let out a low growl, its sharp teeth gleaming as it stalked forward.

Chris edged closer to Eleanor. "Tell me that's just an actor."

The creature tilted its head, its movements unsettlingly real. Then, with a sudden snarl, it leapt into the shadows, vanishing.

Chris exhaled hard. "Okay. Yeah. Definitely just an actor."

They turned a corner, only to be greeted by a crooked old witch bent over a bubbling cauldron. Wisps of smoke curled into the air, carrying the scent of burning herbs. Her long, gnarled fingers stirred the thick potion, eyes gleaming beneath her tattered hood.

"Beware the path ahead," came a raspy voice behind them.

Eleanor and Chris spun around to find hooded figures— ghouls and demons—lurking in the mist, their cloaks billowing as if caught in some invisible wind.

"Many have entered..." one whispered, their breath unnaturally cold against Eleanor's skin, "...but few have returned."

Eleanor narrowed her eyes at Chris. "Okay, maybe this is a little creepy."

Chris swallowed hard. "A *little*?"

Suddenly, from the corner of their vision—a figure lurched forward.

A zombie.

Its decaying flesh and hollow eyes sent their hearts racing. It staggered toward them, its limbs jerking unnaturally.

"Nice costume!" Eleanor called out, trying to keep her voice steady.

The zombie groaned in response, its mouth opening in a lazy, hungry moan. "Braaaains..."

Chris leaned closer. "That costume is way too realistic."

Eleanor chuckled nervously. "They really went all out this year."

Just ahead, a group of ghostly phantoms circled around a steaming cauldron, their spectral forms twisting in the dim light.

"Care for a taste of my potion?" one crooned, holding out a ladle of shimmering, green liquid.

Chris wrinkled his nose. "Yeah, I'll pass."

Finally, at the trail's end, two imposing figures awaited. Dressed in long gold capes, their faces completely concealed by intricately moulded masks, they held out a wand and cane—each sending bursts of fire and crackling sparkles into the night air.

Eleanor didn't need to think twice. She knew *exactly* who they were.

"Stop there, mere mortals!" one intoned dramatically. "You are about to enter the realm of sorcery and witchcraft."

Eleanor smirked. "Nice costume, Tom."

One of the masked figures lifted their mask just enough to reveal a familiar smirk. "Hey, don't break my character. I'm winning the bet against Jenny."

Eleanor sighed. "What bet this time?"

Jenny, still masked, pointed toward a tally board beside them. *Tom—21, Jenny—20.*

Chris narrowed his eyes. "Do I even want to ask what that's for?"

Even though she couldn't see their faces, Eleanor could feel the twins silently giggling.

"Scaring first-years," Tom said smugly. "It's ridiculously easy."

Chris snorted. "Of course. I might have known you two would be working the spooky trail. Was this your idea?"

"Surprisingly, no." Tom shrugged. "But after the prank we pulled on Dougan earlier, she made us work the maze all night."

Jenny added, "Honestly? I think she's losing her touch. Not only are we not in detention, but she's letting us terrorize people."

Eleanor and Chris exchanged knowing smiles. Classic twins.

As they left the haunted trail, the cold air faded, replaced by the warmth of candlelight spilling from the ballroom doors.

Stepping inside, they were met with a transformation that took their breath away.

The great hall had been turned into a nineteenth-century ballroom. Dark wooden benches lined the walls, heavy velvet drapes hung from the ceiling, and chandeliers flickered overhead with an eerie glow.

Classical, spooky waltz music filled the air, and couples in elaborate costumes twirled gracefully across the makeshift dance floor. The haunting melodies added an air of mystery and elegance to the scene, making it feel like they had stepped back in time.

Chris's attention was quickly drawn to the back of the room, where a long table was laden with an array of delicious treats. His eyes lit up as he spotted a platter of chocolate, and he couldn't resist helping himself to a generous portion. As he savoured the rich, sweet taste, he glanced around the room, taking in the details.

Jack-o'-lanterns lined the windowsills, their carved faces flickering with the light of real candles. The breeze made their flames dance, casting shifting shadows across the walls. Chris found the effect mesmerizing—and slightly eerie.

Eleanor glanced away for just a moment, but when she turned back, Chris was gone.

Her pulse quickened as she scanned the room, the flickering candlelight making it harder to pick out faces in the crowd. Then, movement caught her eye—a dimly lit hallway at the far end of the ballroom. She hesitated before stepping forward, pushing deeper into the shadows.

Out of nowhere, a figure appeared—a student in a fortune teller's outfit, their velvet robes swaying as they reached for Eleanor's wrist.

"Come," the fortune teller said, their voice smooth and beckoning. "Let me read your fortune."

Eleanor hesitated. Something about their presence felt off. But the fortune teller's grip was firm, guiding her toward a small, elaborately decorated tent.

Inside, thick incense curled into the air, mixing with candlelight to cast long, stretching shadows across the walls. The fortune teller sat shrouded in deep black robes, their face completely hidden beneath the hood.

At first, the reading was light-hearted—talk of adventure, choices, opportunity. Eleanor relaxed slightly, even letting out a small laugh.

Then—the atmosphere shifted.

The fortune teller's voice dropped, their tone now slow and deliberate. "You have known loss," they murmured. "You have felt betrayal."

Eleanor stiffened.

The candlelight flickered.

"And you possess something powerful." The fortune teller leaned forward, lowering their voice to a whisper. "An object hidden inside your pocket."

Eleanor's stomach twisted. The Light Element pressed against her ribs, concealed in the inner lining of her jacket.

There was no way they could know that.

Her throat went dry. "Who are you?" she asked, barely more than a breath.

The fortune teller didn't answer. Instead, they straightened, their layered robes shifting. And then Eleanor saw it.

Beneath the black fabric, they wore an inner robe, made of stark white fabric.

Her pulse pounded in her ears and her eyes swirled in and out of focus. But before she could say another word, the tent flap burst open and Eleanor shot her head around.

"There you are!" Chris's voice cut through the air. "I've been looking everywhere for you."

The tension snapped like a rubber band. Eleanor exhaled hard, turning to Chris as relief flooded through her.

Chris took one look at her pale face and frowned. "What are you doing in here?"

"The fortune teller..." Eleanor trailed off, shaking her head, only to find the seat opposite completely empty. She was confused Where had they gone? Something didn't feel right.

Chris blinked, batting his eye lids as thought trying to clear dust from his eyes, "You mean Lindsey?" he asked.

From behind the tent, a girl emerged—a third-year ballerina dressed in fortune teller robes.

"She's working the fortune teller booth," Chris explained. "I was just chatting with her on her break."

Eleanor stared at Lindsey. "Then... it must have been someone else working the booth."

Lindsey tilted her head in confusion. "I'm the only fortune teller here."

Chris glanced between them, then gently grabbed Eleanor's wrist. "You're coming with me."

Eleanor let him lead her away, still shaken.

"That was weird," she muttered under her breath.

Chris tried to sound reassuring. "It was probably a first-year messing around with you. You know what they're like. They say one thing that can be generalised to everybody. And then suddenly you think they are psychic... or something like that."

Eleanor nodded slowly. "Yeah... you're probably right."

Chris grinned. "Now—more important matters."

He spun around, pointing toward the banquet tables, where rows of chocolate fountains gleamed under candlelight.

Eleanor couldn't help but laugh. The eerie encounter still lingered in her mind—but right now, chocolate sounded like the perfect distraction.

Chris practically sprinted toward the table, his excitement impossible to contain.

A server threaded marshmallows and strawberries onto skewers, dipping them into the cascading layers of dark, milk, and white chocolate. Toffee pieces and biscuit crumbs sprinkled over the glossy coating, the smell alone enough to make Eleanor's stomach rumble.

Chris took a bite, eyes going wide. "This is life changing."

Eleanor laughed, finally letting some of the tension ease from her shoulders.

Chris dipped another marshmallow into the fountain before glancing up at her. "Feeling better?"

Eleanor nodded, the small smile returning to her lips. "Chocolate helps."

Chris chuckled. "Science would agree. Endorphins and all that."

But for Eleanor, it wasn't science—it was nostalgia.

The taste reminded her of the Swiss chocolate bars her mother used to bring home when things were good. Sweet, rich, comforting. That was before things changed—before birthdays were forgotten, before the drinking started.

Now, the only time she ever tasted something close was when the kind old woman at the bakery handed her a chocolate muffin every Saturday. No words, no expectations—just warmth and generosity.

Chris nudged her playfully. "You just zoned out real hard. If you're thinking about eating all the chocolate, please know that I will fight you for it."

Eleanor rolled her eyes, shoving him lightly and let herself drift in the music, watching the dancers twirl beneath the flickering candlelight. Shadows stretched and swayed across the walls, the whole scene feeling like something out of a dream.

Then, she frowned.

"Have you seen Maddison anywhere?" Eleanor asked, scanning the sea of masked faces around them. The crowd had become a blur—familiar voices swallowed by waves of laughter, costume disguises blending together until everyone felt like a stranger.

They hadn't seen Maddison since the Haunted Trail, but that wasn't surprising. The party sprawled across nearly every corner of the school, with a disco and a live band drawing most of the students to the main hall. Eleanor supposed they should wander over there at some point that evening, but there was no rush—it wasn't even nine o'clock yet.

The grandfather clock in the corner ticked steadily toward the hour, its deep chimes swallowed by the noise around them.

Chris shrugged, still stuffing his face with food. "She's probably wherever Daniel is. Have you noticed those two lately?"

Eleanor smirked. It was true—Maddison and Daniel had grown undeniably close. Some moments, their sweetness was heartwarming. Other times, it was so saccharine it bordered on nauseating.

Eleanor smirked, catching the way the candlelight made Chris's pale blue eyes look almost silver. "What?" he questioned.

"I thought you hated Daniel?" She raised an eyebrow, recalling his very strong reaction to seeing Maddison arrive with him at last year's winter ball.

Chris sighed, rubbing the back of his neck. "What can I say? He's grown on me."

Before Eleanor could press further, Chris abruptly held out his hand. "Do you want to dance?"

Eleanor hesitated—just for a moment—then slipped her hand into his. "Sure, why not?"

Together, they stepped onto the dance floor, letting the haunting melody take control. Their movements fell effortlessly in sync—the gliding steps, the measured turns. The hem of Eleanor's coat swished around her ankles, catching the warm candlelight, while Chris's tailored jacket rippled beneath the ice-blue spotlights.

For a few fleeting moments, they were lost in the rhythm, lost in the sheer magic of the masquerade.

Then, it struck.

A violent pounding in Eleanor's skull.

Her vision blurred, the world around her twisting, warping. She staggered, pressing her hands to her temples, forcing her eyes shut as flashes of imagery slammed into her mind.

Grass. Branches.

Then—stone. A towering structure.

The stone path leading up to Bleakwood School.

The images flickered too fast to grasp—disjointed, fleeting, yet impossibly real. Her breath hitched, knees threatening to buckle beneath her.

"Eleanor!"

Chris's voice cut through the haze. Strong hands gripped her arms, anchoring her, holding her steady.

"Are you okay? Did you see something?"

Eleanor's fingers trembled as she pried her eyes open, the vision fading, leaving her breathless.

She knew this feeling.

She had felt it before.

"It was like... like when I used the Light Element," she whispered, struggling to find air.

Chris's grip tightened. "Wait—what does that mean? Did you-?"

But before he could finish, the world detonated in sound.

A thunderous crash shattered the air and the oak doors at the far end of the hall exploded open.

Figures spilled into the room—cloaked in black, faces masked, movements sharp and calculated. Each one armed.

The masquerade screeched to a halt.

Gasps. Screams. Tables overturned in the chaos.

And Eleanor's pulse thundered in her ears.

21

Mercenaries

"**N**obody move!"

Eleanor froze.

The command rang through the ballroom like a gunshot.

The man at the far end of the room stood—clad in black, masked, every movement screaming *control*. His presence alone was enough to crush the air from the room. Instinctively, Eleanor shrank into the shadows, gripping Chris's arm tighter and pulling him closer.

Their masks helped in concealing their identities for now, but the bright silver feathers attached to hers made her feel exposed. It wouldn't protect her for long.

The music had died. The murmurs, the laughter—gone. Fear spread like wildfire.

"Listen up, all of you. If you have any plans of seeing tomorrow, you'll do exactly what we ask."

A ripple of terror ran through the crowd. Some students backed against the walls, others clutched their partners like lifelines. Chris edged in front of Eleanor, his grip firm on her wrist.

"Stay behind me," Chris murmured, voice taut with urgency.

The men in black hoods moved with precision, eyes sweeping the room. No insignias. No distinguishable features. Only black uniforms and the deadly weight of the shotguns in their grip.

Not props. Not cheap plastic replicas. Real weapons.

Eleanor's stomach twisted.

"Where is Eleanor Walker?"

Her pulse thundered in her ears. Gasps rippled through the crowd. The whispers came fast—frantic—barely above breaths.

Why Eleanor? Why her?

The leader didn't wait. He reached into the nearest group, grabbed a boy at random, and yanked him forward.

"Let me make myself clear—where is Eleanor Walker?"

The barrel of his gun pressed against the boy's spine.

Instant screams.

Eleanor's mouth parted. She was seconds from stepping forward—seconds from surrendering herself—when Chris squeezed her hand in warning. A sharp, urgent shake of his head.

She stopped.

The intruder's gaze swept across the room.

For a heartbeat, Eleanor was certain their eyes landed on her.

Her fist clenched, slick with sweat.

They knew. They had to know.

She could feel it—the weight of their gaze. They were hunting her. And everyone else in this room? Collateral.

"Very well." The leader turned. "Search them."

Chaos erupted.

Mercenaries pushed forward like a wave, weaving through the sea of bodies—searching, grabbing, forcing students to remove their masks.

Every exit was blocked. Every window locked. There was no escape.

A figure approached—bigger than the rest, moving with quiet determination. Coming straight for her.

Eleanor's breath hitched. Her feet refused to move, rooted in place by panic.

They'd found her.

Then—a hand.

Chris's. Grabbing her wrist. Yanking her down.

"Eleanor—use it!"

The air thickened with panic, bodies pressing against each other, frantic whispers rising and fading like waves. Eleanor's mind reeled.

Use what?!

Chris turned, his expression desperate. "NOW—before they find you!"

The Light Element.

Her fingers brushed against the book hidden inside her jacket, its familiar weight pressing against her ribs. A lifeline. But—Chris.

"What about you?" she whispered, fear catching in her throat.

"Don't worry about me." His voice was firm, urgent. "They're not after me. They'll kill you right here if they get the chance."

He was right. The mercenaries weren't here for destruction—they were hunting. And their prey was her.

The crowd split apart, clearing a path for the advancing men.

Eleanor forced herself to focus, shoving back the terror clawing at her throat.

Eyes shut. Breath held.

She whispered the incantation.

A cold, rough hand slammed down on her shoulder.

Eleanor's eyes snapped open.

She turned—face-to-face with the barrel of a gun.

"Take off that mask!" The man's voice was sharp, commanding.

Her vision blurred between his hollow stare and the black abyss of his weapon's muzzle.

"NOW!" His grip tightened—too hard, too cruel—and Eleanor was certain her arm would snap.

She reached up, fingers trembling as she pulled at the knot behind her head.

The mask fell away.

Every flaw. Every speck of redness. Every feature exposed.

Silence.

The man hesitated.

Eleanor fought to keep her breathing steady, her mind racing. Had it worked? Had the Light Element warped his perception enough to keep her hidden?

She couldn't be sure.

His stance remained stiff, the shotgun still trained on her.

Then—his leader muttered something under his breath.

"She's not here."

The armed men shifted uneasily, exchanging glances.

"You said she was here!" the leader barked at one of them, a shorter mercenary with the skinny frame of a boy. "You said your information was reliable!"

"It was! She must still be in the building."

Eleanor's chest burned with the need for air, but she held it— held it until the last possible second.

The Light Element hadn't altered her appearance like Nyx's Dark Element could. But it had bent perception—just enough to make her unrecognizable.

How long would it last?

A gunshot ripped through the air.

The leader had fired into the ceiling, the deafening blast silencing the room in an instant.

Screams. Instinctive panic. Some ducked. Others froze.

The leader's jaw tightened. "Clear out!"

He turned sharply to his men.

"Split up—search the building. Nyx will have our heads if we fail to find the girl."

Cold. Final. A warning wrapped in steel.

Then—they moved.

Like a tide crashing against rock, they spilled out of the ballroom, weapons drawn, carrying both the precision of soldiers and the recklessness of assassins.

Eleanor barely breathed.

But they weren't gone.

Not yet.

And time was slipping through her fingers.

22

Tunnels

Sweat clung to Eleanor's forehead, gathering along her hairline in damp beads. The pulsating lights blurred in her vision, and the heat pressing in from all sides felt suffocating. Every frantic heartbeat slammed against her ribs like a warning. The Light Element was weakening—she could feel it draining from her, slipping away like water through her fingers.

Without it, she was vulnerable. But all eyes were turned elsewhere for now. This room was safe. They wouldn't come back knowing they had already searched it. At least not straight away.

As far as they were concerned, *Eleanor Walker was somewhere else in the building.*

But of all the people, she felt a sharp tug on her arm from Chris, who steadily pulled them through the crowd. His touch wasn't rough, but there was no space for hesitation either.

"Come on, we need to get out of here," he urged, voice low but tense.

Eleanor barely registered the sensation of moving—only the cold bite of stone walls as they passed through the narrow hallway, Chris steering her along. The contrast between the suffocating press of bodies and the isolation of the corridor left her disoriented.

She stumbled. Chris caught her mid-fall, hoisting her upright with practiced ease.

"Chris, slow down," she whispered, though she wasn't sure if it was her body or her mind that needed the extra second to process.

His gaze flicked from one shadow to the next, scanning for any movement beyond their own. The hallway stretched ahead like a maze of unseen threats. They rounded the corner—

Eleanor froze.

Her stomach lurched, twisting itself into knots.

Mercenaries.

Their movements were precise—too precise. The black-clad figures blocked every exit, their formation tightening like a web meant to ensnare them.

"We're trapped," she breathed. The words barely made it past her lips.

Chris's fingers tensed slightly around her wrist, but he didn't let go. His expression didn't shift, but she knew better—knew the storm of thoughts whirling behind his eyes. Calculating. Weighing options. Searching for gaps that didn't exist.

"We need to find another way out," he said, though his voice was noticeably strained. "Let's check the doors."

They rushed to the nearest exit. Eleanor's fingers fumbled over the handle. Locked. She pressed her forehead against the cool metal, inhaling sharply through her nose. Outside, she glimpsed armed figures stationed along the school grounds. It was a deliberate trap. There was no running.

Chris ran a hand through his hair, exhaling sharply. His frustration was clear—but beneath it, there was something else.

"They're not just keeping us in. They're making sure you have nowhere to run."

Eleanor swallowed against the rising fear in her chest.

"Maybe that's a good thing," she murmured. "We can't just leave everyone."

Chris turned to her, eyebrows knitting together. His voice was quieter now. "Eleanor, they will kill you. Don't you realise how much danger you're in. You're the one they're after."

Eleanor knew. She wasn't trying to be brave, nor was she seeking recklessness—but how could she live with herself if something happened to her friends because of her? How could she just stand back and watch while they put their lives at risk for her sake?

No. That wasn't even the worst of it.

Nyx was here. She was certain of it. She didn't know where, didn't know what he was planning, but this attack wasn't just about her. If it were, he wouldn't need an army of mercenaries armed to the teeth. He could have killed her anywhere, at any time. This chaos, this siege—it was a distraction from his true goal.

And Eleanor had a gut feeling she knew exactly what that was.

The Time Element.

This was happening right now, right here in Bleakwood, and no one—neither the professors nor the other students—were prepared to stop him.

Despite the adrenaline storming through her veins, despite the shiver of fear tickling her spine, she forced herself to steady her trembling hands against the cover of the Light Element. Drawing in the energy like a lifeline, she focused on her breath, slowing her racing heart until her mind sharpened back to rational thought.

If they wanted to warn the others, they had to get there before the mercenaries did. But that wasn't going to be easy—not with the school's main corridors already crawling with armed soldiers, every exit under lockdown, each enemy ordered to shoot on sight. They weren't bluffing.

"I have an idea," Eleanor said suddenly.

Chris glanced at her, his expression taut with urgency but willing to listen.

"Do you remember the blueprints Oliver and I found of Bleakwood?"

Chris nodded once, fast.

"What if there's a route underneath the school leading straight to the main hall?"

It wasn't a perfect plan. But it was the best one they had.

The only problem? Eleanor didn't know where Oliver had left the map—or even if he still had it.

Chris, however, barely hesitated.

"I know where it is."

Eleanor didn't have time to question how, nor did she particularly care. She only nodded, trusting him, and took off after him without another word.

They ran all the way to the prefects' locker room. Hurry. Hurry. Hurry.

Standing in the open like this felt too vulnerable—like a sniper might be lurking in the shadows, waiting for the perfect shot.

Chris reached the end of the row, stopping in front of Oliver's locker.

Locked.

"Damn it," he muttered under his breath.

Eleanor scanned the room, thinking fast. "Break it."

Chris didn't hesitate. He lunged at it, ramming his shoulder against the metal.

Nothing.

He bounced back, groaning as he rubbed at his shoulder, looking—for the briefest moment—like an angry Chihuahua.

Eleanor bit back her frustration. Every sound, every impact against the locker risked alerting the mercenaries. They had to be careful.

Then she spotted a steel nameplate wedged in the office door.

She ripped it free and handed it to Chris.

At first, he frowned at it, uncertain—until realization dawned. He wedged one end of the metal between the locker frame and levered all his weight into it.

A sharp *snap* echoed through the room.

Clothes spilled onto the floor. Eleanor batted away a stray shirt from her face, watching as Chris tore through the heap of personal belongings.

Finally, from the bottom of the locker—he pulled out the map.

Chris spread it across the desk, fingers flying over the markings.

"There," he murmured, tapping the map.

A tunnel leading directly beneath the main hall.

Eleanor exhaled. Relief warred against the creeping unease still pressing in on her.

If they moved fast enough, they could make it without crossing paths with the mercenaries.

But they had to move *now*.

As they crept through the school, Eleanor couldn't shake the feeling of unease. Too focused on the possibility of a mercenary lurking just around the corner that she barely noticed when Chris stopped abruptly in the hallway.

She collided into his back with a sharp *oof.*

Steadying herself, she frowned, glancing down at the map in his hands, then at the space ahead.

This was it. The tunnel entrance should be here.

But all she saw was an old bookshelf, worn and crammed with dusty, neglected tomes.

Chris wasted no time, yanking out books one by one.

But Eleanor knew better. The entrance to a secret passage wouldn't be something as cliché as a hidden lever behind a loose book. That was pure fiction. They needed something permanent. Something subtle.

"Look here," Eleanor said, pointing to a faint marking printed on the map.

She knew it—she knew it—but in the rush of adrenaline, her mind was blanking, unable to make the connection.

Chris, however, recognized it instantly.

His eyes lifted to the bookshelf—and froze. "There."

At the top of the shelf, the same engraving was carved into the wood.

"Give me a boost."

Eleanor crouched down, gripping Chris's leg as he stepped onto her hands for leverage.

He reached up—fingertips brushing against the hidden notch—pressing inward.

A metallic clunk sounded.

Then—the entire bookshelf shuddered.

Bolts shifted. The structure swung outward, revealing a long, narrow passage beyond.

Chris and Eleanor exchanged a glance—a silent confirmation—before stepping inside. Their footsteps echoed softly in the confined space.

Then—the bookshelf slammed shut behind them.

Trapping them inside.

There was no turning back now.

They bolted through the tunnels, Eleanor storming ahead, the Light Element illuminating the passage.

Neither of them knew for certain if this was the right way—but Eleanor felt it. With each step, the glow of the Light Element grew in intensity ever so slightly that it gave her some hope that they were heading in the right direction.

101... 102... 103...

Chris had been counting every step, his voice quiet but persistent. At first, Eleanor ignored it—focused on the task at hand—but after a while, the constant counting started to grate on her nerves. She was just about to tell him to stop when she suddenly froze.

Chris wasn't paying attention. He walked straight into her with a startled grunt.

"Why are you stopping?" he whispered.

Eleanor pressed a finger to her lips, then pointed upward.

Above them, the pulse of bass vibrated through the ceiling—a rhythmic thump, steady and unbroken. Voices hummed in a distant blur, laughter and song weaving into the music.

They were directly beneath the main hall.

Where students danced, oblivious. Where excitement filled the air, untouched by the creeping danger that slithered through the corridors as they spoke.

Unseen.

But coming.

It was clear by the sound of laughter above that the mercenaries hadn't yet reached this part of the school. If they worked quick enough, they still had a chance of warning everyone before it was too late.

Her stomach twisted.

"We need to get up there," she murmured. But there was no obvious escape. It wasn't like there was a big flashing sign marked EXIT!

Chris immediately ran his hands along the tunnel walls, fingers searching for anything—an opening, a switch, a loose brick.

Eleanor held the Light Element high, its glow flickering against the cold stone.

That's when she saw them.

Carvings—covering every inch of the tunnel walls.

Chris paused, brushing a hand over the etched patterns. "What's this?"

Eleanor leaned in, tracing the surrounding symbols. As the Light Element's glow touched them, the markings shimmered, shifting, twisting—until they became words.

She read them aloud.

"Raise the level."

Chris frowned. "Raise the level?" He repeated the words under his breath, confused. "What's that supposed to mean?"

Eleanor bit her lip, mind racing. How could they raise anything? They were deep underground, beneath layers of solid rock.

Then Chris snapped his fingers. "Wait! Isn't 'raise the level' something people say about water? Like dams and reservoirs?"

Eleanor's heart skipped.

Water.

Chris slowly glanced around the tunnel, suddenly looking nervous. "Oh gosh, I *really* hope there's no water down here. I don't feel like drowning."

Eleanor let out a breathy laugh, shaking her head. "I don't think it means *actual* water... but maybe it's telling us how to open the tunnel."

She scanned the wall again—then froze.

Just below the inscription, near the ground, was a different carving. This one hadn't translated the instant the Light Element touched it. The symbol remained as two wavy lines, like ripples.

"Chris," Eleanor whispered, pointing. "Don't you think this looks like water?"

Chris crouched down, nodding. He reached toward it, brushing away dust. As his fingers explored the edges, a small chunk of rock slid free—revealing a hole no bigger than the neck of a bottle.

He squinted inside. At the very back, something glinted.

"What is that?" Eleanor asked.

"I'm not sure." Chris stretched his arm closer, fingertips just barely squeezing through the gap. He chuckled. "Good thing I've got narrow wrists."

He fumbled blindly for a moment, then his fingers snagged something.

A lever.

Without hesitation, he pulled upward.

The entire wall trembled. Stone groaned and scraped against stone.

Above them, something shifted.

With a heavy *clank*, a narrow spiral staircase unravelled from the ceiling, jutting downward like a bridge leading them out of hell.

Eleanor exhaled. "Nice work, Chris."

He grinned, though there was still unease in his eyes.

They climbed swiftly, each step sending a fresh ripple of nerves through Eleanor's chest. At the top, she pushed hard against a small metal hatch, straining against the weight until—

Click.

The latch swung open.

A burst of flashing strobe lights blinded them.

Eleanor and Chris poked their heads above the surface.

The tunnel had led them directly beneath the stage. The main hall was packed by dancers. Each in a vast array of costumes, smiling, laughing and complete unaware of the danger that was heading for them.

23

Followers of Nyx

T he crowd was a sea of movement—flailing arms, shifting bodies, the thick scent of sweat masked beneath whiffs of perfume and the sticky sweetness of glazed candy apples.

Eleanor and Chris were swept into the mass of dancers, squeezed between bodies, their footing barely steady on the vibrating floor. The Light Element was tucked securely under Eleanor's shirt, its glow hidden, but its presence weighed heavily on her thoughts.

Her mind raced—flashes of her visions blurring past her eyes. The tunnels. The armed mercenaries. Nyx lurking in the shadows.

Chris suddenly grabbed her arm, gripping tight. "Over there! I see Dr. Asterio."

Eleanor snapped her gaze in the direction he pointed. Amidst the chaos, she spotted the professor near the side entrance. Relief surged through her—but they had to reach him.

They shoved forward, pushing against the current of moving bodies, but the crowd was thick, unpredictable. Eleanor kept losing sight of him.

"Dr. Asterio!" she called, trying to keep her voice steady, above the noise.

But the music drowned everything.

Stomping feet. Thunderous bass. Laughter and cheers swallowed her voice entirely.

Then—

Silence.

The music cut off.

Darkness devoured the hall.

The sudden shift sent a chill through Eleanor's spine. Mutters rippled through the room—soft, uncertain.

A voice boomed through the speakers, slicing through the eerie quiet.

"GOOD EVENING, ALL."

Every breath jumped.

Eleanor gripped Chris's hand tighter.

"Listen long and hard... we are *The Order of Shadows*... and we have control of this building."

The mercenaries had hacked into the school's technology. Everything—the air vents, the security systems, the automated locks, the cameras, even the cell networks. They had sealed them inside, cut off any escape. No calls for help. No way out.

"So, you think you all know the truth about the events from last year..." The voice was smooth, deliberate, dripping with mockery.

Eleanor's skin prickled with the unmistakable sensation of being watched, a suffocating awareness pressing in from all sides as students spun around wildly, scanning the dimly lit hall for signs of hidden infiltrators. But with everyone adorned in elaborate costumes—faces masked behind layers of intricate design and misleading disguises—identifying imposters was an impossible feat, each figure blending seamlessly into the sea of restless bodies.

The voice pressed on.

"Did you know your own headmaster knew all along how to stop the attacks? That despite possessing the knowledge to end your suffering, he chose instead to guard his reputation, his career, his standing—your safety be damned? That he kept his silence, not to shield you, but to shield himself?"

Suspicious glances darted upward, toward the balcony where Headmaster Singleton stood rigid and unmoving, his expression unreadable, his posture betraying nothing.

Then, the voice lowered, curling into the space like thick smoke unfurling in slow, ominous waves.

"As we speak, some amongst you conspire against us. There are those who wield powers beyond your wildest imagination, forces you could never comprehend—but instead of stepping forward, they choose silence. They choose cowardice."

Eleanor forced herself to remain perfectly still, resisting the urge to flinch, to run, to make herself disappear entirely. Slowly, carefully, she edged backward, her movements measured, until the familiar warmth of Chris's presence anchored her in place. His fingers closed tightly around hers, a silent reassurance, his grip pulsing in erratic beats that mirrored the frantic rhythm of her own heartbeat.

She felt watched.

Exposed.

The Light Element rested heavily against her hip, half-poking out of her pocket, its presence impossible to ignore—as if urging her to act, begging to be noticed.

But she couldn't.

Not now.

Not when the Order was somewhere in this very room. Watching. Listening. Lurking in the shadows.

Maybe even standing right beside her.

"The lies end today—with us. And those who betrayed us... will finally get what they deserve."

Suddenly, scattered cheers erupted—not from everyone, but from select voices throughout the hall, their triumphant cries cutting through the murmurs like jagged glass.

Her grip tightened around Chris's arm, fingers pressing deep into his sleeve, grounding herself against the growing dread clawing at her chest.

Everything about this moment felt wrong.

Maybe Chris had been right. Maybe they should have run when they had the chance—slipped away into the night, warned someone, called for help.

But now, that window had slammed shut.

They were trapped.

Just like everyone else.

And worse—Eleanor was powerless.

She couldn't move. Couldn't risk being seen. If she made a single misstep—if she so much as breathed in the wrong direction—Nyx would seize the Light Element, and that was a fate she couldn't allow.

She had sworn to protect it.

Yet standing here, frozen in place, watching as chaos erupted around her, made anger simmer beneath her skin, hot and relentless. Helplessness burned in her veins, but she forced herself to stay still, to hold her ground, even as her instincts screamed at her to run.

Then, like a sudden storm breaking over the gathering, a flood of armed mercenaries stormed down the staircases, pouring from the balconies as they cut off every possible exit.

Chris muttered something beside her, but the words barely registered. Her focus had already shifted, locking onto the trap door beneath the stage—the only chance they might have. If they could just—

A sharp crack split the air, shattering any fleeting hope.

Gunfire.

A bullet tore into the grand chandelier above, sending a deafening explosion of glass cascading through the hall. Shards rained down in dazzling, dangerous bursts, scattering in violent sprays across the stage and blocking the only way out. Eleanor instinctively flinched, throwing up her arm to shield her face as shrieks rippled through the panicked crowd.

The Order had eyes everywhere.

Their warning had been unmistakable—this was not a game to them, and they weren't leaving until they got exactly what they came for.

"Stop this now!" A voice, low and commanding, cut through the screams.

Students turned their heads, breath hitching in their throats.

The leader of the mercenaries sneered, his dark eyes gleaming with twisted amusement. "You want to play the hero, do you?"

Dr. Asterio stood his ground, his expression firm, his voice steady. "No, I just want you to leave these innocent students unharmed."

The mercenary leader hummed mockingly, his smirk widening. To him, this *was* a game.

"Very well," he said slowly, savouring the tension. "No one will be harmed... *if.*"

He paused deliberately, dragging out the moment, letting the fear settle deep in the students' bones.

"...You tell me where Eleanor Walker is."

Eleanor's stomach twisted violently. She could feel the eyes shifting toward her, wary glances exchanged between students. Some looked at her directly, suspicion flickering behind their fear, but none of them said a word. Perhaps they weren't certain, or perhaps they didn't want to draw attention to themselves.

She forced herself to keep still, blending into the crowd as best as she could.

But Eleanor knew that when faced with the choice between saving themselves or saving her, instinct would always take over. It was only a basic animal instinct to do whatever it took to survive.

The except of which seemed to be Dr. Asterio, who didn't hesitate before stepping forwards with his head held high, "Never!"

The mercenary leader's smirk vanished. "Very well."

The gunshot cracked through the air like a whip and Dr. Asterio crumpled to the floor, clutching his bleeding arm.

Screams erupted as the professors rushed toward him, Professor Dougan pressing her hands against the wound, trying to stop the flow of blood.

But Eleanor—Eleanor felt frozen.

The world around her blurred as the madness fading into the background. She stared, fixated, at the mercenary gripping the smoking weapon—the same one who had fired as the scent of burnt metal lingered in the air.

"That was a warning shot," the mercenary leader declared, his tone dripping with menace. "Anyone else who wishes to get in our way won't be so lucky."

Silence crashed down over the hall.

Even the murmurs of fear had quieted to hushed whimpers. The leader now took slow, deliberate steps forward, his gaze sweeping over the terrified faces before him.

"Can nobody tell me the whereabouts of Eleanor Walker?"

A sickening pause. The room held its breath.

"Fine."

His voice darkened. "Then I'm afraid you'll all die with her."

The words sent another ripple of panic through the crowd. Students clung to each other, pressing into the walls, searching for an escape that didn't exist.

Then—sudden movement.

Henry Kensington shoved his way forward, knocking frozen students aside. Eleanor's stomach plummeted.

A shot fired—sharp, fast—striking the ground at Henry's feet which caused him to stumble back with eyes wide with terror.

Then, in one desperate motion, he grabbed Maddison's arm and yanked her forward.

Henry's voice was frantic. "She—she's friends with Eleanor!"

A mercenary seized Maddison roughly by the arm. "Where is she?"

Maddison pulled back fiercely, but the grip on her was unshakable.

Another bullet ripped through the air—an inch away from her shoulder which made Eleanor stiffen.

The shooter on the balcony wasn't missing by accident. From twenty feet away, they could pick off a fly on a glass and leave the glass untouched.

But even as heat coursed through Maddison's veins, she refused to show fear. "*Eleanor Walker?*" Maddison hummed, tilting her head slightly. "Let me think," she drawled, feigning ignorance—though everyone knew Maddison was anything but.

She let the silence stretch, dragging it out just long enough to make them uneasy. Then, with deliberate slowness, she tapped a finger to her chin, her expression sharpening as she turned toward the man.

"Oh, you mean the girl who sent you all running and screaming like terrified children when you tried to abduct me?" She smirked. "Unsuccessfully, might I add."

Recognition flickered in her eyes.

The mercenary's face twisted in fury and he raised his hand, high and sharp, ready to strike her down with one powerful blow.

Maddison braced herself, but before the hit could land—

Daniel moved.

His hand shot out, gripping the mercenary's wrist mid-air. "Don't lay a hand on my girlfriend." He growled. Then, without hesitation—Daniel drove his fist into the mercenary's face, sending him sprawling to the ground.

Chaos erupted as the students fought back. A surge of bodies crashed against the mercenaries, scrambling for control. But amidst the madness, a group of figures moved swiftly through the crowd.

Long black cloaks. Hoods pulled low, faces obscured.

They were heading toward the staircase.

The traitors.

The *Order of Shadows.*

Still on the ground, the mercenary leader wiped the blood from his busted lip, his expression twisting into a snarl as his voice cutting through the screaming. "Light it up!"

Without hesitation, mercenaries raised his weapon, the cold steel glinting under the flickering lights. A single round fired, the bullet striking the speakers with brutal precision. Sparks erupted instantly, igniting the exposed wires and triggering a chain reaction of small explosions that sent shockwaves rippling through the room.

Beneath their feet, the stone floor quaked with growing intensity, each eruption rattling through the walls as one by one, the detonations burst to life, their relentless force tearing through the once-celebratory hall.

Students screamed louder as bodies were thrown across the room, tossed like weightless figures.

As the dust slowly settled, leaving behind a haze of destruction and unsettled debris, the mercenaries and their cloaked allies moved swiftly, their dark forms slipping toward the upper balconies. Then, with a deafening finality, the great doors slammed shut, the locks clicking firmly into place, sealing every last terrified soul inside.

Their mission was nearly complete.

And now—

The deathtrap had been sealed.

24

Perilous Decent

The world was crumbling around them—stone breaking against stone, glass shattering into dangerous shards. The mercenaries were gone, but their destruction remained. The stage had been obliterated, and the professors wasted no time rushing toward the doors, attempting to force them open.

But it was no use.

The exits were sealed.

Then, through the chaos, Singleton emerged, his voice cutting through the panic.

"This way, everyone!"

With the help of ten others, he tore down the massive historic tapestry hanging at the back of the hall. Dust and fabric fluttered to the ground, revealing a small, nearly invisible latch carved into the stone wall.

Singleton pulled out his ring of master keys. His fingers trembled slightly, but his movements remained swift and sure. He found the oldest, rusted copper key and jammed it into the lock. With a rough turn, the ancient mechanism clicked open.

The students wasted no time. They pressed their full weight against the stone door, heaving it open as it groaned against its hinges. A tunnel stretched beyond—leading directly toward the lake. One by one, bodies piled through the entrance, desperate to escape the collapsing hall.

But there were too many students—over a thousand to evacuate—and the building wasn't going to hold much longer. There wouldn't be enough time.

Eleanor and Chris stood frozen in the middle of the destruction, unable to move, their eyes locked onto the chaos unfolding before them. The rush of fleeing students, the frantic shouts, the fear—everything blurred together.

Then—

A sharp pounding erupted in Eleanor's head. It was sudden, a forceful pressure against her skull—like hands grasping at her mind, clawing their way in.

The chaos of the Halloween Ball melted away.

In its place—

Nyx.

She saw flashes. Disjointed images.

A grey, overcast sky stretched above Bleakwood's lake. Nyx stood high above the water, perched on a cliff's edge, surveying the distant forest and town below.

Then—a shift.

Six police officers lay unconscious, sprawled across the ground, surrounded by broken stone and debris.

Nyx was inside the school.

Eleanor recognized the corridors immediately—familiar stone walls, narrow passages, dim lighting. The mercenaries moved beside him, their presence ominous and unyielding.

She felt her breath flutter in her chest as her vision locked onto the chained door—the entrance to Singleton's office.

Chris's voice snapped her back to reality.

"We have to do something." His tone was urgent, his eyes sharp. "We need to warn Singleton—tell him where Nyx is, what he's planning—stop him before it's too late."

Eleanor's resolve tightened.

"No! Chris, you need to get out of here with the others. I'm *not* risking putting you in harm's way again."

She shook off his grip, but he held firm.

"You're not putting me in harm's way, Eleanor." Chris scoffed, frustration flashing across his face. "And I'm *not* just going to leave you here."

"I have to stay." She exhaled sharply. "Nyx *has* to be stopped."

"Not alone, you're not."

Eleanor grabbed his arm, pulling him close, her voice low and fierce.

"You *don't understand.* If Nyx gets the Time Element, we're all doomed. I need to stop him now, while we *still* have the chance."

Chris's eyes softened, but determination burned behind them. "And *you* don't understand that I'm not letting you face this alone. We're a team, Eleanor. We always have been. And this is my choice to stay, only mine."

Eleanor swallowed hard, staring at him.

He was right.

But the thought of putting him in danger—like last year—nearly suffocated her.

"Chris, this is different." Her voice was barely above a whisper. "This is more dangerous than anything we've faced before."

Chris nodded.

"I know. But that's *exactly* why you need me." His grip tightened slightly. "We're stronger together. If Nyx is as dangerous as you say, then you need all the help you can get, no matter how useless I might be."

Eleanor exhaled sharply, running a hand through her hair, frustration and fear tangling together.

"Alright." Her voice was firm. "But we have to be smart about this. We can't rush in blind."

Chris smiled slightly, relief flickering in his eyes. "Agreed. First—we warn Singleton. He needs to know what's happening."

Eleanor nodded.

"And then—we find a way to stop Nyx before he reaches the Time Element."

In the next breath, neither of them were prepared for the ground to erupt beneath them.

A shockwave sent students flying in every direction.

Eleanor felt herself lifted from the floor, her body weightless for a brief, terrifying second—

And then—

She crashed onto her back.

Her breath blew out of her nose like a deflating airbag, staring at the ceiling as fresh cracks splintered across the stone.

Stars blinked through the gaps—starlight shining into the ruined hall.

Objects slid past her, tumbling faster, gaining speed.

Eleanor turned her head, but was met by nothing but an endless blackness.

The dance floor had vanished, swallowed by the earth. It made her stomach flip. Yet the ground beneath her was tilting.

Rotating.

Students were still clinging to whatever they could, half of them falling deeper into the collapsing pit, half hanging on to the walls, the surface twisting vertically.

Tables and chairs screeched as gravity pulled them upside down.

The stone she lay on was cracking—ready to *split* under its own weight.

Her throat was dry.

Upon creeping to the edge, she saw that it wasn't a sheer drop—but close enough.

A ten-foot fall.

At *least* enough to break a bone.

Panic surged through the room as students shoved and climbed over each other, desperate for an escape.

A deep, primal instinct to survive had taken over.

But Eleanor—

She ran *toward* the danger.

Her blood pumped with adrenaline, pushing her forward like a force beyond her control.

She streamlined her body down the incline, picking up speed as a fresh wind whipping against her face.

The blast had destabilised the foundations, meaning there was no part of the room untouched by destruction.

Chunks of the ceiling ripped free, crashing down, trapping students under the rubble.

But Eleanor *didn't stop.*

She sprinted past the overturned high table, now half-submerged in the ditch, barely registering its presence.

The entire floor had folded into a precarious V-shape, teetering on the edge of total collapse. Smoke thickened, burning her throat, stinging her eyes. She forced herself to push harder, lungs straining—

Then—

"Help me! Please!"

The voice cut through the chaos, raw with desperation.

Eleanor's muscles tensed. Without hesitation, she veered toward the sound, heart hammering.

A first-year boy was wedged against a pile-up of chairs, his ankle trapped—bent at a sickening, unnatural angle.

No blood, but the way the bone jutted beneath her skin made her stomach twist.

She crouched beside him, forcing her voice to stay steady. "What's your name?"

Sniffling back tears, the boy whimpered. "Corey."

"Okay, Corey." She tightened her grip on the debris. "This is going to hurt a little."

A voice called out—

"Need a hand?"

Tom appeared beside her, slightly breathless but unwavering, determination written all over his face.

Eleanor nodded, relief flooding through her. Together, they gripped the wreckage, straining against the weight, lifting it just enough for Corey to pull himself free.

Panting, she turned to Tom.

"Why didn't you get out with the others?"

Tom smirked. "Ran into Chris—he filled me in. Besides, you know me. I never miss out on the action."

Above them, Chris appeared, lowering a rope towards them. Bit by bit, getting closer and closer. "Come on!" he screamed over the drop.

Eleanor grasped Corey's hand first, steadying him as she guided his grip onto the rope.

It was impossible for all three of them to climb at once—the rope wasn't built to hold that much weight. They'd have to take turns. But Eleanor had learned to bury her fear deep, keeping it locked within her core. And Tom—well, chaos and destruction were practically second nature to him. If anything, he seemed to be enjoying this a little too much.

"Hold on tight," she murmured.

Tears-streaked Corey's cheeks as he squeezed his eyelids shut, his fingers tightening around the rope.

Eleanor and Tom watched as his body lifted, rising steadily through the air.

From below, they tracked his ascent, holding their breath as he finally vanished over the edge.

Then, their focus snapped back to the ground beneath them—unstable, shifting, threatening to give way.

The floor was rising—tilting past sixty degrees.

If they didn't move *soon*—

They were going to be *trapped.*

Eleanor's eyes darted across the wreckage, searching for another way out. Maybe a fallen beam, a lodged scrap of metal—anything they could use to climb out. But there was nothing.

The only way up was by rope.

Above them, smoke thickened, swirling between the students being pulled to safety and those still stranded below. The grey haze blurred the faces of their rescuers, making it difficult to see how many had escaped.

A voice called down.

"Eleanor! Tom!"

Another bundle of rope flew over the edge, unravelling as it dropped—only to stop several feet out of reach.

"What now?" Tom muttered.

A sharp grinding noise pricked their ear. It was the sound of stone scraping against metal.

Eleanor felt it before she heard it—a deep, eerie rumble shaking the air around her. Titanium supports were ripping from the ceiling.

"Get *down!*"

She and Tom threw themselves sideways just as the structure crashed where they had been standing moments before. Dust and debris exploded around them, choking the air with thick clouds of stone and shattered metal. Tom coughed, clearing his throat.

"I've got an idea—follow me."

Eleanor didn't hesitate. They scrambled onto the fallen metal shards, climbing up the slanted wreckage, gripping anything stable enough to hold their weight. Tom balanced on the tips of his toes, barely reaching the hanging rope. He stretched out, fingers grasping the end, then turned to Eleanor, offering it to her first.

She shook her head. "You go. I'll be right behind you."

Tom hesitated, tightening his grip on the rope. He wasn't going to leave until he was sure Eleanor had a hold of it too. But something had pulled Eleanor's focus away.

A deep, rumbling vibration.

The stone beneath her groaned, shaking violently. The destruction was worsening—if anyone else was still trapped, this was their last chance to escape. She scanned the wreckage once more, searching, listening, her pulse hammering in her ears.

"Eleanor, come on!" Tom shouted. "What are you waiting for? There's no one left to save!"

She hesitated a second longer. "Right."

Finally, she turned away from the rubble. Relief flooded Tom's face as Eleanor grabbed hold of the rope. She tugged it once, testing the grip.

Then—a sharp pull on her ankle.

Eleanor gasped, looking down.

A cloaked mercenary—one who had failed to escape in time— had somehow fallen in with the rest of them and now clung desperately to her leg.

"STOP!" Eleanor screamed, kicking furiously.

Tom couldn't hear her over the chaos—the screams, the shuddering rock, the deafening destruction.

"I've got her!" the mercenary shouted, his fingers clawing their way up her boot.

Despite the crumbling world around them, he still focused all his effort on dragging Eleanor down with him, even if it was the last thing he did.

It was clear he'd already caught sight of the Light Element. Its cover was poking even further.

His eyes gleamed like he had struck gold.

Eleanor tugged at the book, struggling against his grip. They were evenly matched in strength as he reached up to grab it.

She needed a way out. She needed to break free somehow, or she was going to be brough down with him.

No time to think.

Her hand shot toward a lodged shard of glass wedged into the rocky sides. She yanked it free, gripping the jagged edge.

She couldn't reach the mercenary directly—not while he was still clinging onto the Light Element. So, she did the only thing she could.

In one swift motion she sliced through the rope. But it was too late to take it back, even if she'd wanted to.

A voice called her name. It was distant and frantic. But nothing could stop her from falling.

Wind rushed past her ears.

Eleanor twisted her body midair, facing the vertical stone wall hurtling toward her.

She *slammed* the glass shard into the rock.

Her descent slowed—but not enough to stop the impact from sending splinters of glass flying, slicing her fingers open.

Eleanor clenched her jaw against the pain, calculating her fall.

Three seconds.

Two.

One.

The last of the glass shattered, allowing her just enough time to adjust her position and land hard, feet first.

The valley's floor had cracked completely down the middle like an open wound splitting through the earth.

And she and the mercenary were headed straight for it.

The void below stretched endlessly, swallowing anything that fell.

Eleanor had only seconds—precious, fleeting seconds—before it was too late.

She tore the Light Element from her belt, feeling the energy pulse from its pages, shifting her trajectory just enough to land on solid ground instead of tumbling into the abyss. Her shoulder slammed against the rubble, sending a shock of pain through her body, but she barely registered it. The mercenary landed a few metres away, recovering quickly.

Lifting her head slowly, Eleanor sucked in a breath, forcing herself to focus. Below, the darkness stretched endlessly—a chasm blasted straight through the room like an open wound, jagged and unforgiving. She was right at the edge. One wrong move, and she would slide straight into the pit. Every swallow sent needles scraping down her throat, the taste of blood thick on her tongue. Her muscles trembled as she tried pulling herself toward higher ground, but the vibrations through the rock beneath her hands made her freeze.

The tremors deepened, rumbling like some ancient force waking beneath her. She exhaled sharply, willing her heartbeat to slow, to steady. As she stared into the abyss, she imagined her life flashing before her eyes, every moment, every decision that had led her here.

But strangely—somewhere, buried deep in the back of her mind—an unfamiliar voice whispered.

Jump.

Eleanor gritted her teeth, shaking the thought away. Instead, she sprang onto the vertical slab of rock, gripping its surface like an insect. Her heels dug into the uneven terrain, each movement precise, calculated.

Slow. Steady. Slow. Steady.

But the mercenary was climbing too—right behind her. Closing in fast.

The rock face was jagged, each crevice offering only the slightest grip. Her fingers scraped against the rough surface, nails catching, skin burning as she fought her way higher. It was unbearable. But she pushed forward, forcing herself onward, ignoring the screaming protest of her muscles.

The mercenary's laboured breathing grew closer, each breath a warning, each second bringing him nearer. Her pulse pounded, matching the urgency of her climb. She could not afford a mistake. Not now. Not when one misstep—one slip—would send her plunging into the abyss.

Eleanor had to stay focused on the climb, no matter what her other senses were screaming at her. The mercenary was closing in fast, his ravenous stare sending shivers racing down her spine, but she refused to let fear take control. She kept her grip firm, her breathing steady, even as she heard the scrape of his boots against the stone, the harsh sound reverberating in the confined space.

The drop below felt impossibly far away, a void stretching endlessly beneath her. But the top—salvation—was just within reach. One final push, one last burst of strength, and she would make it.

With the Light Element clutched under her arm, she felt the mercenary lunge, his hand darting forward in a desperate attempt to snatch it away. Without hesitation, Eleanor hurled it over the ledge, watching it disappears beyond sight, trusting that someone above would catch it.

Her muscles burned, her limbs heavy, as if weighted by lead bricks. She could feel the exhaustion threatening to take hold, urging her body to give up, to surrender to the downward pull. For a brief second, she wondered if she would lose her grip entirely, if her hands would betray her and let go.

A powerful gust of air surged up from below, icy and relentless, dragging at the debris and pulling everything downward like a hurricane sucking in its surroundings.

A horrible thought crept into her mind—maybe she *should* let go.

If she aimed for the air vent grating below, her weight alone might be enough to knock the mercenary loose, sending him tumbling into the abyss instead.

Before she could decide, a deafening roar ripped through the cavernous space beneath her. The foothold she had been clinging to was suddenly torn from the wall, vanishing into the void.

She was dangling now, her feet kicking at open air, nothing left to support her except for the shallow groove her fingers were desperately clinging onto.

Heart hammering, Eleanor glanced down—just in time to see the mercenary's grip falter.

His scream ripped through the air as his body plummeted, swallowed whole by the endless darkness below.

Her fingers ached, shaking, slipping. She couldn't hold on much longer.

Then, as if her body had made the choice for her—her fingers spasmed.

And she fell.

For a second, everything seemed to move in slow motion.

The wind whipped against her face, sent her hair flying wildly in every direction. She could feel the pulse beating in her fingertips, every sensation magnified by sheer adrenaline. Before a sudden, painful jolt tore up her shoulder.

She wasn't falling anymore.

Instead, she hung limply, suspended midair like a rag doll caught on a thread.

Dazed, she turned her gaze upward, expecting to see only smoke and destruction—

But instead, she locked eyes with *Chris.*

His entire body was sprawled over the ledge, his arm stretched down, gripping her wrist with all the strength he had left.

"I've got you!" he shouted, his voice frantic yet firm.

His skin was clammy, his palm slick with sweat, but his grip remained tight.

Eleanor gasped for breath, barely able to force out the words.

"Chris—where's the Light Element?"

"It's safe!" he called back. "Maddison has it. I told her to go with the others."

Relief flickered through Eleanor's chest—but only for a moment.

"But what about you?" she cried. "You need to get out, too!"

Chris shook his head, his expression unwavering.

"I'm *not* leaving without you, Eleanor."

But deep down, they both knew what was coming. His grip wouldn't last forever. Sooner or later, his muscles would fail, his strength would falter, and she would fall. He wasn't strong enough to pull her up—not on his own.

The world around them was still collapsing, debris sucked toward the abyss, vanishing into the void below. The wind was stronger now, an unstoppable force tearing apart everything in its path.

Eleanor tightened her grip, pulling herself closer, fighting against gravity. Her cracked lips tasted of blood, her breath shallow. If this was their last moment, there was something she needed to say.

"Chris," she whispered hoarsely. "I need you to know—"

The ground beneath them ruptured.

A deafening roar shattered the air. A shockwave burst upward, hurling dust and rubble in every direction. Eleanor felt herself lift—weightless, like a feather caught in the wind. Her hair whipped around her face, her limbs tingling with numbness, her vision blurring at the edges. She fought against the pull, tried to stay conscious. But the force was too strong.

Her grip slipped.

She fell.

The void swallowed her whole.

She had no sense of how far she was plummeting, no way to tell if the drop would end in an instant—or if she would fade into unconsciousness long before she ever hit the ground. A strange detachment seeped into her thoughts. The world above shrank to a tiny pinprick of light, barely visible in the abyss.

Then—movement.

Eleanor's pupils dilated.

Chris.

He was falling too.

Her breath caught. Had he jumped after her? Was it a reckless attempt to save her—or something more?

She reached out, her fingers brushing against his in the freefall. The darkness below stretched endlessly, infinite. But with him beside her, the fear felt less suffocating.

"Whatever happens—"

His voice was barely audible over the roaring wind, but it rang clear through the void.

"We stick together."

25

Paradox

W hen you're falling to your death, there are many things that might race through your mind beyond the looming thought of your own demise. Some people think about their family and the ones they'll leave behind, others reflect on all the things they've achieved in life—wondering whether they've done enough, whether they've left a mark. But Eleanor didn't regret the decisions that had brought her here. Because those choices had led her to her friends, to the Elements, and ultimately—to the truth.

The air around her grew warmer as she continued to plummet, her entire life flashing before her in fractured, fleeting images. The rough, rocky walls of the cavern flew past in slow motion, a blur of jagged stone that felt like it should have scraped against her skin—but somehow didn't.

And yet, despite the rapid descent, Eleanor was certain she should have hit the bottom by now.

As time stretched on, her mind defaulted to calculation, grasping at logic, at survival. At this speed, how much longer could she fall before impact became fatal? A human hitting solid rock at ten meters per second could be killed instantly. Terminal velocity—where gravity and air resistance balanced out—was five times that speed. That meant their chances of survival were close to zero.

A sudden wind billowed beneath her jacket, forcing her sleeves to flutter wildly before filling with hot air.

She could feel it—the heat, thick and suffocating, like a furnace burning from the inside.

But heat was good.

Heat meant rising air.

An updraft.

Not enough to save her completely, but maybe enough to slow her descent—just a little.

Reaching out instinctively, she searched for Chris, hoping to find him within arm's length.

One strange comfort in terminal velocity was that it was the maximum speed an object could travel through the air without accelerating further. It meant she wasn't getting *faster*. But what it didn't mean—was that she wouldn't hit the ground at all.

She had lost sight of Chris entirely.

Not even a million carrots could help her see in the pitch-black void, and the longer she searched, the more hopeless it felt. But then—

Something flickered below.

A dim, eerie glow.

At first, she thought it was a trick of the mind—a desperate illusion formed from exhaustion and fear—but as the seconds passed, the light grew stronger, sharpening into focus like a beacon guiding her through the darkness.

She strained her eyes, forcing herself to recognise it, to understand.

The walls around her narrowed, slanting inward like a slide—but this wasn't the kind of slide with a soft landing at the bottom. Over the next few minutes, she kept falling, the glow beneath her intensifying. Chris had to be somewhere, either ahead or behind, but judging by the eerie silence, he was most likely unconscious.

As her eyes fell below, a shimmering surface came into view. It was growing larger. Faster. And suddenly—Eleanor stopped watching the tunnel walls race past her and tightly shut her eyes, bracing herself for impact. She forced her body into a feet-first position, preparing for the worst.

Her breath was stolen the instant her feet struck the surface—cold and rigid, but not the unforgiving stone she had expected. Water. Ice-cold, fresh, crystal-clear. It swallowed her whole, pulling her deep, crushing her lungs with the sudden force of impact. She gasped instinctively—only for her chest to flood with water. The shock sent searing pain through her throat, every muscle locking in resistance, but it was too late. She was sinking now, twisting downward into the denser layers.

The pressure built, hammering against her ribs. Breath came in shallow gasps. Thought—impossible. Through sheer will, Eleanor forced her eyes open. The world blurred, distorted, painful. Her skin stung from the brutal impact, her limbs numb, as though the freezing temperature was already leeching sensation from her hands, feet—even her eyeballs. Time had slowed. This was her chance. If she didn't reach the surface now, her oxygen-starved brain would betray her. Unconsciousness would take her.

She kicked hard, pumping her arms in sluggish yet determined strokes. She was rising—slowly, fighting against the water's grip. Then—a burst of air met her lips. She surfaced, lungs screaming for oxygen, gulping each particle greedily through ragged gasps.

Chris was close. So close she could hear his heartbeat in her ears, his slow, uneven breaths barely audible against the cavern's stillness. Darkness surrounded them—vast, suffocating. Not even the screams from the school above could reach them now. How far had they fallen? And how were they still alive?

Even if she didn't understand it, she couldn't question it. But relief—however sweet—wouldn't last forever. Two minutes? Two seconds? A day? A week? A year? Even if the others believed she had miraculously survived, the fact remained—she shouldn't be breathing. Would they even try to reach her? Would they know where to start?

Eleanor had no idea how far underground they were. And if the fall itself hadn't killed them—starvation surely would. There was nothing down here. Nothing but stone and dust. That was—if they didn't suffocate first. The tiny pocket of oxygen that had fallen with them might be all they had left.

Still numb, barely able to twitch her fingers, Eleanor stared into the black void ahead. Death consumed her thoughts. Would suffocating hurt? Would panic overwhelm her before her body shut down? Or would she remain aware—through every agonizing second—until her very last breath? She imagined it—sand pouring into her lungs, filling them, burying her from the inside. It was useless thinking about it. But what else could she do?

Then—a flicker.

Faint. Green. Unnatural.

She steadied herself. "Chris! Wake up!"

She shook him gently, and a muffled groan escaped his lips— familiar, like the sound he made when caught sleepwalking toward the bathroom. Relief spread through her chest. He was alive.

Slowly, carefully, she waded toward the tunnel entrance— toward the light. Her fingers traced the ground beneath her.

Smooth. Not rough. Not ridged like she had imagined. If anything, the stone felt too perfect.

Suddenly, the glow intensified, revealing a vast opening filled with fireflies and strange, skittering creatures. Water trickled down rock faces, pooling below. But none of that compared to the most head-spinning sight—

A thin humanoid silhouette stood near the edge. Motionless.

Eleanor instinctively reached for Chris—

But found only emptiness.

"Eleanor Walker."

The figure spoke. Deep. Certain.

Her limbs froze. "Yes?" she answered, voice wavering.

Silence stretched between them as the stranger stepped forward, pulling something from his cloak. Eleanor wasn't too sure what it was until the soft green glow radiating from the object's centre dimmed to a candlelight brightness.

"Welcome."

His voice was calm. Almost expectant.

She stiffened. She didn't move—didn't breathe.

"And should I know you?" Eleanor asked, her voice brittle.

The figure shook his head. "I'm sure you're wondering how I know who you are."

Eleanor shrugged. "Not really." She had long since grown accustomed to strangers knowing her name. It came with being John Walker's daughter.

"Yet, even in spite of my warnings... you still jumped into danger."

Eleanor's mind stalled. Her pulse pounded.

But the words—

They sent a chill deeper than the cold water had.

"It was YOU!" She gasped, realisation dawning on her. As her eyes grew accustomed to the absent of light, their features came into focus. He wore a long white cloak that fell all the way down to his ankles and a brown leather satchel strung from shoulder to waist.

It was unmistakable—the same white cloak vanishing around every corner, a fleeting spectre she had dismissed as a trick of the mind. The figure who had deceived her, who had pretended to be the fortune teller at the ball. If it had done all that just to deter her from the ball, then it had done a very poor job at it.

She swallowed hard, heart pounding against her ribs.

"I thought I was *going mad!*" she exclaimed, the weight of her experiences with Nyx pressing down on her. "I kept seeing you, but I could never be sure." But now that he was standing here—right in front of her, she was sure he was not a figment of her imagination.

Her voice was sharp with accusation, but beneath it lay confusion, disbelief, a desperate need for answers.

The stranger remained composed, unmoving, his gaze unwavering as if he had expected this confrontation—had *prepared* for it.

"But you still haven't answered my question," Eleanor continued, her voice laced with suspicion. "*Who* are you? And how on earth did you get down here?"

She and Chris had fallen by accident, dragged into the abyss, battered and bruised with aching limbs and a metallic taste of blood clinging to the back of her throat. Yet this person—this figure before her—stood without a single scratch.

Untouched.

Unscathed.

How?

The stranger tilted his head slightly, as if considering his words carefully before speaking.

"I haven't got time to explain," he said finally, his voice remarkably steady, carrying an authority that sent a ripple of familiarity through Eleanor's chest. "You need to trust me, Eleanor. Your life depends on it."

Something about the way he spoke—the firm yet measured urgency in his tone—made her hesitate. There was something familiar in his voice, a sense of recognition she couldn't quite place. For a brief moment, she wasn't thinking about the pain in her body, the aching weight of exhaustion pulling at her limbs. She was simply listening.

Her clenched fists slowly relaxed at her sides. She stepped forward cautiously, trying to see more of the figure standing before her, but even as she moved closer, his face remained completely hidden. No hair, no distinct bone structure visible beneath the mask that clung to his features, woven from a futuristic-looking nano fabric that distorted his voice ever so slightly, giving it an almost mechanical edge.

Despite that, there was a presence about him—something undeniably human. Something familiar. His frame was slender, no bigger than hers, his movements controlled and precise. But his eyes—those piercing blue eyes—were what unsettled her the most. There was depth in them. A story waiting to be told.

With her mouth still half open, she scoffed, masking the unease curling in her stomach. "And why should I trust you?" she challenged, crossing her arms.

"Because you're the only one who can stop Nyx."

Eleanor's jaw tightened, frustration sparking to life inside her. "In case you haven't noticed, we didn't choose to fall down here," she shot back. "We're trapped."

The stranger didn't flinch. "Not with my help, you're not."

Eleanor narrowed her eyes.

"You *know* a way out?"

"Better," he answered without hesitation. "I know how to navigate the tunnels."

Eleanor's pulse quickened.

She had explored the depths of Bleakwood enough times to know how labyrinthine its underground passages were, but *Nyx*— he had an advantage.

The stranger seemed to sense her thoughts before she voiced them.

"Nyx and his followers are already moving through them," he continued. "He has the Dark Element, which means he can use it as a beacon to guide his way. But don't worry—he's not the only one in possession of an Element."

His hand lifted, the dim green glow reflecting off his fingertips. Eleanor squinted, her focus shifting to the round-shaped object in his grasp.

It was attached to a chain around his waist—a pocket watch, old and peculiar.

A lump formed in Eleanor's throat.

Her breath quickened, her mind racing.

Could it be?

Was it *possible*?

Her thoughts swirled in frantic uncertainty, her heart thumping wildly as she fought to process what she was seeing.

"That's the *Element of Time!*" she gasped.

She couldn't see the stranger's expression beneath his mask, but she *knew* he had a smug expression curling at the corners of his lips.

"How can you *have* that?" Eleanor demanded, unable to contain the sharp edge in her tone. "It was buried beneath Bleakwood! My father made sure of it—he *destroyed* his entire life's work to keep it from ever being found again!"

Her voice carried a rawness, an emotion she hadn't expected.

Her fingers twitched at her sides, itching to reach out, to grab the watch—to *prove* to herself that it was real.

But the stranger remained unmoved.

"True," he said simply. "In your time—right here, right now—this pocket watch is lost beneath a pile of rubble, buried underneath Bleakwood, untouched for the past fourteen years. And that is what Nyx seeks. Even as we stand here talking, he is growing closer to digging it up."

A sudden weight settled in Eleanor's chest. Her mind grasped at the impossibility of his words, at the notion that she was somehow standing before the very thing her father had sought to hide. Her breath slowed.

And then—

It clicked.

Her eyes widened. "You're from the future."

She didn't ask the question. She knew.

The stranger gave the faintest tilt of his head, acknowledging her words without surprise. Eleanor's pulse pounded, a thousand possibilities flooding her mind.

Who was he?

Why was he here?

And more importantly—what else did he know?

Adrenaline thrummed through Eleanor like a drug—intoxicating, unstoppable—until a single thought struck her like a stone to the chest. Her stomach churned.

"But... if you're from the future, and you have the Time Element, doesn't that mean Nyx succeeded in finding it? That at some point in the future, it was recovered from the wreckage? Does that mean he wins?"

The possibility made her pulse falter.

After everything her father had sacrificed to keep Nyx from getting his hands on the Light and Time Elements, after all the destruction that had followed, Eleanor couldn't shake the sickening idea that it had all been for nothing.

She had let Nyx walk into Bleakwood, into her school, without any real power to stop him—she had held the Light Element in her hands and still hadn't been able to stop him.

What help could she possibly be now?

Now that she was well and truly *powerless*?

The stranger stood still, the dim green glow of the pocket watch barely illuminating the sharp angles of his mask. His voice was calm, unfazed, as if he had answered this question before.

"The future is… foreign. Time isn't as simple as you were taught in school. Foreknowledge is a dangerous thing, Eleanor. One who meddles too much with the natural order can find themselves in deep waters—waters far deeper than they ever intended to swim."

Eleanor swallowed, lips pressing into a thin line.

"That sounds… lonely," she admitted softly.

For a fleeting moment, he nodded.

Something about him fascinated Eleanor.

He carried an air of authority, absolute certainty in every word, but beneath that certainty, she sensed something else that Eleanor was very familiar with.

Baggage.

"You're quite a paradox yourself," she mused, studying his stance, his measured movements. "I don't know whether to believe you or not."

The last sliver of vulnerability disappeared from the figure, replaced by something else—a knowing amusement that curled in his voice as he stepped forward.

"If you *don't* believe me," he said smoothly, a sly chuckle threading through his words, "then tell me, Eleanor—how do you think you survived a fall of over fifty feet?"

Her breath caught.

She *hadn't* considered that.

She must have looked dumbfounded, because Paradox began rambling to himself, humming thoughtfully, as if she were a child who had just asked a particularly amusing question.

"A paradox, you call me," he mused, voice carrying lightly through the dimly lit tunnel. He hummed some more, a soft sound that bounced against the stone walls, stretching into the silence between them.

"I think I rather *like* that."

Meanwhile, Eleanor was still grappling with the idea that she had come inches away from death—not just herself, but Chris as well.

She couldn't fathom *how* this stranger had saved their fall, what exactly he had done, but she was *grateful* all the same.

They had survived.

And that was all that mattered—her curiosity aside.

"From now on," the stranger declared, straightening slightly, "you may call me *Paradox.*"

The name settled into the air between them, unfamiliar yet strangely fitting.

Eleanor forced herself to focus, shaking free of the whirlwind in her thoughts.

"Alright then, *Paradox.* How do we stop Nyx?"

Paradox's head tilted slightly, unreadable behind the mask.

"We can't," he said simply. "Only *you* can."

Eleanor blinked.

A sharp, incredulous laugh escaped her lips.

"Me? *Me!* What could *I* possibly do? You know these tunnels better than anyone, you can *travel* anywhere—to *any* time! Why would you need *me*?"

Her voice carried traces of desperation, raw confusion, the pressing weight of hopelessness.

Paradox didn't react.

His voice remained unwavering.

"I *can't* interfere in the course of events."

"Then *how* can you be here?" Eleanor pressed, frustration creeping into her tone.

Paradox exhaled slowly, as though he had answered this question before, perhaps hundreds of times.

"It's... complicated," he admitted. "When you've travelled as long as I have, the Elements become a part of you. You start to understand that some moments in time are soft—malleable. Changing them won't shift the timeline significantly. But *fixed* points in time... those are dangerous to tamper with. Change one... and you could alter *everything*."

His voice was laced with experience, with years of witnessing things Eleanor couldn't begin to understand.

Paradox stepped forward, reaching out and taking Eleanor's hand.

He pressed something small into her palm.

"Take this," he instructed, urgency laced in his tone. "It will help you find your way through the tunnels."

Eleanor glanced down at the unfamiliar object—a small, delicate device resting against her skin.

"What is it?" she asked cautiously.

"A radiation counter," Paradox explained.

Eleanor furrowed her brows. "A... what?"

Paradox studied her reaction before elaborating.

"When the base collapsed fourteen years ago, all the radioactive waste was sealed inside. The thick layers of rock protected Bleakwood from exposure. But down here—beneath the surface—it's different. Radiation spikes are far more common."

Eleanor stiffened. "Isn't that dangerous?"

Paradox shook his head. "No. Most of the radiation will have decayed by now. But there's still enough to get a reading on that device. Follow the paths where the meter light turns from green to red—that's how you'll know you're going the right way."

Eleanor barely glanced at the device.

Her eyes remained fixed on him—on the last glimpse of Paradox's figure.

"The future is in your hands," he murmured.

The pocket watch in his grasp pulsed with a brilliant green glow, illuminating the edges of his mask.

Eleanor stepped forward. "Wait!" Her voice echoed off the stone. "What should I do?"

But before she could blink—

Paradox was gone. He had vanished into thin air with the pocket watch disappearing with him. And for a fleeting second, it was as if no one had ever been there at all.

26

Into the Unknown

What had just happened? Had any of it been real? For anyone else, they might have believed they'd gone mad. But Eleanor knew better. The biting chill wrapping around her was a cruel reminder that she was very much alive, stranded deep underground, with danger pressing in on all sides.

She pressed her hands against her head, fingertips brushing against the radiation meter clutched in her palm. It buzzed lightly—a constant, mindless drone she hadn't even noticed until now. Every sense was heightened, her body locked in survival mode, adrenaline still coursing through her veins.

Then—movement.

Her muscles tensed as she turned sharply. A dark outline emerged from the shadows, staggering slightly. Recognition flickered across both of their faces at the same time.

Chris.

Relief hit Eleanor like a wave, her chest tightening with emotion. She barely hesitated—her feet moved before her mind could catch up, closing the distance between them in seconds. She threw her arms around him, gripping him tightly, feeling the solid weight of his presence anchoring her in reality.

Chris let out a muffled grunt of surprise but quickly steadied himself, returning the embrace. For a few fleeting seconds, nothing else mattered. The fear, the exhaustion, the uncertainty— all of it melted under the overwhelming gratitude surging through Eleanor's body.

They had survived. Against all odds, they were alive.

When they finally pulled apart, Eleanor's eyes darted over Chris's face, assessing him. Her gaze landed on a thin trail of dried blood trickling from a gash near his ear. She let out a breathy chuckle, the humour oddly soothing against the chaos.

"Guess your ears are still big enough to get you into trouble."

Chris blinked, bewildered, before a tired laugh escaped his lips. "What happened?" he asked, voice uneven. "Why aren't we... Not that I'm complaining, but shouldn't we be dead?"

Eleanor glanced upward. The abyss stretched into nothingness above them, an endless void where pitch-black obscured any sense of depth. She exhaled slowly before murmuring, "A stranger."

Chris furrowed his brow. "Who...?"

"It doesn't matter." Eleanor shook her head, pushing the thought aside. "We need to find the Time Element before the Order of Shadows does."

Chris stiffened. He knew as well as she did—without an Element, they were fighting a battle they couldn't win. Their enemies outnumbered them, outmatched them. Nyx alone was formidable, but now, with the Dark Element, his strength had only grown.

It had taken sheer luck—and a lot of help—for Eleanor to defeat him last year. But that had been six months ago. He had changed. He had adapted. And Eleanor wasn't sure they were prepared for what came next.

Still, she kept those fears to herself. Chris didn't need to carry that weight too. He already had enough to worry about.

"Let's get moving, then." His voice was firm and steady. "No time to waste."

Suddenly, the radiation meter in Eleanor's hands flickered—its faint glow shifting from green to orange.

Eleanor raised it higher, scanning the area.

"What's causing this?" she muttered, pacing as the light dimmed.

She waved it in the air, testing its response, only for Chris to shoot her a sceptical look, clearly wondering if she had lost her mind.

Just as she was about to give up—the light flared orange again.

This time, pointed at the wall.

Eleanor leaned in, running her fingers over the rocky surface.

She stopped when a cold trickle slid down her palm.

"Water?"

Chris copied her, touching the dampness before bringing it to his nose.

He sniffed cautiously, then nodded. "Looks like it."

Eleanor frowned. "Radioactive water..."

Chris exhaled through his nose. "That can't be good."

"No," Eleanor agreed, "but it might lead us to the Time Element."

Chris glanced down the narrow passageway where the stream trickled off into the dark.

"I'm guessing we're going *that* way."

Eleanor tightened her grip on the rad meter. "We don't have a choice."

Chris sighed, casting one last glance toward the empty void behind them before murmuring, "Into the unknown."

His voice was quiet, but Eleanor caught the thread of uncertainty beneath it.

Still, he nodded, resolve settling in his expression.

Together, they pressed forward.

The passageway twisted and narrowed, the walls slick with damp moss, curling inward as if nature itself wanted to keep them from continuing.

The flickering glow of the radiation meter cast eerie shadows along the stone, stretching into the darkness ahead, making the journey feel more treacherous with each step. Their boots splashed through shallow pools as the water level slowly rose, creeping up to their ankles. Their movements were steady—slow but relentless, their breaths uneven in the damp air. The cavern pulsed with sound. Soft. Haunting. A lonely symphony of dripping water rippling through the underground, echoing off the walls like whispers from the void. Eleanor's heartbeat quickened with every step.

She could feel it.

Up ahead, a deep, guttural moan echoed through the darkness. Her pulse jumped, her body instinctively tensing—

But as she turned to Chris, he was already doubling over slightly, hands pressed against his stomach. A low groan rumbled again.

Chris groaned. "Oh, come on." He winced, straightening slightly. "How long do you suppose we've been down here?"

Eleanor blinked, thrown off by the sudden shift in tone. "I don't know..." She frowned. "Three—maybe four hours tops?"

Chris groaned louder. "I knew I should've eaten those pumpkin pies when I had the chance."

Eleanor let out an amused sigh, shaking her head despite herself. Down here, where no sunlight existed, where the world had faded into damp stone and flickering shadows, time had lost meaning. Minutes stretched into hours. Hours blurred into an uncertain before and after. She glanced at Chris, watching him carefully. Despite his exhaustion, his fear, his nerves—he was determined.

The radiation meter flared brighter as they entered a cavern, casting eerie light into the dark. Eleanor barely had time to register the shift before Chris stopped abruptly. His body stiffened, his breath hitched, and his eyes widened.

Eleanor followed his gaze until her stomach plummeted at the sight of a writhing mass clinging to the ceiling.

Bats.

Hundreds of them.

Chris's terror thickened the air between them—palpable, pressing. Eleanor swallowed, instinctively placing a reassuring hand on his shoulder.

"Quietly," she whispered, voice barely above a breath. "We'll get through this."

Chris clenched his jaw and nodded once. His steps slowed and measured, with each movement being heavier than the last.

"Why did it have to be bats?" he groaned, but they still pressed on.

The discovery of bats in these tunnels wasn't surprising—caves and underground passages running beneath Bleakwood's lake made the perfect habitat for creatures of the night. What was surprising, however, was the sheer number of them clustered together in one place. Hundreds clung to the jagged ceiling above them, tucked away in thick, shifting masses. One wrong step, one careless movement, and they would awaken in a frenzy.

The dust from the crumbling walls drifted lazily down, forming a hazy curtain in the dim glow of the rad meter. Eleanor tightened her grip on it, holding her breath, praying they could slip through unnoticed. But just as they were almost clear, the fine powder fluttered down and landed on Chris's nose.

He sneezed.

The sharp sound ricocheted through the chamber like a gunshot, reverberating across the uneven stone. Eleanor's heart stopped. Above them, the bats stirred. A rustling, whisper-like movement swept through the air—bodies twitching, claws flexing, wings stretching.

Until—

Chaos.

A wave of shrieking, flapping bodies erupted from the ceiling in a violent storm. Eleanor barely had time to react.

"Chris, run!"

She grabbed his arm, yanking him forward with every ounce of strength she could muster. Before he could respond, the bats descended—an engulfing cloud of wings, claws, and screeches closing in around them.

They sprinted through the narrow passageway, dodging blindly, frantic and panicked as the swarm closed in. The relentless mass tore at the air around them. Tiny claws scraped against Eleanor's cheek, wings brushing past her ears, sending cold bursts of air against her skin.

Chris let out a high-pitched, strangled sound—not quite a scream but nowhere near dignified—as a bat swooped past his face.

"Keep going!" Eleanor shouted, her voice barely carrying over the cacophony.

Chris stumbled forward, half-dragged, half-guided by Eleanor's grip. They ran, vision blurred by the flurry of movement, driven only by the desperate need to escape.

Just when Eleanor thought the tunnel might stretch on forever, it abruptly widened into a larger cavern. The sudden shift in space threw the bats into confusion—their movements faltered, their chaotic momentum dissolved, and soon, the swarm scattered, retreating into the safety of the darkness above.

Panting heavily, Eleanor and Chris collapsed against the damp cavern wall, their bodies trembling with exhaustion. For the first time since entering the tunnels, silence surrounded them. Chris, still gasping for air, wiped the sweat from his brow.

"I think I hate bats even more now," he panted, voice shaking slightly.

Eleanor let out a breathless laugh, though her nerves remained taut, every muscle still tingling with the lingering effects of adrenaline. They took a moment to recover, allowing their breathing to even out before pushing onward. The steady flicker of the radiation meter guided them deeper into the cavern, illuminating the slick stone and casting eerie shadows along the dripping walls.

As the air grew colder, Eleanor felt the weight of everything pressing down on her—the exhaustion, the uncertainty, the fear. Then—Chris spoke. His voice was quieter than before, hesitant.

"What are we going to do when we find Nyx?"

Eleanor didn't answer immediately. She knew the weight of his question, understood the doubt underlying it.

"What if we can't stop him?" he pressed, eyes searching hers for reassurance. "What if it's already too late?"

Eleanor exhaled slowly, forcing herself to remain composed despite the storm brewing in her chest. "I don't know," she admitted finally.

Chris shook his head firmly. "We can't think like that. We've come too far to back out now."

Eleanor sighed, knowing he was right but still unable to shake the doubt gnawing at her thoughts. "If Nyx gets his hands on the Time Element..." She hesitated. "Who knows what kind of devastation he could unleash. But we can't just confront him head-on. We are no match without a well-thought-out plan."

Chris nodded slowly, his expression serious. "What kind of plan?"

Eleanor frowned, shaking her head. "I... I don't know." Her gaze dropped to the ground. "Everyone keeps calling me a hero, but it was pure luck I stopped Nyx last time. I don't have all the answers. I feel like a fraud."

Chris studied her for a long moment before offering a weak grin. "Maybe you feel like that now, but at least you didn't scream like a baby running from bats."

Eleanor let out a short laugh despite herself, some of the tension easing just a fraction. But before she could reply, something shifted in the darkness ahead.

A sound.

Dripping water.

Chris stiffened. "You hear that?"

Eleanor nodded, all amusement forgotten as her senses sharpened.

They followed the sound, footsteps slow and careful, the rhythm of dripping water growing louder with each step. The passage twisted, then abruptly widened into a vast cavernous chamber. A still, deep pool stretched across the stone, its surface undisturbed, reflecting the dim light like a mirror.

Above them, stalactites hung like jagged teeth, their shadows sharp against the flickering glow of the radiation meter. The buzzing intensified. The soft pulse of orange light flared into deep red.

"This has to be it," Chris murmured, voice barely above a whisper.

Eleanor swallowed, her pulse quickening. Together, they scanned the cavern, taking in every shadow, every movement. The silence pressed down on them like a weight, thick and suffocating.

"Look." Chris pointed ahead.

An old, wooden bridge stretched across the water. It didn't look entirely stable, but it was the only way forward. Eleanor hesitated, unease curling in her stomach.

"We have to cross," Chris said, already moving toward it.

Eleanor nodded. She knew it was the only way across, but that didn't mean she had to like it. Keeping her eyes locked on the drop below—half expecting it to shift under her feet—she reached for the rope railing and gripped it tightly.

They stepped forward, slowly, carefully, feeling every creak and groan beneath their weight. Chris moved ahead, his pace cautious but steady. He was almost across when—

CRACK.

The sound shattered the silence like lightning.

Eleanor froze.

The wood beneath her feet splintered violently, and the next thing she knew, the bridge had collapsed.

Before she could react, they were falling.

Icy water rushed up to meet them, stealing the air from their lungs, dragging them down into suffocating darkness

27

Deep Waters

E leanor barely heard Chris's voice over the deafening rush of water, but the urgency in his tone was unmistakable.

Her body was tossed violently through the torrent, spun and battered by the unforgiving current. The freezing water seeped into her bones, stealing the last remnants of warmth from her skin and numbing her limbs until she could barely tell where her body ended, and the river began. Every time she fought to lift her head above the surface, the waves crashed down mercilessly, pulling her back into their chaotic embrace.

She gasped for air, coughing as icy droplets sprayed against her face. Somewhere in the distance, Chris's voice echoed—frantic, desperate—but the roaring river swallowed his words before she could process them.

"Chris!" Eleanor screamed, her voice raw, swallowed instantly by the rush of water.

The current surged, dragging her through a stretch of violent rapids. She slammed into jagged rocks jutting from the riverbed, the impact jolting through her like lightning, sending sharp pain ricocheting through her ribs and shoulders. Her lungs burned as she struggled to stay afloat, her fingers grasping wildly for something—*anything*—to hold onto before the current dragged her under for good.

Just when she thought her strength would give out completely, her hand brushed against something solid.

A rock.

Jutting out from the riverbank.

Clenching her jaw, she reached out, gripping it with every ounce of energy she had left. Her muscles strained, screaming in protest as she pulled herself toward it, clawing her way free from the grasp of the current.

When she finally heaved herself onto the damp ground, she collapsed against the stone, her breath coming in uneven gasps. Water dripped from her soaked clothes, pooling beneath her as she lay there, panting.

The rad meter flickered weakly on her wrist, its glow barely surviving the brutal conditions.

Through the blur of exhaustion, she scanned the dark river, searching desperately for Chris.

"Chris!" Eleanor's voice was hoarse, shaking with lingering panic.

For a moment, nothing. Before Chris's head broke through the surface, his arms flailing as the current carried him toward her. His expression was contorted in effort, water choking his every breath.

Summoning the last of her strength, Eleanor reached out.

"Chris, *grab my hand!*"

His fingers caught hers just as the current threatened to pull him under again. Digging her heels into the mud, Eleanor pulled with everything she had left.

With one final, strained effort, Chris tumbled onto the riverbank beside her.

They lay there, shivering, drained, soaking wet.

"That was close," Chris wheezed through chattering teeth. "Nothing like a *refreshing swim* to wake you up."

Eleanor let out a breathless laugh, though her chest still tightened with lingering fear.

"That was so foolish of us. We could have drowned!"

Chris groaned as he sat up, "Yet alas we didn't." tugging at his soaked clothes, which clung to him like dead weight. His first layer—a Halloween costume completely ruined—stuck to his skin in a way that made pulling it off resemble a comical battle against fabric. He flapped helplessly, resembling an injured bird, and Eleanor found herself laughing again despite everything.

Chris's ability to joke—even now, even after nearly drowning—was a strange comfort.

But Eleanor's attention quickly shifted to the rad meter, its hum punctuated with weak crackles. The water had nearly fried the electronics; its light flickered unevenly, casting ghostly shadows against her hand.

Her fingers brushed the screen, and the red glow reflected in her palm.

They were running out of time.

"We need to keep moving," Eleanor murmured, her voice steadier than she felt. "The Order of Shadows could be close. Or worse... *ahead of us.*"

Chris's humour disappeared instantly.

His expression hardened.

He nodded, wringing out as much water from his clothes as possible, though the heavy fabric still clung stubbornly.

They couldn't afford to be weighed down.

Not now.

Not when Nyx's agility—his raw power, sharpened by the Dark Element—made him unstoppable.

Every second counted.

Chris led the way forward, each step careful on the uneven ground. The rad meter's dim flicker was their only source of light, forcing them to strain against the darkness ahead. Each shadow felt dangerous, each shift in the air carried the promise of something lurking just beyond sight.

Then—Eleanor walked straight into Chris's back. Her hands instinctively grabbed his shoulders to steady them both.

"What's the holdup?" she whispered.

Chris didn't answer immediately. Instead, he bent down, picking up a small pebble. Holding it at arm's length, he let it fall. The silence stretched out until a faint splash, barely audible, made Eleanor's stomach sink.

"Please don't tell me—"

"There's another river beneath us," Chris cut in, his voice tight.

The tunnels wound and twisted unpredictably, intersecting the same underground rivers again and again. But judging by how long it had taken the pebble to hit the water—this drop was fatal. Chris crept forward, feeling along the ground until he found a sharp turn in the path.

No bridge. No safe crossing.

"We need to get around this," Chris said, his breath coming short and sharp.

Eleanor nodded, her mind racing. The distant roar of rushing water grew louder with every step they took toward the edge. Then—Chris spotted it.

A narrow ledge ran along the cavern wall—barely wide enough for a single foot. His lips pressed into a firm line.

"It's our only option," he said, forcing certainty into his tone. "Slow and steady. One foot at a time."

Heart pounding, Eleanor stepped onto the ledge. She pressed her hands flat against the jagged rock, bracing herself for balance.

The uneven surface bit into her palms, sharp enough to sting, but she ignored it.

With every careful step, the sound of the river below seemed to grow louder.

A menacing reminder of what awaited them if they slipped.

As they edged forward, the distant roar became deafening, drowning out the faint hum of the rad meter, suffocating Eleanor's shallow breaths, as each movement sent her nerves into overdrive.

"Careful, the ledge is sloping to the *left!*"

Chris's voice barely carried over the noise.

Eleanor fought against the instinct to move faster, forcing herself to stay slow and deliberate so that her fingers scraped against the rough cavern wall, each touch grounding her.

Her eyes locked on Chris's silhouette ahead.

"Just a little further," he urged, his voice steady despite the tension etched into every line of his body.

Eleanor exhaled sharply, her pulse thrumming in her ears. They had no choice but to keep going.

As they rounded the corner, she was struck by a sudden gust of cold mist rising from the depths below, wrapping around her like icy fingers. She held her breath as the source of the sound came into view—a towering waterfall, at least twenty feet high, cascading violently from the cavern wall, its relentless surge creating an impenetrable veil of mist that swallowed everything in its reach.

"We need to find a way around it!" she shouted, struggling to make herself heard over the deafening torrent.

Chris squinted through the swirling vapor, scanning the cavern for an escape. Then, just beyond the waterfall's relentless spray, a faint outline took shape—the shadow of a narrow tunnel, barely visible through the haze. His eyes widened as realization struck.

"There!" he yelled, pointing toward the opposite side of the cavern. His figure was little more than a blur through the mist. "That's our way across!"

Eleanor kept her shoulder brushing against the jagged rock face, forcing herself to stay focused, her gaze fixed on Chris's movements. Droplets clung to his damp hair, glistening under the fragmented light like strands of a delicate spider's web. Her instincts screamed at her to turn back, to find another way, but she knew better—there *was* no other way.

The ledge narrowed even further as they inched toward the waterfall, ending abruptly at a sheer drop into the unknown. Below them, darkness yawned like a hungry void. Their only option was to jump.

Eleanor swallowed hard, her eyes flickering between the tunnel ahead and the unforgiving gap standing between them and escape. There was no room for hesitation, no time to second-guess.

"I'll go first," Chris said, inhaling deeply as he steeled himself. His voice was calm, but Eleanor could hear the resolve straining beneath it. Without another word, he pushed off, leaping into the mist-filled air.

For a fraction of a second, he seemed weightless, suspended against the backdrop of roaring water, before landing heavily on the far side. His feet skidded over slick rock, nearly losing his balance, but he threw his arms out, catching hold of the edge just in time to steady himself. He turned, breathless but intact, and gestured for Eleanor to follow.

"Your turn!"

Her pulse pounded, beating a frantic rhythm beneath her skin. She wiped her damp palms against her trousers, forcing herself to breathe through the fear. The ledge offered little space for a run-up.

She had *one* chance.

With a burst of strength, Eleanor pushed off from the edge, propelling herself into the air. The wind roared past her, cold and unforgiving, whipping through her hair as she soared across the gap. For a single, terrifying moment, she felt as though she were floating—adrift, untethered—but then her fingers brushed the edge of the far side.

Desperately, she clawed for purchase, but the slick rock gave no mercy. Her body tilted, threatening to plunge into the abyss below. The waterfall's roar seemed to mock her, growing louder as she slipped—

Then—

Chris lunged forward, his hand locking around her wrist in an iron grip. Eleanor gasped as he hauled her upward, her legs scrambling against the rock face for footing. With a final, strained effort, she pulled herself over the ledge and collapsed beside him, both of them gasping, hearts racing. The waterfall thundered behind them, relentless and untamed, but they had made it.

Eleanor barely allowed herself a second to recover before glancing down at the rad metre which had deepened into an even deeper red. Something had changed.

They were close.

She pushed herself to her feet, brushing damp strands of hair from her face, the determination in her eyes unwavering. "Come on," she said, her voice steady despite the unease tightening in her chest. "The Time Element is near. I can feel it."

Chris didn't argue. He nodded, pushing forward as they carefully made their way into the tunnel, each step carrying them deeper into the unknown. The air grew colder, dampness clinging to the walls like a ghost's breath. The roar of the waterfall faded behind them, replaced only by the quiet hum of the rad metre and the steady beat of their footsteps—

28

Unearthed

Following the guidance of the rad metre, Eleanor and Chris pressed forward through the tunnel and emerging on the far side of the waterfall. The sound of cascading water filled the cavern, an unrelenting roar that bounced off the stone walls and spilled into a deep, swirling pool at its base. The damp air clung to their skin, and their breath misted faintly in the cold. Across the cavern, a pile of rocks and debris blocked what appeared to be another tunnel entrance—but that wasn't the only thing they saw.

A metallic clang echoed through the chamber, followed by the heavy stomping of boots against stone. Eleanor stiffened, eyes darting toward the movement below. Several hooded figures, their postures sharp and deliberate, gathered near the rubble, their presence sending a fresh wave of unease down her spine.

Chris crouched lower, his breath shallow.

"How did they get here before us?" he whispered, barely audible above the thunderous waterfall.

Eleanor didn't answer, but her mind raced. Even after fourteen years, Nyx hadn't forgotten these tunnels—every twist, every passage, every hidden path. He had navigated these depths before, and his precision meant he would have no trouble finding his way now. Her jaw tightened, frustration coiling in her stomach.

Together, they ducked behind a jagged outcrop along the cliff top, their vantage point offering some cover while allowing them a clear view of everything unfolding below. As they watched, more figures slipped into the cavern, their movements seamless, silent. At least twenty members of the Order of Shadows had arrived, their black cloaks blending into the darkness. At their centre stood Nyx, towering, composed—his presence thick with quiet authority. Even from this distance, Eleanor could feel the chill of his calculating stare, his sharp eyes scanning his surroundings like a predator searching for its prey.

She held her breath as the Order began hacking away at the debris blocking the tunnel entrance, each heavy strike sending small fractures spiderwebbing across the cave walls. It wouldn't take long for them to break through. Then, through the thinning cracks, a faint green glow began to seep into the cavern, casting an eerie brilliance against the rock. Eleanor's pulse quickened, the sight momentarily stealing the breath from her lungs.

The glow wasn't just light.

It was *power,* emanating from the Time Element which had been waiting to be found for the past fourteen years.

Suddenly, two members of the Order burst into the chamber, their footsteps frantic, their breaths uneven as they rushed straight to Nyx.

"Leader Nyx! Leader Nyx!" they called, almost stumbling in their haste. "We have a problem!"

Nyx turned slowly, his expression unreadable, his presence suffocating.

"Well?" His voice was cold, controlled, carrying an edge sharp enough to draw blood.

"We found footprints in the tunnels," one rebel panted. "Fresh and wet."

A flicker of dark amusement touched Nyx's eyes.

Without a word, he shoved the two rebels aside and stretched his arms wide, tilting his chin upward—as if already knowing where to look.

Eleanor's breath hitched.

His gaze landed directly on the cliff top.

Right where she and Chris were hiding.

"I *know* you're here, Eleanor."

His voice cut through the cavern, smooth yet venomous, curling into the air like smoke.

"Come out, and *maybe* I'll spare your lives."

Eleanor's muscles locked in place, her body frozen as adrenaline surged through her veins. Beside her, Chris's grip tightened around her arm, his pupils blown wide with fear. They exchanged a glance, both silently willing each other to stay still, to breathe, to *think.*

Nyx shifted, his voice lowering into something sickly sweet.

"Come now, Eleanor, don't make this harder than it needs to be," he coaxed, feigning patience. "I've been *looking forward* to this reunion. Isn't it rude to keep someone waiting?"

Then—a pause. A smile.

"Didn't your father teach you manners?"

Eleanor clenched her teeth so hard her jaw ached. Her nails bit into her palms, sharp enough to draw blood. Nyx was toying with her, playing a game he had won a thousand times before. She had to ignore him. She had to stay focused.

"Oh, right... sensitive subject."

Nyx chuckled—hollow, cruel—the sound curling through the cavern like a blade dragging against stone. It rattled something deep inside Eleanor, threatening to crack the fragile control she clung to. She inhaled sharply, forcing herself to remain calm. To think.

The Time Element was close—too close. They couldn't risk losing it to the Order of Shadows.

Beside her, Chris shifted, his voice barely more than a breath. "We can't stay hidden forever."

Eleanor nodded slowly, her mind already scrambling for a plan. "If we can create a distraction," she murmured, "we might have a chance to get to the Time Element before they do."

Chris exhaled sharply, then a mischievous smile tugged at his lips. "Then it's a good thing I found these."

He reached into his bag and pulled out two long black cloaks, their heavy fabric swaying slightly in the damp air. Eleanor stared for half a second before realization struck.

Her expression shifted instantly. "That's brilliant."

They slid into their disguises quickly, adjusting the material to cover their faces. The fabric smelled faintly of damp stone and dust—its weight unfamiliar, but enough.

It had to be enough.

Chris tugged his hood up, his hands steady despite the tension thrumming beneath his skin. "Just act natural," he instructed, scanning the cavern carefully, analysing their options. "I'll distract them. You go for the Time Element."

Eleanor hesitated. A thousand possibilities, a thousand risks— What if he got caught? What if they saw through the disguise? What if—

But Chris was right.

She squeezed his hand briefly, her grip firm despite the cold sweat clinging to her palms. "Be careful."

Chris nodded, unreadable but determined. "You too."

And then—they moved.

Chris veered right, melting into the shadows. Eleanor swallowed hard, shifting her focus to the glowing fissures in the rubble below. The light pulsed—beckoning her forward.

No room for hesitation now. No time to second-guess.

Summoning every ounce of courage, she steeled herself—

And prepared to descend into the chaos.

29

The Time Element

E leanor moved with calculated accuracy, weaving seamlessly into the crowd of hooded rebels, her black cloak merging with the sea of identical figures that swarmed the cavern. The dim glow spilling from the cracks in the rubble masked her presence, allowing her to slip past prying eyes, though she knew the illusion of invisibility was fragile—one careless glance, one wrong step, and she would be exposed.

Her fingers tightened around the cold handle of a pickaxe, mimicking the rhythmic strikes of those around her as they hacked away at the obstruction blocking the glowing Time Element. Every motion, every breath, was measured, controlled, and carefully disguised.

The light spilling through the gaps in the stone grew brighter, pulsing with unnatural energy, bathing the cavern in an eerie green haze.

The roar of falling debris, the relentless hammering of tools against stone, and the distant thrum of the waterfall masked the tension rising between her shoulders, but she felt it nonetheless—

an awareness sharp and unforgiving, warning her of the danger that lurked mere inches away.

Before a loud clatter shook the ground beneath her feet.

Rocks tumbled from the far end of the chamber, crashing against the cavern floor with startling force. The noise ricocheted through the tunnel like a gunshot, breaking the rhythm of the excavation, snapping heads toward the disturbance. But the sound wasn't coming from the dig sight.

"Over there!"

One of the rebels gestured sharply in the direction of the sound, his voice cutting through the stale air. Half of the workers abandoned their posts instantly, moving toward the noise with swift precision.

Eleanor's pulse thundered as she pressed forward.

Chris! What are you doing? She thought to herself, feeling a flipping in her chest as if all the people around her could read her thoughts.

Still, she continued like the others to chisel away at the rock. And bit by bit, the rubble crumbled beneath the relentless assault of pickaxes, until the blockage was nothing more than dust and scattered stones beneath their feet. The passageway had opened, and through the shifting remains of the blockade, the green glow surged outward, illuminating the cavern with an almost ethereal brilliance.

This was her moment.

Amid the chaos, she seized her opportunity.

Dodging falling debris, weaving through the disarray of moving bodies, Eleanor darted toward the entrance with unwavering focus. Before she'd gotten a few steps a sharp and commanding voice yelled out. "*Stop her!*"

The sound alone sent ice through Eleanor's veins, but she refused to falter.

Several figures lunged toward her, their movements fluid, trained, lethal—but before they could reach her, Chris struck.

He tore through the crowd, ripping his hood free as he tackled two rebels to the ground in one swift motion. The hood flew from his face, revealing his identity to the entire Order. Eleanor had only a split second to react—she gripped his wrist tightly, pulling him toward her as they fought back against the oncoming attackers, fists colliding with cloaked bodies, each movement fuelled by sheer emotion.

Until a few seconds in, the hooded figures froze.

A presence, weighty and suffocating, pressed down on the space between them, forcing them still as a single figure stepped forward, emerging from the mass of rebels like a shadow rising from the depths.

Nyx.

Eleanor's eyebrows fell as she locked eyes with him, her every nerve electrified.

In his hand, the Dark Element crackled with twisted energy, its tendrils writhing like living shadows, shifting and pulsing against his skin.

A slow, deliberate smile stretched across his lips.

"Hello, Eleanor."

Up close, Nyx was worse than she remembered.

Dark scars slashed across his face like claw marks, etched deep into his pale skin, a grotesque reminder of the battles he had endured, of the power he wielded. His hollow white eyes burned with something unspoken, something old and cruel, something that made the air around him feel colder. His lips—stained red, like blood—curved upward as he examined her, as if savouring the moment.

"You've come a long way," he murmured, his voice silky, sharp. "But, alas, you're *too late.*"

Eleanor swallowed, her mind racing.

She clenched her fists, forcing herself to push aside the fear clawing at her insides. Without the Light Element, she felt naked—*exposed.* The absence of its power left a void inside her, a chasm where her supernatural strength once resided, and the sheer weight of that emptiness made her limbs feel impossibly heavy.

Still, she refused to waver.

"Why are you doing this?" she demanded, her voice steady despite the storm raging in her chest.

Nyx chuckled, the sound empty, haunting.

"The Time Element is the key," he answered smoothly. "It will grant me dominion over time itself. Why waste my efforts reclaiming the Light Element when I can reshape the *entire future*?"

"The *FUTURE!*"

The rebels echoed his words, their voices rising in blind worship, a chorus of devotion that made Eleanor's stomach turn.

Her gaze sharpened as she scanned their faces.

"And what do *you* gain from this?" she challenged, her voice cutting through the fervour.

"Hope," one of them replied, their conviction unwavering.

Eleanor's breath caught in her throat—more in frustration than disbelief.

"Hope?" she repeated, incredulity laced into every syllable. "He doesn't offer *hope*—only *lies.* He doesn't want to *save* the world. He wants *power.* And he's been feeding you false promises just to get it."

Nyx's smirk widened, a dark tendril slithering from the Element in his grasp.

Before she could move, it coiled around her neck, tightening, stealing the breath from her lungs.

The pressure spread—pins and needles prickled across Eleanor's skin, squeezing against her throat—but even as the world blurred at the edges, she forced the words through her teeth.

"He wants... power. He'll destroy... everything."

Nyx laughed, hollow and cruel. "Such a fragile little girl without her Light Element."

Chris stepped forward, fists clenched. "You can't play God, Nyx," he spat. "Tampering with time will have consequences beyond your control."

Nyx's gaze darkened, his grip tightening. "You underestimate the Elements. Combined, they can accomplish anything."

Eleanor and Chris exchanged a glance—silent, understanding. Nyx was dangerous, but more than that, he was convincing. The rebels, the young faces surrounding him, were children—manipulated, convinced, swayed by his words. But they weren't the enemy. Nyx was.

Eleanor inhaled sharply, ignoring the sting in her throat. "You're wrong, Nyx." Her voice rang clear, unwavering. "The Elements belong to no one. We won't let you misuse them. Not now. Not ever."

Chaos erupted before Nyx could speak.

Smoke bombs detonated. Gunfire ricocheted against the cavern walls.

Eleanor lunged, knocking the Dark Element from his grasp. It skidded across the stone floor—teetering on the edge of the cliff.

"No!"

Nyx's roar shook the cavern.

But then—

An explosion tore through the air above. Over a dozen red lasers cut through the smoke, sweeping over the battlefield like searchlights.

Everyone was disoriented as a high-pitched ringing shook their ears. Figures in tactical gear dropped into sight, SWAT written in bold white letters across their vests.

Chris grabbed Eleanor's wrist. "Eleanor—Nyx is getting away!"

She turned to find him already gone, along with the Dark Element.

"He's going after the Time Element," Eleanor breathed.

They had to follow him. They had to stop him. Before it was too late.

30

The Hidden Chamber

Bodies tumbling through the chaos as the SWAT team stormed the chamber. The air was thick with smoke, the scent of burning rock mingling with the acrid sting of gunpowder, and the dim light of the glowing Time Element barely pierced through the blinding fog. Shouts of surrender, orders barked through gas masks, and the rapid-fire crackle of stun rounds filled the space as rebels either dropped their weapons or were forced to their knees, their defiance stripped away by sheer force.

Eleanor barely registered their arrival before she was moving again, ducking and weaving through the battlefield, her heart pounding like war drums against her ribs. Chris had hold of her arm, pulling her into cover as a blinding light pierced through the haze, just about grazing their heads. The SWAT team's voices continued to bark commands over the chaos.

"DROP YOUR WEAPONS! ON YOUR KNEES—NOW!"

Gunfire continued ricocheting against stone in a deafening frenzy, and Eleanor knew they had *seconds* before Nyx reached the

Time Element. He had already entered the tunnel and was at least a minute ahead of them by now.

"We have to move!" Eleanor shouted, shoving Chris toward the narrow passage, its eerie green glow pulsing ahead.

They took off, sprinting faster than their bodies should have allowed, diving behind collapsed pillars and slabs of rock as they raced forward. Every footstep echoed against the damp stone, every breath burned as they pushed toward the brilliant glow.

The air grew colder. The tunnel narrowed.

And then—

Eleanor saw him.

Nyx was already at the far end of the passage, framed against the green brilliance of the Time Element. His movements were unnervingly quick, almost insect-like, as he darted toward his prize with predatory precision.

Eleanor didn't think—she acted.

"NYX! STOP!" Her voice rang through the tunnel, but she knew her plea was futile.

Nyx glanced over his shoulder, his expression twisting into something between anger and amusement before quickening his already inhuman pace.

Eleanor's stomach lurched.

They had seconds.

She couldn't let him reach it.

Panic surged through her veins, turning thought into instinct. Before she could even process the movement, she yanked the radiation meter from her belt—its flickering light barely functional. She didn't hesitate.

With every ounce of strength, she hurled it toward him.

The impact struck hard, smacking against Nyx's outstretched hand, knocking him off balance, sending him stumbling backward away from the Time Element.

Chris didn't waste a single second.

He tackled Nyx to the ground with enough force to send both of them skidding across the cavern floor. The fight was feral, relentless. Chris gritted his teeth, grappling with everything he had as Nyx twisted beneath him, clawing for control.

Eleanor didn't wait to see who won. She ran. Straight for the Time Element.

Her fingers closed around it the same moment Nyx's hand lunged for it.

The contact sent a shockwave ripping through her body— lightning surging through her veins, electric and raw, locking her muscles, hitching her breath. But she refused to let go.

Nyx's eyes blazed, fury flashing across his features.

"You think you can STOP ME?!" he snarled, his voice dripping with venom.

Eleanor tightened her grip, ignoring the pain tearing through her. "Chris, hold on!" she shouted, forcing her mind past the panic threatening to consume her.

The Time Element flared—its energy pulsing like a heartbeat, its glow overwhelming, pushing back against the suffocating darkness like the universe itself was responding to Eleanor's call.

Nyx's expression shifted—his rage cracking into fear.

"No—NO! YOU CAN'T—"

His voice faltered, desperation breaking through his arrogance. But it was too late.

The Time Element obeyed Eleanor's will, its power surging through her, roaring through the chamber like a tidal wave, warping the cavern walls, twisting space itself.

Reality buckled—

Dissolving—

Colours bending—

Time folding—

Eleanor lost herself in the chaos.

Her grip on the Time Element failed, its vibrations too violent to hold until it finally slipped out of her hand—into the swirling vortex that had swallowed her whole.

The world spun, unravelling—

And then—

Like a hurricane ripping through her body—

She was pulled through time.

PART 2

The separation between past,
present and future is an illusion
clear to only those who cannot see.

31

Chasing Through Time

After a whirlwind of spinning, whirling, and disorienting chaos, everything finally settled—but Eleanor's mind remained in turmoil.

She opened her eyes, but nothing about the world felt familiar. The air was warm, carrying the crisp scent of fallen leaves and fresh earth. The golden light of the setting sunbathed everything around her in an ethereal glow.

Her breathing was uneven, and the ache in her limbs reminded her just how much she had been fighting against time itself. Slowly, she forced herself upright, blinking rapidly, trying to process where—*when*—she was.

Chris stood beside her, equally dazed, his chest rising and falling in rapid bursts. His gaze darted wildly across their surroundings, searching for something—anything—that made sense.

"What... What happened?" he gasped, struggling to steady his breath. "Where are we?"

Eleanor opened her mouth to respond, but before she could speak, a voice, smooth and sharp as a blade, slithered through the air like venom.

"You *fool!*"

Eleanor's body stiffened instantly, instinct forcing her into high alert.

Nyx stepped forward, emerging from the shadows with his usual calculated elegance. He looked utterly unbothered by their sudden displacement, his presence still as dark, as suffocating, as ever.

"You've *stranded us here!*" he sneered, though there was no anger in his voice—only cruel amusement.

Eleanor's stomach turned at the way he smiled slowly and deliberately, like he was savouring the moment.

He scanned their surroundings, his sharp eyes gleaming with something unmistakable—*delight.*

"Brilliant," he murmured, stretching his arms slightly, drinking in the view. "Perhaps the gods *do* favour me after all."

Eleanor swallowed hard, dread pressing against her ribs.

He already had a plan.

Before she could even begin to figure out where they were, Nyx had already decided what came next.

His laughter echoed around them like a haunting melody, reverberating through the air, wrapping around Eleanor like a noose tightening around her throat.

She felt it before she saw it—

The Dark Element pulsed with malicious energy in Nyx's hand.

"*Chris! Get down!*" Eleanor screamed, instincts kicking in faster than thought.

Chris barely had time to react before tendrils of shadow erupted from the Dark Element, lashing out, twisting and constricting around him like a snake coiling around its prey.

Eleanor's breath hitched in her throat. Chris thrashed against the binds, his body locked in a desperate struggle, muscles straining, face contorted with pain. But the tendrils tightened, squeezing, pulling every last ounce of breath from his lungs, crushing his attempts to fight back.

Nyx watched with satisfaction, his smirk widening, his voice dripping with false sympathy. "And as for you, my dear Eleanor," he drawled, tilting his head slightly, daring her to move. "If you value his life, I suggest you don't follow me. Consider this... insurance."

Eleanor stood her ground, fists clenched so tightly her nails bit into her palms. But she refused to show weakness.

"You're not going anywhere," she seethed, her voice low and steady, her entire body coiled like a spring, ready to strike.

Nyx's expression sharpened into something more dangerous. "Oh, Eleanor." He sighed dramatically, shaking his head. "You still don't understand, do you?"

He stepped back, gripping the Dark Element tighter, and the shadows constricting Chris grew darker, denser, suffocating the little resistance he had left.

"Say your goodbyes," Nyx hissed, his voice smooth, certain. "In two days, the world you knew will cease to exist."

Then—

The smoke erupted. Thick. Heavy. Swallowing everything in its wake.

"NO!" Eleanor surged forward, reaching out, trying to grasp something—anything. But the dark fog contracted and pulled both Nyx and Chris inward before it collapsed into nothingness.

LOST IN TIME

Eleanor hit the ground, the impact knocking the air from her lungs, pain shooting through her limbs. And for a moment, all she could see was darkness.

3 2

Shadows of the Past

"Do you think she's alright?"

A brief silence followed before another voice answered, hesitant and uneasy. "I don't know. She was just lying there in the middle of the road, all by herself."

"Where do you think she came from?"

"I don't know. She just came out of nowhere."

The words faded as Eleanor's consciousness sharpened, the dull ache in her skull throbbing harder with each breath. When she finally forced her eyes open, the world around her swam for a moment, shapes and colours bleeding into one another before settling into clarity.

She was lying on a makeshift bed in a small, dimly lit room. The warmth of a crackling fire nearby sent soft waves of heat toward her chilled skin, but the harsh glare of an overhead lamp made her squint, worsening the pounding in her head.

A gentle voice broke through the silence, soft but firm.

"It's alright, love. Just take it easy."

Eleanor turned her head slowly, wincing at the sharp pain that radiated through her skull. A woman stood beside her, her expression lined with concern.

"Where am I?" Eleanor asked groggily, her throat dry and raw.

"You're in our living room," the woman replied, placing a damp cloth against Eleanor's forehead. The sudden sting made her flinch.

"You've got quite the nasty gash," the woman continued, dabbing gently at the wound. "You might need stitches. Did someone do this to you?"

Eleanor didn't answer. She struggled to sit up, her muscles sluggish, weighed down by exhaustion. A blanket had been draped over her, and the soft fabric felt oddly foreign against her fingertips. Her surroundings remained hazy, disjointed pieces of reality trying to slot into place.

A man stood a few feet away, his gaze flicking between Eleanor and the woman.

"Was there anyone else out there with her?" the woman asked, turning toward him.

"No. Not that I could see," the man responded, his tone unsure.

Eleanor barely heard him. Her breath quickened as memories surged back—the tunnels beneath Bleakwood, the glow of the Time Element, Chris's terrified face, Nyx's twisted smirk. She nearly threw off the blanket and bolted upright, but the woman beside her steadied her with a firm hand, pressing against her shoulder.

"Chris?" Eleanor rasped, her voice barely audible.

Silence.

She swallowed, then tried again, louder this time.

"Chris!"

The name hung in the air, unanswered. Eleanor's chest tightened, panic clawing its way through her ribs. Nyx had taken him. And now, Eleanor was stranded. Alone.

Her legs trembled as she forced herself to stand, though every movement sent fire through her limbs. A wave of dizziness hit her, and she stumbled slightly, catching herself against the arm of the couch. She thought nothing could make her feel more lightheaded than she already did—until her gaze landed on the man beside her.

She hesitated. Something about him felt familiar. Too familiar.

The breath in her lungs turned razor-sharp as realization crashed into her like ice water spilling through her veins.

The fireplace crackled softly, shadows shifting across a worn brown couch and a dusty cream carpet. The scent of firewood lingered in the air, warm and grounding, but Eleanor felt nothing but cold. Her vision tunnelled. Her heart thundered violently against her ribs.

The man stepped forward, brows furrowed in concern. "Careful," he murmured. "Are you alright?"

Eleanor stared at him, her lips parting slightly, her hands trembling. She opened her mouth, but no words came.

Finally, she whispered.

"...Dad?"

Her fingers reached out instinctively, brushing against his arm before she could stop herself.

The touch was real.

Solid.

Living.

John Walker tilted his head slightly, watching her reaction with quiet confusion. "You don't look too good," he said, his brow furrowed. "It's like you've seen a ghost."

Eleanor's body swayed, her mind spinning wildly, trying to grasp the impossible truth staring her in the face.

Her father.

Her father was alive.

How?

Was she dead? Was this the afterlife? If so, she was sorely disappointed by the lack of grand enlightenment—and the drab furnishings.

Her gaze darted around the room in frantic desperation until she spotted it—a newspaper sitting atop the coffee table.

She grabbed it, her fingers trembling as she scanned the date.

British Telegraph, commemorating its 25th anniversary.

Her breath stalled as she lowered her gaze toward the top of the page.

October, 1996.

Her jaw slackened.

"1996?" she repeated, her voice barely a breath.

"Yes, love," John replied slowly, concern creeping into his tone. "That's the year."

Eleanor staggered toward the window, flinging the curtains open. Snowflakes drifted gently against the glass, settling over the cars parked outside.

She stared. The vehicles looked old—boxy, outdated—some with registration plates from the eighties.

Her pulse kicked into overdrive.

She pinched her arm—hard.

"Ow!"

But the realization hit her harder than any physical pain ever could. She wasn't dreaming. She wasn't hallucinating.

She was in the past.

She had stranded herself—had stranded Nyx—had stranded Chris in 1996.

The woman took her under her arms and seated her beside the embers of the fire. The warmth licked at her cheeks, drying off the last traces of damp clothing.

"Do you think she has memory loss?" the woman murmured, gazing into the spitting flames with a distant haze.

But Eleanor could barely process her words. Her mind was consumed by a singular, gut-wrenching thought.

What if Chris was already dead?

What if Nyx had killed him? Chris wasn't a direct threat to Nyx—he held no power that could be stolen, no advantage Nyx could use. He wasn't useful to Nyx—except as leverage against Eleanor.

The thought sent ice through her veins.

She had to find him.

The woman gently rubbed Eleanor's shoulders and pressed a glass of water into her trembling hands.

"You need to take a breath, love," she urged, her voice kind but firm.

Eleanor forced herself to sip the water, though her hands shook violently.

"What's the date today?" she asked, her voice raw, fragile.

"The 30th of October, 1996," the woman answered.

Eleanor's blood ran cold.

She slowly looked up at her.

Young. Glowing. Familiar.

It was her mother.

Not the version Eleanor had known, but a woman fourteen years younger than the mother who had raised her.

Eleanor swallowed hard, forcing herself to steady her thoughts.

But that meant—if she had gotten her dates right—it was one day away from the 1st of November. One day away from her father's death.

In the span of a single heartbeat, a lifetime of thoughts flooded Eleanor's mind, crashing into her with relentless force.

Most people spend their lives trapped in the what ifs of their past, imagining what they could do to change a moment, to undo a mistake, to rewrite history. They relive these fantasies over and over, indulging in the idea but never expecting it to become reality.

Yet here she was.

Standing in the past.

With her father—alive, right in front of her.

A chance of a lifetime.

Was this the reason she had been sent here? Was this fate aligning her steps, leading her to this exact moment? Out of all the possible timelines, all the infinite paths history could have led her down, why had she landed here—right in her father's path?

Her mind twisted with possibility, excitement, uncertainty.

If she was truly in the past—if time itself had bent to place her here—then she had power. She had agency. She could do what no one else could.

She could change history.

She could save her father.

But then—

Chris.

Her chest tightened.

In 1996, nobody had ever heard of the Elements—except for the few, like her father. But what if telling him about Nyx, about her real identity and purpose in this time, was the very thing that caused his death?

But Eleanor couldn't live with herself without Chris. She couldn't lose them both.

Her thoughts swirled, tangled in chaos. Her conscience tugged her in two directions—one urging her to focus on what stood right before her, the impossible chance to save her father, while the other screamed for her to act now, to find Chris before it was too late.

Her lips parted, and before she could stop herself, words tumbled out.

"I need your help to find someone." Eleanor's voice trembled, but she kept it steady and vague. "Someone dangerous. Someone evil. Bad things will happen if I don't stop him—bad things to people I care about. Will you help me?"

John—her father—exchanged a glance with his wife, hesitation flickering in his expression. "Of course," he said, though caution lined his tone. "But first, why don't you start by telling us your name, love? Surely your parents wouldn't want you out here, running around alone at night. They must be worried sick."

Eleanor flinched.

That word.

Parents.

It punched the air out of her lungs and sent ice crawling up her spine. She didn't answer, blinking hard against the tears threatening to spill over.

"I don't have parents," she whispered, her voice cracking—fragile. "Not anymore. Not in any way that mattered."

Silence stretched between them. John's expression softened, concern deepening in his features as he exchanged another look with his wife.

"If this person is as dangerous as you say," he said carefully, "don't you think we should call the police? Or take you to the hospital? You've clearly been through something awful."

Eleanor shook her head immediately, gripping the blanket still draped over her shoulders. "No," she said firmly, her voice sharp, unyielding. "The police wouldn't understand, and they wouldn't believe me. This—this is beyond what they can handle."

She exhaled slowly, forcing herself to stay composed. "I just..." Her voice faltered.

She turned away, trying to collect herself—but instead, her gaze landed on a tall mirror in the corner of the room.

She froze.

Her reflection stared back at her—smirking.

No. Not now. This was the last thing she needed.

A voice slithered into her mind, low and venomous.

Do you really think you can save him?

Eleanor stiffened, fingers digging into her palms.

You've already failed once. Nyx has him now, and he's stronger than you'll ever be. What makes you think Chris is even still alive?

"No..."

She barely recognized her own voice, barely felt the way her throat tightened, barely registered the air leaving her lungs.

The grin in the reflection widened.

Face it, Eleanor. You've doomed him. You're the reason he's in Nyx's hands. And if you hesitate for even a second longer, you'll lose him. Forever.

Her stomach twisted.

Her pulse hammered.

"No!" she snapped, spinning away from the mirror, her body rigid and boiling.

The woman near the fireplace startled, her brow furrowing, concern flickering in her eyes. "Are you alright, dear?" she asked, stepping closer.

Eleanor squeezed her eyes shut, forcing herself to steady her breathing.

Focus.

She had to focus.

She took a deep, shuddering breath, drawing strength from the urgency pressing against her ribs. When she opened her eyes, her expression was steeled with purpose.

"I don't have time," she said.

She turned back to John and his wife, her words urgent yet precise. "Please. I need to find him."

John studied her closely, his gaze sharp, calculating. He wasn't convinced—yet.

Finally, after a long pause, he nodded. "Alright," he said, his voice calm but filled with expectation. "Tell us what you need."

Eleanor inhaled deeply, steadying herself. "Do you have a phone?"

33

A Father's Suspicion

J ohn directed her the hallways. Eleanor rushed toward the giant wall-mounted telephone, her fingers trembling as she lifted the receiver. The world around her spun slightly, her thoughts tangled from the effects of time travel, her brain struggling to piece together fragments of numbers and memories.

She tried to recall it—the phone number.

Her hands felt clammy against the receiver as she pressed the numbers one by one, praying that they were correct, hoping that the haze clouding her thoughts hadn't interfered with her memory.

The dial tone rang once. Then twice. Then—

A gruff voice finally answered, cutting through the static.

"Hello?"

Relief crashed over Eleanor so forcefully she nearly forgot to breathe.

"Dr. Asterio?" she said quickly, her voice edged with desperation.

A pause.

"Yes, it's me," the man replied slowly, as though trying to place the voice speaking to him. His tone carried an edge of disbelief, wary but listening.

Eleanor swallowed hard, forcing herself to steady her words.

"I need your help."

Silence. The kind that stretched too long, too tense—thick with unspoken thoughts.

Then, finally, his voice returned—firmer this time, more cautious.

"Who is this calling? And how did you get this number?"

There was something in his voice—an unease, a nervousness, like he was suddenly aware that whoever had called him knew too much.

"You won't know me," Eleanor admitted, willing him to trust her even though she sounded just as cryptic as he probably feared. "But it's about the Elements."

A sharp, muffled sound on the other end of the line. A gasp? A choke?

Dr. Asterio audibly stiffened, his voice dropping into hushed tones.

"How do you know that name?"

Eleanor gritted her teeth, forcing herself to push past the fear threatening to slow her down.

"Please," she said, gripping the phone tighter, her pulse hammering. "You have to trust me."

The line went dead for a long, hard ten seconds. The kind of silence that made her stomach twist, that made the weight of everything settle deep in her chest.

Then—

Finally—

"You can find me at 365 Old Birch Road," he said, his voice quiet but unwavering. "Beneath the old Bleakwood Library. Come alone."

The urgency in his voice sent a chill down Eleanor's spine.

She didn't hesitate.

She hung up the phone and turned back, only to find John standing by the doorway, watching her.

Eleanor blinked a couple of times, trying to steady herself, trying to ease the weight pressing against her ribcage. It was difficult—almost impossible—to look him in the eye.

She swallowed past the lump forming in her throat, attempting to sound composed, polite.

"Thank you for your help," she said, forcing control into her voice. "I need to leave now."

John's expression tightened, concern flickering in his eyes.

"But it's snowing heavily," he protested. "You can't just go out there on foot."

Eleanor clenched her fists. She had to go. There was no time. Chris was in danger.

Her father exhaled slowly, rubbing his hands together, thinking.

"All right," he said after a long pause. "How about you spend the night here with us?" His tone was calm, measured—not demanding, but reasoning with her. "You need to rest. You're in no condition to go after anyone right now."

Eleanor opened her mouth to argue, but the fight died in her throat. She knew he was right.

Her body ached. Her limbs were sluggish. Her vision swayed when she moved too quickly.

Eleanor's fingers curled around the fabric of her sleeves, frustration coiling inside her. But she nodded.

Because no matter how much she needed to go, she wouldn't do Chris any good if she collapsed in the street again while trying to find him.

Reluctantly, she eased back onto the makeshift bed, resting her head against the pillow. Her muscles ached with exhaustion.

She closed her eyes—but she didn't sleep.

She couldn't sleep.

Her mind raced with thoughts of Chris. Of Nyx. Of the screams that haunted every corner of her subconscious—Chris's voice, fractured and desperate, rattling through her bones like torture.

34

Knowledge

F or hours, she tossed and turned on the couch beside the slowly dying embers of the fire. Part of her expected to wake up, as if all of this was just a dream – but that was wishful thinking.

Her gaze drifted toward the grandfather clock standing rigid in the corner of the room, its hands ticking forward in slow, deliberate movements. She watched as the hour struck five in the morning, and that was it—she couldn't wait any longer.

Swinging the blanket off her legs, Eleanor sat up, the silence of the house pressing in around her. Every creak of the floorboards, every distant rattle of the plumbing, sounded unnaturally loud against the stillness.

She had always thought, since she was a child, that something *lived* in the pipes.

Maybe it was just her imagination, the way the metallic clanking resembled footsteps pacing through the drains. Or maybe it was the way the sound always seemed too precise, too patterned, like some nocturnal beast lurking unseen beneath the floors, waiting—watching—until vigilance gave way to vulnerability.

The thought sent a chill down her spine.

Then, a realisation struck her.

Brilliant.

Sharp.

Sudden.

She had to go.

Checking the hallway carefully, ensuring no movement stirred from the bedrooms upstairs, Eleanor moved toward the coat rack. She grabbed one of the heavier winter coats, thick with wool lining, and quickly pulled on a pair of sturdy boots, hoping they wouldn't mind her borrowing them.

She crept to the door, hesitating only briefly to listen for any sign of movement above.

Silence.

Good.

With one final glance back at the house—the place where her parents stood, alive—she slipped out into the night.

The town of Bleakwood was eerily still, blanketed in untouched snow, undisturbed save for Eleanor's hurried footsteps crunching against the frozen ground.

The cold bit at her cheeks, sharp and merciless, while her breath formed delicate clouds in the air as she walked. The wind carried with it a biting chill, howling between the buildings, rattling the old wooden signs that hung outside shops she had once known in the future—places that looked different now, faded but intact, before time had worn them down.

She pressed forward, her thoughts locked on one thought until at last, she reached the address: 365 Old Birch Road. The building loomed dark and tall, its windows reflecting the faint glow of streetlights. She expected it to be locked, expecting that she would need to knock and hope Dr. Asterio hadn't changed his mind about meeting her. Yet when she reached out, the door creaked open slightly as if someone had left it ajar, waiting for her arrival.

Was this some kind of trap? She hesitated for only a moment before pushing the door open fully and stepping inside. The door swung shut behind her with a soft thud.

Inside, the porch smelled of aged paper and dust, a thick, ancient scent that felt almost alive. Early morning light filtered weakly through the windows, sending hazy golden streaks across the room and illuminating dancing dust motes. The silence was heavy and expectant, making Eleanor swallow back a dry, gritty taste.

"Hello?" she called out. There was no answer—only the sound of her own voice. Then, a click broke the silence.

Eleanor stiffened.

"Stop right there!"

The unmistakable sound of a round being chambered sent shivers through her. She turned slowly, raising her hands in a universal sign of surrender. Standing before her was Dr. Asterio. He was rigid, holding a small handgun aimed directly at her temple. His rugged brown coat hung loose over his shoulders, worn with age, and streaks of white ran through his stubbly beard. Despite the tired look in his eyes, the Dr looked exactly like the photograph she'd seen—a young, timeless version of the man in his prime.

Forcing herself to remain calm, Eleanor spoke carefully. "Dr. Asterio," she began in a steady voice despite the fear prickling under her skin.

His expression was unreadable, yet his grip on the gun did not falter. "Who are you?" he demanded.

It felt strange for Eleanor to see a man she had spent the whole summer living with and getting to know now appear as a complete stranger. His younger self seemed different—as if she were watching an old video of someone who hadn't fully grown into themselves yet.

Eleanor slowly lowered her hands, keeping her movements measured. "I can't tell you that," she admitted, hoping that even a partial truth would earn his trust. "But I know you believed what I said on the phone. Otherwise, you wouldn't have agreed to meet me here."

Dr. Asterio narrowed his eyes as he weighed her words. Then, without warning, he lowered his hand and tossed the pistol to the ground. Eleanor flinched, bracing for the possibility of an accidental discharge. But the gun lay still and silent, unused.

"It's not real," Dr. Asterio said simply, shrugging. "Just a replica. I wanted to see if you were really being truthful."

Eleanor exhaled shakily, trying to process everything. "But I'm afraid if you're looking for the Elements, I can't help you," Asterio continued. "I left all of that behind a long time ago. I want nothing to do with it."

Eleanor's expression hardened. "But you still have connections with the Royal British Museum, don't you?"

Dr. Asterio paused, his eyes flickering with something unreadable. "That I do," he admitted, though scepticism tinged his tone. "But I don't see how that could help—"

"Has the expedition happened yet?" Eleanor pressed. "The expedition to Athens? For the Time Element?"

Dr. Asterio froze. His face paled slightly. "How do you know about that?" he asked.

Eleanor's pulse pounded in her ears. She had his full attention now.

"I need you to tell me, where they are planning on taking it? Where is it now?" She didn't have a full timeline of the events that took place in 1996, but Nyx did. That was his advantage over her. But if she could track down the Elements, if she would figure out where his next move might be, she could use it to track down Chris.

"I don't know exactly where it is now. But if they are transporting the artifacts in any way like they did when I was a part of it. They should be transporting them in an unmarked truck or car to Bleakwood.

"And then, where?" Eleanor pressed.

Again, he nodded. "There is a base beneath Bleakwood. After discovering a network of old passageways running beneath Bleakwood, we rewired everything to turn it into our own secret hideout, allowing us to travel about out of the eyes of the police... the maze of the dead they call it. But you can't get in there on your own." He explained curtly. "Only one of the four members in our team would know how to navigate the tunnels, with at least two sets of DNA prints required to get past the security scanners."

Eleanor puzzled. She didn't remember seeing any security scanners in the tunnels back in the future. Perhaps they had long rusted and withered away, back in her time, after fourteen years of sitting around in the moist tunnel air. But then she remembered when she'd first gone exploring the tunnels at the start of the year with the twins, Chris and Maddison. And how after resting her hand of the screen, the locked doors connecting to one of the chambers had immediately opened. Of course, her DNA could trick the scanners, especially when it was similar to her father's.

"Two DNA print?" Eleanor confirmed.

The Dr nodded, "They were added in case any outsider came snooping... but that's as much as I can help you with. I vowed never to return."

Eleanor lowered her head, "Thank you, Dr. Asterio." It didn't matter that he wasn't willing to help her get through the tunnels. She had been down there once, surely, she could do it again. But then recalled that she'd had the help of Chris and the Radiation scanner, which had acted like a compass, both of which she had lost.

As she neared the door, her body betrayed her, freezing mid-step. Something gnawed at her consciousness, urging her to turn. Swivelling on her heel, her gaze locked onto the Dr's eyes, now pools of profound sorrow that seemed to whisper a thousand unspoken truths, "We are all human, Dr and we all make mistakes ..." Upon hearing this, some sense of resolve brightened in his eyes, "... what matters is what we do to make it right."

The frozen streets of Bleakwood stretched before Eleanor like a lifeless wasteland, silent and unmoving beneath layers of untouched snow. The place she had once known, the town she had walked through a thousand times, felt wrong—off-kilter in a way she couldn't quite place. Buildings loomed over her, their windows dark and watchful, empty eyes peering into the night. Curtains twitched as she passed, and though she could see no one outright, she *felt* the weight of their gazes, the suspicion thick in the air.

Her boots crunched against the ice-covered pavement as she pressed forward, breath forming small clouds in the frigid air. The wind wailed through the brittle streets, rattling old wooden signs as though whispering warnings she didn't want to hear.

She couldn't focus on the eerie stillness around her—couldn't afford to let the unease settle in her bones. She had one goal. Find Chris.

Eleanor tightened her coat, ignoring the cold biting at her exposed skin. She turned left onto Thatch and Thistle Alley. The cobblestone path should have brought some comfort.

But it didn't.

Something was wrong.

Something unseen.

Something waiting.

She glanced over her shoulder—once, then again.

Nothing.

Yet the hairs on her neck prickled. Instinct urged her forward. She quickened her pace, breath curling into the icy air.

Just as the tension in her shoulders began to ease—

A sudden grip.

A hand lunged from the shadows, snatching her and lifting her off the ground. She barely had time to register what was happening before she was slammed against the cold brick wall, feet barely grazing the frozen pavement.

The impact stole the breath from her lungs.

"You!"

The voice was rough, edged with panic and fury—the kind of fear that made people reckless.

Eleanor's pulse jumped. She twisted against the grip, arms pinned, body straining.

"What are you up to?" the man snarled, wild-eyed, his gaze darting across her face, searching. "What are you doing out here?"

Then—his expression shifted.

Recognition.

Not of her, but of something else.

"I know," he breathed, realization striking like lightning. His grip tightened.

"You're one of them, aren't you?"

Eleanor's pulse hammered.

"One of who?" she choked out. She kicked, fought, but his strength held her fast.

"You know who!" he spat, voice rising with hysteria. "Those people—those things—who toy with demons and magic!

"We warned you before—we don't want that dark magic here. You'll damn us all!"

His calloused hands pressed through the fabric of her coat, iron-tight.

Her breath came fast—short, sharp bursts.

The stench of stale beer clung to him—sharp, pungent—the reek of a mind too clouded by alcohol to reason.

She couldn't even speak.

How could she explain that she wasn't from this time? That she wasn't part of some secret group meddling with magic? That she was here by accident?

But she knew that anything she said would make it worse.

His breath was hot against her skin, a sharp contrast to the biting cold curling through her body. His feverish eyes burned with something primal.

Fear. Not just of her. Of something else. Something ancient.

The same fear lurked in the faces of the townspeople watching from behind frost-covered windows. None of them came to help. None of them moved.

They were afraid. Afraid of whatever they believed lurked beneath Bleakwood.

Eleanor swallowed, her throat raw, mind racing. She needed an escape.

Then—

"Let her go!"

A voice cut through the thick air.

Eleanor twisted her head, pulse thundering.

For the first time since waking in this timeline, relief flooded her.

Her father.

John.

Emerging from the snow, solid and unwavering.

The man holding her stiffened, his grip faltering for the briefest moment.

"*You!*"

His voice crackled, fury laced with something darker—resentment.

He released Eleanor roughly, shoving her back as he turned his full attention to John.

"We *don't* want you here! With you around, it's not safe for *us* or *our children!* You bring nothing but misfortune!" The word spit from his mouth like poison.

John's expression remained calm and unreadable. "This town isn't so big," he said, voice level but firm. "I've *heard* the words whispered behind my back. I've *seen* the hateful letters shoved through my door. But might I remind you that I have a *family*, too? Just like you, I have *every right* to live here."

The man hesitated, his fists clenching at his sides.

The man still kept his distance, as if he believed John carried something infectious, an unseen threat lingering in the air between them.

"Then shame on you!"

His voice cracked under the weight of his fury, his outrage folding into something more uncertain. He held his fist in the air for a final, wavering moment, then turned on his heel, disappearing down the alley without another word.

Eleanor let out a breath she hadn't realized she was holding, the tightness in her chest easing just slightly.

John reached for her, his expression unreadable at first, though his eyes carried something steady, something searching. His gaze lingered, skimming over her face, as though assessing whether she was truly unharmed.

For a moment, neither of them spoke, but the relief was palpable, settling between them like the first hint of warmth on a cold morning.

Eleanor let out a strained chuckle, though the fear still clung to her skin like frost in the air, refusing to fade completely.

John studied her for a beat longer before shaking his head with a faint, amused sigh.

"What is it with you?" he mused, his voice carrying the ghost of a smile. "Why do I always seem to be rescuing you from danger?"

Eleanor exhaled a small, breathy laugh, the tension in her muscles still reluctant to release. She rolled her shoulders slightly, trying to shake off the unease that sat beneath her ribs like a weight refusing to be dislodged.

"Just a habit, I guess," she admitted, her voice lighter than she felt.

John let out a slow sigh, rubbing the back of his neck, his gaze shifting toward the street. The silence stretched, thicker now, heavier.

"I suppose part of it is my fault," he admitted, his tone more subdued. "Ever since I returned from that archaeological dig in Egypt, people in Bleakwood have believed I'm cursed."

Eleanor furrowed her brows, uncertainty flickering across her features.

"Cursed?"

John nodded, his expression tightening as he pressed his lips into a thin line.

"In a town this small, superstition runs deep," he explained. "Some folks believe the things we uncovered—things we weren't meant to find—brought bad luck with them, something unnatural, something that doesn't belong in our world."

His gaze drifted down the abandoned street, a place that had once hummed with life, now reduced to frost-covered doors and shuttered windows, each one sealing itself off from the world beyond its threshold. The silence felt heavier here, pressing against the empty storefronts and casting long shadows beneath the dim glow of streetlamps.

"That's why finding you alone in the street last night surprised me," he said after a pause, his voice carrying a quiet edge of suspicion, the words settling uncomfortably between them.

Eleanor stiffened, sensing the shift in his attention as his gaze flickered back to her, sharper now, more intentional. His posture changed, almost imperceptibly—a subtle shift in weight, a slight narrowing of his eyes—but she felt it. He was watching her differently. Assessing her. Reading her in a way that made the air between them feel suddenly charged with unspoken questions.

"What are you doing here?" he asked again, though this time, the weight in his voice was unmistakable.

Eleanor's pulse skipped—a sharp, uneven beat against her ribs—as she swallowed carefully, her mind scrambling for an answer that wouldn't pull her deeper into the web of suspicion, wouldn't invite more questions she wasn't ready to face.

"I could ask you the same thing," she said finally, keeping her voice measured, steady, resisting the urge to look away.

John didn't respond right away. Instead, he simply waited. Watching. Expecting something.

Eleanor forced a tight smile, her expression deliberately neutral as she gestured vaguely toward the street she had come from. "Just taking a walk."

John arched an eyebrow, unimpressed. "You crept out at five o'clock in the morning for a walk?"

Eleanor blinked, trying to find something, anything, that wouldn't sound completely absurd. But her mind stalled, blanking under the pressure.

"It's five o'clock?" she blurted out, immediately regretting it. She forced another smile, this one strained, a little too rehearsed, and grasped at the only explanation that made sense. "I'm not from around here."

John's frown deepened slightly, though his gaze never wavered.

"Well," he said slowly, withdrawing just a fraction, his tone carrying an edge of scrutiny, "when my wife heard you leave this morning, she insisted I follow you. She was worried. She wanted to make sure you were alright."

Eleanor's pulse quickened, a flicker of unease creeping into her limbs.

John let the silence stretch between them, deliberate and heavy, before he finally spoke again, his voice sharper now, more precise, cutting through the space between them like a blade.

"So," he said evenly, his words laced with quiet certainty, "now that I've explained myself—do you want to tell me why you were visiting my old colleague Dr. Asterio and how you know about the Elements?"

Eleanor's heart stumbled.

Her breath hitched, catching painfully in her throat.

"What... how?" she stammered, though deep down, she already knew the answer before he gave it.

John smirked knowingly, tilting his head just slightly, his expression carrying the quiet satisfaction of someone who had uncovered what he had been searching for.

"I recognized the phone number and followed you to his address," he said simply.

Eleanor felt the blood drain from her face.

There was no point in lying now.

He had overheard. He knew everything.

And yet—he was still waiting.

Waiting for her truth.

She swallowed, her mouth dry, her mind scrambling for something to say, some explanation that could make any of this seem less impossible, less like something torn from a story far beyond rational belief.

"I don't think you'd believe me if I told you," she admitted finally, the words barely above a whisper.

John's smirk lingered, though something in his eyes softened just slightly, a flicker of something unreadable passing through his expression. He knew secrets better than most.

But even he would struggle to grasp this one.

A long, stretching silence settled between them, neither of them moving, neither speaking, the weight of the moment pressing in from all sides.

Then—finally—John sighed, shaking his head, exhaling a slow breath like someone resigning himself to the inevitable.

"Come with me," he said, resting a hand on her shoulder, his touch grounding, steady, carrying an odd sense of familiarity despite the uncertainty lingering between them.

"You can tell me all about it over breakfast."

35

Halloween 1996

T he grandfather clock had just struck six when Eleanor and John arrived back at the house, the warmth inside melting away the chill that had settled deep in Eleanor's bones.

John kept a close eye on her as they stepped through the door, his gaze shifting between quiet curiosity and careful calculation. He wasn't just watching her—he was studying her, piecing together fragments of an unspoken puzzle, searching for the missing details in the silence between them. He knew something wasn't quite right. He could sense there was more to Eleanor than she was letting on, something left unsaid, something just beyond his reach.

From the kitchen, Mrs. Walker's voice rang out, bright and welcoming, carrying the warmth of a home Eleanor had never truly known.

"Bacon or eggs, dear?"

Eleanor blinked, momentarily thrown off by the simplicity of the question.

"Sorry?" she asked, unsure if she had heard correctly.

Her mother chuckled softly and stepped into view, her expression kind, filled with the effortless warmth that Eleanor had always imagined but never experienced.

"Or you can have both," she said with a knowing smile, her eyes flickering over Eleanor's face as if searching for something familiar. "You look like you could use a proper home-cooked meal."

Eleanor hesitated.

She wasn't used to seeing her mother like this—happy, carefree, and free from the heavy grief that would eventually way her down. The last time Eleanor had seen her like this was a distant memory, no more than faint echoes from when she was five years old.

Before everything had fallen apart.

Before her father's death had drained the joy from their lives and her aunt had twisted her mother into someone unrecognizable.

Across the room, her father's movement caught her eye.

John strode across the kitchen and pressed a quick, affectionate kiss to his wife's lips, the gesture so easy, so familiar, so impossibly normal that Eleanor felt something stir inside her— something warm, something aching, something dangerously close to longing.

It was perfect.

Everything she had ever wished for.

Everything she had imagined when she was younger, when she had desperately clung to dreams of a family that was whole, a life untouched by grief. She wasn't sure whether any family was truly as perfect as she had imagined.

And yet—

For every second she sat in this room, she felt more and more like an outsider.

She wasn't part of this warmth, wasn't woven into the fabric of this life. She was merely watching it unfold, observing something she had never truly been a part of, something that had been stripped away from her before she had ever had the chance to hold onto it.

These people—her parents—didn't know who she was.

They didn't know she was their daughter.

Because to them, she was nothing more than a stranger.

Swallowing hard, Eleanor shifted against the backrest of her chair, forcing herself to appear casual and normal, as though she belonged here.

Her mother beamed at her as she turned back to the stove, cracking eggs into a sizzling pan, the scent of butter and salt filling the air with something familiar, something painfully distant.

Eleanor wondered if she saw it—the resemblance between them, the faint similarities in their features, the small details that hinted at a truth too impossible to voice. Was that why her mother kept looking at her with quiet curiosity, as if her instincts were pulling at the edges of a realization, she couldn't quite place?

Across the table, John poured himself a cup of coffee, settling into his chair, flipping open the morning newspaper.

But he wasn't reading it.

His eyes barely flickered over the words before lifting— watching her, measuring her every movement with careful scrutiny.

He was waiting.

Expecting something.

Eleanor tried to ignore the weight of his stare, but the silence between them was thick, pressing against her ribs, wrapping around her like something tangible.

Finally, John leaned forward slightly, resting the newspaper flat against the table, breaking the silence with a voice that was steady, deliberate—casual, yet far too calculated to be innocent.

"So," he began, the pause between them stretching just long enough to make Eleanor's pulse quicken.

"Now that we're alone..."

Eleanor swallowed, feeling the tension tighten around her throat.

"...you can finally tell me—where are you really from?"

Her fingers tightened slightly around her mug, the warmth of the ceramic grounding her, steadying her.

She looked up, startled, uncertain.

"I already told you," she said carefully. "I'm not from here."

John shook his head, his expression unchanged, his gaze sharp, knowing.

"No," he corrected, leaning back slightly, assessing her with quiet intensity. "What I really meant to ask was—you're not from this time, are you?"

Eleanor's heart skipped a beat.

He had figured it out.

She had hoped to keep her true origins secret, at least for a little while longer—but clearly, her father was far more perceptive than she had anticipated.

She hesitated.

Then—

"Yes," she admitted, forcing herself to meet his gaze. "I'm from the future."

John's expression remained unreadable at first, but his eyes widened slightly, a flicker of something—shock, intrigue, disbelief—passing through his features.

"The future?" he echoed, as though testing the word in his own mouth, trying to grasp its meaning, trying to make sense of the impossible. "How... how is that possible?"

Eleanor exhaled slowly, carefully choosing her words as she explained everything—the Time Element, Nyx, her desperate mission to stop him. But even as she spoke, even as she shared fragments of the truth, she kept pieces of herself hidden.

He didn't need to know about her—not yet.

Or maybe she wasn't ready for him to know.

John listened closely, his expression shifting between quiet awe and careful concern, his hands tightening slightly around his coffee cup as he absorbed each detail, as he weighed the reality of her words against everything he thought he knew.

"I've only met a time traveller once before," he murmured eventually, his gaze drifting slightly, lost in thought, his voice quiet, almost distant.

Eleanor's pulse quickened. Her father had met someone else? Her mind raced with the implications, but before she could ask, he continued.

"But they weren't like you," John said slowly. "They spoke in riddles—always saying they couldn't interfere with the course of events, always warning of consequences."

Eleanor's gaze dropped to her hot chocolate, watching the marshmallow floating at the surface slowly dissolve, breaking apart into pale, gooey streaks.

Paradox.

She knew that was who he was talking about. Unlike her, Paradox knew the rules of time travel. Unlike her, they had control. Unlike her, they had a purpose.

John studied her carefully. "I'm guessing there are rules to time traveling, right?"

Eleanor bit her lip, unsure how to respond. She didn't know. She had never known. She wasn't even supposed to be here.

Had her presence changed the past? Or had all of this happened before? Was she merely walking in the footsteps of fate?

She looked up, locking eyes with John. His gaze was sharp— nearly identical to hers.

A plate of fresh food was placed in front of her.

"Thank you," she said softly, glancing at her mother, who smiled warmly, unaware of the storm brewing in Eleanor's mind.

She took a bite, trying to ground herself, trying to ignore the gnawing guilt clawing at her stomach.

She should tell John everything. Who she was. Why she was really here. Who she was really up against.

Should she warn him? Could she?

She caught her reflection in the glass counter and, instinctively, the wicked voice in her head returned.

Time can't be cheated, Eleanor. The universe doesn't make bargains.

But who's to say it didn't? Why did she have to lose a father? What possible gain was there in that?

A small squeal came from the corner of the room. Eleanor lifted her head, just as Mrs. Walker rushed over to a tiny crib.

"Is that..." Eleanor began to say, as Mrs. Walker lifted up a baby swaddled in a soft pink blanket that looked no older than three months.

She stopped shovelling food into her mouth, staring at the baby, so small and helpless.

John smiled, pressing a kiss to the baby's forehead. "This is our little one," he murmured.

And then Eleanor felt her hands tremble, like a tremor starting at her fingertips and racing up her shoulder.

The baby's wide brown eyes blinked up at him, full of adoration.

The baby—

Was *her*.

Somehow, it hadn't even crossed Eleanor's mind that her younger self had existed in 1996—not in any meaningful way, at least. She had spent so much time focused on her mission, on stopping Nyx, on finding Chris, that the actual *logistics* of her time travel had barely settled into her thoughts. But now, as she sat in this home—her home, though it wasn't hers *yet*—watching her mother carry the tiny bundle of her infant-self upstairs, the realisation hit her like a stone dropped into deep water.

She had landed in *her own past*..

"She's just a little tired," Mrs. Walker explained gently, cradling baby Eleanor in her arms as she walked toward the staircase. "I'll go and put her to bed."

Eleanor couldn't take her eyes off the small, swaddled figure, watching as her mother disappeared upstairs with the baby—*her*.

John, who had remained oddly silent, leaned forward, elbows resting on the table, gaze locked onto Eleanor with quiet intensity.

Eleanor, still processing the moment, barely realized her fork was suspended mid-air, forgotten between her fingers.

John's voice was calm, expectant.

"When you've finished eating," he said, glancing briefly at the staircase where his wife had disappeared, "there's something I want to show you."

Eleanor nodded absently, her movements mechanical as she shovelled the last few bites of scrambled eggs into her mouth.

Her mind was spinning.

Her father knew something.

Something about Nyx.

And Eleanor needed to know *everything*.

*

283

LOST IN TIME

John's office felt like a different world compared to the rest of the house—filled with old paper and the scent of well-worn leather, a space moulded by years of knowledge, research, and secrets.

Wooden shelves towered from floor to ceiling, packed with books ranging in age and condition, their spines frayed from use, their titles faded but still holding fragments of untold stories. A large oak desk stood at the centre, cluttered with notes, ancient-looking documents, and an assortment of trinkets, each item seemingly whispering pieces of history. I looked eerily similar to Dr. Asterio's cluttered office back in the future.

A soft desk lamp glowed warmly, casting elongated shadows over the mess, illuminating scattered artifacts that John had clearly collected throughout his travels.

Eleanor inhaled deeply, taking in the space, the weight of it.

This room—this collection of knowledge—it had been her father's whole *life*.

John moved toward a wooden desk in the corner of the room. A dusty old box sat atop it, edges worn from age. He opened it carefully, revealing a disordered collection of photographs, handwritten letters, and mementos—fragments of the past, of a life spent chasing truths buried beneath centuries.

Eleanor's fingers grazed the edges of a particular photograph, one that seemed to capture a moment of pure, unfiltered joy.

Her father and mother stood together in front of ancient ruins, their faces lit with excitement, their posture relaxed, as though the weight of the world had momentarily lifted from their shoulders.

John held a small artifact in his hands, pride shining in his eyes, while Mrs. Walker stood beside him, her arm wrapped around him, smiling *radiantly*.

Eleanor's heart ached in a way she wasn't prepared for.

She wished she could have been there.

John noticed her lingering gaze and smiled, though there was something slightly wistful in it.

"That was taken during one of our expeditions," he said softly, nodding toward the image. "We were so young, so full of dreams back then."

Eleanor nodded, still staring at the photo.

"You look happy."

John's smile faded slightly, and he glanced down at the box of memories, running his fingers over the edge as if grounding himself.

"We were," he admitted. "Those were some of the best times of our lives."

There was a pause, long enough for Eleanor to sense *something* shifting in the air between them.

John exhaled slowly, glancing toward the shelves that surrounded them, his eyes scanning the room like he was seeing it for the first time.

"These memories," he murmured, almost to himself, "are all pieces of our story."

Then, more directly, he added, "And I think they might hold the key to what you're looking for."

He guided Eleanor toward another desk in the corner, pulling out a different box—this one dustier, heavier.

"Last night," he said, his voice dropping slightly, "you mentioned that the person you were chasing after went by the name *Nyx*?"

Eleanor nodded.

She had been careful not to use Nyx's real name—*Nicolas Cipher*—when explaining everything to her father. She didn't want to accidentally shift history in a way she couldn't undo.

John watched her closely, measuring her response.

Eleanor felt a surge of excitement and urgency.

"Nyx... You *know* about Nyx?"

John sighed, pulling out a photograph from the box and laying it flat on the desk.

It was an image of him with a group of people—men and women dressed for an expedition, each holding what appeared to be ancient artifacts.

Eleanor's stomach twisted.

"That was taken during an expedition to uncover the Elements," he explained, his tone heavier now, layered with something unspoken. "It was one of my most challenging assignments. Not just the journey itself, but the languages I had to learn, the histories I had to *decipher*."

Eleanor scanned his face, waiting, listening.

John hesitated—just briefly—but then he spoke again.

"Do you know what the name *Nyx* means?"

Eleanor shook her head.

John's expression darkened slightly, a shadow passing over his features.

"Nyx is the Greek god of the night," he said, his voice quieter now, more measured. "A powerful and enigmatic figure, often associated with darkness and mystery. In mythology, they were one of the primordial deities—born from *Chaos* itself. Their presence was so formidable that even Zeus, the king of the gods, feared them."

Eleanor stiffened.

Chaos.

Nyx.

Darkness.

She had thought the name was *random*, something Nyx had chosen for *himself*, but now—

Now, she realised it wasn't just a name. It was a *declaration*.

John studied Eleanor's face, reading the tension in her features.

"There's more to this," he said finally.

Eleanor inhaled sharply, knowing—*without a doubt*—that he was right. And somehow, she sensed that her father knew more than he had ever admitted before.

"But human beings are neither completely bad nor good," she said, her voice measured but firm. "They are a mixture of both, giving them the ability to reason and make logical decisions. But with the Dark Element, their most fatal flaw is their unpredictability. They thrive on chaos, disorder—making it nearly impossible to anticipate their next move."

She exhaled slowly, folding her arms across her chest.

"But in chaos... there are also mistakes."

John sat back, rubbing his chin thoughtfully. He studied her, his fingers tapping absently against the wooden table, as if weighing her words against his own lifetime of knowledge.

"So, what?" he murmured, eyes narrowing. "We just *wait* until they make a mistake?"

Eleanor opened her mouth to answer, but before she could speak—

A sharp, buzzing noise rang throughout the office, startling them both.

John stiffened, instinctively reaching into his pocket.

A phone.

Not a modern one—nothing like the sleek, glass-covered devices Eleanor was used to—but an older, bulkier model. He flipped it open, pressing it to his ear without hesitation.

Eleanor strained to hear the voice on the other end, and the moment the first words came through, her stomach dropped.

Singleton.

But his voice—

It was *lighter* and less worn than she remembered. But the urgency in his tone was *palpable*, crackling through the line so sharply that Eleanor could almost *see* his expression, feel his tension bleeding into the space between them.

"John, we've got a *problem*," Singleton's voice rasped, hurried, uneven. "I was on my way from London with the Time Element when—"

A pause.

"We were *knocked off the road*."

John's grip tightened around the phone. "What?" he said, his voice calm but edged with controlled panic. "Singleton, what are you saying?"

"The truck's overturned," Singleton continued, his voice strained. "I—I don't know how long we can keep everything hidden from the police."

John's jaw clenched. This was very, very bad. "Stay calm," John ordered, his tone shifting into something more authoritative. "Where *exactly* are you? Are you and the Time Element safe?"

Singleton hesitated—long enough for Eleanor's pulse to spike.

"We're shaken but okay for now," he finally responded, his voice quieter now, more clipped. "We're about twenty miles north of Bleakwood town—near the old farm road."

A pause.

"But I *don't* think it's safe to stay here for long."

John glanced at Eleanor, his expression dark, unreadable—but there was something unspoken in his gaze.

He knew they had no time to waste.

Eleanor was still staring at him, still absorbing the shock of Singleton's voice from years before she had known him, still trying to process what was happening. But there wasn't time to process it.

"Hold tight, Mike," he instructed, his voice firm, unwavering. "I'll be there as soon as I can. Keep the Time Element *secure*, and *don't* tell the police any more than they need to know."

36

Off Road

A s Eleanor climbed into the passenger seat of John's car, she pulled the coat tighter around her body as the biting morning air seeped through the cracked windows. The hum of the engine was the only sound for nearly twenty minutes, a steady drone beneath the rhythmic crunch of tires against the frost-covered road. Neither of them spoke, the weight of the impending confrontation pressing against their silence like an invisible force.

It wasn't hard to tell where the crash had happened.

Even from a mile out, warning signs and barricades lined the roads, flashing lights casting reflections against the icy pavement. The detour stretched far in either direction, forcing them to take a shortcut through the cornfield that bordered the town.

John revved the engine, pushing the vehicle through the thick crops, yellow and green stalks slapping against the windshield as the wipers batted them aside. The narrow path carved through the field was uneven, forcing Eleanor to grip the edge of her seat as they bounced over stubborn roots and half-frozen soil.

Upon resurfacing onto a secluded country road, the full scale of the wreckage came into view.

Just a few meters ahead, a seven-ton cargo truck lay overturned, its frame crumpled and warped from the force of the impact. It had flipped one-hundred-and-eighty degrees, its undercarriage now exposed to the sky, twisted metal jutting out at odd angles.

The truck's driver was strapped into a stretcher, his face pale, his arm secured with thick gauze. First responders moved with trained urgency, loading him into the back of an ambulance as fire engines and police cars encircled the wreckage like vultures surveying a fallen prey. The chorus of sirens filled the quiet countryside, their wailing tones slicing through the crisp morning air, a stark contrast to the otherwise empty roads.

John parked a safe distance from the chaos, giving them a moment to assess before making their way in.

As they stepped out of the car, Eleanor's boots crunched against the icy gravel, her breath forming small clouds as she exhaled, eyes sweeping across the scene. The acrid smell of burning rubber stung her nostrils, mingling with the sharp tang of spilled gasoline that had pooled beneath the truck's twisted remains. The flashing red and blue lights cast fractured shadows against the surrounding trees, throwing distorted shapes across the frost-covered ground.

She barely had time to fully take in the devastation before John strode forward, his movements deliberate.

An officer stepped toward them, prepared to stop their approach, but the moment John came into view, hesitation flickered across the man's face. He faltered mid-step, exchanging a brief glance with a nearby colleague, before both men wordlessly took several steps back.

Even this far from the centre of Bleakwood, John was well known.

And not for a good reason.

Eleanor filed that observation away for later, keeping her wits about her as they approached the wreckage.

The cargo truck's wheels pointed uselessly to the sky, its body crushed inward, the heavy steel caved in where the force of the accident had been strongest. She spotted Singleton standing near the wreckage, his posture stiff, his expression drawn.

He was pale beneath the flashing lights, his hands tight at his sides as he spoke with an officer, no doubt trying to explain the impossible situation unfolding around them.

"Singleton!" John called out, cutting across the space between them. His voice carried over the noise, sharp enough to pull Singleton's attention away from the officer. "Are you alright?"

Singleton didn't respond immediately.

Instead, he shifted slightly, turning just enough to face them fully, eyeing John with a mixture of relief and frustration.

He walked a few steps to the left, just far enough out of sight of the authorities, before letting out a low grunt.

Eleanor studied him carefully.

Back in 1996, she had often wondered what Singleton had been like before he had hardened into the stern, unrelenting headmaster of Bleakwood School.

Now, standing here, seeing him bruised and shaken in the aftermath of the crash, she realized that *this* version of Singleton— the younger, more vulnerable side of him—was something she had never imagined witnessing.

It was jarring.

John pulled a handkerchief from his coat pocket, passing it to Singleton without a word.

A thin trail of blood dripped from a cut on Singleton's brow, the crimson stark against his otherwise pale skin. It wasn't deep—nothing a few stitches wouldn't fix—but he winced slightly as he dabbed at it, muttering under his breath.

"I'm glad you got here quickly," Singleton admitted, squinting a little as he worked to clean up the wound. His voice was strained but intact, his tone carrying more relief than Eleanor had expected.

She glanced around, scanning the area for any signs of danger, any lingering threats beyond the immediate wreckage.

Singleton followed her movement, then turned his attention back to John, his eyes flicking toward Eleanor with mild suspicion.

"Who's this?" he asked abruptly, lowering the handkerchief.

Eleanor stiffened slightly but kept her expression neutral.

John, however, didn't hesitate.

"She's just a student from Bleakwood," he said smoothly, the lie rolling off his tongue with practiced ease. "She's interning as my assistant."

Eleanor forced herself to remain composed.

From her perspective, it *wasn't* entirely a lie.

She *had* been a student at Bleakwood.

Singleton raised an eyebrow, cynically.

"You have an *assistant* now?" He scoffed, crossing his arms. "Has the *sensitivity* of our work completely skipped your mind, or have you finally *lost* it?"

John barely acknowledged the jab, brushing it aside with a shrug.

"Where's the Element?"

Singleton's expression shifted instantly, the weight of the situation pressing back into his features.

He gestured toward the wreckage, pointing at the rear of the overturned truck.

"It's still in the containment unit," he said grimly. "We need to move it *quickly*. I don't want the joy of explaining why we were transporting a fully armoured cargo truck across the countryside at six o'clock in the morning."

John exhaled sharply, scanning the scene once more.

"Alright," he said, his tone clipped, decisive. "Let's get to it."

Eleanor swallowed hard, forcing herself to stay sharp.

This was *happening*.

The scene was chaotic, but John moved through it with practiced precision, cutting through the flashing lights and the hum of emergency responders like a man who had done this more times than he cared to admit. The firefighters had stabilized the wreckage just enough to allow access to the cargo hold, and after a brief, tense explanation, they stepped aside, letting him and Singleton through.

Eleanor followed close behind, her pulse thrumming in her ears. She could feel it—the weight of the moment pressing down on her, thick and suffocating. As Singleton disabled the security system, the containment unit hummed softly, its energy rippling through the air. And then—

The *Time Element*.

Its green glow pulsed faintly, casting unnatural shadows over their faces as they carefully extracted it from the wreckage. The light twisted and refracted, bathing their hands in shimmering streaks, illuminating their expressions—John's unwavering determination, Singleton's quiet urgency.

Eleanor inhaled sharply.

They had to protect it.

At *all* costs.

Singleton secured the Element in a reinforced portable case, snapping the locks into place with deliberate movements. But before Eleanor could exhale in relief, the atmosphere shifted.

She *felt* it before she saw it—the change in the air, the sensation of something approaching.

A rustling from the tall grass near the road, the faint shuffle of footsteps, the presence of something—or someone—moving toward them.

She turned quickly, her senses sharp, her muscles tense, and then—

Her stomach *dropped*.

Emerging from the fog-drenched roadside was a figure, hobbling slightly as if injured, their form half-obscured by the rising sun.

Her heart pounded as recognition hit her like a punch to the ribs.

Nyx.

But—

Something was *different*.

She stared, her breath catching.

The man before her was *not* the scarred, monstrous version she knew. He didn't had any deep gashes across his face, or unnatural gleam in his hollow eyes. No wicked, knowing smirk curling at his lips.

This was Nyx's younger self.

Nicolas Cipher.

The man who had once lived in Bleakwood, who had worked alongside her father, Singleton, and Dr. Asterio. The man who had yet to become the villain—the nightmare—that Eleanor had spent her entire life trying to fight.

She could barely process it.

John and Singleton turned at her warning, tension flaring briefly in their shoulders—until they saw who was approaching.

Their expressions relaxed instantly.

Singleton scoffed lightly, stepping forward.

"Don't worry, it's just one of our partners—Nicolas Cipher."

The name echoed through Eleanor like a gunshot.

She watched, numb, as Singleton approached the man—the man who, fourteen years from now, had *killed her father*, terrorized Bleakwood school and be known as *Nyx*. A man who had tried to kill her on countless times.

But here—now—he looked nothing more than... *ordinary*. But it took all her concentration just to resist the urge to remain still. Especially when every instinct in her strike him down.

"Nic, where were you?" Singleton asked, scanning him briefly for injuries.

Nicolas Cipher took a slow breath, glancing around, disoriented.

"Something knocked me off the road," he said. "I didn't see it coming. It was like it appeared out of nowhere. I didn't have time to swerve."

His voice was calm but strained, as if still piecing together what had happened.

"I must've been thrown from my vehicle and landed in the farmland," he continued. "If I hadn't been wearing *this*..."

He paused, lifting his hand slightly—revealing a sleek black ring circling his finger.

Eleanor's blood *ran cold*.

The *Dark Element*.

Her jaw clenched so tightly she could feel the pressure in her teeth.

Eleanor's heartbeat pounded in her ears, loud and relentless.

She wanted—no, *needed*—to rip the ring from his hand.

But she couldn't.

Not yet.

Not now.

He wasn't the Nyx she knew.

Not yet.

Her breath came shallow and uneven as she forced herself to stay calm. She clenched the edge of her coat, grounding herself, steadying the tremor in her hands.

Her gaze swept across the crash site, scanning the wreckage with a renewed sense of urgency. Something was wrong— something beyond the obvious.

A few meters away, near the deep skid marks left by the overturned truck, something glistened in the fractured concrete.

Eleanor knelt down, brushing her fingers over the rough surface. When she pulled her hand away, her fingertips were stained—black, slick, coated in an oily residue.

John stooped over her shoulder, peering down at the substance with quiet curiosity.

"What's that?" he asked.

Eleanor stared at the dark stain, her mind racing as she traced its origin, recalling the only place she had seen this before.

John followed her gaze as it snapped back to Nicolas Cipher.

The ring.

The Dark Element.

Pressing an ice pack to his temple, Cipher barely noticed the gleam of the ring beneath the dim morning light.

Eleanor exhaled slowly, steadying her thoughts as a realization settled deep in her bones.

"This wasn't an accident," she murmured, voice low, edged with certainty.

There was only one force capable of leaving behind a substance like this—only one power that could summon matter from nothing, could send a massive truck skidding like a toy across the pavement.

The Dark Element.

But—this wasn't wild, uncontrolled magic. This was calculated. Precise.

A memory surfaced—Nyx's last words to her before everything had collapsed. Her stomach clenched.

If Nyx was trying to change the past—slowly, subtly shaping the future—then where was he?

Something wasn't right.

She looked back at the track marks, her brain moving quickly, flipping through fragments of logic and memory, searching for the missing piece.

Then, like a lightning strike—

"There's only one set of skid marks," she said suddenly, her voice tight, sharp with realization.

John frowned slightly, his mind catching up, trying to grasp what she meant. "So?" he asked.

Eleanor inhaled deeply, trying to keep the panic from clawing its way up her throat. She turned to John, forcing herself to keep her voice steady.

"Was Nicolas Cipher inside the truck carrying the Time Element?"

John blinked, confusion flickering briefly across his face. "No—just the driver and Singleton. Why?"

Eleanor swallowed hard, her pulse hammering. She didn't respond immediately, because now she knew what had happened.

She knew what Nyx was doing.

And worse—

"Didn't Nicolas say that he was thrown off the road?"

John froze. "Yes, he did."

She turned her gaze to the road, scanning for any sign of wreckage—skid marks, broken glass, anything that might indicate that Nicolas Cipher's vehicle had crashed like he claimed.

But there was nothing.

No twisted metal buried in the tall grass, no black streaks of burnt rubber on the pavement, no shattered headlights glinting in the morning light. Just an unbroken stretch of road, empty and untouched, as though no second vehicle had ever existed in the first place.

Eleanor's stomach twisted.

If Nicolas had truly been thrown from his car, there should have been *some* evidence—an impact point, a trail leading into the field, even a lingering scent of gasoline in the cold air. But there was none of that.

She turned sharply toward John, the urgency in her expression enough to snap his attention to her.

"Then where's the vehicle he was in?" Eleanor asked, her voice low but firm.

John blinked, caught off guard.

Eleanor gestured toward the long grass, keeping her movements controlled. "If he was thrown off the road, there should be another set of tire tracks. We'd see smoke, fire— *something* from his crashed vehicle."

Eleanor's gaze flicked toward the crooked speed limit sign standing near the roadside—50 miles per hour. A crash at that speed doesn't just *vanish*. Something was wrong.

John followed her gaze, his brows drawing together, piecing together the logic in her expression as he studied the wreckage.

"What are you saying?" he asked, his voice quiet, cautious.

Eleanor inhaled sharply, steadying herself before answering.

Nyx had been here. The one who had travelled back in time with her. The one who had kidnapped Chris. He had caused the crash. That much was obvious.

But now—now, the situation had shifted.

Something bigger was happening.

Nyx wasn't just manipulating events. Someone else was, too.

Her eyes flicked to Nicolas Cipher—the younger version of Nyx, the man before he had fallen into darkness.

But had he already fallen?

Had Nyx reached him before this moment? Had everything that led them here been orchestrated long before they arrived?

A deception, carefully crafted, slipping seamlessly into their timeline to mask its true intentions.

Eleanor stood abruptly, wiping the slick black residue from her fingers onto her trousers, barely pausing before she spoke.

"Do you think you can get the Dark Element off Nic?" she murmured under her breath, ensuring that only John could hear her. She kept her lips still as she spoke, barely moving them, controlling the sound so that it wouldn't carry beyond the two of them.

John's jaw tensed slightly, his expression darkening. "Are you sure about this?"

Eleanor gave a swift nod, and in response, his gaze hardened.

As they walked back toward the others, everything felt stiff, unnatural, as though every movement had to be carefully calibrated to prevent suspicion. They couldn't afford to tip off anyone watching. They had to act as though nothing was wrong.

John called for Singleton to help him secure the Time Element back in the portable case, sealing the reinforced locks into place with careful precision. Meanwhile, Eleanor kept her eyes trained on Nicolas, analysing every detail—the tension in his posture, the way his grip tightened slightly around the ice pack, the way his breathing seemed just a little too controlled.

He looked disoriented. Injured, even.

But Eleanor knew better than to underestimate him.

The Dark Element was already working its way through him, threading itself into his mind, its influence growing stronger with each passing second.

She couldn't afford to let her guard down.

John turned to Nicolas, keeping his voice calm, steady.

"Nic, can you help us with the containment unit?"

Nicolas pressed the ice pack harder against his head, nodding slowly. "Yeah. Just... give me a moment."

It was an ordinary response. But Eleanor didn't trust ordinary.

She had to find a way to separate Nicolas from the Dark Element, but she knew it couldn't happen here. Not with so many people watching. Not with so many variables she couldn't control.

He didn't know her. He didn't trust her. And there was no way he would willingly give up the Element—not to a stranger, not when he believed it was his to keep. And how could she possibly explain what was happening? There was no way to tell him without revealing secrets she wasn't ready to share, secrets that might change the course of everything if spoken too soon.

Moving swiftly, they secured the containment unit and loaded it into the back of John's car, the heavy weight of it settling into place like an unspoken warning of what lay ahead.

Then—

"Nicolas," John said carefully, his voice even, measured, the tone of someone approaching a situation with precision. "Can I see your hand for a moment?"

Nicolas turned just as he was about to close the car door, his expression flickering with confusion as he studied John's face. "Why?"

John forced a small, casual smile, the kind designed to ease suspicion, to make the request seem harmless. "I just need to check something."

Reluctantly, Nicolas extended his hand.

John moved quickly, firmly—his fingers closing around the black ring encircling Nicolas's finger.

The Dark Element.

And the moment his hand made contact—

Nicolas snapped.

His grip shot forward like lightning, his fingers clamping around John's wrist with unnatural force, his body shifting as something primal and uncontrollable surged through him. His eyes darkened, a hypnotic stare overtaking them, something inside him stirring, something Eleanor recognized.

John barely had time to react before Nicolas twisted his grip.

A sickening crunch echoed through the space, cutting through the quiet hum of voices at the crash site, sharp enough to silence everything around them.

John let out a cry of pain, his hand bent backward at a vicious angle, bolts of agony radiating through his arm, the sound so visceral, so brutal that it sent him dropping to one knee, his breath coming in ragged bursts between clenched teeth.

"Nicolas—stop," he ground out, his voice tight, strained, desperate.

But Nicolas's grip didn't loosen.

It tightened.

With every passing second—

The Dark Element was claiming more of him.

And Eleanor knew—

She had to act.

Now.

Before it was too late.

Suddenly, the police officers had their weapons drawn, voices cutting through the charged air as they aimed at the two men.

"Let him go!"

Singleton backed away from Nicolas, looking as if he was watching a rabid wolf turn on its own pack, horror flickering in his eyes as he tried to understand what was happening.

"Nic—what are you doing?"

"What I have to," he said, voice steady and deliberate," To get what I *need*."

The moment the words left his mouth, the world shifted. It was subtle at first—a faint rumble beneath their feet, the kind that could have easily been dismissed as an aftershock from the wreckage. But then, as if responding to the change, the sky darkened unnaturally, a black cloud thickening above them, swirling with malevolence.

Within seconds, the temperature dropped sharply.

The air turned heavy, charged with electricity, and the first drops of rain began to fall—icy needles that pierced the skin upon contact, soaking through fabric like it was nothing.

Eleanor shivered violently, her breath catching as the cold settled deep into her bones, relentless and unforgiving.

The rain intensified at an unnatural speed, shifting from thin droplets to a torrential downpour, pounding against the ground with a force that made the earth itself tremble.

It was deafening.

A roar so loud that it drowned out everything else—the police sirens, the shouting of officers, the distant crackling of radio static.

Thunder rolled overhead, deep and guttural, shaking the ground beneath them. Lightning ripped through the blackened sky, illuminating the chaos in brief, blinding bursts. Each flash revealed shapes within the swirling darkness—*writhing*, *twisting*, stretching out like unseen hands reaching for everything below.

Eleanor's pulse hammered.

"What's *happening*?" John shouted over the storm, his voice barely cutting through the noise as he braced against the violent winds whipping through the wreckage.

The wind tore at their clothes, clawed at their faces, made it impossible to focus, impossible to move without force.

It wasn't a storm.

It was *him*.

Nyx.

"He's *here!*" Eleanor shrieked, her head snapping from side to side, searching wildly through the chaos, trying to find him—trying to *see* him.

He had to be close.

She could *feel* him.

The suffocating weight of the storm pressed down on her like an invisible force, heavy and deliberate, soaking her to the core. The scent of ozone thickened, mixing with damp earth and gasoline, clinging to her lungs like a warning she couldn't ignore.

The storm *expanded*.

Bodies dropped to the ground instinctively, hands braced over their heads as the whirlwind above them began to *tighten*, sweeping dangerously low, brushing just above their hair.

Dust kicked into the air, swirling violently in the wind's grip, forming a cyclone so fierce it was impossible to see beyond it.

It *collided*.

A shockwave rippled through the air, blasting outward with enough force to send debris flying in all directions.

And just as quickly as it had come, the rain had stopped and the wind had died. Instead, a bright ray of sunlight broke through the clouds, which pierced through the darkness.

Silence.

Slowly, one by one, they reared their heads up.

Singleton was the first to speak, his voice hoarse, cautious.

"...Is it *over?*"

Eleanor remained standing, staring up at the sky, at the remnants of storm clouds thinning into the early morning light.

"It *seems* so," John murmured, still catching his breath, wiping the rain from his face.

Singleton let out a heavy sigh, relief mixing with exhaustion.

"Thank goodness for *that*."

Eleanor's gaze snapped back to the bodies around her. But the nagging in her chest hadn't gone away.

Her heart seized in her chest as her mind counted—too quickly, too frantically—until she noticed they were *one short*.

She scanned the wreckage, the broken road, the damp earth, twisting around sharply, searching—

But Nicolas Cipher was *gone*.

John noticed her panic first.

"What—?" His head jerked up, his eyes widening as he followed her line of sight.

Eleanor swallowed thickly. He'd taken *both* the Dark and Time Elements.

37

Confession

E leanor paced frantically, her breath coming in uneven bursts, her mind spinning so violently she could hardly hold onto a single thought.

Nyx had been *here*.

Right in front of her.

And she had let him slip through her fingers.

She kept reciting it under her breath, the words tumbling out of her mouth in a spiral of frustration—like an incantation, as though saying it enough times might somehow undo it.

"He was here. He was *here*. *Nyx was here!*"

Her voice cracked on the last repetition, and before she could stop herself, she let out a sharp, guttural scream, grabbing at her own hair, yanking at the strands as if physically forcing herself to process the failure.

"How could I have been so *stupid*?" she spat, turning sharply on her heel, her movements erratic, unhinged. "He's *always* been two steps ahead—and now, how can I hope to stop him when there are *two* of them?"

A sharp, painful twist coiled in Eleanor's stomach at the thought of what had just happened.

Nyx had taken the Time Element.

And Nicolas Cipher—his younger self—had helped him.

Whether he had done it knowingly or not hardly mattered anymore. The result was the same.

She had failed to stop them.

Before her thoughts could spiral further, John moved quickly, gripping her shoulders with firm hands, steadying her before she lost herself completely to panic. His touch was grounding, urgent, but not unkind.

"So that's who you're after?" he asked, his voice tight with barely contained frustration, his words edged with something raw—betrayal, disbelief. "Why didn't you tell me that the person you were chasing—Nyx—was Nicolas Cipher?"

The moment he said the name, Eleanor saw the realization begin to settle, watched as the weight of the truth pressed down on him, shifting everything he thought he understood.

His posture stiffened.

His face turned pale, the blood draining from his cheeks as if ice had suddenly washed through his veins.

"I let him take both the Dark and Time Elements," John whispered, his voice barely carrying over the relentless roar of the storm outside. His grip tightened around Eleanor's arms, his breath coming shallow, uneven. "I might as well have *handed* them over to him. Now he has two of the most powerful objects in this world."

Eleanor shook her head furiously.

"It's not your fault," she said, her voice urgent, pleading.

But John wasn't listening.

His mind had already latched onto the guilt, refusing to let it go.

"It *is* my fault," he muttered, his voice breaking slightly, raw with regret. "Everything—it's all on me."

Eleanor's chest tightened at the sheer desperation woven into his tone, at the way his expression darkened with realization, with remorse.

"Asterio warned me not to trust Nic," he continued, each word sounding heavier than the last, laced with something bitter. "I didn't want to believe it could be true. I didn't want to believe that the Dark Element had started to change him."

And then—

As if the thought had ignited something deep within him, John *ran.*

Straight for the car.

Eleanor barely had time to process it before instinct kicked in, forcing her into motion, sending her rushing after him. Her boots slipped slightly against the slick pavement, her pulse hammering wildly in her chest and her breath coming too fast.

"Where are you going?" she called, struggling to match his pace, trying to catch up before she lost him completely.

John didn't hesitate.

He yanked open the driver's side door, his movements sharp, determined, fuelled by nothing but urgency and fear.

"To my home," he said, his voice tight, shaking with conviction. "If Nic has truly lost all reason, there's no telling what he'll do. He could go after my family—my *wife*, my *child*!"

Eleanor froze mid-step, the words hitting her like a violent wave.

But the shock only lasted a split second.

Then, without hesitation, she threw herself toward the passenger door, climbed inside and slammed the doors shut. Before she had even settled, John pressed his foot hard against the gas pedal, launching the car onto the main road. The tires fought against the slick, rain-soaked asphalt, skidding briefly before finally gripping and propelling them forward.

The storm had worsened, howling violently through the darkened sky. Rain hammered against the windshield in thick, merciless sheets, rendering visibility almost impossible.

Eleanor clenched her fists, digging her nails into her palms, trying to steady the terror clawing at her chest.

She knew Nicolas wouldn't John's family, at least not yet. After all, she was living proof that her younger self survived. But John? John's future was uncertain. And the thought of losing him—again—sent a suffocating weight crashing into her lungs, pressing against her ribs like something physical, something unbearable. She had to stop him before he made a fatal mistake. She had to keep him from dying.

"John, wait!" she screamed, bracing herself against the dashboard as the car lurched violently into a sharp turn. John barely glanced at her, his grip white-knuckled against the steering wheel, his jaw locked, his focus unrelenting.

"Stop the car!" Eleanor tried again, her voice rising, thick with desperation. "We can't go back to your house!"

John snapped his gaze toward her, his expression fierce, determined. "What? Why not?" he demanded. "Did you not see what he could do?"

Eleanor's breath hitched, her worst fear clawing its way into the forefront of her mind, refusing to be ignored. She couldn't shake the thought—What if this was it? What if this was how John

Walker died? She couldn't let it happen. She had to change the future. She had to stop him.

"He's counting on that!" she blurted out, the words spilling from her lips before she could stop them, cracking under the weight of her fear.

John didn't slow down.

"I don't care!"

Eleanor squeezed her eyes shut, frustration building rapidly, twisting painfully in her chest. She couldn't lose him. Not again. Not when she had the power to stop it.

And then—before she even realized she had said them—the words spilled from her mouth.

"I'm your daughter!"

The sentence seemed to hang in the air, suspended in the moment before reality snapped back.

The tires screeched, the car jerking violently as John slammed on the brakes. Eleanor barely braced herself in time before the car skidded to a halt, the wet pavement slick beneath them, the engine rumbling like a frustrated beast. The rain pounded against the hood, drowning out the silence that now filled the space between them.

John turned slowly, his face unreadable—his eyes wide, disbelieving.

"What...?"

His voice was barely a whisper, but Eleanor heard every ounce of weight it carried.

She took a deep breath, her hands trembling. "I'm your daughter," she repeated, forcing herself to meet his gaze. "I'm Eleanor. I came back from the future to stop Nyx and to save you."

John's face went pale. His chest rose and fell in uneven bursts, his mind struggling to grasp the impossibility of what she had just said. Eleanor swallowed hard, fighting back the emotion choking her throat.

"I missed you so much."

John's eyes filled with tears. His grip tightened around her hand—his hand that had once held her when she was just a child, long before time had taken him from her. He pulled her into a fierce embrace, shaking slightly, rain soaking into his jacket, his breath hitching against her shoulder.

"Oh, Eleanor..." His voice broke.

"I can't believe it."

Eleanor clung to John, holding onto him as if he might disappear at any moment, as if she could somehow make up for the years, she had spent wishing for this moment but never believing it would happen. The rain poured around them, soaking into their clothes, dripping from their hair, but neither of them cared. They stood in the middle of the empty road, father and daughter reunited across time, across impossible circumstances.

John cradled her face gently, pushing a wet strand of hair from her cheek, his expression soft despite the storm raging around them.

"This is the best gift in the world," he murmured, voice thick with emotion, "to see my little girl all grown up."

Eleanor let out a shaky breath, her heart aching at the tenderness in his voice.

"You look just like your mother," John added, smiling faintly.

Eleanor blinked up at him, surprised. "Everyone always said I looked like you."

John chuckled, the sound warm even in the cold night air. "Well, you definitely have my stubborn streak. I'm sure I taught you plenty of bad habits growing up."

For a second, the weight pressing against Eleanor's chest eased.

She wanted to laugh—*really* laugh—but something about the moment felt too fragile, too precious.

Instead, she forced a small chuckle, nodding lightly. "Yeah... *so many.*"

But her smile wavered, her gaze drifting past his shoulder, staring into the shadows beyond.

Her arms tightened around him, pulling him closer, burying her face into his shoulder as the emotion overwhelmed her.

She hadn't realised how badly she needed this—how much she had *longed* for it, for years, for *forever*.

"Oh, I *can't wait* to get to know you," John said suddenly, pulling back just enough to look at her properly. His eyes shone with excitement, as if a thousand questions had just flooded his mind all at once. "Am I a good father? What do we enjoy doing together? I mean—"

He hesitated, his breath catching as a realization settled in. "No," he murmured, shaking his head slightly. "*Don't* tell me. I already know too much. It's dangerous to know too much about one's future."

Eleanor swallowed hard, her lips pressing together as she fought the urge to tell him *everything*.

John sighed, rubbing his temple lightly, trying to compose himself as he struggled to process everything. "So, if you're here," he said slowly, choosing his words carefully, "it means that everything must turn out okay in the future, right?" His gaze settled on her, searching for reassurance, for any sign that she carried the answers he desperately needed. "You must know how to stop Nicolas."

Eleanor's throat tightened, hesitation gripping her before she could form a proper response. "Ermmm... kind of." The words barely left her lips before John frowned, catching onto her uncertainty. She could feel his rising suspicion, but before he could press her further, she quickly checked the time—past eleven o'clock. Time was closing in. She had to move.

She might not know exactly where Nyx was at this moment, but she knew where he would be. The last time anyone had seen Nicolas Cipher was the night of November 1st, 1996—the same night her father had... died. The thought sent a deep, sinking weight into her chest, but she swallowed hard, pushing aside the emotions clawing at the edges of her resolve. She couldn't afford to dwell on the pain. Not now.

Today was still the 31st, which meant she had an entire day to find Nyx—both of them—and take back the Time and Dark Elements before it was too late. Steadying herself, she inhaled sharply, forcing her voice to remain steady. "We need to get to Bleakwood School."

John raised an eyebrow, suspicion flickering across his expression. "The school?" His tone carried both doubt and intrigue. "Why there?"

"Not in it," Eleanor clarified, shaking her head. "Beneath it. That's where we'll find Nyx. He'll be in the tunnels under Bleakwood—inside the base where you keep all of your artifacts."

John hesitated, his posture stiffening as his sharp gaze locked onto hers. In that moment, something unspoken passed between them. He knew she was right—but he also knew she shouldn't know that information. A light flush crept up his neck, his jaw tightening slightly, but he didn't argue. Instead, after a long beat of silence, he exhaled deeply and nodded. "Very well," he said, his voice calmer now, more resolute. "Then I'm coming with you."

Eleanor snapped her gaze up. "No," she said quickly, almost too quickly.

John recoiled slightly, startled by the urgency in her tone. "Why not?"

"I—" Eleanor hesitated, struggling to find the right words. She couldn't tell him. Not like this. Not yet. Taking a steady breath, she finally said, "I think you might be in danger," her voice barely more than a whisper.

John's expression shifted instantly. "What?"

Eleanor forced herself to meet his gaze, determination hardening in her chest. "Nyx is dangerous," she said firmly.

John let out a breath of laughter, shaking his head in disbelief. "I saw."

Eleanor clenched her fists, frustration flaring beneath the surface. "I don't think you do," she murmured. "Not like I do."

John studied her for a long moment, his brows knitting together, his mouth set in a firm line. "You know the version of him who was your friend," he said, his voice lower now, filled with a quiet gravity. "But you can't imagine the person he turns into. The wicked, soulless version who followed me back through time to wreak chaos and destruction."

Then he exhaled, shaking his head firmly which made Eleanor's heart sink.

"If you think I'm going to let my daughter run headfirst into danger after the mess I created, then you've got another thing coming," John said, his voice unwavering, filled with quiet determination. His gaze was steady, firm, carrying the weight of a man who had lived too many mistakes to let another unfold before his eyes. "Besides, only I can get through the security system. You'll need my DNA, so I'm coming whether you like it or not."

Eleanor's chest tightened, the weight inside her pressing down like a deflated balloon. She knew that look—the hard-set resolve in his expression, the sheer refusal to back down. She knew it because it was her own. And there was no convincing him otherwise. Letting out a defeated sigh, she rubbed her forehead, the exhaustion creeping in. "Fine," she muttered, the word tasting like resignation. "But please—just be careful."

John offered a small smile, though it didn't quite reach his eyes. "Don't you worry about me," he said, voice lighter but no less firm. "That's my job."

But Eleanor did worry. Because she knew what the future held if she didn't succeed.

John pressed the ignition, the engine roaring to life with a sharp backfire that echoed through the quiet stretch of road. The tires shifted slightly as the car reversed, angling toward the west, cutting through the darkness of the rain-slicked streets. Outside, the storm deepened, rain pouring heavier now, drumming against the roof in rhythmic urgency, each drop hammering home the weight of what lay ahead.

Eleanor stared out the window, watching the droplets race down the glass, their fleeting paths dissolving into the blur beyond. She tried to ignore the overwhelming pressure settling in her chest, the suffocating fear curling into her ribs. But now—now she had told him the truth. There was no turning back.

She had to stop Nyx.

She had to change fate.

She had to save her father.

No matter what.

Meanwhile

6 hours earlier ...

38

Prisoner

C hris shivered violently, his body hunched against the damp, suffocating cold that filled the tunnel beneath Bleakwood. Every breath he took came out in a ragged exhale, the air thick with mildew and stagnant moisture, clinging to his skin like a second layer. His wrists throbbed from where the heavy chains cut into them, the iron biting deep, leaving raw, reddened rings of flesh. The cold crept into his bones, hollowing them out, twisting through his muscles until even the smallest movement felt like fire licking across his skin.

He had lost track of time.

Hours. Days. They blurred together, swallowed by the oppressive darkness.

The walls around him loomed, slick with condensation, long trails of moss clinging to the stone like veins—alive, breathing in the damp underground air. Stalactites hung menacingly from the ceiling, their jagged forms resembling fangs poised to sink into whatever unfortunate thing ventured beneath them. The uneven floor, littered with small stones and forgotten debris, made every shift of his body painful, the sharp edges digging into his legs where he sat.

And then there was the machinery.

Embedded into the cavern walls, units of metal pulsed with strange, flashing lights, the low hum of motors vibrating against the ground beneath him. The whirring sound was constant, a slow mechanical breath echoing through the space.

He seemed to be somewhere underground. He was sure where exactly, but something about everything around him seemed familiar, but different at the same time.

Chris squeezed his eyes shut, forcing his mind to stay focused.

He scanned the cavern as best he could, searching for *anything* that could aid his escape. His wrists burned, the iron digging cruelly into his flesh, but he ignored the pain. He had to find a way out—no matter how impossible it seemed.

As he shifted against the floor, something small and metallic grazed against his fingertips.

His breath caught.

Squinting in the dim light, he carefully maneuverer his fingers, curling them around the tiny object, his heart pounding as he realised—

A *screw*.

Hope surged inside him, sharp and immediate.

He forced his frozen fingers to move, cradling the screw carefully in his palm, his hands trembling both from the cold and the sudden rush of adrenaline.

Slowly, painstakingly, he worked the screw into the lock of his chains, careful not to make any sudden movements. His fingers were numb, barely responsive, each twist agonizingly slow.

His breath came out in ragged gasps, teeth clenched so tightly his jaw ached, sweat mixing with the grime on his skin.

The screw scraped against the metal, the sound sharp and deafening in the silence.

Chris winced, pausing briefly, his chest tightening in fear.

Had anyone heard that?

Seconds stretched into minutes, every movement agonising, but he refused to stop.

He had to get out.

He had to find Eleanor.

Finally, after what felt like *hours*, the lock *gave way*.

A small click—subtle, barely noticeable, but enough to send his pulse rocketing.

The chains loosened *just enough* around his wrists to bring circulation back into his fingers, the dull ache slowly replaced with sharp, agonizing tingles as feeling returned to his limbs.

Chris breathed deeply, shaking his hands, trying to suppress the pain. His gaze flicked over his shoulder, catching sight of the deep markings around his wrists—raw, red, skin broken where the iron had dug too deep.

But there was *no time* to dwell on pain.

With everything he had, he yanked on the chains, hoping to dislodge the bolts from the wall.

Nothing.

They held fast.

His pulse quickened as frustration burned through him.

As the reactor beside him kicked into action, the floor *rumbled*, sending small vibrations through the cavern.

The screw—his only hope—rolled just out of reach.

"No—no, no, no!"

Chris lunged, fingers scraping desperately against the cold stone floor, reaching—grasping—but the object had already tumbled too far out of reach. His body sagged, defeat pressing heavily against his ribs, threatening to drown him in hopelessness. But he couldn't give up. Eleanor wouldn't, and neither could he. There had to be another way.

Clenching his fists, he forced himself to stay focused, to push aside the rising panic clawing at his mind. There had to be a way out of these chains—one that didn't involve amputating his wrists, because the idea of severing both hands was far from appealing. He thought back, digging through everything he had learned over the years, searching for something useful, anything that might help. Most of it felt irrelevant, scraps of knowledge buried beneath the suffocating weight of his desperation. But then, just as he was about to give up, a seemingly random thought crystallized in his mind.

A year or two ago, the twins had played a prank on Professor Dougan, swapping the soles of her shoes for banana peels. The result had been disastrous—she had skidded straight into the fire escape and ended up in the hospital with a broken arm. But the memory wasn't what mattered. It was what it reminded him of. Lubricants. They were everywhere—in everyday life, in machines, in the world around him. They were what made a car engine run smoothly, coating the gears and pistons with oil, reducing friction, preventing them from grinding against each other and locking in place. And just like that—an idea sparked.

His eyes darted to the slimy, thick green mildew clinging to the walls. It smelled absolutely revolting, but the slick sheen of its surface looked slippery enough to help slide his hands through the chains. Without hesitation, Chris shuffled backward, pressing his hands into the muck, rubbing it thoroughly into his skin, forcing himself to ignore the slimy sensation and the stench threatening to turn his stomach. He pulled. His skin rolled beneath the metal straps, the slick film creating just enough lubricant to let him twist, just a little, just enough—

"Almost," he whispered, his voice trembling, hope clinging desperately to his ribs.

Then—

Footsteps.

Echoing through the tunnel.

Heavy.

Approaching.

Chris barely had time to react before hands grabbed him from behind, yanking him hard, throwing him off balance. He thrashed violently, twisting, kicking, hoping to catch whoever it was off guard, but before he could gain any leverage, he was shoved to the ground, his breath torn from his lungs. The metal straps snapped back around his wrists—tighter this time, digging unforgivingly into his skin.

He gasped, chest heaving, trying to catch his breath, panic surging through his limbs like wildfire.

Then—

A shadow moved toward him.

Slow.

Predatory.

Chris stiffened as the figure emerged from the darkness, and dread curled in his stomach as he met the piercing gaze of his captor.

Nyx.

The man moved with an unsettling grace, his posture relaxed, but his eyes gleaming with cruel satisfaction.

"Comfortable, *Chris*?" Nyx murmured, voice smooth, mocking.

Chris glared at him.

"What do you want, Nyx?"

Nyx chuckled, stepping closer, his expression unreadable.

"Oh, *just* a little chat," he mused, crouching down slightly. "You see, I've been *thinking*—about your dear friend, Eleanor."

Chris's jaw tightened instantly.

"Leave her *out* of this!"

Nyx's smirk widened.

"Why?" he asked, tone deceptively casual. "Do you *really* think she cares about you? You're nothing but a pawn to her—a means to an end."

Chris clenched his teeth.

"That's not *true*," he snapped, but doubt gnawed at the edges of his resolve.

Nyx leaned even closer, eyes gleaming.

"Isn't it?" he whispered, low and insidious. "Think about it, *Chris*. Why would someone like Eleanor be friends with *you*? You're weak. Insignificant. She doesn't need you."

Chris's heart pounded violently against his ribs.

His breath came faster, shallow, shaking.

Nyx's words cut deeper than he wanted to admit.

"You're lying."

Nyx tilted his head slightly, his smile unwavering.

"Am I?"

His voice slipped through the air like a poisoned thread—slow, deliberate, *relentless*.

"What have you ever done to prove your worth?" he whispered.

"You're just a burden, Chris."

"A weight around her neck."

"Holding her back."

Chris felt something inside him *fracture*—not physically, but something deeper, something woven into the fabric of who he was. A quiet, vulnerable part of himself he had spent years trying to bury, trying to silence. But now, under Nyx's scrutiny, under the weight of those words, the fragile pieces of his confidence splintered, cracking apart like old glass beneath an unforgiving pressure.

Memories of failures and insecurities stormed through his mind, each one carrying an unbearable weight. The times he had fallen short, the moments when he had hesitated, when doubt had gotten the better of him. Every mistake played on repeat in his head—the voices, the disappointments, the reminders that maybe he had *never* been enough.

He tried to fight it, to push it away, but Nyx's voice was a venomous thread slipping into the gaps of his defences, winding around his thoughts like a suffocating coil.

"Face it, Chris," Nyx murmured, his tone steeped in false pity, soft enough to sound like understanding, sharp enough to slice deep. "Eleanor doesn't *need* you. She never did."

Chris flinched.

Nyx's eyes gleamed, sensing the impact of his words, feeding off it like a predator playing with wounded prey.

"You're just a liability," he continued, stepping closer, his voice nearly a whisper now, pressing into Chris like a blade. "A weak link in her chain."

Chris felt his chest cave slightly, his shoulders slumping under the weight of it all.

He wanted to deny it—to throw the words back, to fight, to prove Nyx wrong—but when he opened his mouth, his voice betrayed him.

"You're wrong," Chris whispered, his voice barely audible, fragile, uncertain. The words slipped from his lips, carrying no weight, no conviction—only doubt.

And Nyx heard it.

That slow, curling satisfaction flickered across his expression, victory settling effortlessly into the sharp lines of his features. He straightened, stepping back with deliberate ease.

"We'll see, Chris," he mused, his tone casual, yet edged with quiet amusement, as if he had already won. He gave a small, knowing smirk, one that widened ever so slightly, deliberate in its arrogance. "Sit tight. I'll be back soon enough."

And just like that, with no further words, no hesitation, he turned and walked away, his footsteps echoing against the cold, unyielding stone walls, fading slowly into the suffocating silence.

Chris remained perfectly still, his body unmoving, swallowed whole by the darkness Nyx had left behind.

His thoughts spiralled into chaotic fragments that twisted deep into his mind, tangling into knots too tight to loosen. Doubt wrapped itself around him, creeping in like a relentless tide, pulling him downward, deeper, drowning him in questions he wasn't sure he wanted to answer.

Had Nyx been right?

Had he ever truly mattered in the grand scheme of things, or had he merely been a fleeting presence—something temporary, something replaceable?

Was he nothing more than a burden?

A meaningless piece in something far greater than himself, easily discarded, easily forgotten?

Had Eleanor ever truly needed him, or had he simply been there—just convenient, just another name written into the pages of her story? The thought cut deep, unearthing doubts he hadn't dared to voice before. The weight of the chains pressing into his wrists felt heavier now, more suffocating than before, as if the cold metal had absorbed Nyx's words and transformed them into something stronger, something unbreakable.

He clenched his teeth, forcing himself to steady his breathing, pushing past the tightening in his throat, the pressure mounting in his chest like a vice. He needed to think. He needed to focus. He had to find a way out—had to escape before his mind became its own prison. But more than that, he had to prove—

Chris hesitated, the thought catching like a snag in fabric, unravelling something deeper. What, exactly, was he trying to prove? His worth? His purpose? His place beside Eleanor? The questions weighed heavy, each one pressing into his ribs like stones, making it harder to breathe. He inhaled deeply, his breath unsteady, fingers twitching against the freezing stone floor beneath him, as if trying to grasp at something solid, something certain.

No.

This wasn't about proving anything to Nyx. Nyx was the manipulator. The deceiver. The one who spun lies into truths, who twisted weaknesses into weapons and wielded them with precision. Chris knew this. And yet, the words had still wormed their way beneath his skin, planting doubts like seeds waiting to take root.

But he refused to let them grow.

Chris had already earned his place. Whether Nyx saw it or not didn't matter. What mattered was getting out. Finding Eleanor. Getting home.

He forced himself to sit up straighter, ignoring the aching pull in his wrists. But in the suffocating darkness of the tunnel, surrounded by silence so thick it felt almost alive, it was hard to hold on to that belief.

39

Seeing Double

Nyx moved like smoke through the undergrowth, each step calculated, silent. The chill of the pre-dawn hours clung to the forest, thick with pine and promise.

He knew Eleanor was hunting him. Perhaps she'd sensed the shift. Perhaps she was piecing it together. But she was already too late.

He remembered this night—how the truck carrying the Time Element had crashed. He'd watched it unfold once before, wide-eyed and unsure.

But now? He was the one about to make it happen.

Nyx crouched behind the brush. The Dark Element thrummed beneath his skin, volatile and hungry. A low wind stirred the leaves, whispering secrets he already knew. He narrowed his eyes at the empty road.

Soon.

Then—headlights. Twin beams slicing through the dark. The truck.

Right on schedule.

Nyx inhaled, raised his hand. And struck.

A surge of invisible energy slammed into the front tire. The vehicle shrieked, skidding out of control. Metal twisted, rubber burned, and the truck flipped mid-air—crashing down in a roar of shattered steel.

Debris blanketed the road. The driver was out cold, slumped inside the wreckage. Nyx didn't look twice.

This wasn't about him.

Another set of lights approached. Slower. Hesitant.

Nyx's pulse quickened as the second car came to a stop—just as it had before. He stepped from the shadows, deliberate and slow.

Nicolas Cipher got out. Alarm painted his face.

Nyx studied him carefully. His younger self. So close to knowing. So close to breaking.

"Who are you?" Nicolas asked.

Nyx let the moonlight touch his face, casting deep shadows across familiar features.

"You already know," he said softly.

Recognition flickered in Nicolas's gaze—uncertain, impossible.

"I'm you," Nyx said. "From the future. And I need your help."

Nicolas froze.

"This can't be real," he whispered.

"Oh, but it is," Nyx replied. "And if you want to survive—if you want to win—do exactly as I say."

Nicolas hesitated, searching for logic in madness.

"Why should I trust you?"

Nyx smiled.

"Because I know what you're capable of. And I know how *you*, how *we* can get exactly what we've always desired."

The silence hung heavy, like the pause before a storm.

"First," Nyx said, voice low and steady, "we get the Time Element. Then we rewrite everything."

They walked toward the twisted wreckage together.

Soon, the world would bend to their will.

40

Cooperation

The green glow from the Time Element pulsed between them, steady and sinister, lighting their faces in sharp contrast. Nyx stood still as stone, his eyes fixed on the younger man just inches from the containment unit. He felt the power humming through the metal—alive, vibrant, almost breathing. It tugged at the atmosphere like gravity, promising control over time itself.

"Not yet," Nyx said, voice taut with command.

Nicolas froze, hand halfway to the casing. The hesitation showed plainly in his posture, tension rolling across his shoulders. His glance toward Nyx was uncertain, questioning—not just about the plan, but maybe about who he was becoming.

"Why?" he asked quietly, the edge in his voice dulled by doubt.

Nyx didn't answer right away. He simply lifted a finger, pointing to the wreckage where a faint sound stirred. Glass crunched. Metal shifted.

A figure crawled from the wreck—dazed, limping. Singleton.

Nyx's pulse didn't rise. He barely blinked. He hadn't forgotten this moment; it had already happened once—only now, he was steering it.

Without a word, he gripped Nicolas's sleeve and pulled him down behind the cargo door. They pressed into the steel shadows, hidden by darkened metal and the tall grass swaying around them. Nyx could feel Nicolas's breath beside him—shallow, uneven. Nervous.

Singleton staggered toward the driver, calling out through cracked lips. He sounded like a man piecing himself back together mid-collapse, trying to sound in control while everything screamed otherwise.

Nyx watched it all unfold. Every slow step. Every strained word. And then Singleton turned toward the back of the truck.

Nicolas shifted beside him, shoulders tight, body barely contained.

"Why stop me from taking it?" he whispered, frustration bleeding through.

Still Nyx said nothing. He simply motioned toward Singleton again—watching as the man reached into his coat and pulled out a key.

A small click. Lights flashed red for a second, then vanished.

"Security grid disabled," a robotic voice confirmed.

Nyx's lips pulled into a quiet grin.

"That's why."

He felt Nicolas beside him ease slightly, his voice softer now.

"I didn't know they'd upgraded the truck."

"Of course you didn't," Nyx replied, his tone laced with dry amusement. "I've already lived this."

And yet—it wasn't just about knowledge. It was about control. Nyx wasn't just ahead of the curve; he'd designed it.

Then—movement on the far ridge.

John Walker. And Eleanor, just behind.

Nyx's stomach knotted—not from fear, but anticipation. They didn't know he was here. Not yet.

"What now?" Nicolas asked, the impatience in his voice starting to fray.

Nyx turned and looked at him for a long moment. In that sliver of moonlight, Nicolas looked so much younger than Nyx remembered—caught between doubt and longing, tangled in a reality too surreal to grasp.

Nyx studied him. His posture, his tone. His hesitation.

"You blend in," he said carefully. "Your car's hidden. Take the path to the main road. Wait for them."

Nicolas nodded, half turning. But Nyx grabbed him again—and this time, the punch came hard and fast.

A crack to the temple. Nicolas dropped to one knee, groaning, blood sliding between his fingers as he clutched his face.

"What the hell was that?" he spat, his voice raw.

Nyx didn't flinch. "They need to believe you've been attacked."

Nicolas stared at him, fury blazing in his eyes.

But beneath the anger... was understanding.

"I need you focused," Nyx said, quieter now. "This moment matters. More than you know."

There was silence between them. Not cold, exactly. But distant. A mirror stretched across time—one man sculpted by consequences, the other still unravelling his place in it.

Then Nicolas turned, limping toward the road, adjusting his expression as though slipping into character.

Nyx stayed behind, hidden in the dark.

He watched everything unfold—John's approach, the concern in Eleanor's voice, the way Singleton gestured toward the cargo.

And then... John reached for the ring.

Nyx moved.

A single flick of his fingers. A roar of wind erupted, swirling dark energy into a storm so fierce even he felt the drag of its pull.

The chaos wrapped around him, and then—

Nicolas was there.

At his side.

Smiling.

Cruel and familiar.

The Time Element gleamed in his hand.

Nyx stared at him, heart steady, satisfaction simmering beneath his skin.

"Now," he said softly, reverent. "We begin."

He reached out, brushing his fingers across the bronze casing. Power pulsed beneath the surface like a second heartbeat. Every second from now on would bend to their will.

"Together, Nicolas," Nyx whispered. "We'll become unstoppable."

41

The Reactor

C hris's thoughts churned in a fevered haze, slipping in and out of consciousness as the suffocating darkness pressed against him from all sides. The cold damp of the tunnel clung to his skin, soaked through his bones, numbing him until the boundaries between his own body and the stone beneath him blurred. The numbness spread, creeping through every aching muscle, dulling the sharp edges of his pain until he could no longer tell where the agony ended, and the raw chill began.

He had no idea how long Nyx had been gone. Minutes? Hours? Time just seemed to pass into a haze of discomfort and silence.

The heavy chains around his wrists kept him bound, the iron biting into his flesh, his pulse weak beneath their crushing grip. Every shift, every slight movement sent sharp waves of fire shooting through his arms, but he barely noticed anymore. His mind was trapped elsewhere adrift in fading memories, pulled into fleeting fragments of warmth that flickered against the backdrop of his suffering.

Eleanor's voice stirred inside his mind, so distant it might have been a dream.

Hang on, Chris. We need you. I need you.

He held on to her words, as if they were a rope that could pull him out of the pit he found himself in. The doubt that Nyx had planted in him crept into every thought, threatening to undo everything he once believed.

Had Eleanor ever truly *needed* him?

Had he ever been more than just *another piece* in the story—an extra set of hands, a name among many, a presence that could be easily replaced?

He remembered every moment of hesitation, every time he had faltered, every instance where she had picked him up, steadied him, pushed him forward when he had doubted himself.

Had she ever needed him the way he had *needed her*?

He forced himself to hold onto the memory of her words— words she had spoken long before everything had fallen apart.

"You're stronger than you think, Chris. Don't ever forget that."

Now, he clung to her words like a lifeline. Slowly, Chris's eyes fluttered open, his vision blurred and wobbly. The soft glow of the moss-covered walls cast strange shadows across the chamber, turning the tunnel's edges into eerie, shifting shapes. He could feel the damp air wrap around him, heavy with the growing smell of mildew and rust. He tried to steady his breathing and clear the fog from his mind, but exhaustion weighed him down, pulling him deeper into sleep.

Just hang on a bit longer, Chris.

Eleanor's voice again.

That beacon of hope and the promise that he wasn't alone. But the darkness around him swallowed everything, leaving him feeling *small*, leaving him feeling like the pain wasn't worth fighting through anymore.

"You've got to stay with me, Chris."

Eleanor's voice was now desperately pleading for him to get up.

"Please, Chris. For me..."

Then—

Footsteps.

Echoing through the tunnel.

Chris's body tensed instinctively, every remaining ounce of warmth draining from him. His blood ran cold as he strained to see who was approaching, even though every bone in his body already *knew* the answer.

The voice sliced through the silence with theatrical delight, venom disguised as charm.

"Hello honey—I'M HOME!"

Chris swallowed hard, forcing his head up, his heart hammering against his ribs.

The dim glow of the moss-covered walls revealed him—Nyx, standing in the entrance of the chamber, his grin wide, teeth bared like a predator that had cornered its prey.

But—he wasn't alone.

Chris stiffened.

Nyx moved forward, carrying something with practiced ease.

A tray—food, water.

He set it down in front of Chris, his smile never faltering, disturbingly gentle, dripping with mock kindness.

"Hungry, Chris?" he asked smoothly, his voice like silk. "I thought you might need a little sustenance."

He spoke as if he was offering a meal to a sick child, his tone disturbingly parental.

Chris *glared* at him, refusing to let even an ounce of weakness show, even as exhaustion weighed him down.

"What do you *want*, Nyx?" he demanded, spitting the words through clenched teeth.

The harsh, flickering light of the chamber cast jagged shadows across his face, accentuating the sharp angles of his jaw, the defiance in his stare.

Where had he been? What had he been doing?

Nyx's grin widened, his eyes glowing with mirth—dark, cruel, *enjoying* this.

"Let me introduce you to someone," he mused.

He gestured to the figure lingering just behind him.

Chris's breath caught.

A younger, brighter and more gentle-looking version of Nyx stood awkwardly in the shadows, his posture stiff, his gaze flicking uncertainly between Nyx and Chris, a trapped animal caught between two forces he didn't understand.

"This is my younger self," Nyx continued smoothly. "He's going to help us with our plan."

Nyx's younger self, Nicolas Cipher, shifted under the weight of the words, his discomfort evident.

Everything had changed so fast. Just moments ago, he had stood by his friends, a young man trusting and trusted. But now he found himself following a plan that wasn't even his own—well, at least not yet anyway.

Chris saw this doubt and conflict in Nicolas's eyes. "But he's just a boy," Nicolas murmured, almost to himself, his voice unsure. "What threat could he be?"

Then Nyx let an amused chuckle. "Oh, he's not," he said,

Chris clenched his fists and braced himself as the cold, final words came: "He's just the bait." Nyx replied.

Those words cut through the air, and Chris felt his stomach sink.

"One thing you should know about your enemy is their greatest weakness." Chris swallowed hard, his heart pounding as he thought of Eleanor—signals of hope that would soon come. But he didn't know if he wanted them too. Nyx crouched down and whispered' into Chris's ear, "And when she comes to save you, she'll walk right into a trap," Nyx continued.

Trying to stay calm, Chris forced himself to meet Nicolas's eyes, searching for any sign of a sane man who would still listen to reason.

"Just look at him!" Chris snapped in desperation. "Look at who he has become! Do you really want to end up like that?"

Before Nicolas could answer, a low, hollow laugh echoed off the cavern walls.

Nyx grinned sharply and said, "You hope to appeal to my better nature." Then turned straight to Nicolas just to confirm that Chris's words hadn't swayed him from their plan. "He is me. My will is his will."

Nyx stared at his younger self with an expression carefully moulded into something soft. It was an echo of the way he used to speak to Eleanor, back when he pretended to be their chemistry professor. Back when he pretended to care.

His tone was gentle, deceptively sincere, laced with the kind of reassurance meant to lull someone into obedience and trust. But Chris saw through it instantly. He saw the glimmer beneath the facade—the faint, almost imperceptible trace of slithering deceit woven into the edges of Nyx's voice, the undertone of something predatory and calculated.

"This is our chance, Nicolas," Nyx murmured, his voice barely above a whisper but steeped in conviction, in quiet promise. His gaze remained unwavering, holding Nicolas's with an intensity that suggested inevitability.

"To get everything we ever wanted."

The words hung between them, stretching impossibly long in the stale underground air.

A pause.

A breath.

"Trust me."

And that was all it took.

Nicolas's brief moment of doubt disappeared almost as quickly as it came. His stance shifted, and his face grew firm and determined, as if Nyx's words had steeled him. Without another look, he stepped back and vanished into the tunnels with clear, steady resolve.

Chris's stomach dropped—it was happening again. Yet Nyx only turned away, completely unfazed, his attitude casual and almost bored, as if Nicolas's decision was just another part of a plan set long ago.

Chris watched, his breath growing quick and his pulse pounding in his throat, as Nyx's fingers slowly curled over the reactor controls with deliberate care. He pressed down on some of the buttons, typed across the keypad and flipped the switches.

A grin spread across Nyx's face, deepening into something sharp like a blade dragging through flesh. Then the chamber *trembled*.

A deep, resonant vibration shuddered through the walls, rattling through the ground beneath them. The reactor was coming to life.

Chris *fought* against his restraints, his body twisting, straining, every muscle in him burning with exertion, with the desperate need to move and *stop this*.

He felt the iron dig deeper into his wrists, felt the sharp sting of metal cutting against raw skin, but he *didn't care*.

Panic surged through him, blinding and consuming.

"You *can't* do this, Nyx!" he gasped, voice breaking under the sheer force of desperation clawing at his throat.

Nyx barely spared him a glance.

Instead, he tilted his head slightly, his smile stretching impossibly wider, his eyes gleaming with something unhinged—something untethered by morality or restraint.

"Oh," he purred, his voice sliding through the air like silk, rich and dripping with amusement.

"But you should know by now, *Mr. Knight*—"

He leaned in slightly, fingers shifting over the reactor's interface, the glow of the controls casting sickly green hues against the cavern walls. From his pocket, he pulled out the Time Element and placed in the core of the reactor, followed by his own ring. Without the Dark Element pulsing on his finger anymore, the unnatural darkness in his eyes seemed to disappear, but it didn't remove the delight within them.

"I can do *anything* I want."

The reactor whirred beneath his touch, the hum deepening into something ominous, something *final*.

"And there is *nothing* you can do to stop me."

42

Traps

Eleanor and John were already moving cautiously through the tunnels, they had been for the last hour. It hadn't taken them long to find the entrance to the tunnels beneath Bleakwood. In fact, it was easier to find now because the branches hadn't overgrown, not unlike they had in Eleanor's own time. It reminded her how much could change in just fourteen years—both in people and in nature. Life simply carried on.

Their footsteps echoing off the damp stone walls, the only sound breaking the suffocating silence beneath the foundations of Bleakwood school. The deeper they ventured, the more oppressive the atmosphere became, pressing in around them like unseen hands.

It wasn't just the narrow, winding pathways, the low-hanging stalactites, or the slick moisture coating the uneven floor that made it unnerving. It was the feeling—the sensation creeping along Eleanor's spine, a whisper in the back of her mind, telling her they weren't alone.

John's presence beside her was steady, reassuring, his movements precise and deliberate, navigating through the labyrinthine with the familiarity of someone who had walked these tunnels countless times before. He turned every few minutes, casting quick glances over his shoulder to ensure Eleanor was still following, his expression tense but protective, the way a parent might check on a child walking too close to a ledge.

"We need to find Nyx before it's too late," John muttered, his voice carrying just enough weight to break the silence. It bounced off the stone walls, swallowed up by the cavernous space, lost somewhere in the darkness ahead.

Eleanor opened her mouth to respond, but before she could form the words, a loud crash tore through the tunnel, the violent *crack* of shifting rock reverberating around them.

John moved faster than Eleanor could process, yanking her back just as debris came raining down in jagged slabs, striking the earth where she had been standing only moments before.

"*Watch out!*"

The tunnel shook under the force of the collapse, dust billowing in thick clouds, making it difficult to see, difficult to breathe. Eleanor coughed against the sudden wave of grit in the air, her heart hammering wildly against her ribs.

John ducked instinctively, his arms shielding both their faces as loose stones tumbled, clattering noisily against the hard-packed ground.

Finally, the tremors subsided, leaving behind a cloud of fine dust and fragmented rubble.

Eleanor pulled herself upright, her breathing still uneven.

"Thanks," she gasped, shaking her head as if that would clear the adrenaline flooding her veins. "That was close."

John hummed low in thought, brushing dust from his jacket. His eyes roamed the collapsed section of the tunnel with something beyond concern.

"Yeah," he agreed slowly. "A *bit* too close." His gaze narrowed. "Nothing like this has ever happened before. The reactor is supposed to keep the passages stable."

Eleanor lowered herself carefully, fingers grazing the ground where she had almost been crushed, her hand brushing against something rough, foreign.

A coarse thread.

She tugged it gently, lifting it from the debris, squinting in the low light.

"What's this—"

Before she could finish, John's hand grabbed her wrist, gripping tight as he *pulled* her back against his chest.

"Trip wire!"

He barely had time to say it before another *trap* triggered.

"Duck!"

Eleanor barely caught her breath before both of them slammed onto the ground, bodies pressed flat against the stone floor as a *plate of metal* ripped from the walls, slicing through the air just above them in a deadly arc.

It missed them—*barely*.

A few strands of Eleanor's hair fluttered in its wake.

For several beats, neither of them moved, their bodies rigid, their breathing fast and shallow.

"That was *definitely* not an accident," Eleanor muttered, finally managing to sit upright, her pulse still rattling through her frame.

John exhaled sharply, pressing a hand against his chest as if physically forcing his heart rate to slow.

"Nyx has booby-trapped the tunnels," he said, his voice grim, his tone carrying a weight that made Eleanor's stomach drop.

Which meant one thing.

"He *knows* we're coming," Eleanor replied, swallowing hard.

John nodded, rubbing his temple before straightening fully. "Which just means he *feels* us closing in on him."

Eleanor didn't respond, her mind racing with too many possibilities at once.

John continued speaking, his voice laced with frustration, his words carrying the tension they both felt in their bones.

"But that still doesn't explain how we can *safely* navigate through the tunnels. Every step could mean life or death. We have no way of knowing where or how many traps have been set."

Eleanor heard his words, but her thoughts were drifting somewhere else—towards her reflection. She had been catching glimpses of it in every mirror, every shiny surface they passed. That reflection bore a knowing, almost taunting smirk and a piercing gaze. And now—now it whispered, *I know where HE is.* The voice, soft as silk, echoed at the back of her mind. *I can feel it.*

Eleanor inhaled sharply, a shiver running along her skin. *Trust me.* She clenched her fists, hesitating only long enough to question herself before taking a step forward. "This way," she said.

John blinked in surprise. "What?"

"This way," she repeated more firmly, her voice steady despite the uncertainty creeping beneath her skin. John's brow furrowed. "Are you sure?"

She nodded. "I just know."

She couldn't explain how she knew the route, and she couldn't justify it logically. But deep down, she trusted that inner voice— even if it sometimes felt like an irritating earworm. It had never let her down before. It had always given her the information she needed.

Maybe it was crazy or even reckless to follow a voice that was only inside her head. But as they approached the first security checkpoint without triggering another trap, she knew they were going the right way.

A high-tech scanner flickered on as they drew near, casting a clinical blue glow over their faces. "DNA required," the mechanical voice stated in a precise, emotionless tone. John placed his hand flat on the glass screen, and the panel lit up with his touch. "DNA acquired," the scanner confirmed.

Before they could proceed, another light flashed on the screen. "Security breach detected. Second DNA print required." The extra security measure was now active. How were they going to get through this?

In the very next breath, the reflection whispered another urgent command: *Place your hand!*

Eleanor didn't hesitate and pressed her own hand on the scanner. As the light took a moment to scan it, the light glowed blue a second time.

"Second print acquired... Access granted."

Eleanor wasn't sure how her print had worked. That was until she realised that her DNA must be so close to John's that I was able to trick the scanner.

A hiss came out from its hinges and the door slid open, revealing the chamber beyond.

"One down," John muttered, stepping inside.

As they moved deeper into the facility, the reflection continued to guide Eleanor. Each security system presented a new challenge. The reflection's guidance was invaluable, its knowledge of fighting and navigating the complex tunnels giving Eleanor the edge she needed.

"Stay close," she said, her voice steady. They pushed forward, the tunnel twisting and turning, each step bringing them closer to the reactor chamber—and to Nyx.

But as they moved forward, a sudden, sharp snap echoed through the chamber.

John collapsed to the ground, his leg caught in a vicious metal clamp. The teeth of the trap were open wide, ready to bite into his flesh. Eleanor inhaled a breath that made her chest set on fire, almost as if she'd inhaled boiling water into her lungs. As she knelt beside him, her mind was an out-of-control race car. Every neuron was firing away, like a shock she never wanted to end, the adrenaline pumping into her bloodstream making every sense sharper, every moment longer and every instinct stronger. She had to figure out a way to free him before it was too late.

"Hold on," Eleanor said, her voice trembling. "I've got to get you out of this."

She examined the trap, her fingers tracing the mechanism. It was a sophisticated device, designed to hold its victim fast and inflict maximum pain. She knew that if she didn't act quickly, John could lose his leg—or worse, his life.

She looked around the sides, hoping to find some inscription or instructions describing how to dismantle the trap. But there was nothing. At least nothing she could see.

Beads of sweat collected on John's temple. His foot was already shaking, hovering over the trigger, not daring to make any sudden movement for fear of slicing his leg off. Yet his ankle had already begun to turn numb; he couldn't hold out much longer like this.

Eleanor took a deep breath, focusing on the task at hand. She could do this. Even without instructions, she had to do this NOW.

"Just keep holding still a little while longer." Eleanor encouraged, "I think I can see the release." She bent down, inspecting the trap a little closer.

She needed to hurry. The paralysis had already spread up his legs, causing John to shudder and cause the sweat on his forehead to drip into his eye – burning like acid rain.

Eleanor reached for the edge of the release lever, hidden beneath the trap, but it was jammed with debris.

Time was running out; she could see the blood pooling around John's leg, the colour draining from his face.

"Hang in there," she whispered. Grabbing hold of a jagged metal blade from the ground, she began to pry at the debris.

Her hands were slick with sweat mixing with the dust and grime, creating an uncomfortable layer that clung to her like a second skin.

The vibrations from the reactor seemed to intensify, the hum growing louder as if mocking her efforts. The air was thick enough to cut through, each second feeling like an eternity.

"Eleanor, listen to me. If something happens to me..."

"Don't say that." Eleanor cut him off before he could finish.

"It's going to work. I've almost got it,"

She brushed off the dirt beneath the trap, trying to get a clearer view of its intricate design.

The way the gears moved, the way the trap was structured.

She had to *break* it.

Had to *force* it open.

Finally—

With a desperate shove, Eleanor managed to clear the last piece of debris.

She *pulled* the lever, putting every ounce of her strength into the motion.

A groan.

A *snap*.

The trap *released*.

The metal jaws loosened, the pressure easing, the springs shifting as they finally yielded.

John let out a guttural noise, his body sagging slightly in relief, his leg trembling but *free*.

Eleanor swallowed hard, barely able to process the moment.

"We need to move, now," Eleanor said, helping John to his feet. He leaned heavily on her, his leg trembling but free from the trap.

"Thank you," John whispered, his voice weak but grateful.

Eleanor continued to stare at her reflection, the sharp metallic edges of the blade shimmering, like something of beauty.

As her mind was lost in thought, John was watching her every move.

"You seemed like you knew what you were doing with that blade," John observed, noticing the precision and accuracy with which she manoeuvred it under the trap. The confidence in which she held it between her fingertips was unmistakable.

"You've had to fight before, haven't you?" he asked, but Eleanor didn't need to answer; her expression said everything.

Her gaze drifted away from the blade as she slowly slid it into the safety of her back pocket. She thought it might come in handy later. But there was another reason for her hesitation—John had noticed the blade, even though she had tried to ignore it.

Since the moment she'd seen Nyx's younger self, a thought had been growing at the back of her mind. At first it was just a quiet background thought, but as midnight approached and the first of November neared, it grew stronger. The clock was ticking, and John's time was running out.

In those moments, Eleanor wondered how far she was willing to go to save her father. Could she really take a life, even if it was someone who deserved it, if it meant saving countless others? Her reflection in the blade seemed to taunt her, its grin widening as if it knew the dark thoughts swirling inside her. The weight of the blade in her pocket was a constant reminder of the choice she faced.

As they pressed onward through the tunnels, the vibrations in the stone grew stronger. Eleanor could feel them deep in her bones, humming through the soles of her feet and resonating in the walls.

Then she saw the entrance. It was unmistakable. The structure before them and the chamber beyond were the very same place where she had first found the Time Element in the future. She had stood before this door before—she knew this place.

But something was wrong. The door was partially open, revealing a sliver of deep blackness through the crack. Its metal edges were twisted, as if forced apart instead of simply unlocked.

The sound of machinery clanking—like wrenches caught in a malfunctioning motor—echoed through the cavern, filling the tunnel with sharp, shrieking noises that made Eleanor's ears ring.

Something felt off. Beside her, John's posture stiffened protectively as his eyes swept over the broken doorway and the stretching shadows that led into the chamber beyond. His voice dropped to a barely audible whisper:

"Let me go first, Eleanor."

She turned sharply, noticing how his expression had hardened, and his shoulders squared, ready for what was coming. He shot her a brief, tight-lipped glance and said steadily, "My life is far less precious than yours."

Her chest tightened and her pulse quickened at his words' implication. She reached out, trying to hold him back, but she wasn't quick enough. John had already moved forward. Determined, and staying close—too close—she stepped into the chamber beside him.

43

The Unfolding of Fate

The sight that greeted them was terrifying. A countdown flashed on a massive overhead screen, its numbers steadily ticking toward disaster, while alarms screamed in discordant bursts, filling the room with chaotic noise. But it was the reactor that truly held them in its grip—a nuclear heart trembling violently at the centre of the room. Its metallic frame groaned under the strain of unstable energy, emitting a low, ominous hum that seemed to seep into their bones and press down on their lungs, making each breath a labour. The chamber's suffocating heat only deepened the sense of dread, wrapping around them like an unyielding, oppressive force.

"Something's wrong," Eleanor said, her eyes wide with fear. The reactor shouldn't be behaving like this. It was built to keep the whole base together, but if it continued like this, it would eventually tear itself apart.

John was already at the control panel, his fingers moving in sharp, practiced motions across the flashing buttons and emergency switches, trying to decipher the urgent warnings that flooded the monitors. His brow furrowed deeper with each passing second, his throat dry as he took in the numbers blinking at him in furious red.

"The reactor is *set* to overheat," he muttered, a note of panic creeping into his voice as his fingers raced across the console. "The readings are *off the charts*. It's like it's going to—"

Before he could finish, the shadows near the reactor shifted, pulling away to reveal a tall, imposing figure stepping forward with slow, measured movements.

Nyx.

His grin was wide, sharp, almost *inhuman*, stretching across his blackened, deformed features in a way that sent an immediate wave of nausea twisting through Eleanor's stomach. His eyes— luminescent blood-red, burning with a grotesque delight—locked onto them, soaking in their shock, *feeding* off their fear.

His presence alone was enough to drain what little warmth remained in the room, replacing it with a suffocating chill that clung to Eleanor's skin like a parasite.

"You're *too late*," Nyx declared, his voice unnaturally smooth, dripping with malice. Every syllable was deliberately drawn out.

Eleanor stiffened, her muscles coiling with instinctive tension.

"Nyx!" she forced out, her heartbeat thundering in her chest. "What have you *done*?"

John stumbled back slightly, knees threatening to buckle as he took in the *monstrosity* standing before him. The man—if he could still be called that—was barely recognisable now. His skin was black as tar, unnaturally warped, veins pulsing with something dark and unknowable, stretching like cracked fault lines beneath the surface. His grin, his stare—it was as if something else *lived* behind his face, something hollow and insatiable.

Nyx let his grin deepen, enjoying the reaction, feeding off their disbelief like a beast admiring its prey before the kill.

"I've added *both* the Time and Dark Elements to the reactor," he purred, lifting his chin slightly, the flickering black and green glow of the unstable energy reflecting off his distorted features. "It's going to *overheat* and *explode*, taking *everything* with it."

Eleanor's mind whirled in a tornado of chaotic thoughts as every worst-case scenario fought for dominance.

Her voice was barely steady as she forced herself to speak.

"*Why?* What do you hope to gain from this?"

Nyx's expression barely flickered, his posture relaxed, as if they were discussing the weather.

He shrugged, a casual roll of his shoulders, his voice almost *bored*.

"Chaos. *Destruction.* A *reset* of sorts." He tilted his head slightly, studying them as if they were lab rats caught in an experiment. "Sometimes, to build something *new*, you have to destroy the *old*."

His grin twitched as his gaze settled on Eleanor fully, his amusement deepening.

"You two must be feeling *very* nostalgic right now. Well—more *you*, Eleanor." He took a step forward, slow, deliberate. His voice twisted into something mockingly childlike. "Isn't it *wonderful* how such *big* moments bring *family* together?" He gestured to John with a smug flick of his fingers. "In a way, you should be *thanking* me, Eleanor. Just *look* at the two of you—father and daughter—together *again*."

He paused just long enough for his smirk to turn sharp.

Then—

He spat at the ground.

"It makes me *sick*."

The moment was fleeting, but Eleanor caught it.

Something in his *posture* changed.

Something in the *way* he held himself.

It was as if he had flicked a switch in his mind, shifting from deranged glee to something *empty* and *cold*. No emotion. No reason.

Just *void*.

Eleanor barely had time to process it before Nyx moved again. "Speaking of..."

A sudden, sharp *snap* of movement. Nyx reached behind the monitors and *dragged* Chris forward. Half-conscious, barely responsive, his body limp in Nyx's grip.

Eleanor's breath hitched violently as her stomach dropped with nausea swirling through her core.

"Chris!" The name left her mouth before she could stop it, desperation clawing at her throat. "What have you *done* to him?"

Nyx barely blinked.

He lifted Chris slightly, shaking him like a ragdoll, almost *casual* in his movements.

"Say *hello* to your little friend," Nyx murmured, his tone drenched in cruelty.

Eleanor felt tears sting her eyes, burning, raw.

Nyx tilted his head, shaking Chris again, harder this time, enjoying the *lack* of response.

"Well, go on, Chris—don't be *rude*." He laughed, a wild and inhuman sound. "Your dear *friend* has come to *rescue* you. You'll want to *watch* this..."

His laughter twisted into something unhinged.

"You can watch me snap her body in half and drop it at your feet," he sneered.

Eleanor trembled, every part of her urging her to move, to act—to stop this before it was too late. Her heart pounded in her skull, and adrenaline surged through her veins. "You're insane! You're beyond insane!" she shouted, struggling to hold herself back from charging across the room and tackling him.

Then, slowly, she noticed a change in him. The darkness that had filled his veins was beginning to fade, and the soulless sheen in his eyes flickered—black, then red, then back again—like a light fighting to stay on. Her breath caught as her eyes fixed on his hand, on his bare index finger. The ring mark—the cylindrical imprint where the Dark Element had been—was gone.

The power had shifted. It was now inside the reactor, where both the Dark and Time Elements were locked in an unstable fusion. Black and green energies fought against each other, casting erratic shadows across the cavern walls.

Eleanor's thoughts raced. Nyx no longer possessed the Dark Element. This meant that, for the first time, she had a real chance to fight him. Without the Dark Element, he was just an ordinary person—albeit one who was still twice her size and cradling Chris's head in his hands, too weak to resist. With Chris still in harm's way, she knew she had to act, even if the odds were stacked against her.

Eleanor's mind raced, calculating her next move. The heat from the reactor made her skin feel like it was on fire, the sweat dripping down her raw and weathered skin. She could feel her heart pounding in her chest, each beat echoing in her ears like a drum.

Nyx's eyes locked onto hers, a cruel smile playing on his lips. "What's the matter, Eleanor? Feeling a bit overwhelmed?" he taunted, his voice dripping with sarcasm.

Eleanor's grip tightened on the blade in her hand, her knuckles turning white.

She knew she had to act fast.

The countdown on the screen was ticking away, each second bringing them closer to disaster. She took a deep breath, steeling herself for what was to come.

"Let him go, Nyx," she demanded, her voice steady despite the fear gnawing at her insides.

"Or what? You'll try to stop me?"

Eleanor's mind raced, searching for a solution. She glanced at John, who was now working frantically at the control panel, trying to find a way to stop the reactor from overheating. She knew they were running out of time.

"Can you do anything to slow down the countdown?" she asked, her voice urgent.

John shook his head, his expression grim. "I'm trying, but it's not looking good. We need to get those Elements out of the reactor."

Eleanor tore her gaze away from the flashing warnings on the screens, turning her full attention back to Nyx.

She knew what she had to do.

Her fingers flexed instinctively at her sides before she took a deliberate step forward, squaring her shoulders, steadying her breath, locking her gaze with his.

"Let him go," she ordered, her voice firm, unwavering despite the fear gnawing at the back of her mind. "And I'll give you what you want."

"Oh?" he mused, his grip on Chris tightening just a bit. "And what exactly do you think I want?"

Eleanor swallowed hard, forcing herself to remain calm and controlled. She felt his intense gaze press against her, watching every movement and breath for any sign of weakness.

Taking a careful step forward, her pulse pounded in her chest. "You want me," she said deliberately. "Let Chris go, and I'll come with you willingly."

Nyx's grin widened unnaturally, predatory in its satisfaction. "Oh, Eleanor," he purred, amusement heavy in his tone. "You always were the clever one." He paused, his smile twisting into something sharper. "But I'm afraid it's too late for that."

Eleanor's stomach tightened. "The countdown has already started," Nyx continued, shifting his stance with a controlled air. "And there's no stopping it now."

Determined not to show how much his words rattled her, Eleanor took another step forward. "Then let him go," she pressed, her voice steady, "and I'll help you."

For a brief moment, Nyx's amusement faltered. "We can control the power of the Elements. We can reshape the world." His gaze darkened as he searched her face for any sign of deceit. "And why should I trust you?"

Eleanor inhaled deeply and steadied herself. She had to make him believe her—just for a moment, long enough to gain his trust. "Because you know I'm right," she said in a low, unwavering voice. "You know that with my help, you can achieve your goals. But you need me alive to do it."

The chamber seemed to shrink around them as the moment stretched out. A single bead of sweat dripped slowly from her nose, falling silently onto the stone floor. Nyx studied her intently, and for a heartbeat, he considered her—then he laughed. The sound was sharp, empty, and hollow.

His grip on Chris remained unyielding. "Do you really think I'm that easy to fool?" Nyx sneered, his voice curling around the words like venom. His expression hardened—cruel and merciless. "I don't have a beating heart worth appealing to."

John clenched his fists, his body rigid and his breath coming in sharp bursts. "We won't let you get away with this," he declared. Nyx simply smiled. "You don't have a choice."

The reactor groaned as the shaking worsened, and the countdown ticked on, marching relentlessly toward disaster. "In a few minutes," Nyx said, his voice soaked in quiet satisfaction, "this entire facility will be nothing but rubble."

Eleanor turned sharply toward John, her mind racing. "We have to find a way to stop it," she urged.

John nodded without hesitation, his fingers already moving frantically across the console.

"There *has* to be an override—something we can do to stabilize the reactor," he muttered, his mind working furiously. "That's our last hope."

Nyx chuckled under his breath, folding his arms.

"Good luck with that," he mused, watching them with ease, with amusement. "You'll *need* it."

Eleanor ignored him.

She darted toward the control panel beside John, their hands moving in a desperate attempt to find *anything*, some sequence, some fail-safe, some way to stop the countdown before it reached zero.

The reactor's shaking grew violent, the warnings flashing *red*, filling the screens with urgent alerts, every possible system signalling failure.

"*Come on, come on,*" John muttered, his eyes scanning every line of data, searching, digging, *hoping*.

Their minds were focused on *one* goal—

Stopping the explosion.

"We can't let him *win*," she growled, her voice a razor's edge.

As the countdown ticked closer, the reactor trembled on the brink of catastrophe—its massive structure groaning under the weight of unstable energy pulsing through its core. Every alarm in the chamber shrieked in warning, as the countdown got closer and closer to deviation.

Eleanor could feel it all—the world teetering dangerously close to collapse. The walls around them shuddered, deep cracks splintering through the stone as if the very fabric of reality threatened to come apart. For a split second, she feared that time itself was unravelling, that reality itself was breaking down. But no, it was still the reactor, desperately fighting to contain the two Elements as it pushed itself toward critical failure.

Still—anything could happen. As long as the reactor remained active, the future was in flux.

Then Nyx's voice cut through the chaos, cold and bitter, carrying something deeper than mere rage.

"I am *tired* of playing in the hands of fate," his voice carrying through the chamber, curling around them like smoke. "Tired of following the *rules*. I never wanted to be the *bad guy*."

The reactor shuddered even more violently, sending waves of tremors through the cavern floor, but Nyx barely seemed to notice.

"But fate *made* me the bad guy."

The walls *burst apart*.

Metal hinges tore free from stone as the ceiling cracked, spilling debris into the chamber in thick, suffocating clouds. The weakest pressure point—right by the entrance—collapsed completely, sending jagged rock and twisted steel crashing down with brutal force.

Eleanor barely had time to react before John yanked her backward, both of them hitting the ground as the air filled with splintered fragments. A deafening *boom* drowned out their cries, scattering shards of metal across the chamber like shrapnel. The dust was suffocating, clogging Eleanor's throat, turning the world into a haze of dim lights and fractured rubble.

When the dust finally began to settle, the sight before her made her blood run *cold*.

The reactor doors—

Blocked.

Trapped beneath layers of fallen rock and heavy steel.

There was no way out.

Eleanor gasped, her body tense, scrambling to steady herself.

"I'm going to take *everything* precious away from you..."

Nyx's voice drifted through the smoke, slow, deliberate.

Through the thick clouds of dust and flickering reactor light, Eleanor caught sight of him emerging from the chaos, his grip tight around Chris's shirt.

"*...Starting with this one.*"

He yanked Chris forward, fingers curling harshly around his collar.

Eleanor's stomach twisted violently as she caught sight of Chris's face—bruised, his lip split, his eyes struggling to stay open.

Nyx leaned closer, sneering.

His breath reeked of something *rotted*, something *dead*.

"Say *goodbye*."

Eleanor surged forward instinctively, but—

A single blink—

And Nyx was *gone*.

Chris, too.

Eleanor clenched her teeth, frustration surging through her in a sharp, unbearable wave. She slammed her fist against the ground, her mind racing in search of a *solution*.

"He's locked us out of the controls." John's voice rose above the clanging of engines. His fingers flew over the damaged console, searching—*digging* for an opening. "There's *only* one way to stop this. A complete system override."

Eleanor stiffened, pushing herself upright.

The walls around them had started to cool slightly, but without shielding, the radiation would begin *seeping* in. If they didn't act now—if the shielding *failed*—they would hardly last ten minutes before the exposure became lethal.

John turned toward her sharply, urgency flashing in his expression.

"Eleanor—I need you to input the same codes as me," he instructed, nodding toward the far end of the console. His voice was steady, but his movements betrayed the strain—the *fight* against time. "We *have* to work together."

Eleanor *ran.*

She reached the terminal, fingers hovering over the keyboard—

But the screen was filled with *lines* of code, flashing in erratic bursts, completely unreadable to her.

"I don't know what to do!" she yelled, panic edging her voice. The alarms blared and the reactor groaned in response. Then, a third voice cut through the chaos: "I do."

For a moment, the room fell silent except for the steady hum of the reactor. John turned, surprised to see the young face of Mike Singleton standing in the doorway, silhouetted against the flickering glow of the control terminal. He had been watching them, quietly piecing together their plan. Eleanor wasn't shocked—Singleton always had a knack for sniffing out lies.

John's breath caught. "What are you doing here?"

Singleton stepped further into the chamber, his tone steady and unwavering. "I followed you," he said simply, sounding just like the Singleton Eleanor remembered, which made her chest tighten.

John opened his mouth, ready to explain, but Singleton quickly interrupted. "Save the sympathy act. I already know what you two are trying to do."

John sighed, his shoulders dropping a little. "Now, Mike— before you say anything—"

But Singleton barely paused. "I know there's only one way to stop the reactor from overheating."

Eleanor inhaled sharply, bracing herself. "What?" she whispered.

Singleton's expression hardened as he replied, "We need to destroy it."

The words settled over them like a final sentence. Without pause, Singleton moved swiftly. His fingers danced over the keyboard as lines of code blurred across the screen. Yet the reactor's defences were strong, layered behind complex, calculated barriers—a testament to Nyx's meticulous planning.

John turned to Eleanor, urgency in his eyes. "Go after your friend," he urged, his voice strained but determined. "We can handle this."

Eleanor hesitated, her chest tightening as she felt the pull of duty and concern for Chris. But she knew what she had to do. Swallowing hard and with uneven breaths, she nodded. Without another moment's hesitation, she ran.

She sprinted out of the chamber, her heart hammering with each step, breath coming in ragged bursts. The tunnel blurred around her—the winding path, damp stone under her boots. The roar of rushing water filled her ears, drowning out everything else as the waterfall came into sight.

And there—

Under the relentless cascade—

Nyx stood.

His grip was tight around Chris's arm.

But he had nowhere to run.

Nowhere to go but down.

44

The Edge

"It's over, Nyx, there's nowhere to go!" Eleanor shouted.

In a desperate move, Nyx grabbed the rope securing the temporary overhead lighting and looped it around Chris's arms. With a fierce tug, he dragged Chris toward the edge of the waterfall. Eleanor watched in horror as Nyx dangled Chris over the abyss, the rope the only thing keeping him from plummeting into the churning waters below.

"Let him go, Nyx!" Eleanor screamed, her voice raw and harsh. She reached into her back pocket and pulled out the blade.

"You have a choice, Eleanor—save your friend or catch me," Nyx replied coolly. Eleanor stood her ground, weapon drawn while Chris squirmed, his hands bound by the rope. Nyx's eyes gleamed with dark malice, though the supernatural glint had faded. In the blade's reflection, Eleanor saw her own face mock her. A voice repeated in her mind, sharp and fierce as if jeering like a ravenous lion, "Say it again!"

"I said, LET HIM GO!" she shouted back with the same ferocity. Nyx glanced at Chris before shifting his focus back to her. "Poor choice of words," he taunted, loosening his grip on the rope.

Eleanor's stomach dropped as she lunged forward, but it was too late. Nyx released the rope, and Chris disappeared behind the cliff face. As Nyx scurried one way, the rope flailed through the air, inch by inch getting pulled over the edge. Time seemed to slow as Eleanor watched him fall, her mind racing.

With a burst of adrenaline, she drew her blade and drove it into the earth, pinning the last meter of rope into the ground just in time. Chris's body jolted to a halt, dangling precariously over the edge, his eyes wide and his breath coming in ragged pants.

"Hold on, Chris!" she shouted above the roar of the water. Eleanor slipped onto her stomach and inched her way over the lip of the opening. Lowering her hands onto the rope for a better grip, her muscles strained as she grasped the rim tightly and began pulling Chris up. He was far heavier than she'd expected—the rope squealed, and its threads frayed under the pressure.

Though Chris was only two feet away, it felt like an impossible chasm. He dared not look down. With every desperate pull from Eleanor, Chris inched closer to the summit, fighting off dark thoughts of failing limbs, a slipping grasp, and the void waiting below. He counted to three in his mind, timing every pull with the rhythm of his heart. Every muscle screamed in protest, every breath was a battle, yet the top was tantalizingly close.

Just as Chris reached for the rocky surface, a coarse rope snapped back around Eleanor's neck, knocking her down and pinning her to the ground. Chris's scream was swallowed by the roar of the water as her grip released the rope—its ends burning through her fingertips.

Before she could recover, Nyx was on top of her, his hands closing around her throat. Eleanor struggled, gasping for air as his grip tightened and his eyes burned with malevolent fury. "You're too late," Nyx hissed. "You'll never save him."

Her vision blurred while she clawed at Nyx's iron grip, the world around her slowing as the roar of the waterfall became a distant echo. With each passing second, her strength waned. But then a surge of adrenaline flooded through her.

She couldn't give up.

Not now.

Summoning every ounce of strength left, Eleanor reached for a jagged rock beside her. With a desperate swing, she smashed it against Nyx's head. The impact stunned him, and his grip loosened just enough for her to push him off.

Gasping for breath, Eleanor scrambled to her feet and glanced over the edge. Chris still dangled precariously, his eyes wide with fear. "Hold on, Chris!" she shouted hoarsely. She grabbed the rope and began pulling again, her muscles straining with effort. Chris's eyelids fluttered as he fought to keep hold.

"Hold on, Chris! Hold on!" she screamed, but his body hung there like a dead weight. She knew she couldn't pull him up alone—not in her weakened state.

In the next moment, she felt a sick crunch as Nyx, still dazed but not defeated, jumped forward and crushed her fingers under his boot. Pins and needles burned away all feeling from her hand as her vision darkened with tears, her strength fading.

Nyx reached down and pulled the blade out of the ground. "No!" Eleanor screamed as she watched the rope vanish completely over the edge. "This is where it ends, Eleanor!" Nyx roared as he raised the blade over his head, its razor-sharp tip glinting silver, ready to slice into her bones.

But then, with a sudden burst of energy, an unexpected fist swung over the edge and struck Nyx's chest. His body reeled backward—not enough to knock him down, but enough to give Eleanor a chance to escape. She quickly snatched hold of Chris's outstretched, blistered hands. They collapsed on the ground together, panting and trembling with relief.

"I thought I'd lost you," Eleanor cried, her voice breaking as Chris's breath whispered in her ear. "You can't get rid of me that easily."

Before they could catch their breath, a figure darted at Eleanor, lunging and throwing her aside in a tumble of dirt and mud. Both Nyx and Eleanor rolled down the ledge and hit the ground with a heavy thud. Seizing the opportunity, Nyx swiftly drove his blade into Eleanor's leg. A searing pain shot through her body as the blade sank deep, nearly toppling her. She fought to remain upright despite the hot, pounding pain coursing through her feet, while Nyx's sinister grin widened as he circled her like a predator.

Gritting his teeth, Eleanor pulled the blade from her leg, blood staining the ground beneath her. She could feel his strength waning but refused to give up. Nyx lunged again, this time pulling out a second blade, but Eleanor was ready.

The two clashed fiercely, the sound of metal against metal filled the air, each movement a blur of deadly precision.

Nyx was formidable, his strength and speed making each strike dangerous. But with every exertion, his movement seemed to become more and more human. Eleanor deflected a swift slice aimed at her face, countering with a back hand of her blade.

Summoning all her strength, she pushed herself off the ground and launched into a series of rapid, precise strikes. Her movements were a blur, her blade a whirlwind of steel as she drove Nyx back, away from the edge.

Eleanor clutched hold of Chris' hand and pulled her behind her own body.

"Stay close," Eleanor whispered to Chris.

This was their chance.

Nyx was growing weary, the weight of an ordinary human existence pressing down on him. His legs felt like lead, his muscles ached, and the more he exerted himself, the more he struggled to catch his breath.

Chris tightened his grip on his weapon, shifting into a fighting stance.

"I've got your back."

As Nyx advanced, Eleanor felt the oppressive weight of his presence bearing down on her.

She inhaled deeply, centring herself.

She had to stay focused—

For Chris.

For her father.

For everyone depending on them.

Nyx struck first, his movements a blur. Eleanor parried his attack, the force of the blow reverberating through her arms. Chris moved in from the side, aiming a strike at Nyx's flank, but Nyx twisted aside, sending Chris stumbling forwards with the force of his own momentum.

Nyx's attacks were relentless, but Eleanor wasn't about to give up. They couldn't afford to lose. Not now.

The roar of the waterfall seemed to amplify the yawning chasm as they backed against the edge, water sprayed in Eleanor's face – temporarily blinding her.

Nyx's sinister laughter echoed in her ears as he loomed over her, his blade poised to strike.

"Eleanor, duck!"

Feeling the air fly over the top of her head, Eleanor swung beneath Nyx's blade. With one slice, Eleanor's heart dropped as she watched her own blade knock clean out of her grasp.

Eleanor scrambled to look over waterfall, hoping it had landed on a ledge nearby - somewhere within reach. But all she could see was the crashing white foam at the water's abyss. With a sudden, brutal move, Nyx grabbed Eleanor by the scruff of her jacket and slammed her against the rocky wall. The impact knocked the wind out of her, and she gasped for breath, Nyx gripped her tight. Before she could react, he dragged her towards the waterfall, the icy water crashing down around them.

Eleanor struggled, her vision blurring as the water pounded against her. Nyx forced her head under the torrent, trying to drown her in the relentless cascade. She thrashed and kicked, her lungs burning for air, but each breath was filled by a mouthful of water. The world around her began to fade, the roar of the waterfall drowning out all other sounds.

Just when she though she couldn't hold on any longer, the pressure on her head released, allowing her head to resurface; lungs gasping for air.

Nyx, enraged, thrashed about at Chris who was on top of his shoulders, like a jockey mounting a riled-up horse. As he rammed his back against the cliff face, Chris tumbled to the ground.

But this time, Eleanor was ready. Before Nyx could launch himself towards her, she snatched hold of his blade and sliced through the air with deadly accuracy. Nyx roared in pain, clutching his gaping wound.

Now hand-in-hand, Eleanor and Chris moved in unison; their attacks perfectly synchronized.

Nyx's body crumbled to the ground, weak and groaning. The remnant power of the Dark Element had almost all but drained from his body. Now, he looked just as human as the two of them.

Eleanor couldn't help but release a sigh of relief. She reached out and pulled Chris into a brief, tight embrace. "Are you okay?" she asked, her voice shaking.

Chris nodded, his voice hoarse. "I am now. I'm so glad to see you."

A delirious screech tore from Nyx's throat.

Despite everything, he still managed a wicked laugh which caused Eleanor and Chris to clench their teeth, just enough to bear Nyx's sneering.

"Enjoy it while it lasts, Eleanor," he rasped, coughing up spurts of blood. "Time is a fickle thing. If you don't know what you're doing, fate always has a way of coming back to bite you."

A choking gurgle filled his throat before his eyes fell shut.

Eleanor and Chris exchanged a brief glance.

Then—

Realization struck.

"John!" Eleanor gasped, spinning on her heels like a hurricane and bolting toward the reactor room.

Panting, drenched, she arrived just as Singleton cracked the final layer of the reactor's defences. The system beeped in acknowledgment, its motors humming to a gentler rhythm.

They all exhaled, watching as the reactor lights slowly powered down.

Eleanor raced across the room, her footsteps echoing in the now-silent chamber.

Reaching the reactor, she carefully lifted its casing—revealing the two Elements nestled inside.

Their energy pulsed beneath her fingertips.

With a determined look, she pulled them free, feeling their power thrumming in her hands.

She turned to her father, pressing the Time Element into his grasp. He accepted it with a solemn nod of gratitude.

Then, silently, she slid Nyx's Dark Element into her own pocket—

Resolving never to make the same mistake he had.

Was that it? Eleanor thought.

Had they done it?

Were they safe?

Were they ALL safe?

A chilling voice echoed through the chamber, followed by the unmistakable sound of a weapon being loaded.

Eleanor's heart skipped a beat.

She turned slowly, eyes widening in shock.

Standing in the shadows opposite them was Nicolas Cipher—but not the one she'd just defeated.

His eyes glowed with an eerie light, his presence even more menacing than before. He stepped forward, the weapon in his hand gleaming ominously.

"Not so fast!" he said, his voice unsteady.

Eleanor had all but forgotten about Nyx's younger self.

Up close, his skin was clear, unscarred—a stark contrast to the monstrous future version she knew, lying unconscious in the tunnels. More than that, his eyes still held something she had thought long lost—hope.

This younger Nicolas had never held a gun in his life.

He hadn't yet been worn down by the weight of the atrocities he would commit.

Eleanor was about to act—until John raised a hand.

She froze beneath a pile of rubble near the entrance, keeping her head low, trying to stay out of sight.

On hands and knees, she crawled forward, pressing herself flat against the ground to get a better view. Dirt and grime clung to her arms—a mixture of burnt metal fragments, radioactive rocks, and leaking oil from smashed equipment. The rough surface scraped against her skin, leaving small cuts and bruises.

"Nic, please," John pleaded, his voice steady but laced with desperation. "We can talk this out... just put the gun down."

Nicolas's gaze flickered to John's hand—where the pulsing green light of the Time Element glowed in sync with his heartbeat.

"Hand it to me," Nicolas ordered, his voice sharp and unwavering.

John stood firm, his stance unyielding.

"I can't do that, Nic."

Nicolas's expression tightened, frustration flickering in his eyes. "I need it, John. Now more than ever. Nothing will ever be the same again."

John exhaled slowly, keeping his voice measured, trying to deescalate the situation. "Everything can be fixed."

"No!" Nicolas's voice cracked, raw with emotion. "Not this time. Some things can't be fixed—only changed."

His grip on the gun tightened, knuckles white from the strain.

"I'm going to go back in time and make sure we never found the Elements," he continued, his breath ragged. "I can't live like this—with the constant whispering inside my head. I hear them wherever I go, making me think horrible things."

His voice trembled, the weight of his confession pressing into the space between them.

John's brow furrowed, his concern deepening. "What voices?"

Nicolas's haunted gaze locked onto him, desperate, pleading.

"Can't you hear them too? Just listen," he whispered, his eyes wide, lost in something unseen.

Silence stretched, thick with tension, wrapping around them like a suffocating force.

John inhaled slowly, choosing his words carefully. "Nic, you're sick. It's the Dark Element that's made you like this. Please—just give it to me, before you do something you'll regret."

Nicolas shook his head, an eerie certainty creeping into his expression.

"That's just it. I have no regret," he said, his voice growing steadier, conviction burning through his words. "All those pathetic feelings only held me back. The Dark Element is the cure. It pulled the veil back and showed me the truth of humanity."

His fingers flexed around the weapon, his confidence hardening into resolve.

"We are made to believe we are tiny, insignificant, without purpose. But I... I do have a purpose."

His voice carried a raw edge, sharpened by years of resentment. "While those in power exploit the free will we've been given, taking advantage of the desperate, twisting their choices for their own gain—"

He paused, a deep and unsettling silence settling between them.

For a moment, his expression hardened, reflecting on his own words. Whether tainted or misguided, they came from a place of anger, of bitterness—a pain Eleanor might never fully understand.

But no amount of pain should ever be replaced by more pain.

It was an endless, futile cycle.

"But I can put a stop to that," he said, conviction growing in his voice. "Imagine it—no more war, no more sickness, no more greed."

Then, rising above all other voices—John's.

"But what about the freedom to choose our own life? The right to be unique? Each of us—individuals. If you take away our choice... you take away our humanity. And without that—what would be the point of life?"

His voice burned with passion.

Eleanor clung to the shadows, gritting her teeth. She had to do something. But Chris had his hand tightly gripped around her arm, as if he could read her mind. She was no match for a bullet.

"Please, Nic, let me help you," John pleaded, his voice breaking.

Nicolas' frown softened a little a well of tears glistened in his eyes. A struggle was tugging inside Nicolas' mind, the best part of him that John had always been able to reach.

But just in the corner of their eyes, Eleanor noticed Singleton creeping behind them, his eyes set on the control panel. The bright red activation light was now flashing like a steady pulse. The reactor still needed a manual override before it could fully shut down; otherwise, the reactor would start up again, this time with no way of stopping it. Singleton was going to make a move for it, ready to break out into a run.

Nicolas' thoughts must have locked onto Singleton's plan, for the next moment his attention swung to the flashing button.

Nicolas' and Singleton's eyes met. Focusing hard, until his legs kick-started into a sprint.

"Mike, no!" came John's voice, wavering and unsteady.

It didn't take Nicolas more than a second for the darkness to take control of him once again. As if his whole body were possessed by some external force, his hand spun around, and his arm raised up to shoulder height.

Singleton stared down the barrel of the gun. Sweat poured off their temples, the tension in the air thick enough to cut with a knife.

A bang ruptured the air, and a spurt of blood showered Singleton's face.

Singleton looked down at his body, but there was no wound, not even a scratch, for the bullet had plunged straight into John's body instead of his.

45

Out of Time

John staggered, his hand clutching his side where the bullet cut through him. Blood seeped through his fingers, staining his clothes a deep crimson. He fell to his knees, his face contorted in pain.

"Dad!" Eleanor screamed, her voice filled with anguish. She tried to rush to his side, but Chris held her back, his grip firm.

"John! Why did you do that!" yelled Singleton, catching him in his arms and lowering him to the ground.

Nicolas's eyes widened in shock, the gun trembling in his hand. "No... no, this wasn't supposed to happen," he muttered, his voice breaking.

John looked up at him, his eyes filled with a mixture of pain and sorrow, "Nic...what have you done?" he gasped, his voice weak.

Nicolas' hand shook, the gun slipping from his grasp and clattering to the ground. Tears streamed down his face as he fell to his knees, his body wracked with sobs.

In the next moment, as if a thousand sighs of anguish had been injected into his blood, his eyes turned a furious red.

"This is all your fault!" he screamed, his voice filled with rage and aimed at Singleton.

The Dark Element buzzed ominously on his finger, black energy building up in full force.

"And it will be the last mistake you ever make."

A sudden burst of energy spiralled across the room, but it didn't come from Nyx. The light was green, like a fireball. In an instant, it crashed into Nyx's face, blinding him and sending him hurtling back into the remnants of the low-humming reactor.

With every last morsel of strength, John had focused all his remaining energy into the Time Element. But he didn't have the strength to hold on any longer. It was as if the Element had extinguished the last flame from his body.

As his head fell forward, the glow from the Time Element slowly faded in his hands, transforming back into an ordinary-looking pocket watch.

Eleanor broke free from Chris's grip and rushed to John's side, her hands trembling as she tried to staunch the flow of blood.

"Dad, look—*look at me*," Eleanor begged, her voice tight, thick with emotion. "Stay with me, please. *Stay with me.*"

John's breath was shallow, each inhale weaker than the last. His eyes fluttered open—just barely—as he struggled to remain conscious, his body limp against the ground.

"Eleanor..." His voice was barely more than a whisper, strained and fading. "You have to—stop the reactor... It's the only way..."

Eleanor clenched her teeth, shaking her head violently, refusing to accept the words.

"Save your breath," she pleaded, repositioning herself, trying *again* to lift him, to get him *out of here*. "We have to get you *help*—you *can't* stay here."

She hooked her arms beneath his shoulders, straining against the weight. Her muscles burned, trembling with effort, but no matter how hard she tried— she knew. She *knew* she wasn't strong enough.

But she refused to stop trying.

Blood dripped from his mouth, staining his lips red as he struggled to speak again, his voice barely audible beneath the alarms and the hum of the reactor.

"The truth..." His breath shuddered. "Is in the light."

Eleanor froze.

Her mind fought to process the words, fought to make *sense* of them.

The light?

Was he delirious?

Confused?

Had the rush of adrenaline from the shock damaged his ability to think?

"Dad—"

His eyes fluttered—

Then closed.

Gone.

The world shattered around Eleanor in an instant.

Screams tore from her throat, raw and broken, drowning out *every* other thought, every alarm, every sound in the room.

Singleton, standing over the reactor's controls, barely spared a glance in her direction. His jaw clenched as he fought against the urgency pressing down on him, his fingers hammering the final override sequence into the terminal.

A single, final slam of his fist against the emergency shutdown.

The reactor hummed one last time—

Then fell *silent*.

A dead, suffocating silence.

The heat still lingered, pressing into Eleanor's skin like fire, but the rhythmic vibrations beneath them—the constant threat pulsing within the chamber—had ceased.

But Eleanor—

Eleanor was *still*.

She didn't move.

Her knees pressed against the ground, her hands curled uselessly into fists, her body rigid, staring—*just staring*—at her father's lifeless frame.

The walls around them shuddered.

The power from the reactor—the containment energy keeping the radiation at bay—was *gone*.

The chamber was collapsing.

Chris's voice broke through the static of her thoughts, urgent, desperate, loud.

"Eleanor, we have to go!"

But she didn't move.

"No!" Her voice cracked, sharp, raw.

She could see Singleton by the reactor again, typing viciously at the screen. The blast from the Time Element which had sent Nicolas flying across the room had also hit the reactor. The wires sparked like fireworks compact inside a small tube – building up a mass of energy – ready to bring the entire structure crashing down upon them.

"I *can't* stop it now," he hissed, his eyes flashing toward the screen. "The emergency procedures have already been activated."

The terminal flickered—

'H-2100.'

Singleton's breath *hitched*.

"Oh, *crap*."

Chris turned sharply, catching the change in Singleton's expression.

"What does *H-2100* stand for?"

Singleton's fingers hesitated over the keyboard.

His eyes widened slightly, and his throat tightened.

"H stands for *Halon*," he answered, his voice clipped, his words coming faster, rushed, urgent. "It's a fire suppression system—it's going to *pull all the oxygen* out of the room to contain the explosion."

Chris's mouth parted slightly, blood draining from his face.

"All of the *oxygen*?" His voice wavered.

The next moment the engine began to rev. Something was happening. A sharp mechanical groan echoed through the room as the massive steel panels began sliding shut, locking them in, sealing them within the suffocating heat of the chamber.

Singleton *bolted* forward, urgency flashing across his face.

"*We need to go—NOW!*" he shouted, his voice barely cutting through the chaos.

Eleanor didn't move.

She didn't *hear* him.

She barely even registered the words.

The alarms blared—

The reactor shuddered—

Chris's voice broke through, ragged and frantic—

"*Eleanor! Eleanor!* Did you *hear that*? We're going to *die* if we stay here!"

The words landed—reached her ears—but they felt distant, disconnected, like something *floating* on the edges of consciousness.

She wanted to move—she *needed* to move—

But her limbs refused to move.

Her body rejected her mind's desperate commands, muscles locking in place—paralyzed, frozen, refusing to obey.

She couldn't tear her gaze away.

Away from the lifeless form lying before her.

Away from her father.

From John.

Gone.

Everything around her blurred into meaningless chaos—the crumbling ceiling, the crashing debris, the dust and shrapnel slicing through the air. None of it mattered.

Stopping the reactor didn't matter.

Nothing mattered.

Because Nyx had still won.

Her father was still dead.

And no force on Earth—not the Time Element, not fate, not anything—could change that.

A scream tore from her throat, raw and unrestrained, ripping through the chamber with such force that Singleton flinched.

Her voice shattered through the noise, desperate, agonized—filled with something so broken, so utterly destroyed, it hardly sounded human.

She couldn't leave him.

She wouldn't.

But then—

Arms wrapped around her. A firm grip yanked her backward.

Singleton grabbed her under the arms, pulling her forcefully, dragging her toward the exit with every ounce of strength he had left.

Her body fought against him, her heels digging into the ground, her hands clawing at the earth, struggling to break free. But it wasn't enough—her strength was nothing against the force hauling her away.

She lashed against him, furious, frantic—

But he wouldn't let go.

He wouldn't leave her behind.

And as the chamber collapsed around them—

As the walls buckled and the oxygen drained from the room—

Eleanor felt herself being ripped away from the only thing she had left and now even he was gone. She screamed again—

46

Paradox Again

S o many times, Eleanor had pictured her father's death, imagining his body dropping to the floor. But with every thought, she had still hoped that maybe there was a chance he could have been saved, that maybe he wasn't truly gone. But actually, watching her father lifeless body fall to the ground like a lead brick, carved away at her chest even more than she'd expected. The reality of his death hit her like a freight train, leaving her breathless and hollow inside – taking away every morsel of hope from her.

Eleanor believed she'd wake up from this nightmare at any moment. But with each passing second, time seemed to stretch into an eternity.

The sharp, piercing ring of alarms continued to reverberate through the maze-like corridors, the shrieking sound drilling into her skull with painful intensity. Every tunnel looked the same— twisting paths of stone and collapsing earth, thick with dust, void of familiarity—but Eleanor no longer cared. She was running on instinct, on raw determination, on a force much deeper than fear.

It felt as though *nothing* truly mattered anymore.

Her father was gone.

That truth settled inside her like wildfire, twisting and burning beneath her ribs, setting every nerve alight with unbearable fury.

She had spent a lifetime accepting his death—grieving, mourning, learning to live with it, carrying the weight of his absence through every moment. It had shaped her, carved itself into the very fabric of her existence, pressing against every breath, every choice, every fleeting moment of happiness.

But now—now that she knew the truth, now that she had seen it happen with her own eyes, now that she understood he had never been meant to die—her blood burned with a fury so fierce it threatened to consume her whole.

Not at Nyx.

Not even at Nicolas.

But at John.

It might have seemed strange at first, but the question gnawed at the edges of her mind, refusing to let go, sinking deeper with every passing second—why had he jumped in front of Singleton? Why had he taken the bullet? Why had he chosen to throw himself between danger and a man who was never meant to be saved?

John had been the one with a family, a future, a daughter.

Not Singleton.

John had had everything. A life worth protecting. A life worth fighting for. A life she had needed him to hold onto.

And he had thrown it away—just like that.

How could he have done that to her? How could he have chosen someone else over his own daughter? How could he have looked at her, known the sacrifices she had made, understood the depths of her love—and still decided that Singleton was worth saving more than he was?

But—

Even as her body fought against Singleton's grip, even as her mind screamed furious, blistering accusations, a part of her knew.

Her father had always risked everything to help the people around him. It was who he was, written into his soul, into the very fabric of his existence. He was selfless, reckless in his compassion, willing to sacrifice himself at any moment if it meant saving someone else.

Even if it wasn't always her.

Even if she had always wanted it to be her.

And that truth—unyielding, suffocating—pressed hard against her ribs, with a sense of admiration but tainted by the bitter sting of tears.

And the moment sensation returned to her legs, the moment she felt strength creeping back into her limbs, she forced herself forward, tearing free from Singleton's grasp.

He let go—not because he wanted to, not because he had accepted it—

But because exhaustion had caught up to him, because adrenaline had drained from his body, because Eleanor was moving now, breaking away, pulling herself forward.

But her heart—

Her heart ached.

Deep, agonizing pain settled into her bones, the kind of hurt that couldn't be reasoned with, the kind that *stayed*.

The tremors beneath them worsened.

The base was collapsing.

They ran faster, Singleton leading the way, pushing toward the fading glow in the distance—toward the exit, toward survival. But just before they reached the threshold—

A crack thundered through the chamber.

A massive slab of rock broke free from the ceiling, crashing down with an explosive burst of dust and debris which sealed off the tunnel.

The impact sent Eleanor *sprawling*, knocking Chris off his feet, trapping them both inside as the world crumbled around them.

For the first time, she felt the true weight of *helplessness* settle in. But just as she had started to lose all hope, as if by some miracle, a brilliant flash of light illuminated the crumbling tunnel. The air crackled with energy, and a swirling vortex of shimmering green colours materialised before them. The portal's edges glowed with an ethereal light, casting dancing shadows on the tunnel walls.

The surreal glow of the portal stood in stark contrast to the chaos unravelling around them.

It was Paradox who stepped through.

His figure was outlined by the radiant glow of the Time Element. He extended a hand towards Eleanor and Chris, his voice calm and reassuring amidst the chaos.

"Come with me, *quickly*," he urged, his voice deep, unwavering, cutting through the haze of destruction with an authority that left no room for hesitation.

But Eleanor *did* hesitate.

For the briefest of moments, she froze, her body locked in place, her mind torn between the portal—the only path to survival—and the doorway leading back to her father's lifeless body.

No one would ever know.

No one would ever *remember* what he had done—what he had *sacrificed* to save the world, to save them, to make sure *she* had a future.

The thought made her want to *scream*.

Made her want to tear reality apart with her own hands and *rewrite history herself*.

The ground beneath her shuddered violently, deep cracks splintering through the stone, and the roar of collapsing rock filled the air, deafening, suffocating, final.

She *had* to move.

She *had* to go.

Her heart *screamed* to stay, but her mind *knew better*.

She turned sharply—her fingers latching onto Chris's wrist—and with a single breath, a single movement, she *leaped*.

Together, they dove toward the portal, bodies tense, hands clasped, muscles coiled as the energy swallowed them whole—just as the tunnel behind them gave way, crashing down in an explosion of stone and dust, sending the remnants of the past into oblivion.

A sensation of weightlessness overtook them, consuming them, shifting their bodies into an undefined space where time was no longer linear, where reality blurred into streaks of colour and energy.

*

By the time the smoke cleared from Eleanor's eyes, they were back in the future. The familiar surroundings of their own time stood in stark contrast to the chaos they had left behind. She stumbled slightly, her legs weak from the adrenaline rush, and as she looked around, sunlight poured from above, washing over her with an overwhelming sense of relief. Being back in 2010 had never felt so good.

As the dust settled, the stone passageway stood sturdy before them, its ancient structure untouched by the chaos they had narrowly escaped. Cobwebs lined the ceiling, delicate strands hanging lazily in the dim light, the tunnels unchanged by their absence. It was as if time had reset itself—undoing their presence, their interference—erasing the mark they had left behind.

But then—

Her gaze drifted downward.

There, just a few inches from where she stood, the Time Element lay on the ground, its bronze casing face-up, catching the fading glow of the portal's energy. It had carried them back, had cast her, Chris, and even Nyx back into the correct timeline, ensuring that everything had returned to its rightful place.

The sound of heavy footsteps filled the tunnel, reverberating against the stone walls as armed officers charged through the entrance, descending upon them with practiced efficiency. Eleanor barely had time to register their presence before they surrounded them completely.

Chris stood beside her, weary, battered, his stance barely steady. And at their feet—

Nyx.

Unconscious.

The officers wasted no time.

Singleton followed closely behind, his pace quick, his expression unreadable as he crouched down beside Nyx's motionless form, snapping a pair of reinforced handcuffs around his wrists before gesturing for his men to move. The Order of Shadows was rounded up quickly, forced into position, escorted toward the exit with firm, practiced movements.

Eleanor remained still, watching the scene unfold with quiet, detached focus.

She noticed the way Singleton hesitated slightly as he scanned Nyx's body, his gaze flickering over his hand—his *bare* hand.

The Dark Element was missing.

Gone.

Nyx's features were already changing, the unnatural black seeping from his veins, his monstrous form melting back into something human, something fragile.

Eleanor's fingers curled into her pocket, brushing against the small lump where the ring resided.

It was *with her*.

She refused to touch it directly, refused to let the influence of its power reach her skin. She wondered—just briefly—if the Dark Element was strong enough to twist her emotions, to push her toward something unimaginable.

To make her *kill*.

And right now—

With Nyx standing before her, weakened, vulnerable, subdued—

She wasn't sure she *trusted* herself.

Swallowing thickly, she forced herself to move forward, kneeling carefully, her hands steady as she reached down to pick up the Time Element.

The weight of it felt different in her grasp now.

Not heavy. Not unbearable.

Just... *final*.

She barely had time to process the thought before a wave of dizziness crashed over her, forcing her to stumble.

Professor Dougan had arrived only moments earlier, her presence a blur in Eleanor's fading focus, but the second she wavered, her arms were around her, catching her in a full embrace and just about keeping her upright.

The officers moved fast, barking orders, focusing first on Eleanor and Chris, forcing them toward the tunnel's exit.

"Get them into *fresh air*," one of them instructed, voice firm, authoritative, unyielding.

Eleanor was barely aware of it, barely conscious of the force guiding her forward, of the hands gripping her arms, leading her toward safety. Her mind had already begun spinning, her stomach churning violently as the nausea took hold.

The moment she stepped into the sun's spotlight—

It was *too much*.

A painful, ugly sob wrenched from her throat as she *vomited*, her body rejecting everything at once—her grief, her exhaustion, the toxic influence of radiation poisoning, the weight of everything she had endured in the tunnels.

The others barely reacted.

They spoke of her condition as if it was inevitable—just another effect of prolonged exposure, just another symptom of being starved for clean air, water, light.

But they weren't *there*.

They hadn't seen her father *gutted* before her.

They hadn't *watched* him die.

Eleanor barely had time to wipe her mouth before she was passed to another officer, a harness strapped tightly around her waist.

Slowly, carefully, she was lifted upward, hoisted toward the sunlight that sparkled through the hole blasted open by the SWAT team.

The moment she emerged into open air, she was wrapped in a heat-preserving blanket, her body trembling as she struggled to adjust. As she watched from the sidelines, everything seemed to pass by in slow motion as Nyx and the surviving members of *The Order of Shadows* were loaded into the back of a dozen transport vans, their bodies pumped with high doses of Haldol—enough to tranquilise a horse.

The warmth of the sun pressed against Eleanor's skin, unfamiliar and almost *foreign* after so many hours—maybe days—trapped underground. The contrast between this open air and the suffocating pressure of the tunnels made her stomach churn. A part of her had convinced itself she would *never* feel sunlight again, that she would take her final breath beneath layers of rock and crumbling history. And yet—here she was. Alive. The sheer relief of it threatened to bring her to her knees, but another feeling kept her upright.

Grief.

She clutched the Time Element tightly in her trembling hands, its faint glow pulsing against her palm, a constant reminder of what it had cost her to wield its power. The weight of it was unbearable, heavier than she ever could have imagined. This object—the key to time itself—had pulled her back and forth across reality, had shown her things she never wanted to see, had rewritten destiny in ways she *wasn't ready to understand*.

But it couldn't bring *him* back.

Professor Dougan hovered beside her, a quiet presence amid the chaos. She gently placed a hand on Eleanor's shoulder, her voice low but steady, grounding her.

"You're safe now, Eleanor," she said, her words soft despite the storm of movement and noise around them.

Safe.

Was she?

Eleanor nodded weakly, not trusting herself to speak. Her body was still trembling, the lingering effects of adrenaline making her feel as though she was hovering between two realities—the fight, and the aftermath. The scene around her blurred slightly, her mind struggling to process everything at once.

The officers moved with swift precision, securing the area, checking the wounded, murmuring orders as they ensured nothing else had been left unchecked. Eleanor watched them with dull detachment, her gaze flickering over their sharp movements but never quite focusing on anything.

Singleton approached, his presence commanding as he surveyed the scene. He was exhausted—she could see it in his posture, in the tightness around his eyes—but there was something else there too. Relief.

"The Elements need to be secured," he said, his voice firm but lacking its usual edge. "They *must* be kept safe, away from anyone who might try to misuse them."

Eleanor inhaled deeply, her fingers still curled around the Time Element.

Her grip tightened briefly before she *forced* herself to release it, hesitating as she handed it over to Singleton. Then she reached into her pocket, her breath catching slightly as her fingers brushed against the small lump hidden within the fabric.

The Dark Element.

She didn't dare touch it directly, didn't want to *know* what it felt like against her skin.

Carefully, she slipped it into an evidence bag, ensuring it was completely sealed before passing it to Singleton.

"What will happen to Nyx?" she asked, barely above a whisper.

Singleton secured the bag, his expression unreadable as he straightened.

"He'll be taken to a maximum-security facility," he replied, his voice measured. "He won't be able to harm *anyone* ever again."

Eleanor wanted to believe that.

Wanted to believe that Nyx was *done*, that his influence had been erased, that his cruelty would *never* reach another person.

But she wasn't sure.

Could anyone really contain him?

Would *time* allow it?

Her thoughts drifted, hazy and unfocused, back to her father.

The image of him falling—

The way he had thrown himself in front of Singleton—

The way he had *chosen* to die, as if there had been no other choice.

Eleanor clenched her teeth, trying to *push* the thought aside, trying to tell herself that she would have time to grieve *later*. But deep down, she *knew*—there was no coming back from this.

No amount of time could rewrite what had just happened.

And now, in the most unexpected way, Singleton was the only person she *trusted* to protect the Elements.

Dougan stepped forward, gently guiding Eleanor toward the waiting ambulance.

Chris was already seated inside, his expression tight with exhaustion, his posture slumped as he tried to force himself to relax.

"Let's get you checked out by the medics," Dougan said, her tone gentle, coaxing. "You've been through a lot."

Eleanor barely registered the motion of the vehicle beneath her as it carried them away from the wreckage, away from the battle, away from everything that had led to this moment. The hum of the engine blended into the distant voices outside, a murmur of reality that felt impossibly far away. Her body was exhausted, every muscle weighed down by an aching fatigue she couldn't even begin to process.

She let her head fall back against the seat, her fingers curling weakly into her lap, trying—*failing*—to steady the racing of her pulse.

"It's over," she murmured, almost too softly to hear.

She wasn't sure who she was saying it to—herself, Chris, the universe—but the words carried no relief, no finality.

Just emptiness.

A hollow statement meant to convince her of something that felt unreal.

Her gaze flickered toward the window, watching as the scene of their fight faded into the distance, disappearing behind them like smoke dissolving into the air. It felt so surreal—like she had stepped out of time, like she was floating somewhere between existence and memory, unable to place herself back in the present.

Nyx's reign of destruction had finally come to an end. He was finally gone, but so too was her father. The victory felt tainted by the cost of what it had taken to get here.

She had always imagined that when this moment finally came—when she had fought her hardest against Nyx and won— that she would *feel* something. Satisfaction, closure—*anything*.

But she *didn't*.

She felt nothing at all.

The ambulance carried them around the perimeter of Bleakwood School, toward the hospital wing. It was equipped with everything necessary to treat their injuries, but that didn't stop Eleanor from silently cursing its location.

Ten flights of stairs.

Ten.

She had been here more times than she cared to count—last year, this year—and *still* she questioned what kind of idiot had decided that the hospital *needed* to be perched at the highest point in the school.

She could barely walk as it was.

Now she had to climb *ten floors* with a gash in her leg?

Brilliant.

Students had gathered near the entrance, their whispers rising in a wave as the medics helped Eleanor out of the vehicle. Eyes followed her every movement—some filled with awe, others clouded with concern.

Beyond the barricades, a cluster of reporters jostled for position, cameras flashing in rapid succession, the harsh white bursts cutting through the scene like strobe lights.

"Miss Walker! Miss Walker! Over here! Look this way!"

Their voices screeched over one another, desperate, insistent.

But for once, the attention didn't matter.

She *didn't care.*

She was numb to it all, barely even acknowledging the quiet gasps and hushed conversations as she moved forward, limply resting against the medics who supported her.

The moment she was guided to a free hospital bed, she sank down onto it, letting her body go completely limp.

Her thoughts drifted, blurred, detached.

The nurses worked efficiently, securing bandages, tending to wounds, pressing antiseptic against broken skin—but Eleanor barely felt any of it.

The pain in her leg didn't register.

The needles didn't register.

One injection for the pain, another for dehydration, a third for radiation poisoning—all explained in quiet, clinical voices Eleanor barely absorbed.

The voices outside the ward grew louder, swelling into something insistent—curious, questioning—but it all faded into a distant murmur, like static in the background of a half-forgotten dream.

A curtain was drawn across the window, dulling the movement beyond.

"You'll start feeling better soon," a nurse assured her, though the words barely broke through the fog clouding Eleanor's mind.

She didn't respond, didn't move, didn't *care.*

She was *so tired.*

So utterly, impossibly exhausted.

Until her gaze drifted to the other side of the room, landing on one of the occupied hospital beds.

Dr. Asterio was resting on his side, his arm bound in thick layers of gauze, a drip and a sling holding him together like a stitched-up doll.

He turned slightly, exhaustion weighing on his movements, but his presence remained steady, his eyes locking onto hers with quiet intensity. There was relief there, raw and undeniable, threading through his weary expression. "It's good to see you safe," he rasped, his voice rough but filled with sincerity.

Eleanor stared at him, the weight of everything settling in as if the world had finally stopped spinning. He knew. He knew everything. The battles she had fought, the moments she had clung to survival with everything she had, and the crushing reality of what she had lost. It was all there in his gaze—understanding, acknowledgment, and something deeper that she couldn't quite name. She swallowed hard, the ache in her chest pressing tighter, but she refused to let it consume her now. She had made it. He had made it. And despite everything, they were still standing.

"You did well."

The words were simple, but somehow, they carried a weight far beyond their meaning. They shattered something deep within her, peeling away the barriers she had built up, the silent defences she had clung to for so long. She forced a weak smile, nodding as she tried to hold herself together, to keep from unravelling completely.

"Thank you," she whispered, voice fragile but earnest. "For trying your best to protect me. I'm sorry you got caught in the crossfire..." She swallowed thickly, fighting against the heavy pull of emotion threatening to consume her, blinking rapidly to clear the sting in her eyes. "But I'm really glad to see you recovering."

Asterio gave a faint, tired smile, the warmth in his expression carrying something deeper than just words.

"You and me both," he murmured.

In the next breath the nurse who had been so attentive to Eleanor came rushing into sight and gestured the Dr back against the bedrest.

"That's enough talking for you," she said, her tone kind but unwavering, the authority in her voice leaving no room for argument. With a practiced flick of her wrist, she pulled the curtains between them, blocking him from Eleanor's view before shifting her attention fully to her.

"You need to get some *rest*," the nurse insisted, but Eleanor barely heard her.

Her gaze was already moving elsewhere, shifting toward the opposite side of the ward, where golden sunlight filtered through the window, spilling onto the floor in warm, uneven patches. She focused on it, on the way it illuminated the dust floating lazily in the air, on how surreal it felt to be *here*, in the present, in the light, after spending what felt like a lifetime trapped in darkness.

She hadn't truly believed she would see the sun again.

Had accepted, at some point—deep in the tunnels, lost in suffocating shadows—that she *might not make it back*.

It wasn't long before Chris was brought to the bed beside her. His movements were sluggish, weak, his breathing slow but steady—each inhale shallow, each exhale a quiet confirmation that *he was alive*.

For the first time since their return, Eleanor felt the aching urge to *speak*.

To tell someone—*anyone*—about what had happened, about everything she had seen, everything she had endured, everything she had lost.

But as she watched Chris sink into his bed, his body heavy with exhaustion, his mind slipping in and out of consciousness, she knew she couldn't.

Couldn't *disturb* him.

Couldn't *ask him* to relive it.

Just like her, he was too weak to fight the pull of exhaustion.

Too tired to confront the horrors they had barely escaped.

Eleanor let her gaze drift over him, inspecting every inch of his body in silence—the bruises around his wrists and arms, the swollen darkness beneath his eye, the raw, bloodied skin on his knees, the blisters that had torn open on his fingertips, red and angry.

Even his hair—usually wild and tangled—was stiff with dried blood, the strands clumped together at the ends where his fingers had twisted anxiously through them. It was a haunting sight, a stark reminder of everything he had endured. Eleanor couldn't begin to imagine what Nyx had done to him, how many hours he had spent trapped in captivity, subjected to whatever cruel torment Nyx had devised. There was no doubt that Nyx had dragged him to the very edge of death—not out of necessity, not as collateral damage, but for the sole purpose of hurting her. Of breaking her.

The door to the ward creaked open, the sudden noise slicing through the silence and sending ruptures of sound ricocheting through the room. Voices from the corridor spilled in, overlapping in chaotic layers, a disorienting flood of distant conversation and hurried movement. Eleanor flinched, her body tensing involuntarily as she became acutely aware of everything—the rustle of fabric, the clipped rhythm of footsteps, the hushed murmurs just beyond the threshold. She barely had time to process the intrusion before a familiar figure stepped inside.

Maddison.

Her face was a portrait of relief and concern, a mixture of emotions woven into every hurried step as she moved toward them. Her gaze flickered between Eleanor and Chris as she approached their beds, assessing them with quiet urgency, as though needing to confirm with her own eyes that they were truly there, still breathing, still whole. When she finally reached Eleanor's side, her voice was soft but charged with emotion, carrying the weight of everything unspoken.

"Eleanor. Chris."

Though her words were simple, her voice trembled slightly, barely held together beneath the strain of everything she was feeling. But there was no mistaking the sincerity in her tone. Eleanor barely hesitated. Reaching forward, she wrapped her arms around Maddison, holding onto her with more strength than she realized she still had, clinging to something real, something familiar. The embrace wasn't long enough. Would never be long enough. She hadn't known how desperately she needed it until now—needed proof that she was home, that she had survived, that this wasn't just another fleeting moment before the ground was ripped out from beneath her again.

When Maddison finally pulled away, she kept her hands on Eleanor's arms, her grip steady and grounding, holding her there, present in the moment. "I heard what happened," she whispered, blinking rapidly against the emotion threatening to spill over. "I heard everything. Are you both okay?"

Eleanor forced a weak smile, though it barely reached her eyes. "We're alive, Maddison," she murmured. "That's what matters."

Maddison nodded slowly, lips pressed into a tight line, her eyes glistening with unshed tears. She sank into the chair between their beds, her fingers reaching for Eleanor's hand, holding onto it with an urgency that mirrored Eleanor's own. "I was so worried about you both," she admitted, her voice thick with lingering anxiety. "Everyone said you were dead."

She swallowed hard, exhaling sharply as her grip tightened for just a moment, as though reassuring herself that they were real, that they were here. "But I knew they were wrong. I knew it couldn't be true."

She paused, collecting herself, forcing her breaths to steady even as her chest rose and fell with shallow control. "So, when I heard two students were being treated in the hospital ward... I had to come see you."

A soft, shaky laugh slipped past her lips, one that barely masked the raw emotion still caught in her throat. "I knew it could only be you."

Eleanor wanted to believe Maddison had been that certain. Wanted to trust that someone had never truly doubted her survival. But the truth was, there had been so many moments when she had thought she wouldn't make it—so many times when she had felt death reach for her, claw at her, whisper that it was ready to take her. And so many others hadn't been so lucky.

Not even Maddison's words could truly comfort her. After a while of awkwardly standing, she finally sat beside Eleanor, eyes flickering with thought, her fingers absentmindedly tracing the edge of the blanket draped over Eleanor's legs. "They say they'll need to build an entirely new facility just to contain all of Nyx's followers," she murmured, shaking her head. "I *still* can't believe he was able to gather so many so quickly."

Eleanor inhaled sharply, her chest rising with effort. Something about that statement sent a current of realization flickering through her mind, lighting up every nerve like a spark hitting dry wood. As she waited for the nurse to pass by, she turned ever so slightly toward Maddison, lowering her voice.

"The *Light Element*," Eleanor whispered, barely audible, placing a weak hand on Maddison's shoulder as she leaned closer.

Before she could finish, Maddison reached for her hand, squeezing it reassuringly, cutting her off with a quiet nod. "It's *safe*," she answered, firm and certain. "Don't worry. Although I wasn't much help to you down in the tunnels... I guarded it with my life."

Eleanor exhaled softly, attempting to smile, though the motion barely came through. Groaning slightly, she adjusted her posture, wincing as a sharp pain lanced through her shoulder.

Immediately, the nurse turned from the medical cart, catching the movement.

"Hey, *you*," she scolded, moving swiftly toward her bedside, pressing a steady hand against Eleanor's arm. "Sit *back down*."

She guided her carefully into position, ensuring she remained upright but still, her chest rising and falling with soft, controlled breaths. The nurse hovered for a moment longer, observing, before moving off again, tending to another patient.

Maddison hesitated, her fingers tightening slightly around the blanket in thought.

"There's just *one* thing that's still bugging me," she said, her eyes narrowing in deep concentration. "I *still* can't figure out why Nyx chose to target all the businesses funded by Decker Incorporated. For a man as smart and cunning as he, *that* was a big mistake."

The moment Maddison spoke those words, a sound—low, almost imperceptible—rippled through Eleanor's senses like the static charge of an impending storm.

Her instincts sharpened.

Her pulse slowed.

It was almost as if all the time spent wandering the tunnels had *heightened* her senses, fine-tuned them in ways she couldn't yet understand.

A sound came from behind.

"I believe I can help with that."

Eleanor turned her head just as Singleton emerged from the shadows of the doorway, his posture relaxed but his expression anything *but*.

"We found your missing contact - Mr Graham - from *The British Telegraph* tied up in the tunnels on the outskirts of Bleakwood town," he continued, stepping further into the room.

Maddison immediately perched at the edge of her seat, eyes widening in recognition.

"So, *I* was right..." she murmured, more to herself than anyone.

Singleton nodded. "It seems you were correct, *Miss Morningstar*. Nyx kidnapped him to cover his tracks—trying to stop anyone who could have warned us about his plan and about *The Order of Shadows*."

Chris stirred beside Eleanor, groggy but aware, his voice sluggish as he spoke.

"You mean his plan to *break into the school, kill Eleanor*, and *steal the Time Element*."

Eleanor's gaze darkened.

"Not to mention *kidnapping Maddison*," she added.

Singleton exhaled, nodding. "That *too*."

Chris sighed heavily, pressing his head against the pillow, exhaustion creeping into his bones.

"So... *we did it*."

His tired grin flickered through the dim light, brief but genuine.

"We *finally* won?"

Eleanor watched as Singleton's gaze remained hardened, the weight of unspoken thoughts pressing down on the room. And then, in a slow, creeping realization, she understood—it wasn't just her who felt it. The unease that lingered, the unfinished tension in the air, the sense that something wasn't quite right. She shifted uncomfortably, her fingers tightening around the fabric of her sleeve before she leaned forward slightly.

"Not entirely."

Chris shot her a wide-eyed stare, his posture stiffening. "What do you mean? We got Nyx. We got the Dark Element. We got all his followers."

Eleanor held his gaze for a moment, her thoughts sluggish under the haze of medication, yet still grasping onto the weight of their conversation. Even through the fog clouding her mind, she replayed everything they had just discussed—the certainty in Chris's voice, the unwavering conviction that it was finally over.

And yet—

"Did we?"

47

Loose Ends

In stark contrast to the chaos on the upper floors of the tower block, the first floor felt eerily quiet. The only sound coming from outside the headmaster's office were from two police officers stood nearby, their voices low and hushed. Singleton had personally ordered them to stand guard, ensuring that no one—*not a soul*—would enter the office without his express permission.

Their voices echoed softly against the stone walls, carrying snippets of their conversation.

"Are you *sure* it's safe to keep the Elements here?" one of them asked, his voice tight with unease, his brow furrowed deeply as he scanned the hallway, searching for any sign of movement.

"It's only temporary," the second officer replied with a measured calm, though the uncertainty in his expression betrayed his words. "While they get this whole mess cleared up. It's the most secure place we have right now."

Unbeknownst to them, lurking just beyond the sliver of light spilling from the hallway, a shadowed figure stood perfectly still, concealed within the depths of darkness. Their breath was slow, calculated, controlled—every inhale and exhale measured to blend seamlessly with the quiet of the corridor. They waited. *Listened.* Every word exchanged between the officers became fuel, knowledge, opportunity.

The first officer shifted slightly, a flicker of unease crossing his face. He glanced around, fingers instinctively brushing over the grip of his holstered weapon.

"Did you *hear* something?" he whispered, tension coiling through his posture.

The second officer scanned the hallway again, then shook his head.

"Probably just the wind," he muttered, though he didn't sound convinced. "Let's finish our rounds."

And with that, their footsteps retreated down the corridor, fading into nothingness.

The hidden figure remained unmoving for several long beats, listening as the last echoes of their presence vanished into the distance.

They stepped forward.

Silent as a phantom, gliding toward Singleton's office with the precision of someone who had done this *many times before*.

The heavy door creaked faintly as it was pushed open, but the figure barely hesitated, slipping inside with smooth, practiced motion, closing it quietly behind them.

Darkness greeted them—the office shrouded in shadow, save for the faint glow of moonlight filtering through the stained-glass window. It cast fractured rays across the grand desk, illuminating the edges of papers stacked neatly, books lining the far shelf, the elegant woodwork of the chair.

The figure wasted no time, moving swiftly and methodically, every motion calculated, every decision precise. Gloved hands rifled through the drawers with practiced efficiency, flipping through stacks of documents with sharp intent, eyes scanning each page before tossing aside anything deemed irrelevant. Papers fluttered to the floor, the soft rustle of pages brushing against one another barely audible in the stillness of the room. Books were pulled from the shelves, spines cracked open, covers inspected before being discarded in a growing pile of disregarded material.

And then, their gaze landed on something in the far corner of the room—a large, ornate chest, its intricate carvings catching the dim light in subtle relief. A beat passed as they hesitated, breath shallow, pulse quickening in anticipation. Slowly, cautiously, they approached, every step measured, heart hammering against their ribs as their fingers curled around the heavy latch. The metal was cold beneath their grip, but they wasted no time in flipping it open with a swift, practiced motion—

And immediately regretted it.

The unmistakable clank of metal snapped through the silence like a gunshot, reverberating in the quiet space as thick clasps locked around their wrists with brutal efficiency. The force was unexpected, almost violent, nearly yanking them downward with the sheer strength of its hold. Their breath hitched, pulse spiking as the realization set in.

Their hands—

Bolted together.

Frozen.

Trapped.

A slow, deliberate clap echoed through the room, the measured rhythm carrying a weight that sent a fresh surge of tension rippling through their body. The figure stiffened instantly, their muscles locking in place as an unmistakable presence made itself known.

They lifted their gaze sharply—

And met the unwavering stare of Eleanor.

She sat poised in Singleton's chair, utterly composed, her posture relaxed despite the unmistakable tension hanging thick in the air. Legs crossed, one arm resting lightly against the desk, a smirk tugging faintly at the edges of her lips, her expression was cool, unreadable, but undeniably amused. Her eyes gleamed with something sharp—calculated confidence, quiet amusement, a knowing edge that sent a fresh wave of dread coursing through their veins.

"Looking for something?" she asked, her voice smooth, even, laced with an unmistakable undertone of control.

The intruder's breath came in short heartbeat that began hammering violently against their chest.

It was Theo Decker who stared back at her. But Eleanor wasn't the slightest bit surprised. Inside, her smirk widened slightly and her head tilting as she studied him.

"So, *Theo*—" she drawled, her voice laced with cold amusement, "It seems you've been keeping a *rather* big secret from us. And—" she arched an eyebrow, "from your *parents* too."

The weight of her words *hung* between them, the silence stretching impossibly long before—

The door swung open.

Singleton stepped inside first, followed by Maddison, Chris, and the twins—Tom and Jenny—all wearing expressions of anticipation, their gazes landing immediately on Theo's bound wrists.

Tom grinned, slamming his palm against Jenny's in a triumphant high-five. "It worked!" he exclaimed, practically shaking.

But Theo—

Theo wasn't looking at the others. His eyes remained locked on Eleanor, unblinking, unmoving, as if the entire world had faded into the background, leaving only the two of them in this moment.

Maddison stepped forward slightly, arms crossed, her voice steady, deliberate. "We made a call to your family," she stated, watching him carefully.

Theo's body tensed, the shift in his posture subtle but unmistakable.

"They didn't even know you had transferred to Bleakwood School," Eleanor added, keeping her tone cool, unwavering. She met his gaze directly, searching for the smallest flicker of hesitation, any sign of weakness beneath his guarded expression. "I suppose you were right, though."

Theo swallowed, his throat working against the silence.

"They didn't even notice you were gone."

Eleanor exhaled quietly, shaking her head, her gaze never wavering. "I see how frustrating that must have been," she mused, studying him with careful scrutiny, tilting her head slightly. "Frustrating enough to make one do some... rather bad things."

Something shifted in Theo's expression.

His jaw clenched—his shoulders squared—his entire presence darkened, sharpened, charged with a quiet but undeniable intensity. His eyes burned, something dangerous flickering beneath the surface.

"You have no idea what it was like," he spat, voice lined with deep, embedded bitterness. "Day after day—being belittled, ignored, forgotten."

His fingers curled into fists, trembling slightly against the restraints, the tension in his body coiling tighter.

"How did you find Nyx?" Eleanor asked, her tone unreadable, her gaze fixed on him without a trace of emotion.

Theo's lips curled into a sharp, humourless smile.

"I didn't," he muttered.

Then—his eyes flashed.

"He found me."

Silence stretched between them, taut and suffocating.

"He could sense it," Theo continued, his voice rising slightly, charged with something raw, unfiltered. "My anger—my hatred—my desire for revenge against my family." His breath came in ragged bursts now, uneven, the strain of his past bleeding into the present. "But even then, they didn't pay attention to me."

Maddison scoffed, leaning back slightly, arms still folded. "Plenty of us have crummy childhoods," she stated bluntly, her voice sharp, cutting through the weight in the room. "Get over it. We don't all turn to helping psychopaths and forming a rebel army."

Theo's chest rose and fell in shallow bursts, each breath laced with fury, his entire being consumed by resentment that had festered over years, growing sharper, crueller, more irreparable with every wound left unhealed. He leaned forward, his body taut with barely restrained rage, his movements desperate, as though sheer force of will alone could undo the chains binding his wrists, as though his hatred was enough to set him free.

"It wasn't difficult to convince people to join my cause," he spat, his voice thick with venom, his words spilling out in rapid succession, raw and uncontrolled. "My family had been planning to cut funding to dozens of companies—businesses they had been entrusted to support, enterprises that had depended on them, believed in them, relied on them to keep their livelihoods secure."

His breath hitched slightly, but his glare remained unwavering, drilling into Eleanor as though she herself were responsible for everything he despised. "In a year—maybe less—those workers would have been left with nothing. No jobs. No security. Cast aside without a second thought because of people like them." He exhaled sharply, frustration crackling through his every movement. "And you wouldn't believe how quickly they came running to The Order of Shadows when I offered them something better."

His lips curled into a bitter smirk, dark amusement flickering in his eyes. "All I had to do was give them power—the ability to fight back, the chance to take revenge on the wealthy, the powerful, the ones who had built empires on their suffering and discarded them when they were no longer useful."

Eleanor studied him, expression unreadable, her posture poised, her fingers barely twitching against the desk as she processed his words. Her face remained calm—eerily so—though her mind burned with disgust, with frustration, with something sharp and unrelenting.

She exhaled slowly, her voice carrying no tremor, only cold calculation.

"You manipulated people at their most vulnerable point," she said, her tone slow and deliberate, biting down on every syllable. "You took advantage of their desperation, their grief, their anger, just so you could gather an army—just so you could have enough bodies to fight for your ridiculously childish cause." She tilted her head slightly, her gaze piercing, unforgiving. "Maybe I was *wrong*."

The air shifted around them.

Theo's face twitched, his jaw locking, his breath uneven.

Eleanor leaned forward, her voice sharper now, laced with something darker, something colder.

"Maybe Nyx *wasn't* the greatest monster."

Theo snapped.

A guttural, enraged noise ripped from his throat as he lunged forward, his face twisting in raw, unhinged fury.

"You don't *understand!*" he roared, his entire body straining against the officers holding him back, his muscles coiled with the force of his rage. "They *deserved* it! *They all deserved it!*"

Singleton barely hesitated.

His expression never changed, never shifted, never wavered. His voice was like ice.

"Take him away."

The officers came charging through the office doors and grabbed Theo, who struggled violently against their grip. His face was a mix of anger and defeat, his eyes wild and desperate.

"I'll get you for this. Mark my words—this isn't the last you've seen of me."

As the officers led Theo away, Maddison approach Eleanor, her expression a mix of curiosity and concern.

"Eleanor, how did you know Theo was working with Nyx?"

Eleanor smiled slightly. "It wasn't me," she began by saying, "It was you who helped me realise it."

Maddison looked shocked. "Me?"

"When you mentioned the connection with the Decker Incorporation, I thought back to the Halloween party, about how the mercenaries had known where to find me in Bleakwood school? Well, they would have needed someone on the inside. Someone who had been keeping a very close eye on me and someone who would have already known about the Elements because of their interest in rare historical artifacts."

There was a brief pause as Maddison processed this information.

"But I think the biggest tip-off was your dislike of Theo. And I learned a long time ago to always trust your instincts, Maddison," Eleanor added with a smile.

Singleton remained in the corridor outside his office, carefully watching the officers take Theo to the transport van. Meanwhile, the Chief Inspector approached him and began shaking his hand. Singelton accepted a shower of congratulation for his handling of the situation. Of course, Singleton didn't seem the slightest bit interested, keeping a stern and sour face. His eyebrows resting heavily across his forehead.

Eleanor waited for the conversation to end before her and the others approached him. The weight of everything that had happened pressed down on her, but she knew she needed answers. Taking in a deep breath, she gathered her thoughts. "Professor Singleton, what are we going to do with the Elements now?"

Singleton nodded, finally glad to get out of ear shot of the Chief Inspector. He lowered his voice some more, all so only Eleanor and the others could hear him, "We'll be working with a team of experts to find a secure location where they can be guarded and studied without posing any threat, ever again."

Eleanor's brow furrowed with concern. "Studied? Do you think that's a good idea?" She couldn't shake the memory of what happened to Nyx after spending too much time in contact with the Dark Element.

Nearby, Singleton stood in the dim corridor outside his office, watching as the officers led Theo toward the transport van. His gaze was unreadable, a mask of quiet contemplation, but there was a tension in his posture—something restrained. The Chief Inspector approached, clasping Singleton's hand in a firm shake, showering him with congratulations for how he'd handled the situation.

Singleton barely reacted, his expression remaining stern and unmoved, his heavy eyebrows drawn low across his forehead. He endured the praise but did not acknowledge it.

Eleanor waited patiently for the conversation to conclude, though the weight of everything that had transpired pressed against her with suffocating force. She took in a deep breath, steadying herself, before stepping forward with the others.

"Professor Singleton, what happens to the Elements now?"

Singleton nodded, eager to put distance between himself and the Chief Inspector. His voice dropped lower, careful, meant only for Eleanor and those at her side.

"We'll be working with a specialized team to locate a secure facility—a place where they can be protected and studied without posing any further threat. Ever again."

Eleanor frowned. "Studied?" The memory of Nyx flooded her mind—of the Dark Element's overwhelming influence. "Are you sure that's wise?"

Singleton's gaze softened slightly as he met her eyes. "Only electronically. No physical interaction. We need to ensure that Nyx's connection to the Dark Element has been truly severed." He was firm, resolute. "No human contact will ever be made with it again—not until we fully understand its nature."

Eleanor inhaled deeply, her thoughts racing with the gravity of the decision. The Dark Element was too volatile, too dangerous. But at this moment, she could see no better alternative.

She exhaled slowly, nodding. "I suppose that's the best we can do for now." Her voice carried a quiet resignation, but beneath it, a spark of something fragile—hope.

Singleton leaned in slightly, ensuring his next words reached only Eleanor's ears.

"I know you've never liked me, Eleanor." His tone was steady, even thoughtful. "And I can't blame you. I built a reputation for keeping my distance. But after learning you had lost your father—and knowing I was high on Nyx's list for revenge—I thought it best to distance myself from everyone. I convinced myself it was the only way to keep you safe. Over time, I suppose I became the persona I created."

His voice dropped to the quietest whisper. "And for what it's worth—I know how much your father meant to you. His sacrifice won't be forgotten. Even if I can never repay my debt to him."

His eyes held hers for a lingering moment, unreadable, questioning.

"Don't you agree, Eleanor?"

Her stomach twisted at the sound of her first name on his lips.

Did he know?

Had he remembered their encounter from 1996?

Yet, as Eleanor thought about it more, she realised—perhaps it didn't matter. Perhaps, sometimes, certain truths were never meant to be fully answered. Because, in some ways, it felt good to wonder. And in others—it felt good to still hope.

48

Choices

'We all make our own choices ...

It was a quote from Eleanor's favourite book as a child—something about carving your own path. She had always believed in it. But sitting alone in the sterile quiet of the hospital ward, staring out the window at the sports field below, she couldn't help but feel how deeply people's lives were connected. Fate, timing, consequence—they weren't separate. They were tangled threads, woven invisibly between everyone she loved.

She knew Maddison would be out there in the crowd, bundled up for the cold, waiting to see Chris and Dan play in the final match of the season. The stands were already filling, the buzz of anticipation floating up through the cold morning air.

Everyone would be there—except Eleanor.

Her chest tightened. She had promised Chris she'd come. And she intended to keep that promise.

Glancing toward the door, she saw that the nurse had left. A small pocket of freedom.

Carefully, Eleanor pushed the blankets aside. Pain flared through her muscles, sharp and hot, but she clenched her jaw and kept moving. She wouldn't let it stop her.

She reached for her coat and scarf, wrapping them close, and slipped into the hallway. The hospital was awake now—nurses moving swiftly, voices low behind curtains—but Eleanor walked with confidence. Not one person looked twice.

The moment she stepped outside, the cold hit her like a force of nature, the sharp gust of winter wind stealing the breath from her lungs. For a second, she faltered, but as she inhaled deeply, allowing the crisp, icy air to ground her, she pressed forward. The sports field stretched before her, glistening with a thin veil of frost that shimmered under the low-hanging sun, and in the stands, students and staff huddled together beneath thick scarves and woollen hats, their exhalations drifting in the frigid air like wisps of fog.

Just as planned, Maddison was waiting at the top of the spectators' stand, a spare seat saved beside her, and when Eleanor finally reached her, she slid into the spot without hesitation. They pressed close, seeking warmth from each other, their excitement mounting as the match began to unfold.

Chris and Dan took to the field with a confidence that could only come from unwavering trust—the kind built through countless hours of training, through trial and triumph, through frustration and perseverance. They moved in perfect synchrony, reading each other's movements with unspoken understanding, countering their opponents not with brute force, but with clever strategy, each pass calculated, each play executed with precision. Chris, his reflexes sharp, his instincts keener than ever, intercepted passes with ease, setting up opportunities that Dan capitalized on without hesitation—his raw strength and accuracy proving a formidable advantage as he sent shot after shot sailing past defenders.

Eleanor felt her chest swell with pride, her gaze locked onto Chris as he orchestrated another flawless setup—one that had taken months to refine, hours of practice, endless determination. She could still recall the late-night drills, the countless moments of frustration, the exhausted sighs that came right before breakthroughs. And now, here he was, proving exactly how far they had come.

Beside her, Maddison nudged her with an elbow, a wide grin splitting her face. "Look at them go! They're unstoppable."

Eleanor barely tore her eyes from the game, her smile growing. "Yeah," she murmured, "they really are."

The match grew fiercer with every passing minute, the competition intensifying as both teams pushed themselves to their limits. The stands erupted into cheers and groans with every move—waves of emotion rolling through the crowd as tension built. Bleakwood's supporters, wrapped in blue and silver, screamed encouragement, their scarves and face paint marking their allegiance, while the opposing team's fans, clad in crimson and gold, answered with their own raucous chants. The entire stadium vibrated with energy, the rivalry palpable, electric.

Chris darted across the field, eyes locked on the ball as he intercepted a pass with a deft flick of his wrist. He scanned his surroundings swiftly, calculating his next move before spotting Dan in position, ready and waiting near the goal. Without hesitation, he sent the ball sailing toward him—precise, clean, effortless.

Dan caught it with ease, his grip firm, his gaze locked on the defender standing between him and victory. A heartbeat of silence passed before he dodged, sidestepping the challenge with fluid grace, his focus unwavering. And then—he struck, the ball launching toward the net with all the force he could muster.

The goalkeeper lunged.

But it was too late.

The ball slammed into the back of the net.

For a second, silence hung in the air—then the stadium exploded into cheers. The roar of the crowd swallowed everything else, a sea of voices rising in celebration. Eleanor and Maddison jumped to their feet, shouting with unbridled excitement, hands clapping, arms raised in triumph.

"Yes! Go, Dan!" Maddison yelled, though her voice was barely distinguishable amidst the deafening rush of applause.

Eleanor beamed, watching as Dan turned to Chris, their grins matching, their fists meeting in a triumphant gesture.

he opposing team regrouped with unwavering determination, their frustration palpable as they pushed forward with renewed urgency, every player laser-focused on evening the score before the clock ran out. They launched a relentless counterattack, their movements sharp, precise, and calculated, passing the ball swiftly between them as they tore through midfield, their aggression ramping up with every second that ticked away.

Chris and Dan instinctively dropped into defensive positions, their bodies tense, their eyes locked onto the ball, reading the opposing team's movements with practiced precision, waiting for the right moment to strike. The ball shifted possession several times in rapid succession, neither team willing to relinquish control, the tension thickening as players clashed, feet skidding against the frosted grass, sticks colliding, the sharp sound cutting through the crisp winter air.

With only minutes remaining, the opposing team finally broke through the defence, their star player surging forward, his eyes locked on the goal, his speed unrelenting. Chris reacted instantly, adrenaline coursing through him as he sprinted toward the charging player, his heart hammering against his ribcage. He reached him just in time, his body moving purely on instinct, lowering his stick for a perfectly timed block—just as the opposing player pulled back for the shot.

The ball ricocheted off Chris's stick with force, bouncing wildly before landing near Dan, who wasted no time seizing the opportunity. He scooped it up with expert precision, his grip firm, his stance unwavering, then bolted down the field, weaving through defenders, his strides long and powerful, his breath visible in the cold air. The crowd collectively inhaled, the tension suffocating as he neared the goal, closing the final distance with an explosive burst of speed.

The opposing players lunged, desperate to stop him, but Dan was already airborne, his body twisting in mid-leap as he launched the ball toward the net, his movements sharp, fluid, unstoppable.

The goalkeeper dove, arms outstretched.

But the ball slipped past his fingertips.

And then—it hit the back of the net.

A split second of stunned silence filled the air before the stadium erupted, the stands transforming into a sea of frenzied applause and deafening cheers, voices colliding into a roar of triumph that reverberated across the field. Eleanor and Maddison leapt to their feet, arms thrown around each other in exhilaration, their faces flushed with pride. Chris and Dan sprinted toward the stands, their expressions alight with the thrill of victory, their excitement buzzing through every fibre of their being.

Suddenly, their teammates swarmed the field, lifting Chris onto their shoulders, chanting his name as he raised his arms high above them, soaking in the moment, letting it crash over him in waves of pure, unfiltered joy.

Later, when the energy of celebration became overwhelming, Eleanor and Chris slipped away, weaving through the lingering crowds until they reached the familiar solitude of the cliff top—a sacred space between them, a quiet retreat overlooking the town, far removed from the deafening commotion below.

The night stretched endlessly above them, vast and unblemished, the stars flickering softly against the dark canvas of the sky, their reflection dancing over the glistening water below.

They unfurled a thick blanket, settling into the cold earth as they pulled open a steaming box of pizza, the scent of melted cheese and warm dough curling into the crisp night air. Chris cracked open two cans of pop, the fizz bursting out with a satisfying hiss.

"To victory," he said, raising his can toward her.

Eleanor smirked, tapping hers against his. "To victory."

As she sank her teeth into the crispy edge of the crust, the contrast was almost overwhelming—the warmth, the richness of flavours exploding against her tongue. After days of hospital meals, bland broths, hydration drips that tasted of nothing, the sheer indulgence of pepperoni-spiced oil and buttery dough was like a feast she hadn't realized she'd been craving.

"I can't believe you snuck out of the hospital ward just to watch me play," Chris said through a mouthful of pizza, amusement glinting in his eyes.

Eleanor shrugged, nudging him lightly. "I wasn't about to miss your first match, Chris—who do you think I am?" She took another bite, ignoring the growing certainty that the nurse was going to murder her the moment she got back. "Still, she's going to lose it when she finds out I've been eating all this salty food. She's been hooking me up to a hydration drip all week, trying to get my levels back to normal..."

She chased her words with a mouthful of pop, the carbonation fizzing wildly against her tongue, like a thousand firecrackers bursting in tiny waves.

"...Still, it's worth it."

The crust was everything she'd been missing—golden, crisp on the outside yet impossibly soft on the inside, yielding with every bite, releasing an explosion of rich tomato sauce and creamy, melted cheese. The pepperoni packed just enough spice, the mushrooms added a layer of earthy depth, and the bell peppers cut through with their bright, crisp sweetness—a perfect balance of flavours that she savoured like it was the last real meal she would ever have.

The breeze rustled through the trees, carrying the scent of pine and damp soil, a grounding contrast to the warmth curling in her chest.

She looked down at the glimmering pool of water below, the stars mirrored in its surface like fragments of light scattered across a quiet expanse.

In one hand, she held the Light Element, its soft, unwavering glow illuminating their faces.

The other rested gently against the frost-kissed blades of grass atop the cliff.

The two more volatile, unpredictable Elements had been taken somewhere—somewhere secure, somewhere unknown even to her. Singleton had ensured that. But the Light Element had remained with her, an exception granted after weeks of careful practice, control, understanding. He had seen no harm in letting her keep it—better here, in her hands, than locked away in some vault collecting dust.

She turned it over in her palm, watching as its golden light pulsed gently, steady, certain.

It felt like something she could trust.

With a single, focused thought, she reached for the Light Element, coaxing its energy to life, shaping it with precision and quiet intent. The constellations above seemed to stir, shifting within the vast expanse, unravelling into something new— something living. A majestic lion prowled through the heavens, its silent roar rippling through the stars like distant thunder. A swan, its wings stretched wide, drifted effortlessly across the night, its movements fluid, graceful, ethereal. And then, a playful dolphin leapt from one constellation to the next, weightless, unhindered, basking in the celestial glow.

Chris sat frozen, watching the spectacle unfold before him, his eyes wide with awe.

"That's incredible," he murmured, his voice laced with quiet wonder. "You really have a gift, Eleanor."

She smiled, the luminous light reflected in her irises, casting them in soft gold. For a long while, neither of them spoke, content to sit in the quiet, watching as the constellations twisted and shifted above, their movements effortless, eternal.

Then, Chris shifted, turning to her with an expression that was more thoughtful, more deliberate than before.

"Can I ask you something personal?"

Eleanor glanced at him, nodded without hesitation. "Of course, Chris. What is it?"

He hesitated, exhaling slowly, his fingers tightening slightly around the fabric of the blanket beneath them. "Why are you so close to me?" His voice was careful, cautious, layered with something unspoken. "I mean, you've always been there for me, even when I felt like I didn't deserve it. Why?"

Her smile softened, though something flickered behind her gaze—something quiet, knowing. She glanced down at the Light Element resting in her palm, watching as it pulsed gently.

"Because you matter to me, Chris." Her tone was steady, unwavering. "You've always been there for me too, even when things got impossible. You've shown me kindness when I needed it most, loyalty when I doubted everything—and I value that more than anything." She paused, searching his expression. "Where is this coming from?"

Chris dropped his gaze. His hesitation, the tension in his posture—it was answer enough.

"It was Nyx, wasn't it?" Eleanor's voice was quieter now, edged with certainty. "What did he tell you?"

Chris swallowed hard, his jaw tightening slightly. "You know how he works. How he can—" He exhaled sharply, shaking his head. "Coax out the fear in people. That's what the Dark Element does." He paused, his throat tightening around the next words. "But he wasn't wrong. Maybe I've always wondered why you ever needed me. Because every time you were in danger, I was always—" He hesitated. "A liability."

Eleanor's brow furrowed, but Chris kept going, his voice lower now. "If I hadn't gotten grabbed in 1996—if I hadn't been there distracting you—maybe then, your father would still be alive."

Eleanor shook her head before he had even finished speaking.

"Nyx was wrong," she said firmly. "You, Maddison, the twins— you're the only normal thing in my life. The only thing that's kept me going."

Chris looked at her, his expression tense, his body unreadable. "Eleanor..."

She held up a hand, stopping him gently. "You don't have to say anything, I already know."

"No." Chris's voice was quiet but resolute. "I have to say it. I need to know that I said it."

Their gazes locked, unbreaking, heavy with everything unsaid.

"I'm proud of you, Eleanor." His voice was barely above a whisper now. "I'm proud of us. And I can't imagine my life without you in it."

Something shifted in Eleanor then, something deep, something warm. She reached forward, taking his hand in hers, giving it a gentle squeeze.

"You too."

For a long while, they sat in silence, letting the weight of the words settle around them, thick and certain. Above, the constellations still swirled in their silent dance, casting shifting beams of light across the cliffside, bathing them in a golden glow.

Then, Eleanor moved, reaching for the book beside her and pressing it into Chris's hands.

"Here."

Chris frowned. "What for? You know it doesn't work with me—I'm not like you, Eleanor."

"I think you don't give yourself enough credit." Her tone held something quiet, something sure. "Just try."

Chris hesitated, then took the book, running his fingers along the edges of its worn pages, studying it carefully.

"I want you to focus on the Light Element," Eleanor explained, her voice steady. "Clear your mind. Let yourself connect with its energy."

Chris inhaled deeply, shutting his eyes, his expression tightening in concentration. Eleanor watched him closely, searching for signs—for something, anything.

"Now, imagine the light flowing through you," she continued, her voice gentle, coaxing. "Picture it as a warm, golden glow, filling every part of your being."

Chris's brow furrowed, his fingers twitching slightly around the pages of the book. Eleanor reached forward, resting her hand atop his.

"You're doing great," she whispered. "Now, try to create an image in your mind. Something simple—a bird, a flower. Something that brings you happiness."

Chris exhaled sharply, his body stiff with effort. Then— something flickered.

A faint, transparent image materialised between them—not as strong, not as defined as Eleanor's, but still there, still *something*.

Eleanor's breath hitched in excitement.

"Chris, you did it!" Eleanor's voice was alive with elation, her eyes locked on the shimmering beam of light hovering between them. "Now focus harder—let the memory fill you until it's bursting inside you."

Chris opened his eyes, watching as the energy flickered like a restless ember, electric blue and pulsing with uncertainty, struggling to take full shape.

"What memory did you focus on?" Eleanor asked, curiosity sparking in her voice.

Chris grinned, the image above them gradually sharpening, gaining form.

"Do you remember the first time we met?"

Eleanor let out a laugh, shaking her head. "How could I forget? You turned up on your first day wearing nothing but your underwear and one of Maddison's skirts."

Chris groaned, though amusement danced behind his expression. "Hey! The twins had just dropped a raccoon into my bedroom, and it shredded every pair of trousers I owned. What was I supposed to do?"

Eleanor erupted into laughter as the hazy image above them shifted, taking on the distinct shape of a small, wild-eyed raccoon—its fur bristling as if caught mid-chaos. Chris stared up at it, snorting as he recalled the sheer madness of that morning.

For a moment, the two continued laughing, the weight of everything momentarily forgotten, until the glow of the Light Element dimmed once more, its energy settling into quiet. Chris sighed, handing it back to Eleanor.

Then, his expression grew more serious.

"Do you think our lives will ever go back to normal?" he asked, his voice laced with uncertainty. "Now that Nyx is locked up and the Order of Shadows is gone?"

Eleanor sighed, her gaze drifting to the horizon. "I don't know, Chris. We've seen and done things that have changed us forever. I don't think we can ever go back to the way things were before."

Chris nodded, his expression thoughtful. But maybe that's okay. Maybe they could find a new kind of normal. One where they could still make a difference but also find some sort of peace.

Eleanor smiled, squeezing his hand gently. "I like the sound of that," feeling a sense of comfort in the word, before her expression grew serious. "But you know, now that the world knows all about the Element, it's going to draw more threats to Bleakwood."

This once small and cosy town would become a beacon for the strange and supernatural. Or at the very least, reporters and tourists, looking to get a piece of the fame and glory.

"But we stopped Nyx, the Elements are securely locked away. Surely, the threats over, right?" Chris asked, his voice tinged with hope.

Eleanor wasn't certain. "We can never know for sure. And I have the strangest feeling."

"What feeling?" Chris asked, listening intently.

"... something is coming," Eleanor said, her heart skipping a beat. The words hung in the air, heavy with foreboding.

Chris squeezed her hand tighter. "Well, screw the future. Whatever happens, whatever the future has in store, I am right here beside you, every step of the way. You are never alone."

Eleanor's heart plummeted as a shiver danced across the shimmering surface of the water like quicksilver. In the corner of her eye, she sensed the presence. She didn't need to turn around to know she was being watched—by none other than her own reflection. Despite Chris's unwavering support, the weight of the secret she had carried all her life pressed down on her like a millstone.

Each day that she kept this to herself, the secret gnawed away at her, burning like an unextinguished fire. Ignoring it only made the visions more frequent, more vivid. One day, perhaps soon, she wouldn't be able to go a moment without seeing the sinister stare of her reflection in every reflective surface.

"Do you really believe in premonitions?" Eleanor asked, her voice barely more than a whisper.

"I suppose, given everything I've seen, I'd believe anything," Chris replied, his tone contemplative.

Eleanor paused, her thoughts a tangled web. The urge to unburden herself was overwhelming, but she didn't know where to begin.

"Chris..." she started tentatively. Was this the right moment? But the words flowed out of her, unbidden. "...there is something I need to tell you."

Chris looked up, his curiosity piqued. There was no turning back now. She had to do it—she had to lift this weight from her shoulders.

"Eleanor, whatever it is, you can trust me." Chris' eyes widened, a mix of concern and eagerness etched on his face.

Only now did she begin to understand why Dr. Asterio and Singleton had kept so many secrets from her—secrets about her father, and about the Elements. Carrying such a burden required a strength beyond mere physicality.

But with Nyx finally locked away, she had no more excuses. The truth had to come out.

Eleanor took a deep breath, her heart pounding in her chest. She glanced at her reflection in the water, its eyes gleaming with a knowing light. No hesitation—she poured out everything to Chris about the voice inside her head. And for once, after everything they had witnessed, Eleanor didn't seem so crazy after all.

As the words left her mouth, Eleanor felt a wave of relief wash over her. When she finished, he reached out and took her hand, squeezing it gently.

"Eleanor, I believe you," he said, his voice steady.

"And I'm here for you, no matter what."

Eleanor smiled, feeling a sense of comfort in his words. But deep down, a nagging feeling of guilt gnawed at her. She had put Chris in danger yet again. What if next time they weren't so lucky?

"Chris," she said, her voice trembling slightly. "I'm sorry for putting you in danger, yet again, and although I'm relieved, we both got out of it mostly unharmed," she swallowed back a tough taste in her mouth, "I can't help but wonder if next time we'll be so lucky."

Chris shook his head.

"Eleanor, you didn't put me in danger. It was an accident. WE both fell into those tunnels together. I chose to stand by your side. I went into the fight with my eyes wide open to the danger. Like I said, we're in this together. And that means we'll face whatever comes our way, together."

Eleanor nodded, but the guilt still lingered. "I want to teach you as much as I can about how to use the Light Element. In case one day you need to use it to protect yourself."

Chris looked at her, his expression serious. "I'd like that."

Eleanor smiled, feeling her chest lighten like a feather drifting effortlessly through the wind. Her mind surrendered the weight of responsibility. "We'll face whatever the future holds, together."

Chris's smile mirrored hers, and he leaned back to gaze up at the sky. "Together."

49

Shadows

One week later...

... There was no denying the Elements now. Once thought to be nothing more than myths—whispers of ancient legends—had proven themselves undeniably real. The past few weeks had left an indelible mark on everyone who had been swept into their chaos, changing their lives forever. The truth about the supernatural was no longer something that could be brushed aside, not even by the most disbelieving. Even Chris's parents, who had once dismissed his warnings as paranoia or exaggeration, had been forced to face reality. The moment they heard the news, they booked the first flight back to England.

But now, it was Chris's decision whether he wanted to see them.

Eleanor knew him well enough to be certain—he wouldn't ignore them forever. It wasn't in his nature to hold grudges long-term. Still, for now, he avoided the topic, brushing it aside whenever Maddison brought it up. Eleanor understood why. After everything that had happened within her own family, she knew what it felt like to wrestle with the idea of forgiveness. And yet, alienating his parents wasn't something she would wish upon anyone.

The thought lingered in her mind as she wondered whether it was time to reach out to her own family.

What if they didn't want to hear from her?

What if they had already forgotten her?

A part of her felt unready. She wasn't sure if she wanted to forgive them—not yet. Maybe not ever.

Still, Christmas at Bleakwood School was something worth celebrating.

All her friends were there. She had been discharged from the hospital just a week ago, and the first thing she'd done—without hesitation—was devour the biggest ice cream imaginable. A moment of pure indulgence after weeks of bland hospital food. The nurse had scolded her afterward, reminding her that her body was still weak from the radiation exposure and that she wasn't in any condition to be traveling far.

But that didn't mean they couldn't have fun right where they were.

The twins burst into the room, their faces alight with excitement, hauling a box of homemade Christmas crackers. A grand tree stood by the fireplace, its decorations gleaming in the flickering firelight, while streamers hung loosely from the ceiling, adding a festive charm to the space. Christmas music hummed softly from Chris's new record player—a high-end, expensive piece, courtesy of his parents. They were still trying to make up for their disbelief, for the way they had ignored everything he had warned them about. Perhaps, Eleanor thought, he would finally speak to them. After all, Christmas was the season of forgiveness.

But first—movies.

Eleanor, Chris, Maddison, and the twins all gathered on the worn yet impossibly comfortable sofa, nestled beneath thick blankets. The room smelled of pine needles from the tree, blending with the rich aroma of hot cocoa and the distinct sharpness of eggnog—courtesy of Maddison, who had managed to sneak a couple of bottles from her parents' wine cellar.

The fire crackled, casting long shadows against the walls, adding to the warmth of the moment.

Then—a knock at the door.

The sound cut through the cozy atmosphere, drawing the group's attention.

"What now?" Maddison groaned, already irritated by the interruption.

"It's okay, I'll get it." Eleanor stood, moving toward the door and pulling it open.

Nothing.

Just the soft flurries of snow drifting through the crisp night air.

She frowned, lowering her gaze—and there, sitting neatly on the doormat, was a white, sealed envelope.

"What's that?" Chris asked, leaning forward to get a better look.

"A letter, apparently." Eleanor picked it up, turning it over in her hands.

"Who's it from?"

She scanned the front. "Dr. Asterio. He's asking me to meet him in his office."

"What? *Now*?" Chris exclaimed. "We're just about to open the chocolates and biscuits!" He gestured dramatically toward the tray of chocolate mints Maddison had laid out on the table.

Eleanor sighed, giving him a reassuring look. "I won't be gone long. Just start without me, I'm sure it's nothing."

The walk to Dr. Asterio's classroom was slower than expected, her limbs still not used to exertion after weeks of bedrest. She wasn't surprised that he wanted to talk. They had barely had a chance to properly discuss everything that had happened—Nyx, the Elements, the Order of Shadows. There was too much left unspoken, too much unfinished.

But when she finally stepped into the dimly lit room, she didn't find Dr. Asterio.

She found *Paradox*.

Eleanor stiffened, her fingers tightening instinctively around the edges of the envelope.

"You?" Her voice held a mix of confusion and frustration.

Paradox nodded, his expression sincere. "I'm sorry to have asked you here under false pretences."

Eleanor's eyes narrowed, suspicion crawling up her spine. "I thought you couldn't interfere in the present." There was an edge to her tone now—bitterness, distrust.

Paradox exhaled, looking at her carefully before speaking.

"Your father was smart enough to write three letters before going into the tunnels with you." Paradox's voice was steady, measured, but Eleanor could sense the weight behind it— something hesitant, something unresolved.

"One was addressed to me. Another to your mother."

He paused, exhaling softly, before holding out an envelope between his fingers, his gaze meeting hers halfway.

"And this one—this one was for you."

The words struck her like an echo from a dream, distorted at the edges, distant, as if spoken from somewhere impossibly far away. The simple act of seeing it—her father's handwriting scrawled across the front—sent a slow, creeping unease through her veins, chilling her from the inside out. It wasn't just the envelope itself, or the weight it carried—it was the impossible reality of its existence, the undeniable proof that some part of him had reached through time to leave this behind.

LOST IN TIME

She reached for it, fingers brushing against the paper before curling carefully around its edges, the texture rough yet familiar beneath her touch. But the moment it was in her grasp, doubt seeped in, settling deep in her chest. It didn't feel real. It didn't feel possible.

Paradox hesitated, watching her, his expression unreadable, his presence suddenly smaller, like a shadow shrinking under fading light. "I should have given it to you a long time ago, but—" His voice faltered, cracking in a way Eleanor had never heard before. A rare, fleeting break in his carefully composed exterior. "—I was afraid."

Eleanor barely registered his words. They hovered at the edge of her mind, slipping through the cracks of her focus, drowned beneath the weight of the envelope in her hands. Her fingers trembled as she carefully slid them beneath the seal, pressing against the paper, feeling the fragile resistance beneath her touch.

Its weight was unmistakable. Its finality, undeniable.

And then, slowly—deliberately—she began to open it.

Dear Eleanor,

If you are reading this letter, it means something has happened to me…

Eleanor felt the weight of the words sink into her chest like cold stone. A lump formed at the back of her throat, thick and unrelenting. She wasn't sure she could go on reading—wasn't sure she *wanted* to—but her eyes moved instinctively, grazing over the ink-stained paper, landing on the next few words.

Her father had known.

Deep down, he must have known he wouldn't make it out of those tunnels.

...I'm sorry I won't be there for you growing up.

The world seemed to blur, tears pricking at her vision, threatening to spill over. Still, she forced herself to continue, despite the ache tightening in her chest.

... I couldn't be prouder.

But then, as she reached the final lines, the tone changed entirely.

She read the words aloud, as if hearing them would bring some understanding.

... there is great good in the Elements ...
... but there is a darkness about them.
... Beware, my dear Eleanor, because even in the light there are shadows.

Paradox remained still, silent, watching her carefully. Eleanor stared at the letter, her fingers gripping the paper tightly, her pulse thrumming beneath her skin. What did he mean? Had her father left this as a warning? If these were his last words, surely he would have given her more—something concrete, something useful. Yet all she had were these cryptic phrases, these inked fragments that felt more like riddles than guidance.

She read it again. Then again. Focusing on every detail, every stroke of ink, every letter, as if searching for something hidden between the lines.

"Shadows in light?" she murmured, the words barely audible, lost to the storm of thoughts crashing through her mind. Was he talking about the tragedy that had shaped her life? Was he warning her about Nyx—a message that had arrived too late to matter?

Frustration built, rising like a tide, threatening to drown the fragile hope that had clung to her since the moment she saw her father's handwriting. She turned sharply to Paradox, her voice edged with confusion and anger, desperate for an answer that made sense. "I don't understand. You couldn't interfere in time to save my father, but you can cross time to hand me some letter?"

Paradox met her gaze with a quiet sorrow, his voice steady but weighted with something deeper, something heavier than regret. "You'll soon learn that everything happens at the right time. And I'm sorry, Eleanor. I'm very, very sorry."

He hesitated, just for a fraction of a second.

"But it's going to break you."

Before Eleanor could respond, before she could demand answers, the air around them erupted into a blinding green flash. Instinct took over—she threw her arms up, shielding her eyes against the light.

And when she opened them again—

Dr. Asterio's office.

Empty. Silent.

The only sound was the faint rustle of papers on his desk, disturbed by the sudden shift in atmosphere, their fragile edges fluttering as if echoing the disruption of time itself. Eleanor stood there, breath uneven, gripping the letter as though it might vanish from her fingers, as though it might take her father's lingering presence with it.

Her mind raced, tangled in unanswered questions, each one more suffocating than the last.

And for the first time, she wasn't sure she wanted to know the answers.

50

Dead Message

By the time the new year began at Bleakwood School, the corridors hummed with renewed energy—though it was an energy tinged with something different. Change. Uncertainty. Reflection. Students hurried through the halls, voices merging into the familiar symphony of footsteps, laughter, and rustling paper. Yet beneath the surface, something felt altered, as if the fabric of the school had been stretched, reshaped by everything that had unfolded in the months prior.

The crisp January air still carried the bite of winter, but the heavy snowfall had eased, leaving behind frost-kissed windows and the scent of fresh ink as students grabbed copies of *V.E.N.U.S.*, the school's ever-popular newspaper. Some huddled in groups, whispering about the latest headlines; others scanned the pages with wide-eyed intrigue, eager to digest every word. The past term had forced the school into the spotlight—first as the epicentre of chaos, then as the subject of intrigue. Eleanor wasn't sure how she felt about that.

Despite the fresh start, traces of past destruction lingered like ghosts throughout the building. The main hall, once the beating heart of the school, remained scarred—the collapsed ceiling still partially exposed, its skeletal remains held up by scaffolding. Yellow caution tape cut through the space like jagged wounds, cordoning off unstable areas while cracked tiles and dust-ridden beams sat untouched, a silent testament to everything the school had endured.

And then—there was the hole.

A vast, gaping void in the ground, surrounded by floodlights that cast unsettling shadows deep into its depths. Though reconstruction efforts were underway, progress was slow. The crater remained—a reminder of how close some had come to losing everything. Students moved past it with wary steps, avoiding eye contact with the treacherous darkness below. But some still stole glances, drawn in by morbid curiosity or lingering fear.

Eleanor found herself staring too, her breath catching for just a second.

She could still *feel* it—the rush of air swallowing her whole, the moment her feet lost the ground beneath them, the sheer terror of freefall. The dust in her throat. The fear in her veins. She squeezed her hands into fists, willing the memories back into the depths of her mind.

She was fine now. It was over.

"Eleanor!"

Chris's voice cut through the noise like an anchor, pulling her back into the present.

She turned, spotting him weaving his way through the students. His expression was urgent, his pace brisk, his breaths uneven as he finally reached her.

"Have you heard the news?" he asked, the words spilling out fast, as though holding onto them was impossible.

Eleanor blinked, disoriented by his urgency. The morning haze still clung to her, her body sluggish after barely managing to roll out of bed an hour ago. Her messy hair curled wildly around her face, sleep hanging heavy in her limbs.

"What news?" Her voice rasped, lower than usual.

Chris wasted no time. He shoved a copy of *V.E.N.U.S.* under her nose, the bold black print practically demanding her attention. Eleanor huffed, pushing it away, but Chris persisted, holding it up again.

She'd stopped reading *V.E.N.U.S.* since the start of term. Maddison had turned it into something remarkable, a publication that had gone from small school gossip to something bordering on legendary. But Eleanor had kept her distance. Her name was everywhere in those pages, etched into columns she didn't want to read. It wasn't vanity that kept her away—it was the discomfort of seeing herself reflected through the words of others, through perspectives she didn't recognise.

"What is it *this time*?" she sighed, already bracing herself for whatever answer was coming.

Chris inhaled, then blurted it out.

"Singleton's stepping down as headmaster."

For a moment, Eleanor didn't register it.

Then—"What?" The single word shot out of her mouth like a breath stolen by the wind.

She barely waited for an explanation before they both took off, sprinting through the corridors, dodging other students as their footsteps thundered against the polished floors. Up the spiralled staircase, past the cluttered noticeboards and frost-coated windows, until finally—they reached the headmaster's office.

Chris knocked.

A pause.

Then, a curt voice: "Enter."

But it wasn't Singleton's voice.

Eleanor froze as they stepped inside.

Professors Dougan and Dr. Asterio stood behind the desk like sentinels, flanking Singleton, who sat stiffly in the chair he had occupied for years. The air in the office was different—no longer warm, no longer carrying the scent of old books and coffee. Instead, it was colder. Hollow. Heavy.

At the centre of the room sat piles of luggage, suitcases stacked neatly, waiting.

Waiting for him to leave.

Waiting for everything to shift once again.

"Eleanor," Singleton said, his tone subdued. "I expect you've heard the news."

She nodded slowly, her eyes darting between the professors and the packed bags. "I don't understand," she said, her voice wavering. "Why are you leaving? I thought the police were impressed with how you handled everything this year." A flicker of suspicion crossed her face as she added, "Did the Kensington's have something to do with this?"

Singleton shook his head, though his smile barely reached his eyes. "They were impressed," he admitted. "But I think it's time for me to retire."

Eleanor frowned. If she had heard this news last year, she would have felt nothing but *relief*. She had spent months at odds with Singleton, questioning his decisions, distrusting his authority. But now, the feeling was different.

Everything had only *just* begun to settle again—just begun to feel normal.

"Why now?" she pressed, searching his face for an answer. "With Nyx and his rebels locked away, why would you leave Bleakwood?"

Singleton's expression shifted ever so slightly, his lips pressing into a thin line. Eleanor understood the look—one of hesitation, of withheld truth.

She stepped forward, her fingers curling into fists. "That's not the only reason, is it?"

A silent exchange passed between the professors, unease slipping between them like an unseen current. None of them seemed eager to speak first.

Finally, Dr. Asterio broke the silence, his voice gentle but weighted. "We have reason to believe that Nyx wasn't working alone."

The words stole the breath from Eleanor's lungs.

"What?"

Her pulse thrummed violently in her ears.

Dr. Asterio adjusted his glasses, his gaze dark with something she wasn't sure she wanted to acknowledge. "After we cleared some of the collapsed passages beneath Bleakwood, we found traces of bandages and medical equipment."

Eleanor's stomach twisted.

"You're saying someone helped him?"

Asterio nodded. "We believe that after your confrontation with him last year, Nyx used the tunnels to hide and recover. Someone must have tended to his injuries."

Her mind reeled—flashes of past memories, Nyx's unrelenting presence, his network of followers.

"Couldn't it have been Theo? Or one of the rebels?" she asked, though even as she said it, the doubt tasted sharp on her tongue.

None of them answered.

The silence was louder than any confirmation.

"We need to uncover the truth," Dr. Asterio said firmly. "If someone out there was working with Nyx—if they *still* are—we have to stop them."

Singleton's gaze settled on Eleanor, unrelenting, searching. "Did Nyx ever mention a partner? *Anyone*?"

Eleanor opened her mouth to speak, but the words faltered.

Something flickered in the back of her mind—a conversation she had once dismissed, a phrase that had seemed meaningless at the time.

"There was one thing," she murmured, barely above a whisper.

The professors leaned in slightly, their attention sharpening.

"He said that ever since finding the Dark Element... he heard voices."

Singleton stiffened, his expression darkening. "Yes," he said, the word heavy. "He mentioned them to me once. Constant whispers. Like shadows clawing at his mind."

Professor Dougan scoffed. "That sounds like the ramblings of an unstable man."

Dr. Asterio was less dismissive. "Or it means Nyx was being influenced—by something, or someone—through the Dark Element."

Singleton let out a slow breath, thoughtful. "It's possible," he admitted. "Eleanor, you've seen what the Light Element can do. You know firsthand how it can forge connections."

Eleanor looked up at him, remembering vividly—the glowing butterflies, the messages sent between them, the way the Light Element had reached across time and space.

"How did you do it?" she asked.

Singleton folded his hands together, his gaze steady. "The Light Element responds to positive energy," he explained. "I used ancient symbols and rituals to form a connection. The symbols acted as a conduit—allowing me to send messages through it."

Eleanor absorbed the revelation, feeling its weight settle in her chest.

If the Light Element could be harnessed that way—could the Dark Element be manipulated just as easily?

Her stomach tightened at the thought.

"But you don't have any powers of your own," Eleanor pointed out. "How did you manage it?"

Singleton nodded. "True, I don't. But by focusing my thoughts and emotions, I was able to tap into the Element's energy." He paused. "It's like tuning into a frequency. You don't need magic—you need understanding."

Eleanor's brows furrowed. "So anyone could do it?"

"Theoretically, yes."

"Then who could have known enough to manipulate the Dark Element?" Eleanor asked. "It was hidden for centuries before you found it. *Anyone* who had knowledge of it would be long dead."

Singleton's lips twitched slightly, something unreadable behind his expression.

"Are you sure about that?"

Chris, who had been silent until now, faltered. "Well... yes. No. I mean, I don't know."

A heavy pause filled the space between them.

Dr. Asterio folded his arms, thinking aloud. "We never really figured out how the Time Element ended up separated from the others."

Singleton nodded. "Or how Nyx knew it was buried in Greece. It took us years to find the Light and Dark Elements—but he found the Time Element *without* our help."

A chill swept through Eleanor, raising the hairs on her arms.

Something about Nyx—about his connection to the Dark Element—had always unsettled her in ways she couldn't explain.

Dr. Asterio exhaled, his face serious. "Whoever touched the Dark Element might have opened their mind to..."

He trailed off, uncertain.

Eleanor leaned closer. "To what?"

Asterio hesitated, then murmured gravely—

"...Nothing good."

Eleanor's mind reeled. Her thoughts spiralled back to the letter her father had left her—the words she had tried again and again to decipher.

There had to be something there.

She closed her eyes, thinking hard, piecing together fragments of memory.

"Do the words 'shadows in light' mean anything to you?" she asked abruptly, her voice tight with urgency.

Singleton, Dr. Asterio, and Dougan exchanged puzzled glances.

"No," Singleton said finally. "Why would your father write that?"

Eleanor bit her lip. It didn't make sense... unless it wasn't about Nyx or the Elements.

Maybe—just maybe—it was something her father had known.

A secret *only* he could pass to her.

She gazed at the stained-glass windows, where sunlight spilled in from the east side, scattering colours across the room in shifting, shimmering patterns.

Then, like a spark igniting, a thought struck her.

With shaking fingers, Eleanor pulled the crumpled letter from her back pocket.

"What are you doing?" Chris asked, watching her intently.

"Just wait."

Holding the paper up to the light, she tilted it slightly, watching as the coloured rays twisted across the page—revealing something she hadn't seen before.

Shadows.

Not *in* the words—but beneath them.

Hidden.

The professors crowded around Eleanor, their eyes fixed on the letter as shadows flickered and twisted across its surface. The room was silent, save for the faint rustle of paper beneath Eleanor's trembling fingers.

As she tilted the letter ever so slightly toward the window, the sunlight filtered through, bending across the inked words in shimmering fragments. At first, it seemed random—the interplay of light and shadow forming fleeting shapes with every shift of movement.

But then—something began to emerge.

A pattern.

Slowly, the shapes settled, aligning with one another, and converging to reveal something far more deliberate than a trick of the light. The shadows cast by the folds of the paper stretched outward, forming an intricate pictogram projected onto the stone floor—a luminous design hidden in the very fibres of the letter.

Eleanor gasped, her pulse pounding in her ears.

"Shadows in the light!" She barely heard the words come out of her own mouth, which were breathless with realisation. "It was right here all along."

Chris stepped closer, his face lit with awe. "What is that?"

The projection shimmered, its details sharpening with every subtle movement of the letter. At its core, three distinct objects took shape—a pocket watch, a book, and a ring. They hovered in the ethereal glow, their outlines steady, their presence unmistakable.

The Elements.

But their attention wasn't drawn to the objects alone.

At the very centre of the image, a dark figure loomed, its form spectral, distorted, its ghostly hands stretched wide, casting an eerie shadow over the symbols below.

Eleanor's throat tightened as dread coiled in her stomach.

Her father's letter—his warning—was more than words. It had concealed a secret, one she had nearly missed.

"Where did the original story of the Elements come from?" she asked, turning sharply to Dr. Asterio.

Dr. Asterio shook his head, his brow furrowed deeply in thought. "No one truly knows," he admitted. "It's been passed down through generations, like a legend. But its origin has always been a mystery."

Eleanor's mind spun backward, pulling her to that freezing night last Christmas—when Dr. Asterio had recounted the tale of the Egyptian princes and the mysterious sorcerer who had given them the Elements.

She remembered the fourth brother—the one who had refused the sorcerer's gift, the one who had turned away from the offer that had ensnared the others. She remembered how the sorcerer had simply vanished, slipping into the depths of obscurity, his existence fading into whispered stories and forgotten myths. No one had ever questioned where he had gone. No one had asked who—or what—he truly was.

Eleanor's breath grew shallow, the weight of the realization pressing against her ribs, her voice barely above a whisper as the words slipped free. "What if the sorcerer isn't gone?"

The statement sent a ripple through the room, its impact immediate and undeniable.

Dr. Asterio stiffened, his posture rigid with sudden awareness, while Singleton's gaze darkened, the shift in his demeanour unmistakable.

"My father was trying to warn me," Eleanor continued, the pieces of a long-buried puzzle finally clicking into place. "He knew more about the Elements than anyone ever realized. More than he ever let on."

Chris swallowed hard, his wide-eyed stare locked on the shadowed figure in the projection, his breath uneven. "You mean... something bad is coming?"

Singleton's expression turned ice-cold, the sharp edge in his voice making the room feel impossibly smaller, suffocating in its quiet severity.

"Not just bad," he murmured, pausing as the silence thickened around them, pressing in from all sides.

He exhaled slowly, his voice dropping to something barely above a whisper, but somehow even heavier than before.

"Something far worse."

PART 3

10
months
later...

51

The Island

Somewhere in the middle of the North Atlantic, hidden beyond the reach of any map, lay an island carved from jagged stone—a forsaken place, its silhouette stark against the storm-heavy sky. The sea around it was relentless, waves hammering the eroded cliffs with ceaseless fury, swallowing the rocky shoreline beneath a constant roar. The wind carried the scent of salt and decay, its howling voice an eerie companion to the prisoners locked inside.

This was no ordinary prison. It was built for one purpose—to contain the uncontainable.

The fortress loomed against the tempest, a brutal construct of concrete and steel, its towering walls scarred by time and violence. Razor wire coiled atop the fences like rusted serpents, catching what little light pierced the thick clouds in jagged, menacing glints. Watchtowers stood like sentinels over the compound, their searchlights sweeping across the turbulent waters, sensors twitching at every shadow that dared to move.

This was where the world's most dangerous figures were held that couldn't simply be locked away behind ordinary bars.

Inside the prison's depths, narrow windows—mere slits carved into stone—offered no glimpse of the outside world. The corridors twisted like a maze, their damp walls reeking of cold steel and the ever-present scent of seawater bleeding through the concrete. The cells were bleak, barely large enough for a man to stand upright, their iron bars casting fractured shadows beneath the flickering, unreliable light. The air was thick with sweat, the stench of bodies unwashed for days, their muffled cries and whispers blending into the eerie hum of captivity.

In the control room—the nerve centre of the facility—a group of guards struggled with the radio, its signal cutting in and out, static crackling like distant thunder.

"There it goes again!" The commander cursed under his breath, slamming his palm against the panel. "We've been having technical issues ever since the high-security prisoner was transferred here, but recently, it's been getting worse."

He pressed down on the controls again, frustration tightening his jaw as he fought to clear the interference. "It's like the whole damn island is rejecting him. Ever since he arrived... things have been different."

A younger recruit, barely past his first few weeks, hesitated before leaning in. "You mean Nyx?"

The room fell silent for a long moment before the commander exhaled sharply, shaking his head. "I don't even like saying his name."

The recruit swallowed, glancing at one of the more seasoned officers. "Have you ever met him?"

The officer stiffened, something dark flickering across his expression—something haunted.

"Only once," he admitted, his voice quieter now, as if speaking the memory aloud made it real again. "It felt like my entire body was crawling with something I couldn't shake—like insects under my skin." He exhaled, rubbing his fingers together absently. "None of the guards have lasted more than a week in the maximum-security ward."

The recruit hesitated. "What exactly is he in here for?"

Another officer, who had been listening in silence, turned from the controls, his expression hard.

"You mean, aside from orchestrating an extremist movement, infiltrating a school, and nearly killing half of its students?" He scoffed, shaking his head. "That summary barely scratches the surface."

The recruit nodded stiffly, piecing together the fragments of information he had overheard. Rumours travelled fast in a place like this—whispers of dark energy lingering in the tunnels beneath Bleakwood, stories of bodies piling up, of power that defied science.

And yet—their prisoner remained locked away. Silent. Waiting.

Suddenly, the radio crackled, static breaking through the interference, a voice flickering in and out.

"Control, this is Guard 1. Do you copy?"

The commander leaned forward, pressing the button. "Guard 1, this is Control. Your signal is weak. Repeat your message."

More static. A faint hum. Then—

"Control, we have an off-course boat heading toward the island. We've tried to contact them, but there's no response. This is a restricted zone. Should we send a security team to intercept?"

The commander's eyes flicked toward the viewing monitors, watching the turbulent waves crash against the distant horizon, their relentless movement ominous beneath the heavy sky. His fingers hovered over the control panel before pressing the speaker button again.

"Negative," he said firmly. "There could be civilians on the boat. Send a security team to check all high-security prisoners. Make sure they are accounted for. Over."

The guards mobilized swiftly, their movements precise, practiced. Only the most seasoned officers were sent down to the lower levels, the ones who had learned not to let their fear slow them down.

The atmosphere shifted.

Tension bled into every step as they moved through the dimly lit corridors, their boots echoing off the damp concrete, the heavy silence pressing against them as they passed rows of cells filled with restless inmates.

Guard 1 led the way, descending deeper into the maximum-security wing—a place none of them dared linger in longer than necessary.

Screams echoed through the air, some wild and filled with desperation, others reduced to quiet murmurs of fractured minds. The very walls felt suffocating, pressing inward, weighed down by something more than just stone and iron.

As he passed, skeletal fingers stretched through the bars, grasping at his sleeve. One inmate managed to latch onto the fabric. Without breaking stride, he slammed the butt of his gun down against their knuckles. A sharp cry followed, but he didn't stop.

At last, he reached the final cell. His footsteps slowed as an unnatural silence settled over the corridor, heavier than in any of the previous chambers. Unlike the others, there was no sound—no shuffling of feet, no quiet murmurs, not even the faint rustling of fabric against stone. Nothing.

The guard hesitated for only a moment before stepping forward, peering through the reinforced viewing window. His heartbeat pounded against his ribs, a force he could feel in his throat. The dim, flickering glow of the overhead bulb cast uneven shadows across the small, contained space, illuminating the figure inside just enough to make the sight all the more unsettling.

Nyx sat perfectly still, his back pressed against the cold, unforgiving wall, his hands folded neatly in his lap. He looked as though he had merely settled into quiet contemplation rather than being locked away in the depths of a fortified cell. His eyes remained fixed on the floor—vacant, unreadable, betraying nothing.

Not a single movement.

Not even the slightest rise or fall of breath.

A slow, mocking grin stretched across the guard's face.

"Well, well, well. Look what we have here—the great Nyx, reduced to nothing more than a common criminal. Not so powerful now, are you? No army. No followers. And no precious ring."

His laughter rang through the cold corridors, bouncing off damp concrete walls.

Nyx didn't move.

Didn't react.

The guard had expected anger—a flare of defiance, a snarl, a clenched fist. But all he got was silence.

Every few seconds, the heavy clang of metal doors slamming shut reverberated through the facility, marking the arrival of another one of Nyx's fallen rebels. They had been torn from hiding, dragged from underground sanctuaries, plucked from the remnants of their shattered movement.

Deep beneath the surface of this secret facility—buried in a place that didn't exist on any map—they awaited their fate.

Then—

A low, ominous groan reverberated through the walls, unnatural in its weight. No alarms rang, but something was wrong.

The floor vibrated, faint at first until another tremor came through, stronger this time and enough to spook him.

He turned and ran.

Something was happening outside, but none of the inmates knew exactly what *that* was, until hurried footsteps echoed down the corridor.

The approaching figures slowed as they reached the maximum-security wing, peering through the narrow viewing slot at Nyx.

He didn't react immediately, but when he stepped forward, his gaze locked onto the eyes staring down at him, scrutinizing every flicker of emotion, every involuntary movement, every breath.

The moment stretched unbearably.

Even without the Dark Element anchoring his emotions, he could feel the shift in the air—the unspoken tension laced with something deeper.

A voice hissed from the shadows. "Are we doing this or not? The twins can't keep the guards distracted forever."

A sharp buzzing filled the air as something sliced clean through the lock, burning through reinforced steel as if it were nothing. The scent of scorched metal lingered, bitter and acrid, as the cell door swung inward with a guttural crash.

Nyx hesitated.

For the briefest second, he believed this was a trick—a cruel fabrication designed to test his resolve, to dangle freedom just out of reach.

"What do you want?" His voice was hoarse, edged with suspicion.

"Your help."

Nyx laughed, a hollow sound devoid of humour. "You must be truly desperate if you're asking for my help. What could have possibly gone so wrong in the last ten months that *you*—Eleanor Walker—have come here, to me?"

Eleanor's looked back at him, her from shifting uneasily under the dim light.

"Don't get smug." A pause. "I could just as easily leave you here to rot with the rest of them. My conscience is clear."

The weight in her words struck something deep within him.

"You're going to do exactly what we say. No questions. And if you even think about betraying us, I will personally ensure you end up right back here. Is that understood?"

Nyx exhaled slowly, a smirk forming despite himself. "Crystal clear."

The smile felt foreign on his lips—a forgotten muscle stretched for the first time in months.

Stepping out of the cell, Nyx turned his attention to the high-security ward around him. Behind locked doors, the remnants of the Order of Shadows lay in wait—some steely with defiance, others sunken with despair. The guards had done their job thoroughly. Every last follower had been accounted for, shackled and silenced.

But control was slipping.

The prison trembled again, a vibration rippling through its foundations.

Nyx tilted his head slightly, considering the girl standing before him.

"So, tell me, Eleanor," he murmured, his gaze locking onto hers—brown eyes sharp, unwavering and filled with something she couldn't quite hide.

"What could you possibly have done?"

About the Author

British author Niamh Speakman has continued her passion for writing in this second instalment of The Elements book series. Alongside her passion for science-fiction, Niamh balances her time completing a master's degree in physics.

Visit her social media on Instagram at nspeakman_27.

Acknowledgement

This story is dedicated to all those who have taken the time to read my debut novel, *The Elements*.

Eleanor Walker's journey is far from over.

N R SPEAKMAN

THE ELEMENTS

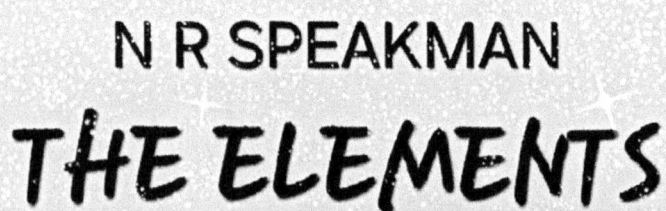

Printed in Dunstable, United Kingdom